Sam's Legacy

BY JAY NEUGEBOREN

Sam's Legacy
Parentheses: An Autobiographical Journey
Corky's Brother
Listen Ruben Fontanez
Big Man

Sam's Legacy

a novel by

Jay Neugeboren

Holt, Rinehart and Winston
New York   Chicago   San Francisco

Published simultaneously in Canada by Holt, Rinehart
and Winston of Canada, Limited.

Library of Congress Cataloging in Publication Data

Neugeboren, Jay.
Sam's legacy; a novel.

"A portion of this book has previously appeared in
the *Massachusetts Review*."
I. Title.
PZ4.N484Sam   [PS3564.E844]   813'.5'4   73–8249
ISBN 0–03–011436–5

First Edition

Designer: Sandra Kandrac
Printed in the United States of America : 065

For Martha Winston and William E. Wilson

and to the memory of Arthur and Doris Bendorf

Contents

And Containing

MY LIFE AND DEATH IN THE
NEGRO AMERICAN BASEBALL LEAGUE:
A SLAVE NARRATIVE

"The Omnipresent," said a Rabbi, "is occupied in making marriages." The levity of the saying lies in the ear of him who hears it; for by marriages the speaker meant all the wondrous combinations of the universe whose issue makes our good and evil.

—George Eliot, *Daniel Deronda*

I

The
Rummage
Shop

These are they that are ineligible to bear witness: dice-players, pigeon-flyers, usurers, traffickers in Seventh Year produce, and slaves.
—*The Mishnah* ("Feast of the New Year," 1:8)

1

Sam Berman was taller than his father Ben by at least half a foot, and his father had been—he remembered this clearly—taller than *his* father; and yet—it was crazy—when he thought of them, things were always reversed: he saw his grandfather as tallest of all, with Ben next, and himself last—like the painted wooden dolls he'd seen in souvenir shops (from Russia, he thought, or Poland), in which, when you opened the largest one, there was one smaller, and when you opened the smaller one, there was one even smaller.

Sam looked down at his stomach—he was standing, applauding as the players were being introduced—and he wondered if he contained anything in the hollow of his body; if not, did that mean that he was empty . . . or solid? It wasn't a question he would let Ben have a chance at. He knew, of course, where questions like that could lead. Religion, he thought—they could use that to mix you up too.

"See the way he fingers his medallion," the man to his left was saying. "That's what did it. He prayed. I read it in the papers."

"Sure," Sam said. "Maybe."

They were talking about one of the players on the New York Knicks, Dave Stallworth, who was sitting on a bench far below, ready to be introduced to the crowd. Everyone in Madison Square Garden was waiting to hear his name: Stallworth, a six-foot-seven-and-a-half-inch black basketball player, had been sidelined for more than two years by what had been diagnosed as a heart attack. He had been twenty-five years old at the time, in his second season with the Knicks, averaging thirteen points a game. Sam had, of course, followed the comeback story in the papers. "It was like somebody was sitting on my chest," Stallworth had told a reporter. Sam knew the feeling, he knew it well. He watched Stallworth finger the medallion.

"I wish the guy well," the man said.

"Sure. Me too," Sam said, and he meant it. "You got to give him credit. He has . . ." He paused, aware that he was embarrassed at the feelings welling within him, at the words that were out before he could check himself. ". . . a lot of heart."

The man smiled. "He said he prayed a lot, and I believe him. A guy doesn't lie about a thing like that."

Sam thought of his father, who still prayed every morning in his bedroom, and Sam could see himself, just before his thirteenth birthday, when Ben had taught him how to wind the black *tephillin* straps around his arm, seven times, and how to pull them through the spaces between his fingers in order to make the letter *shin*, for the name of God, on the back of his hand.

An enormous sound rose around Sam's ears, engulfing him. Over sixteen thousand fans were on their feet, their roar swelling, cresting—and Sam realized that he had, a moment before, heard Stallworth's name. Stallworth trotted out onto the court, took his place at the foul line, shuffled his feet, and let his head drop to his chest. Willis Reed, the Knick captain—six-foot-ten, a black man with a barrel chest—leaned over and slapped Stallworth on the rear-end. Stallworth stood at ease, his hands clasped behind him, and Sam pounded his hands together as hard as he could. *Wasn't this what it was all about?* he thought to himself, not caring that the guy next to him might notice that there were tears brimming in his eyes. He glanced right and left and saw that he wasn't the only one: they called New Yorkers tough, did they? Maybe. But he saw a lot of glassy-eyed guys around him, their mouths pressed tight, their heads held high, clapping their hearts out.

They knew what it must have taken, Sam told himself; they'd followed the story in the papers too: how Stallworth had lain on his back in a hospital bed for twenty-seven straight days without moving, had been told he'd never be able to play again, washed up, a cripple at twenty-five—and they knew what it must have meant to him tonight, to be back in the Garden, slipping his white silk uniform over his long body, trotting out onto the hardwood, warming up with his teammates, hearing his name over the public address system, hearing the hush that had preceded the applause, and then this. The guy next to him—he came to Sam's shoulder, about five-foot-five, Ben's height, only stocky—was banging his hands as hard as Sam was, and the man's eyes were shining. He noticed Sam looking his way, glanced up at him, and the two men grunted at each other.

Why didn't they leave it at that, though, Sam thought. Why did they have to bring religion into it? It gave him the willies. Dave Stallworth looked up now, fingered his medallion nervously, and the applause continued—deafening, swelling. Dave the Rave! The guy was an ace, that was all. Sam's fingers tingled—the papers would exaggerate the next morning, but the applause had lasted for a solid three, three and a half minutes. The noise began to subside, Stallworth's head bobbed up and down—the announcer broke in finally, calling the rest of the team out, some of the Knick rookies making their way to the foul line for the first time in their pro careers—and again, despite himself, Sam saw his grandfather and his father, in the living room on Linden Boulevard, when his grandfather had been living with them. Sam had been nine when his grandfather had died, over twenty years before: it was very early, before Ben left for work, and the two men shuckled back and forth, the black straps fell down his grandfather's collar, from the knot at the nape of his neck. The venetian blinds were drawn, the room dark, warm, and as the two men paced back and forth, murmuring their prayers, their eyes closed, Sam would wonder how it was that they never bumped into each other. He saw his father's jacket, dropped from his left shoulder, the shirt-sleeves rolled up, the straps making ridges on the hairy skin of the forearm; he saw straps emerging from under his grandfather's dark beard, the beard knotted, wild, spreading in crazy curls across the man's chest. Their heads bobbed, as if synchronized.

Sam stuck his first and third fingers into his mouth, to each side of his tongue, and gave a whistle, shrill—Johnny Warren, a Knick rookie from St. John's, ran onto the court, sporting an Afro hairdo. The organ played the Star Spangled Banner, and then Sam applauded again, quickly, and sat down.

This could be the Knicks' year, he thought. After the way they'd handled themselves in the play-offs the previous year, with Bradley finally coming along, and Frazier showing he had real class in the backcourt. Sure. Think about that, he told himself, and forget the other stuff: seeing his grandfather hulking over his father, the three of them inside each other like mummies. He was heading for deep waters if he let his mind dwell on things like that.

The game was good and Sam never had to worry—the Knicks won by twenty-five, going away, which meant that Sam was up by two hundred and fifty for the week. He'd been shaving it pretty close lately, the roughest stretch for him in over ten years. He'd had the Knicks by six and he felt better now, relieved. They told you never to bet opening games, that there were still too many unknowns, but the guys who made the odds were as much in the dark as Sam was. This week Mr. Sabatini would pay him.

He hurried down when the final buzzer sounded, two steps at a time, and reached the first landing before the players had gone through to the underpass and the locker rooms. The cops were there, their arms spread out, keeping the fans away. Everybody was giving Stallworth congratulations. "Way to go, Dave baby—" he heard himself call out, and nobody even looked at him for saying it. Stallworth, a half foot or so taller than Sam, smiled from fat lips. Sam was close enough to see what he'd seen in close-up photos in sports magazines: the five-pointed gold star in the cap on one of Stallworth's front teeth. The light flashed into Sam's face, making him blink. He wanted to reach out, to put his hand on Stallworth's brown arm, to tell him how happy he was for him, that he understood; and he had a feeling that, if they could get together for a few drinks, a few hands of poker—Sam would go easy on him there if Stallworth would go easy on him in some one-on-one in the schoolyard—they would get on together. Stallworth ducked his head, disappearing down the runway; Sam zipped up his jacket and looked for the nearest exit.

On the escalator, descending, Sam listened to three high school kids, wearing their team jackets, tell one another how great the Knicks would be if Willis Reed stayed healthy for the whole season.

Sam smiled, stepped from the escalator, then followed the signs, down and through arcades, to the Seventh Avenue IRT Subway.

"Brother, may I have a word with you?"

It was the guy who'd sat next to him at the game. Sam stopped, his right hand slipping automatically into his sidepocket, where his knife was. "Some other time, yeah?" Sam said. "I got an appointment to see somebody."

Sam moved to his left, but the man moved with him and touched his sleeve. The passageway leading through the Long Island Railroad waiting room was jammed, but Sam wasn't comforted by crowds. "This won't take very long," the man said. "I mean, I saw something in your eyes, brother, when we both—"

Sam stopped, jerked his sleeve from the man's hand. "Look, if you need a hand-out, I'm not the guy." The man's eyes shifted, unsure. Sam relaxed. The city was full of strange birds, but you never knew. He flipped the question out, fast: "You work for Sabatini?"

Then the man's eyes fixed him. "I work for the Lord." The voice was hollow. The man's hand held him again, above the wrist, but Sam didn't move.

"Sure," Sam said. "But I don't got the time."

The man seemed to be an inch or two taller than he'd been at the game; his back was straight, he stared directly into Sam's face. "I was like you once, brother—fearful and alone." The voice was mellow, soothing. "But now I have Christ in my bosom. 'He that covereth his sins shall not prosper: but whoso confesseth and forsaketh them shall have mercy.' Would you be kind enough to read a pamphlet I have prepared, if I were to offer it to you?"

Sam heard the names of Long Island towns being announced on the public address system. In the doorway to a bookstore, two teenagers were necking, the girl pressed back against the window, the guy's leg wedged between her thighs. "Yeah. Sure, sure," Sam said, but when he saw the man smile, shyly, and reach into his inside jacket pocket, he found that he was darting past him, zigzagging through the crowd, bumping into people.

He cut through the lines at the information booth, moved right around the crowd of men looking through the windows of the hut in which you could light up the day's stock prices, passed ticket windows and food counters. He fished in his jacket pocket for a subway token and eyed the turnstiles, measuring the lines. He stopped, looked behind, but did not see the man. He waited his turn, dropped his token in the slot, then took the stairs two at a time and—his luck was running—slipped through the doors of a downtown IRT express just as they were closing.

It was quicker getting home, back to Brooklyn, now that the Garden was at 34th Street. He closed his eyes on the train and tried to think of the game, but instead he remembered how—unable not to think of Ben after the Bible guy had said something about praying—he'd lost his concentration and had missed Stallworth's introduction. He hadn't missed it, really—he'd heard the words—but his mind had been elsewhere. He didn't, he knew, like the feeling.

Sam left the train at Church Avenue. A few black guys got out also. "Ours is a neighborhood in transition," Ben had said, and Sam had to laugh. A neighborhood in transition—that was rich. When he'd been a kid there, growing up, it had been mostly Jews, mixed with some Catholics, Irish and German. Sam didn't mind, though. The blacks never hassled him. Maybe the word was out that he had some kind of business with Sabatini. He touched his sidepocket. Some guys—his buddy Dutch was one—said you were crazy to keep a blade on you, that if you got cornered and they went for you and found it on you, you'd get it ten times worse. But Sam did what he wanted. He liked feeling the blade's weight against his thigh.

He pushed through the turnstile, taking pleasure in the resistance of the wood against his midsection. He stayed in shape—basketball when he had the chance, handball, swimming—it gave him an edge, knowing that his legs were tight, strong, that his waist was the same—thirty-two—as it had been ten years before. Concentration was everything. If you let yourself go to pot, you could get drowsy at a key moment. Sure. He didn't smoke, he rarely took a drink. Who knew how many—the word made him smile—pots he'd won because his body had sustained him just when some other guy's excess baggage had made his mind flabby. . . .

Outside, at the corner of Church and Nostrand, the air was fresh. He saw some guys huddling across the street in front of the Lincoln Savings Bank: he figured he knew what they were selling. That took real brains. It was not even ten-thirty—he was in plenty of time for the eleven-fifteen sports on TV, to see how the other teams had done, to get the word on the football games coming up, to see if there were key injuries that might affect the point spreads.

Half a block ahead, just beyond Phil's Liquor Store, a man stood in a doorway. Sam thought of the Bible man, and he veered very slightly, toward the curb. He wasn't scared—it was early, a lot of cars cruising, his apartment was on the next block; if he had to, he could outrun most guys. He passed the man, crossed Martense Street, and, looking across the street, saw that there were still lights on in the windows of his apartment. With what had happened after the game still on his mind, there was no point, he knew, in going upstairs while Ben was awake. He'd had enough words for one night.

He kept walking, heard music and looked left: two teenage girls, both black, their heads covered in brightly colored silk kerchiefs, were dancing in an all-night laundromat. Sam paused, watched their behinds moving. The girls were shaking nicely, their eyes closed, dreaming—Sam licked his lips, then noticed something yellow come into focus, rising, next to the dryers. A tall black guy, wearing steel-rimmed glasses, his hair fuzzed up, a crazy bright yellow poncho draped over his shoulders, glared at him. One girl bent over slightly, wiggling her shoulders like a stripper, and Sam saw the backs of her legs, muscles rippling under brown thighs. He looked through the window—there was a ledge, where a portable radio sat, next to a box of soap flakes, and Sam figured that the guy had been sitting there before he'd stood. Sam walked away. If the guy had sounded him, he could have thought of a lot of things to say, but it was just as well that he hadn't. The girls had known what was happening, that they'd been putting on a show for him, trying to start something. Sure. Stick to a bitch, end in a ditch.

Sam turned left onto Linden Boulevard, the rock music fading out. Women—! He bet they'd been the ones who'd invented religion in the first place. That was rich, the line the guy had quoted to him, but he wasn't out—the word stuck—to prosper. Sure. He never lived really big, rolling around in fancy cars and expensive women, but he stayed alive, ahead of the game. That was something. Playing it small and smart he could get by from feeding on the others, the dumb ones, the guys who were out for the big kill.

He headed for Flatbush Avenue: the morning papers would be in soon—he could have coffee and a Danish in Garfield's while he waited. The street was dark, an old couple ahead of him, walking arm in arm. He'd lived on this block for almost twenty years; he knew every cellar, every alleyway, every roof. Number 221, his old building, was across the street, inside—one of four buildings which surrounded a courtyard. They'd had a large five-room apartment on the third floor. Now, ever since Ben had become ill five years before, Sam lived with his father in a narrow two-room place on Nostrand Avenue between Martense Street and Linden Boulevard, directly above the Muscular Dystrophy Rummage Shop. At fifty-six dollars a month, rent-controlled, they couldn't complain. What would they do with five rooms? He turned left at Rogers Avenue. When he'd been a kid, this had been the corner he had hung out at. The old stores—Bender's Fruit and Grocery, Klein's Kosher Butcher Shop, Lee's Luncheonette, Dominick's Barber Shop—were all gone. But you couldn't, Sam told himself, go against it. Things changed. He never made any predictions: he played the games one at a time. Play what's there, don't bet on air. . . .

Ahead of him, a man was sprawled on the sidewalk, his head against a garbage can, his left leg folded impossibly backward, under his rear-end. Sam looked left, checking the doorways to see if it was the old trap. Nobody. He walked to the man, smelled liquor mixed with vomit. The guy was Negro, but with a tiny nose, flattened like an Irishman's. His stubble was full of white hairs, he had a sky-blue baseball cap on his head, sideways, and there was something dark clotted along his lower lip. There were no cars parked nearby. Sam bent over quickly, his ear to the man's face—he heard breathing, a low pleasant-sounding gurgle. Sam felt the guy's hands, checked his wrists—he'd be okay the way he was, sleeping it off.

A stranger had once saved a man's life, a diplomat from the United Nations—Sam had seen the story in the *Post*—because he'd stopped when he'd seen him lying in the gutter; the man had had an engraved silver tag on his wrist, stating that he was a diabetic and who to telephone.

Sam moved away, across Martense Street. What if—the thought made him swallow, clench his fists—it had been Dave Stallworth lying there? The cleaning store at the corner, where old Mr. Weiss used to sit in the window, sewing, was now some kind of welfare station—guys hanging out in front of it all day long. This had been the best block for punchball and stickball, and he knew the local kids still used it: not too many cars, only one or two big trees overhanging, and they were far enough apart so that you had to go some, from the first sewer cover, to loft a ball into the branches. He heard the sound of glass—a bottle—splattering on the sidewalk behind him. He crossed over: all the stores had iron grilles across their doors and windows.

Sam walked along Church Avenue, past Holy Cross Church, past the schoolyard where he still played three-man ball some afternoons. Two policemen were walking together on the other side of the street, their walkie-talkies strapped to their sides like silver hip flasks. To the left, across Bedford Avenue, he saw one wall of his old high school, Erasmus, and, next to it, on the far side, where their synagogue used to be, there was now a parking lot.

If religion meant so much to his father, then how come he never even went to synagogue anymore? Answer that, he heard himself saying to Ben—but he knew that Ben would only smile back at him, in the way which drove Sam crazy, and say something clever. Here the man was, though, sixty-seven years old, admitting he didn't believe in God and winding black straps around himself every morning of his life . . . and people thought that gamblers were superstitious!

Sam played the cards, just what was there. If you bluff, it'll get rough. Sure. It was no skin off his back if somebody wanted to believe something—when it came down to it, he bet his old man would have been shocked to find out what he himself believed. Ben didn't know everything.

He passed the post office, the firehouse, and Luigi's, where he and Dutch still went sometimes to split a pizza pie. The parking lot across the street, next to the Biltmore Caterers, had been Harry Gross's place of business, and even though he'd been put in the can almost twenty years before, at the time of the basketball fixes, guys in the neighborhood still talked about him. Gross had been the biggest bookie in Brooklyn, a friend of Bugsy Siegel and Mickey Cohen; and he'd always worked completely in the open. Sabatini's

take was probably one-tenth of what they said Gross had con-
trolled; the man had to be careful, sure, but Sam didn't like it,
never seeing his face, only hearing his voice on the phone.

He couldn't complain, though. If the guy wanted to act as if he
was king of Las Vegas, that was his right. He'd always dealt straight
with Sam, for the six years Sam had been using him. Maybe he felt
he had to impress the muscle men on his payroll, acting like some
kind of Howard Hughes, the guy who owned the state of Nevada
and walked around his penthouse with his feet in Kleenex boxes to
keep germs off. Sabatini could keep himself locked in an iron mask,
for all Sam cared; so long as Sam got his money at the end of the
week, when it was coming to him.

At the corner of Church and Flatbush, Sam could see that the
morning papers had not yet come in—the stacks were all too
low—so he went into Garfield's Cafeteria, pushed through the
turnstile, took his blank check from the machine, picked up a tray,
some paper napkins, silverware. He got his cup of coffee and a
cheese Danish, then sat down by the Flatbush Avenue window.
The kids from Erasmus had probably been rioting again, he
figured: there was tape going across the window in a jagged line. A
lot of old people were sitting around, talking. With triple locks on
their doors and round-the-clock doormen, the old people hung on,
but their kids were all moving out, the way all his old buddies had
done: to Westchester and Long Island and New Jersey, to
California and Florida.

Sam sipped his coffee, watched the kids across the street (they
sat, in rows, on the steps of the Dutch Reformed Church), and he
could see Stallworth moving across half-court, then cutting left
through a pack of players, his body toward the basket, and, at the
last second, his left hand stretching back and swishing a beautiful
hook shot straight through. The guy was right-handed too—an ace.
But Sam would lay off the Knicks for the next game—they would
be playing on the road, and he wouldn't press his luck. The
two-fifty would last until the end of the month.

The man at the table in front of his, next to the window, was
licking a pencil point with his tongue, marking things down in the
margins of *The New York Times*. The guy wore an old brown jacket
over a sweater with holes in it, yet there he was, figuring out the
stock page. The man scribbled furiously along the edge of the

newsprint, stopped, looked at Sam suspiciously, then, with his left hand, stuck a finger through one of the holes in his sweater and scratched his chest. Sam thought of the other guy, reaching into his jacket for whatever pamphlet it was that he'd been selling.

Sam kept his eye on the market now and then, but he never played there. Sure, you could make a big killing if somebody gave you a tip, but where, he asked, was the control? The big boys manipulated everything; you could get your ass cleaned out overnight if some mutual fund decided to dump what you had. All you could do was read the figures in the paper, and they weren't figures Sam could believe in. He'd make his own odds.

He hadn't, he knew, been getting as many games of poker as he needed—that was why he'd put two and a half on the Knicks' first game. He didn't like it. Sure. Maybe, in the way that pitchers were always ahead of the batters in spring training, so Sam could stay ahead of the bookies in the early going; still, the question was there: where was the control? The truth, he knew (remembering how easy it had been, a few hours before, seeing Stallworth, to let his feelings carry him away), was that you were only a spectator. If he could have given up betting on games, he'd have been just as happy.

He felt his fingers tighten into fists. Damn though, he thought. With enough poker he wouldn't have needed anything else. If he could have had one game every night for one year, say—five-card draw, five and ten—he figured he could have retired at the end. But games were harder and harder to come by—he'd had to go out to Newark for the last one, taking the damned tubes—and the game had been only quarter and half-dollar.

The man had switched seats, showing Sam his back. Sam smiled, watched the man's elbow jerking, pushing the pencil round and round in circles. With the Dow Jones average dropping every day lately, the bottom nowhere in sight, the guy was probably eating himself up. Or maybe he traded in the other stuff, which Sam never followed at all: what the fuck were pork belly futures anyway? He laughed—it picked him up, thinking of a line like that. He bit into his Danish. That, and the guys who were always talking about taking losses in order to make gains. You couldn't sell that theory to a man who'd been in Sam's line of work for over a dozen years. Sam knew the guys who'd bet heavy on low pairs, who'd lose hands on purpose, thinking they were setting him up; they'd never taken his money home.

What had he made the last time, though? A hundred and twenty—and it had been his only game in six weeks. There was no point in laughing at the others. He sighed, remembering how easy it had been, playing his hands, small and smart, waiting for the others to make their moves. He could have written the script ahead of time, from the way they ran their mouths so much. When they raised the house, he knew he was home free. If he'd wanted to, in his head, he could have replayed every hand he'd had during that four-and-a-half-hour game. But the thought tired him. There'd been no need to follow the betting pattern: when his own cards were there, he'd stayed in, no matter how many they drew or what they bet. Sam felt himself tense. What good was it, being able to see through a bunch of two-bit players when, in the end, he was the one who was back where he started from, having to bet on things he shouldn't be betting on, having to wonder if he'd get enough games to get by on, having to worry about what he'd tell Ben when his cash reserves were gone, and the bottom dropped away.

Bundles of newspapers flew out of the back of a truck, and two black boys raced each other to get to them. Milt, the old newsdealer, made angry motions at them, but when the kids had dumped the bundles in front of the newsstand, Sam saw Milt give them each some money. The rumble of conversation in the cafeteria relaxed Sam. He remembered when Garfield's had first opened; he remembered the Flatbush Theater, which had been in the spot before—still showing vaudeville long after it had disappeared everywhere else in the city; he remembered—he stopped: heads were lifting, all staring in the same direction, and Sam saw why—the kids on the steps of the church had gone to the corner. A pair of lavender-colored El Dorados, like twins, were parked one behind the other. The roofs, Sam could tell, were made of alligator skin. The roof of the first car began rising, moving backward, and Sam saw the driver, a young black man in a mink-colored fur jacket—and next to him, a girl with a pile of silver-pink hair swirling a foot over her head. They showed you something—he had to admit it. Sure. If he had a wife and kids and a lot of junk in the house, he might want out also—he could understand that—but his old buddies, living out on the Island in their private homes, they missed the chance to see something like this: how often did any of them get to the Garden, as much as they all loved basketball? Sure. When their sons were at a certain age, they'd probably make a day of it once or twice a year—but it wasn't the same thing.

He finished his coffee. The El Dorados turned left and cruised by in front of the window. Along the chrome stripping there were things sparkling like sequins. Sam stood and made his way to the cashier. A girl, sitting near the trays and silverware, had her eye on him. She sat very straight, an empty coffee cup in front of her, and Sam saw, most of all, the ring of black and purple she'd painted around her eyes. He'd seen her here before, waiting, and he was pretty sure he remembered her from high school: he hadn't known her, but he'd seen her, hanging around the Bedford Avenue arch at lunchtime and after school. It would be a treat for her, he guessed, taking him home instead of the old men and the blacks. Sure. Things were rough all over, he said to himself, recalling an old line—even the chorus girls were kicking. He paid, stuck a mint-flavored toothpick in the side of his mouth, and left.

"How's t-tricks, Sam?" Milt asked, stuttering slightly, as he always did.

"Can't complain, Milt."

Milt reached to the side of the newsstand. "*Morning Telegraph?*" Sam nodded. "You want one of Powell's Sheets—he's been h-hot lately."

"Sure," Sam said. Milt's lips were blubbery, his eyes miniscule behind thick, round glasses. He'd been there ever since Sam could remember, a bit of drool trickling out the left side of his mouth, wearing the same green-check lumberjacket, the same baggy brown pants.

"The *Times* isn't in yet," Milt said. "Another f-fifteen minutes maybe."

"What do I owe you?" Sam asked. Milt seemed to concentrate, as if, Sam thought, he'd asked him about the state of the world. "That's one dollar and forty cents—P-Powell is half a dollar."

Sam gave him the money. "I had the Knicks tonight," Sam said suddenly, and felt a warm wave flood across his face.

"I'm happy for you," Milt said. "You're a good boy. How is your f-father feeling?"

"Fine," Sam said, stepping back, indicating he wanted to get away. "He gives you his best. He told me to say that."

Milt seemed to smile, but Sam couldn't be certain: the guy's face was so pasty. "He's a fine man." The words came out evenly, as if, Sam thought, Milt were reading them. "You're a good boy . . . he's a fine man. . . . You're . . ."

Sam had the papers folded under his arm. He walked away, waved, half-turned, "See you around—"

At Rogers Avenue, in the London Hut, there were a few guys sitting at the counter, half-asleep. Ahead of him, people were coming out of the Granada Theater. Some of them, going in the opposite direction, passed him: they weren't afraid, he figured, when there were so many of them. But when they split off, heading in different directions, their numbers thinning until they were alone for the last block or half-block . . .

Sam turned left at Nostrand Avenue, around the subway entrance, the corner cigar store. He crossed over, onto his own block, came to his building, and glanced through the window of the rummage shop. The racks of coats and dresses, and the tables of clothes and odds-and-ends, were pushed to the sides—it had been the night, he knew, for one of their parties, when all the cripples would be wheeled into the store to listen to music and fill their stomachs with soda and food, parents feeding the ones who had lost the use of their hands. There were a few older ones who could still walk in—their legs stiff, their bodies tilted backward as if they were imitating Frankenstein—and when Sam imagined them trying to dance with one another, he cringed.

There was no light on in the back of the store, though, which meant that Mason Tidewater—the janitor, one had to call him, he supposed—was downstairs, in the basement. Sam opened the door. The hall light, which had gone out the night before, was back on. Sam brushed the brass mailboxes with his shoulder, took the steps two at a time, fished in his pocket for his key, and opened the door.

All the lights were out, none coming from under Ben's door. Sam flicked the wall switch and saw that there was something under his foot. Even before he reached down, he had a feeling—it made him set his teeth, angrily—that he knew what he would find. He stared into the man's printed face, and cursed. The pamphlet was printed on glossy paper, three inches square, in blue ink, with the photograph in the middle, and Sam could hear the guy's voice reciting the printed words: *It pleased God by the foolishness of preaching to save them that believe. Hear my story, brother, so you too may be saved.*

Sam took his jacket off, laying the papers and the pamphlet down on the kitchen table. He threw the cushions off the couch, grabbed the leather loop, and jerked: the sofa unfolded, filling his half of the room.

2

When Sam opened his eyes, his head thick with sleep, he saw above him the white silk, and above the silk, two weaving lines of black. He blinked. He felt as if there were a layer of black mesh across his own face, through which he was looking up. His father's head was banded in black, and the Hebrew letters, along the collar of the silk shawl, silver woven on silver, seemed for a moment to be blue. Sam sniffed in, pulled the covers higher, to his chin, rolled his head against the pillow, stretching his neck muscles. A small square of black above his father's eyes dropped toward him, and Sam rubbed his hand across his own eyes, then applied pressure at the sides, with thumb and middle fingers.

He had, arriving home the night before, fallen asleep at once—he never suffered from insomnia—and he could remember nothing except the comforting depth of that sleep. Even now, when he had things on his mind, he did not dream much, and he was grateful: he imagined that people who had dreams all night long, one after the other, worked at half-strength during their waking hours. It would be, he thought, like sitting up through an endless series of Late Show movies. It was all a question of will, of control. When he hit the sack, he put everything out of mind. Sure: out of sight, out of mind.

"What is it?" he asked. Ben lifted his head, smiled, stepped away from the bed. Sam saw the black leather box at the top of his father's forehead, suspended from its straps, the straps circling backward around the crown of his father's head, under a black *yamulka*. Ben's hands were at his sides, his right index finger locked between the pages of an old *siddur*. His left fist was closed around the end of one strap, holding it in place. Sam had read somewhere about holy men in India who kept their fists clenched until the nails grew through the palms and came out through the backs of their hands. He felt a chill wash over his body, but he showed nothing: he lay between the sheets, waiting.

"I wanted to be sure to be here when you woke—before you left for the day."

"Yeah," Sam said. It was all right to move now, he decided. He lifted his right arm from under the cover and rubbed the tip of his nose with the back of his hand. Then he slid backward, on his elbows, until he was sitting.

"I'd like to talk with you."

"I'm not going anywhere."

"Good. May I finish first?" Ben asked, indicating, by flicking the fringes of his silk *talis* with his fingers, his prayers.

Sam shrugged, swung his feet out from under the covers. While Ben prayed, Sam dressed; then he went to the stove and put some water on to boil. The kitchen—a kitchenette actually, with a refrigerator, stove, and sink—was an alcove directly across from his bed. If he wanted to, he could close it off: there were folding doors, with slats in them. In the other half of the room was the square maple table he and Ben used for eating, and behind it, a mahogany breakfront—one of the few pieces Ben had saved from their Linden Boulevard apartment—in which they kept their dishes, glasses, and silverware. The room was, without the kitchenette, about twelve by fifteen feet, and, crowded as it was (in addition to the bed, table, and breakfront, it contained a dresser, desk, coffee table, end-table, and easy chair, a TV set, two stand-up lamps, two small bookcases, a green leather hassock, a newspaper rack, an old costumer for their coats), Sam liked it. He liked it better, in fact, than he'd liked the room—just as big—that he'd had to himself on Linden Boulevard.

He could, as he had once put it to Dutch, be in an entire apartment all at once: living room, bedroom, kitchen, dining room, TV room, study, office—even the bathroom. Since the bathroom he shared with Ben was connected to Ben's bedroom, on the far side, Sam kept a stainless steel hospital pan with him in the living room, resting on its side behind the convertible bed; he used it at night, if Ben were already asleep when he got in.

There was a time when he and Dutch had laughed about the bedpan, but that time had passed. Poor Dutch. You and me, Sam had said to him one time when they'd been talking about their old buddies, we're the only ones who haven't flown off, and we're supposed to be the birds. But Dutch hadn't laughed. What do you think, Ace? he'd replied. Are we different because we stay, or do we stay because we're different? Sam had shrugged the question off; when it came to riddles, his father was the expert. Sure. When Ben left for California—which wasn't too far off, he knew, with the phone calls he'd been getting from his brother lately—Sam figured he'd stay on in the apartment, though he didn't really know what he'd do with the second room. He'd offered it to Dutch, but Dutch had, as expected, said no, and that was just as well. There was something in the idea, not just of living completely in one room, but of living completely in one *small* room, that appealed to Sam. He didn't owe anything to anybody.

Sam's Uncle Andy—Ben's younger brother—was, no secret, fatally ill, and when he died Ben would inherit his apartment in California. That was the only thing Ben was waiting for, Sam knew. The brochure which Andy had sent to Ben over a year before would, if Sam wanted to look, be on Ben's desk: *Pioneer Estates— California's Finest Resort-Retirement Community. Peripheral Privacy Guaranteed.* There, among the full-color pictures of the retirement city's golf courses and swimming pools, Andy had marked with an "x" his window on the seventeenth floor of one of the village's two twenty-story high-rise condominiums.

Sam watched Ben unwind his *tephillin*. What kind of privacy, he wondered, was peripheral. Ben liked to turn that phrase over in his mouth, blowing the "p"s through his lips, but Sam would never ask him to explain. He knew what peripheral meant, of course: Bill Bradley of the Knicks, for example, had more peripheral vision than the normal guy—it was what enabled him to see far to the sides, even behind him, and to get a pass off to somebody you wouldn't think was in his range. Okay. Somehow you saw more than one hundred and eighty degrees, but where did that get you? It didn't, Sam concluded, make sense.

"So," Ben said. "Tell me about the day's doings in the world of sports."

Sam forced a laugh, opened the refrigerator. "You eat yet?" he asked.

"No."

"I'll fix some eggs for us, okay?" Sam looked at his father. "Sure. You can't eat till you pray first, right?" Ben nodded. "See," Sam said. "I know a few things."

Ben smiled. "I've never denied it." He put his *tephillin* in his *tephillin* bag, folded his *talis* carefully, and put that in also. Then he busied himself, setting the table. Sam prepared the toast, poured their coffee, turned on the radio—on top of the refrigerator. The two men sat down at the table.

"I'll tell you the truth," Ben said. "After all this time—living together here the way we have these past five years—you're still a mystery to me, sonny boy."

"Yeah," Sam said. "I'm one for the books."

Ben smiled, cut into the yolk of his fried egg. "Why wait till some other time to say it: it's something I've often wondered about." He watched his son's eyes, open, clear, fixed on his own mouth. "Your—how shall I put it?—not your silence, but your simplicity. If that's the right word." Sam continued to eat, to show interest in what Ben was saying to him. "I've never been sure, though, whether your simplicity comes from the top or the bottom, if you see what I mean. Whether you're simple because you know life so well that you've reduced it to essentials, or the opposite—"

"Meaning?"

Ben laughed. "Ah—there it is. What I mean."

Sam wiped his mouth with a paper napkin, then, touched by his father's confession, he lowered his eyes. "I see things for what they are, that's all." He looked up. "Anyway, what'd you want to talk about—it must be something, you standing watch over my bed." He stirred his coffee. "Don't do that anymore, either, okay? I like to wake up by myself. That's why we have two rooms."

"I'm thinking of visiting Andy," Ben said. "You probably—"

"Fine," Sam said, without hesitating.

"I wanted to tell you first, to—"

"You don't have to make excuses." Sam mopped up some egg with a piece of toast. "He's your brother. You're a free man."

"You wouldn't mind then?"

"Why should I mind?" Sam replied. Then: "What else?"

Ben smiled, slowly. "Yes," he said. "There is something else. I'd like to be able to pay you back, for what you did. You know that."

Sam rolled his eyes. "Here we go round the mulberry bush," he said, standing and taking his dishes and silverware—all but the coffee cup—to the sink. "Look, I told you before: I made my own choices. I live with the results, like always."

"Of course, of course," Ben said. "It's just that, leaving—if I leave, that is—it's not definite—I was reminded: I wish it could be resolved, that you could be paid back."

"I'll get my reward in heaven," Sam said. He thought of guys like Stallworth and he told himself that he had no reason to kick, that—especially with Ben gone—he'd work his way out of things. He'd been in jams before. He shrugged, came back to the table and picked up his coffee cup. "Look at it this way," he said. "How many guys get the chance to put a bet on their own old man in this life?"

"It wasn't a bet."

"What was it then?—an investment?" He drank. "That's even better." He broke off, laughing. "We had some good times, Ben. It's okay."

"No, no," Ben said, as if he were brushing aside the last few things Sam had said. "What's this about heaven?" His voice was stern, forceful. "Come."

"Nothing. Just an expression."

Ben pushed his dishes forward, indicating he had finished eating. "But if you feel that way, then why—"

"Who said I felt any way?" Sam said. "Look, stop confusing me. Your old tricks won't work." He took Ben's dishes from the table and brought them to the sink. "You—that mumbo-jumbo every morning and you don't even believe in—"

Sam stopped; he was turned sideways to the sink, aware of his father's eyes, of the way they gazed at him. Although Ben said nothing, Sam could hear his father's voice, and he defended himself. He set the dishes down, and pointed. "I know all about it. You do it because your father did it and his father did it all the way back to fucking Moses and Aaron—but what's that to me? You don't even believe in God!"

Ben waited, watching his son's face. "What's there to get excited about?" he asked, very quietly. "I don't ask that anybody else believe what I believe. Have I ever urged you to put on *tephillin?*"

"You're too smart."

The light entered Ben's eyes. "You—" His mouth hung open, incredulously. "You mean—all this time, with your—you believe there is a God, a Maker of the Universe?"

Sam expected a laugh, but there was none. He shrugged. "Somebody had to start it all."

"Why?"

"Because—things just don't happen. It had to start somewhere, that's all." He turned away again. "Look—I don't care if you fly to California on an angel's back, just lay off. I got things to think about."

"But it's so simple, Sam," Ben went on, calmly. "All right. Granted. Somebody had to start it all—but then—who started the starter?"

"Come on," Sam said, turning the hot and cold water faucets on, sprinkling soap powder into the sink. He remembered the words which had been in his head the night before: that somebody had to deal the first hand, right?—but he knew what Ben would have done with that kind of line. "It all had to start somewhere," he said again. "That's all." Soap bubbles collected between his fingers. "I mean, it couldn't just keep going on forever. It had to stop somewhere."

Sam faced his father and waited, the water splashing into the sink. He hated the way Ben would drag out the silences. "But why," Ben said again, more as a statement than a question.

Sam waved him off, began washing the dishes. "Like I said, you're out of your mind. Things just don't—" He made a sound with his lips, like that of a motor, but didn't bother to finish the sentence. He'd been stupid to let himself get trapped this way. Seeing the guy all rigged up in his holy shawl first thing in the day, with the straps shining on his arm, those two boxes, one against the heart, one against the head, to show—Sam knew all about it—that one put one's mind *and* heart into prayer: that was what had done it, had put him off stride.

He heard Ben behind him, clearing the table. "Anyway," he offered, "I still say it was a good idea—putting up my money. Win some, lose some—that's the way it goes, you know? If you hadn't gotten sick, we would have done okay together. I stick by that."

"If," Ben said, and then mumbled something in Yiddish. Though Sam could not have repeated it, he'd heard the sounds often enough to know what they meant: *And if my aunt had had balls we would have called her my uncle.*

"That's true too," Sam said.

Ben was next to him, touching his son's arm, above the elbow, firmly. "It's just that—you'll forgive my sentimentality—thinking of leaving here, of—" He paused. "There are things I'd like to say to you."

Sam moved away from the sink, wiping his hands on a dishtowel. "I can understand that," he said, and he meant it. He began making up his bed, smoothing the sheets, tucking the blankets in. He carried his pillow to the closet, dropping it behind the shoes and galoshes. "I mean, okay, when you come down to it, what's it all about, right?"

Ben opened the cabinet above the sink. "My father always gave you credit," he said. "He said you were special."

"Yeah, I'm a bird," Sam laughed. He pulled the loop at the foot of the bed, then folded the three sections backward so that the mattress disappeared and the bed was, once again, a sofa. He lifted the cushions from beside the bed and put them in place.

"You have the right idea," Ben said. "You're like your grandfather—it's a pity the two of you—that he didn't live longer, to know that you had found the—yes—the ideal profession." Sam sat on his couch. "You never work, in the ordinary sense, and yet if you, if—what I mean is, you work for nobody but yourself, you're beholden to nobody. That's why—" Ben's voice had become passionate, but Sam dismissed him with a wave of the hand.

"A lot you know," he said.

Ben stepped back, hung a dishtowel on a hook in the alcove. He was, obviously, upset. Sam understood. Having to go out and be a nursemaid to Andy—Sam didn't figure that Ben had had any real choice, since the guy was his brother—was nothing to look forward to. Especially with the way Andy would try to cover up, to act as if he were still the world's last big spender. But Sam knew that he wouldn't have sent for Ben unless he'd needed him, and probably for cash. Ben forced a smile, spoke in the voice which gave him confidence. "Remember—sunshine and hot competition! Lawn bowling on the lush greensward."

Sam pushed the picture of Andy from his head. "Any more questions?"

"That look in your eyes," Ben said. "I know you don't daydream, sonny boy, but that look—" Ben smiled. "Perhaps from my radio days—the way you fade in and fade out—perhaps that is your inheritance from me. What do you think?"

Sam sighed, as if bored. "Is that all?"

Ben smiled. "You're right again—there is something else you should know." Sam said nothing. "I was worried about how Mason would react to my leaving, you see, and I was thinking of asking you to—well—to look after him."

Sam laughed. "Sure," he said. "Me and my mother."

"I'm serious," Ben said, sharply, and began to speak of his friendship with the man, of their childhood together, of the hours they had spent these past five years in Mason's room below the rummage shop. Tidewater! There was something Sam could never figure—what his father found to talk about so much with a guy like that. The way he slid around so goddamned silently you never knew when he would be there, right next to you. The guy gave him the creeps, that was all. Sure, the two of them had known one another when they'd been kids, growing up in Brooklyn. That counted for something. They could ask one another about people they'd known and what had happened to them and how their lives had turned out, the way Sam and Dutch did with their old buddies. Ben could give Tidewater his life story, and Tidewater could do the same. But then what, Sam wondered. Ben claimed that there was more to Tidewater than met the eye, but Sam only bet what he knew.

He watched his father pick up his *tephillin* bag and turn away, toward his bedroom. At the door, Ben held the bag toward Sam, and his voice shifted, so that Sam paid attention. " 'It's true,' the man said, returning from an illness," Ben declared. " 'The Jews are smarter than we are. How do I know? In the hospital, every morning before the doctors came, each Jewish man would take his own blood pressure—!' " Sam didn't laugh, and watched his father smile, weakly. "But you will do what I've asked you to, won't you? You will let him give you whatever it is he wants you to have."

Sam blinked. "What?"

"Don't ask me," Ben said. "It has something to do with things he would have told me, had I stayed on. But if I'm going, he says you will receive it—"

"Look," Sam said. "Enough riddles. Receive what?"

"I don't know," Ben said, then opened the door to his bedroom. "I just told you. You should pay attention to your father, don't you see? Mason has his secrets—the best your father can make of it is this: that it must be part of what we were talking about before—about your inheritance: you'll receive what had been saved for me."

Thank God for Andy, Sam thought, when Ben was in his room. Maybe, when people got past a certain age they should send them out in the snow with a bag of food, the way the Eskimos did. Live fast, die young, and have a good-looking corpse. That—a favorite line from high school days—was the way it should be, instead of all this moping around and trying to find—to find what?—words, he supposed. To find words all the time, the way Ben had just been doing.

A few minutes later, Ben left the apartment to help out in the store below: it was Saturday morning, and from the living room window Sam could see that the line of shoppers reached almost to the corner. Sleepy-eyed black women, many with their children, stood quietly, waiting. One policeman was there, but usually, Sam knew, if trouble arose—a place in line, who had found a dress first, whether a woman had forgotten to pay for a coat that was on her back when she left the store—Ben's voice would be enough to settle the matter. "I think the manager would like to have a word with you," Flo would say, and a minute later Ben would be there, the richness—the depth—of his voice doing the job.

And if—it happened rarely—there were some real trouble, Ben would bang on the pipes and Sam would come down, for whatever his presence was worth. The policeman was, in the end, useless: the store would not press charges for a twenty-five cent dress or a five dollar suit. In a while, Sam would go downstairs. He liked sitting there, watching the people come and go, and he liked listening to Flo. The people bought, they traded, they looked, they hung around sipping coffee (a nickel a cup, refills free to the regulars), they talked to Flo about their problems, the time passed. It passed more easily, in fact, than it did anywhere else, Sam had decided. Leave it to Flo, he'd heard the local people say, she runs the show. They were right. It told you a lot about the way things were going, for example—Flo had pointed this out to him the first time he'd been in the store—to realize that it was cheaper to buy used clothing than to have old clothes washed and cleaned. Twenty-five cents for dresses, twenty-five cents for a pair of shoes, ten cents for blouses, twenty-five cents for shirts, ten cents for underwear, one dollar for coats, a nickel for a pair of torn nylons. Sheets were twenty cents each, pillows a quarter, pillow cases a dime. Dishes were two for a dime, and eyeglasses were fifteen cents a pair.

Sam thought that Flo slipped Ben five or ten dollars a week—he wasn't sure, and he never asked—but Ben earned the money; it was his voice that helped bring a lot of the merchandise in—telephoning factories, department stores, warehouses, and—the biggest source of gifts, as things turned out—the names he culled from obituary columns. Flo fixed up the tax deduction forms—the shop was, after all, a legitimate charity.

Flo sold to dealers also: they exported the goods, mostly to South American countries. And she would—this got Sam—take orders from the women, according to color and size. Sure. So he could have breakfast and pass the time watching the people trying the stuff on while the kids pored through the comic books (five for a dime), and records (ten cents each), and maybe, toward noon, there'd be a touch football game on Martense Street—but then what? Despite his win the night before, his funds were low, and he hadn't had a card game in six weeks. He felt—the word, as soon as he'd used it to name the feeling, gave him chills—rusty: as if, somewhere inside him, his bones were coated with orange flakes which he yearned to scrape away.

He finished his coffee, rinsed his cup, then went to Ben's room. The *tephillin* bag lay in the middle of Ben's pillow. Sam laughed at his father's theories. If he'd wanted, he knew, he could have said something to Ben about it being forbidden to wear *tephillin* on the Sabbath, but when he had, during their first year together in the apartment, discovered Ben putting *tephillin* on in his bedroom one Saturday morning and said something, Ben had only smiled. He knew the law, he said, but he was entitled in this life to some small transgressions, wasn't he? Even in religion, every man had his own pleasure. . . . The brochure, Sam saw, was there, as always, in the middle of Ben's desk. It unfolded, he knew, with a green map in the center, showing the location of each private home, of Andy's building, of the synagogues, churches, banks, shopping center, and the rest, but what Sam liked most were the captions under the photos. Sometimes, when he was least expecting it, Ben would suddenly look at him and, in his best radio voice, declare: "Grandma Moses started painting at seventy!" or "If you think shuffleboard is an easy game, wait till you take on the pros at Pioneer Estates!"

Across the street, next to the TV repair shop, old Mrs. Cameron sat on the stoop, a large purple cushion under her skinny bottom. The woman was in her late eighties. Maybe Ben could take her with him when he flew off, Sam thought. She could—Sam read the caption in his head—dance the buckles off her shoes. He laughed at that thought. Once, perhaps fifteen years before, during a heavy snowstorm, he'd carried a bag of groceries up to her apartment, on the third floor. But she hadn't let him inside and all he could see, looking through the doorway as he handed the bag in to her, was a dark piano with a gold framed picture of a soldier on it.

Her eyes were very blue: Sam could see that from where he was. He could remember reading, when he was ten or eleven, that Ted Williams had had such good eyesight he could read the titles off 78 rpm records as they spun around. Sam shrugged. He'd been able to do the same, but it hadn't gotten him to the major leagues. In public school his eyes had tested at fifteen over twenty. Big deal, he thought—that and twenty cents would get him a ride on the subway.

In the bathroom he relieved himself, fixed his hair, then walked back through Ben's room, pulled the telephone from its place under the TV table, and dialed.

"Cohen residence. Dutch Cohen, number one son, speaking."

"It's me," Sam said.

"Hey Sam—how's the Ace?" Dutch asked. "I was just thinking of you, did you know that?"

"I picked up two and a half on the Knicks last night—I wanted you to be the first to know."

"Great, Ace," Dutch said, but his enthusiasm—like a teenager's
—irritated Sam. "I mean, with the way things have been going ever
since—"

"Forget it," Sam said. "I just thought I'd tell you."

"Did you get a train schedule last night?"

"Schedule?"

"At Penn Station—for going out to Herbie's, remember? To see
the old crowd."

"I forgot," Sam said, remembering what had happened to upset
his concentration. "But it's still a few weeks away—I'll pick one up
next time."

"I'll be able to go," Dutch said. "Things are pretty good here. I
mean—anytime—it'd be great to see you, Sam."

Dutch's voice, too sweet, made Sam uncomfortable. "I thought
maybe I'd get over your way today," he said, "but I got to see
what's going on in the store—if they need me."

"Sure. I was just thinking about you—did you know that?"

"Yeah. Well, I'll try to come by. I wanted to check if you were
home. And to tell you about the Knicks."

"Sure, Ace."

Sam slipped into his jacket, locked the door behind him, went
down the steps, turned right, behind the staircase, and walked in
the dark until he found the door. He knocked, twice.

"Yes?"

"It's me—Sam."

The door opened. Tidewater was standing there; Sam nodded to
him. "My old man around?"

Tidewater motioned toward the front of the store. Sam thought
of saying something about what Ben had told him, but no matter
which way he worded the question, as to what Tidewater had for
him, it wouldn't come out right. He'd let the other guy make the
first move. When in doubt, wait it out. "Thanks a lot," he said, and
left. What do you think God gave you a tongue for, he wanted to
ask—but he knew where that would have led. The guy would only
have stared down at him from those bulging eyes; Sam had never
seen a guy, except for an albino, with larger whites in his eyes.

The crowd in the back room, where Tidewater stood guard, was
thick with children. They kept the comic books and records and
cartons of junk there—mixed with furniture: chairs (one dollar)

piled upside down on each other; tables (five dollars) full of cartons and dishes and pots; sofas (seven dollars) piled to the ceiling; mattresses and headboards stacked against the far wall. A boy and girl were wrestling under some chairs; at a yellow Formica kitchen table, between two hefty black women who were sorting dishes, an old man, no more than five feet tall, searched the contents of a carton. The man's face was almost green in color, and he stooped over, holding a dull gray handkerchief to his mouth. His eyes were close together, tiny, his nose drooped. Forget it, Sam said to the man silently: Flo checks everything out before she puts it down.

He made his way into the front room, looking for Ben. The blue and white Corning Ware coffee percolator was unplugged: NO COFFEE ON SATURDAYS—SORRY—one of Flo's hand-lettered signs. At the store's entrance, Flo's sister Marion was at the cashbox, taking in the money. Next to her table was a big carton, with paper bags and newspapers and bits of string in it.

Tidewater was only an inch taller than Sam, no more, but Sam didn't like that inch: he remembered the first—and for that matter the last—time he'd had a run-in with him, perhaps two and a half years before, when he had said something innocently enough, he'd thought, about the colored people moving into the Nostrand–to– New York Avenue section of Martense Street; Tidewater had puffed his pigeon chest, risen to his full height, and glared down at Sam, declaring that he was one of them, a black man himself.

Sam believed him, he supposed—why would anyone lie about being black if he could pass for white?—and there was something, once you'd been told, in the way the man's nostrils flared out. Still, the guy gave him the creeps, no matter what stories Ben could spin about what he'd been like when they'd first known one another. Sam heard Flo's voice, from the other side of a rack of coats. He turned, made his way around a table where women were picking through a pile of sweaters and blouses.

"One minute, dear," Flo said, glancing his way. Her eyeglasses were, as always, hanging around her neck on a silver chain. A woman reached over, grabbed something under the rack, and pulled it out: it was a boy, his mouth stuffed with potato chips. She dragged him away. A black woman with dull red hair was helping a man get into a wide-shouldered tweed sport jacket. Men's clothing, for some reason, was always at a premium: jackets were five dollars, suits from five to ten dollars. When a new shipment came in, it would usually be gone within twenty-four hours. Even some of the high-stepping local dudes would come in and go through the stuff, and Sam himself saw nothing wrong with picking up a jacket or a coat in the store. Who would know the difference, after all. The money was better in his pocket.

Flo's hand was on Sam's arm, and Sam smiled at her. She motioned him to a corner. "Did you see the woman I was talking to—?" Sam nodded. Flo smiled and her smile made Sam feel warm, made him smile too; she was probably in her mid-fifties, Sam figured, but it wasn't apparent unless you looked closely. She could have passed for thirty-five, perhaps forty. "She wanted to know if she could return this—" Flo showed him the black dress which was draped across her arm. "She said she didn't need it anymore. Do you know why?"

Sam looked toward where the woman had been standing. "I don't know—a night out, I guess."

Flo shook her head. "It was for a funeral. She didn't say, of course, but I know. It's happened before."

"It takes all kinds," Sam said. Then: "You need any help this morning?"

"No. Things are going smoothly. Marion's here—which helps—and two volunteers from the organization should be along by ten-thirty."

"Ben?"

"He said to meet him at the supermarket. He said to give you the message if you came down—he forgot to tell you upstairs." She looked at her watch. "He left about twenty minutes ago. He said to give him a half hour."

"He wants me to help carry packages home," Sam said, and as soon as the words were out, he felt foolish. "I was supposed to take care of something else, but . . ."

He didn't finish the sentence, and Flo, squeezing his arm slightly, left him. Sam stepped around a rack of dresses and, without glancing behind—he figured he didn't need Tidewater's eyes more than once a day—moved to the front of the store. There was, when he thought about it, nobody he admired more than Flo. She'd had it rough. That she seemed to like him, to take an interest in his life—this meant a lot to him. She was a real queen—to be able to

do all she did for others when her own life had turned out the way
it had.

Marion glanced up. "How's tricks?" Sam asked.

Marion shrugged, embarrassed. Behind her, at Sam's eye level,
was another of Flo's signs: THOSE WHO STEAL FROM THE
HANDICAPPED ARE DOUBLY PUNISHED—BY THE *LAW*
IN THIS WORLD . . . BY THE *LAWD* IN THE NEXT!

"Pretty busy," Marion said.

"Yeah," Sam said. She was younger than Flo, by ten years
perhaps—more attractive at first—but somehow he always thought
of her as the older sister. Her eyes were tired, and her body seemed
to have a sag in it somewhere. She wore a soft wool sweater, pale
blue, but she kept her shoulders so tight to her that the sweater
seemed a few sizes too large. Ben had said something once about
her, and he hadn't paid attention: something about before she was
married, and about what Flo had thought of it all. Flo was always
so full of—energy was the word which occurred to Sam, and
Marion was always so glum, that you had to wonder how, to use
one of Ben's sayings, they could have come from the same womb.

"I got to meet Ben," Sam said. "He's waiting for me." Marion
nodded, but her eyes did not meet his. Sam waited while Marion
took a dollar from a woman—the woman counted out pieces of
children's underwear into a paper bag. "I'll see you around," Sam
said, and gave a half-wave.

He crossed the street, away from the line of shoppers. He didn't
mind the small errands now and then, helping to carry the groceries
home on Saturdays, when Ben usually did their big shopping for
the week—in fact, in this case he was just as glad Ben liked to do it.
The less Sam had to go into stores, the better. Having to do his
shopping by himself would be a small price to pay, though, for the
day Ben would be gone, baking his ass in the California sun. Sam
figured he could get a lot of what he needed at some of the local
delicatessens.

At the near end of Martense Street there was a touch football
game in progress, and Sam stopped, leaned against a tree. The kids
were too young for him—twelve or thirteen, he figured—but they
were good. Sam smiled: a little kid, the shortest player on either
team, took a lateral, got a good block, and jitterbugged past the
corner man, leaving the guy frozen. He ran for ten yards, then got

pinned against a parked car. The kid wore a big grin on his face, laughed at the guy he'd faked out, said something, and the guy went for him; the kid slipped away easily, went back to the huddle rolling his eyes, shuffling his feet to invisible music.

Sam watched another play, this one botched, then left. It picked him up—it always did—just to be able to watch some guys playing. The air was fresh, people were out—there was always a lot of action in the streets on Saturday morning. Some teenagers were pitching pennies in front of the laundromat, and, in the bakery, a fat black woman in an orange bandanna was mopping up. Sam sniffed in, caught the odor of melting butter. Dutch claimed that most of those odors—popcorn, pizza, bread, charbroiled hamburgers—were artificial: little bottles of the stuff set up in front of exhaust fans.

When Ben had been telling him about Tidewater—that the guy had something to give him—Sam had thought of the Bible man. The guy was still on his mind, but Sam figured that was natural: it wasn't every night that some bird followed you from Madison Square Garden and tried to save your ass for Jesus. If he showed up again, maybe he could sic him on Tidewater. Sam laughed to himself: sure—kill two birds with one stone. He liked that idea. He had, before he'd gone to sleep the night before, torn the pamphlet up and thrown it away, but he could remember, nonetheless, just what had been written inside. Not, he thought, because it had made that great an impression upon him—though, for sure, the guy had reached him, with that silk voice, and having known somehow where he lived—but because Sam had a memory like that. He couldn't forget things, even when he wanted to. Ordinarily, in his line of work, it was an asset: in different kinds of card games, he could remember every card that had been played; even in five-card draw, he could increase his edge by keeping track of which pairs from the previous hand—the chances were slightly better than average, the way most guys shuffled—might still be sticking close to each other. It annoyed him now, though, not to be able to forget; he might have had a word or two wrong, but he could still see the guy's blue photo, and hear the smooth voice:

I have been a gambler too, brother. That is why I understand your plight. For over twenty years I wandered in dens of iniquity. Let me help you by leading you to the comfort of our Lord Jesus. For are we not all as an unclean thing, and all our righteousness as filthy rags? I

*have been down and out, I have used women in unnatural ways, I have
defiled my body. But we have all, like sheep, gone astray, and except by
grace, which is the gift of God, are ye not saved. Not of works, lest any
man should boast!*

Like lambs would be more like it, Sam thought, crossing Church
Avenue. The guy's phone number, but not his name, had been there
also, inviting Sam to come and pray. Sam stored the guy's spiel
away, with everything else he had to save: the words would get
weaker in time, especially—and this, he knew, was what made him
so angry—when he could be getting a game of poker again.

Maybe, though, the whole thing was a con and the guy would
make his move just when you were on your knees with your hands
clasped in front of you. But the picture didn't amuse Sam. The guy
had gotten to him—he admitted it. Maybe, he thought, approaching the Bel-Air supermarket, he could have Ben speak with him:
with Ben's voice, the guy might think Sam had God right there in
the room with him. That would be rich, Ben quoting stuff from the
Jewish Bible to Sam's—what should he call him?—to his fellow
gambler. Well, Sam said to himself, this gambler will bet on this life
and take his chances on the next one: you couldn't bet on what you
couldn't see. Play the cards, guard your odds. That was control.

Ben had all week long, when people were at work, to do the
shopping, but he always picked Saturdays, the way a lot of the old
people in the neighborhood did. Maybe they liked meeting each
other there on the weekend, Sam thought, going up and down the
aisles together. Congregation Shaare Torah had moved away, past
Flatbush Avenue, down by Albermarle Road and East 21st Street,
to a better section. When it had been on Bedford Avenue, next to
Erasmus, it was the place most of the people in the neighborhood
had used; the new one was probably too far for most of them to
walk to, unless they were very religious, the way his grandfather
had been. Nothing had stopped him—every Friday night and
Saturday morning, freezing rain or broiling sun, the old guy had
gone.

Sam stepped on the black rubber mat that was embedded in the
sidewalk and the electric-eye door opened for him. The noise inside
the store, mingling with piped-in music, was louder than the street
sounds had been outside. The colors—posters, cans, displays,
boxes—made him stagger slightly, stop: it was as if, coming from

the outside, he was inside a movie which had changed suddenly from black-and-white to technicolor. There were some Christmas decorations up already, silver tinsel hanging from transparent nylon thread, speckling turrets of cereal boxes. He searched for Ben and felt something tug on his jacket. He looked to the right. An old woman, Pygmy-sized, stared into his face. He saw powder pressed into the wrinkles that ran in circles across her black skin, and he thought of the shrunken heads he used to see advertised on the inside covers of comic books. The woman's mouth, toothless, opened: "You all save green stamps?"

Her hand moved from his jacket to his wrist, and he felt the bones of her fingers. "No. Not me, but—"

She smiled, and Sam gazed in at the fleshy red skin in the back of her throat. The woman sat down on an empty Pepsi-Cola case. "I'll wait," she said. "Remember, I asked you all first."

Sam thought of explaining, but decided not to bother. Maybe she'd be gone by the time he left. He walked around the row of empty shopping carts. The store was crowded—people wheeling their half-full carts up and down the aisles, chattering to one another, standing in clusters at the head of each aisle where the specials were. He checked an aisle (vegetables and juices) for Ben. Cartons of canned goods lined the floor from one end of the aisle to the other. A black kid, a pencil stuck behind his ear, was stamping cans of peas and carrots, clicking out an off-beat rhythm with his purple hand-stamper, clickety-click clickety-clickety-click. Two middle-aged black women, wearing heavy winter coats, were debating the prices on several cans of asparagus. Sam walked past them, and they eyed him suspiciously.

At the end of the aisle, to the right, salamis and cheeses were hanging from strings above the delicatessen counter. Sam turned left, passed in front of the meat counter, around shoppers comparing packages of cellophane-wrapped beef. In back of the counter were sliding glass partitions, a recent improvement, and sides of cows were hanging behind it from hooks; chickens were moving along on a conveyor belt. Sam heard a bell ring, calling for a butcher. His mouth watered.

The floor was littered with cigarette butts, candy wrappers. To the right, in the corner of the store, above a display of potato chips, a TV camera moved slowly from right to left, left to right. Sam could remember—he'd been about twelve years old—when the supermarket had opened, the first one in the neighborhood, and how all the women in front of his building on Linden Boulevard had talked afterward about how guilty they felt when they shopped there. He had made some tips, going to the local stores for them—getting a container of milk, a loaf of bread, a half-pound of tomatoes or some soup greens—when they'd been too embarrassed to go themselves.

Where was Ben hiding himself? Sam checked frozen foods, then the produce department. He turned right, around a display of beer in dark store-brand, no-deposit no-return bottles, then cut around a cornucopia of picnic supplies, paper plates and cups spilling into a green plastic basin.

"Excuse me," he said, trying to get through a traffic jam.

"Sure, darling. Here, let me squeeze myself a little this way. . . ."

The woman giggled, and Sam slipped past her, past flour, sugar, salt, baking needs, around and into the next aisle, and Ben was there: in paper goods, his cart almost full. Sam stopped. He was surprised somehow to see how short the man was. Ben had a box of tissues in each hand, balancing them, comparing the weights. He glanced toward Sam but didn't seem to notice him. Hunched up in his raincoat, Ben seemed smaller than ever, his face very gray in comparison with the brown and black faces around him. He was wearing his reading glasses and his nose seemed especially big, hooked out above his thin mouth. Bent over, the man was no more than five-feet-four—he'd shrunk a full inch during the past few years. Sam could see things like that, he could usually estimate somebody's height to within a half inch. He felt dizzy, and he wondered momentarily if it were possible, gazing this way—half-hypnotized by the noise and the warmth, by the music and the colors—to actually see his father shrink. All but the nose and the ears. They were—Dutch had once pointed this out to him—the only parts of the body that continued to grow after the rest had stopped.

A woman's cart banged into Ben's, but he didn't budge. Sam watched him put one box of tissues back on the shelf and place the other on top of his shopping cart. *Don't!* he wanted to call out. *It's too full, Ben!* He felt wide awake now. Ben seemed stuck—between his basket and the shelf. Sam moved forward, past toilet paper, sandwich bags, plastic wrap, aluminum foil, paper toweling, hot cups, paper plates, plastic silverware. Ben turned to the shelf, his elbow knocking the box of tissues to the floor.

Sam moved quickly, but Ben had already bent over—and as he retrieved the box of tissues, Sam saw that his father had had something in his right hand all the while, palmed, and that, shielded now by the tissues and the shopping cart, his face to the shelves, he had slipped it quickly into his coat pocket.

Ben wheeled off, turned right. The guy was out of his mind, Sam told himself. What if . . . he stopped: the questions spun around inside his skull, but they made him angry, not dizzy. He pushed to the end of the aisle, turned right around the stack of cereal boxes, and saw Ben, in front of the gourmet specialties. A small black jar dropped into his left coat pocket. Sam watched Ben's face: it was flushed, happy—the gray color was gone. Sam lagged behind. Ben went past frozen food, ice cream. Sam moved closer. Ben looked over his shoulder, smiled.

"Sure," Sam said.

"I know," Ben said at once. "I said a half-hour. But Mr. Kwestel stopped me on the way here, to talk about his daughter. She's in the hospital. You went to school with her, didn't you?" Ben wheeled away, Sam following him, cutting around cartons filled with boxes of soap flakes. "At any rate, she's in Meadowbrook Hospital, on the Island, and it's such a long trip for him. . . ."

Ben shrugged, let his eyelids close, indicating by the expression on his face the difficulties life could bring. "Listen," Sam began. "As long as—"

Ben's expression changed. "I know. On my trail, Sam Junior—but you didn't escape Ben Berman's eagle eye." He lifted a can of peaches from its pyramid, on sale at forty-one cents, and dropped it into his cart. "I know you don't like to come inside, and that is the reason I apologized."

"Listen—"

Ben shook his head sideways, his eyes closed. He moved an index finger to his lips, the fingertip grazing his nose. "Shh. We'll talk later. Dairy products now—I always buy them last. To minimize spoilage."

Sam breathed through his lips, unable to hide his irritation. The sooner his father flew away, the better. If he loved Tidewater so much, he could take him with him, let him sweep out the shuffleboard courts. Ben put a container of milk, a half-pound of whipped butter, a container of sour cream, and a package of farmer cheese into his cart. "Do you want anything special—some cheese? The longhorn is good, as is the mild cheddar—"

"I just want to get my butt out of here."

"Relax," Ben said.

"Yeah. I'll live longer. I know all about it."

"Some pickled herring, though," Ben said, taking a jar of Vita herring, cream-style. "Nothing else—you're sure?" Sam glared. "I bought a leg of lamb, we can have it tonight. And some—but you're tired of waiting, aren't you? Come."

They moved toward the checkout registers, Ben in front, humming. When it was their turn and Ben had begun unloading the cart, one of the kids who had been hanging around approached them. "Carry your stuff home for you, mister?"

Ben smiled. "I have my son with me," he said.

The kid looked at Sam, showing nothing, then moved away. The old woman, Sam saw, was still there, sitting on her Pepsi-Cola case. He heard the sound of the register, and then their cans and boxes were moving along the counter, on a black conveyor belt.

"Between twenty-one fifty and twenty-two dollars, I predict," Ben said. Sam watched another kid take a paper bag from under the counter, snap it open, and begin to pack their goods into it. Why did they all look so sleepy-eyed? "Want to bet on it?"

"Bet?"

"My dollar to your fifty cents, since I'm an old hand at this. I say twenty-one seventy-five." Ben paused. "Come. Be a sport."

Sam scanned the bags, the remaining items. He was stuck: if he said no, his father would have won anyway; if he said yes, at least . . . "Twenty-three even," he stated.

They stood, side by side, waiting. The girl, black and heavy-set—pregnant? Sam wondered—with scarlet lipstick at the outer edge of wide lips, tapped away at the buttons: total, subtotal, tax. The figures spun, the machine whirred. Ben leaned into Sam, across the counter, his narrow head level with the girl's breasts, and the register rang, stopped: twenty-three twenty-six.

Ben reached up, patted Sam on the shoulder. "You win, sonny boy." He slipped a dollar into Sam's hand. Sam felt warm. Ben paid the girl, and his change exploded into a tin cup. On a machine clamped to the register, high, to the left, the girl typed their total, waited; the machine moved by itself again, and then a strip of green stamps rolled out. The girl tore them off, handed them to Ben, looked toward the next customer.

Ben gave the boy who'd packed their bags a dime. The boy tipped his baseball cap to Ben. "Thanks, Cap'n," the boy said.

"I was first, remember?" The old woman had one of Sam's wrists between her fingers.

"Here," Ben said, loading a shopping bag into Sam's right arm. "Can you take two?" He sighed. "I should buy a carry-cart. I know—"

"I can take another one," Sam said. The woman tugged at his wrist. "She asked me before I went in—for the green stamps."

Ben stared at the old woman, his face blank. "So?" he asked Sam. "Did you buy anything?"

"I chip in. Sure. Fifty-fifty."

Sam stood there, a shopping bag in the crook of each arm, Ben's thin mouth set tight, the woman hissing at his side. "You find them, then, and give your friend your half, all right?" Ben picked up their bag and walked away, the electric-eye door opening for him.

Sam set one bag down on the counter, tried to pry the woman's fingers from his wrist, but her grip was tight, like iron. "You all promised," she said.

Were people staring at them? He shook his head, blinked. He felt furious, dizzy—and he didn't like the mixture. He didn't trust himself when he was this way, when things were blurred and he lost concentration. "I didn't," he said, and looked into each bag. "Not really." Damn his father's beady eyes! He reached into his side pocket. "I have to go. Here—here—" And he pushed the dollar bill Ben had given him into her hand. The woman let go, looked down at the green paper, then shoved it back into Sam's palm. "I want stamps."

Sam had already picked up the bag and was heading for the exit. *"Dumb pickaninny!"* the woman shouted after him. Outside, Sam saw that Ben was at the corner, in front of the Lincoln Savings

Bank, waiting for the light to change. Across the street, in front of Al's Lock Shop, a black policeman was talking to two tall teenagers. They had their hands out, palms up, showing that they were clean. Above them, where Ryan's Billiard Parlor had been, the windows were covered now with posters of ferocious-looking black men and signs saying that black was beautiful.

The light changed. Ben crossed the street. Sam took long strides, feeling the shape of a large can in his left palm, through the bag. The bag in his right hand—boxes mostly, cold cereal probably—was lighter. Sam hurried, but Ben managed to stay ahead of him, by half a block. On his block, the line of people in front of the rummage shop was as long as it had been when he'd left. The cop twirled his billy club, the leather strap stretching from his wrist. Sam had—a mistake—cut diagonally across the street and had to decide now whether to backtrack to the corner and go around the line, or to try to cut through. He saw Ben, in front of the door, waiting.

A woman nodded to him, stepped back. "Let the boy go through—he lives here. I seen him working in the store."

Sam mumbled a thank you. "Man, that boy got himself a real load." It was a man's voice. Ben was holding the door open for him. Sam moved into the dark hallway and mounted the stairs.

Ben unlocked the door and they entered their apartment. Sam put the bags down on the kitchen table—the tear in the bag, he saw, was where the can of peaches had been, but it was only two inches long. He'd been in no danger. "Are you out of your mind?" he said to Ben, his hands on his hips. He was breathing hard, but he wasn't winded. His mind was clear.

"Calm yourself," Ben said. "Here. Let me put the dairy products and frozen food away. Then we'll talk." He went to the refrigerator, opened the door, and put a bag of groceries on top of the stove. "You can empty things onto the table, I'll do the rest. Believe me, Sam, I appreciate your coming. I know I could pay one of the boys, but—"

Sam tore his jacket off, moved toward his father. "Listen, cut the small talk, and don't tell me not to get my balls in an uproar. What the fuck are you trying to do to me? You just tell me that!"

Ben rearranged things in the refrigerator, making room. "To you?—nothing. Your touch is as good as it always was. I have great confidence in you, Sam. When I'm gone, I know you'll get by. I didn't, in truth, expect you to beat me, but . . ."

Sam stepped around the coffee table, in front of his sofa-bed. Ben stood, put his hand up, stopping Sam in his tracks. Ben's eyes danced. "I saw you there, you know, looking for me, before—"

"And you went ahead anyway—?" Sam felt some sweat trickle down the small of his back.

Ben's eyes flickered; he seemed to realize for the first time that he was still wearing his raincoat. He touched the pockets. "Oh *that*," he said, as if he hadn't understood until now what Sam was angry about. "Don't let it bother you, sonny boy. I've been doing that for years—ever since I went on social security. It's nothing to worry about, believe me." He smiled, and Sam saw the kindness in his father's eyes. "I'm sorry you found out. You have your own things—your worries—to think about, I'm sure."

"Not so fast," Sam said, as Ben turned away from him and put the butter onto the top shelf of the refrigerator.

Ben looked at him, steadily, then sighed. "I should have mentioned it before this, not to alarm you." He closed the refrigerator door and walked to Sam, taking his son by the arm, leading him to the kitchen table. "Sit," he said. "Sit," he repeated, pressing Sam's arm. Sam sat. Ben pushed the shopping bags to one side of the table, stroked his chin, then came to Sam again, putting his hand on his son's shoulder, touching Sam's neck with his fingers. "All right. I'll explain: prices rising the way they have, a retired man like myself, living on what amounts to virtually a fixed income—I know you chip in with your share and, believe me, I'm grateful for all you've done, I can never say how much—but it's really, the way I figure it, the only way to keep up with inflation."

Sam blinked. "To what?"

Ben took a can of Alaska king crab meat from his left coat pocket and set it on the table, a bottle of multi-vitamins following it. "Watch: a dollar eighty-nine, and a dollar twenty-nine makes three-nineteen." Sam couldn't believe what he was hearing. Ben produced a bathtub stopper from his other pocket, and a jar of imitation caviar. He read the prices to Sam, adding them up as he went along, putting the tax on at the end. ". . . On a total of twenty-three twenty-six, that's over ten per cent, right? Which puts me well ahead of the annual rate of inflation." He wagged his finger at Sam. "But remember, in the spring and summer, I can't wear a coat without arousing some suspicion—so we can consider this," his small eyes twinkled, "a kind of lay-away plan."

Sam shoved his chair back and stood, the rubber stoppers on the chair legs squealing against the wood floor. "You're out of your mind," he said. He picked his jacket up from the sofa, where he'd thrown it. "You eat by yourself, you hear? And if you do this again, you'll—you'll have more than inflation to worry about. . . . Sure." Sam wanted the words to come out quickly, like machine gun fire, but he felt that his tongue was in the way. His father had the words, the voice. "I don't care what you say, you don't fool me. You're not gonna do me in, do you hear? And that's what you'd like—to have one of those TV cameras spot you and then—and then—" He searched for words.

"Do *you* in? Listen, sonny boy, I'm not out to take anything that's not coming to me." Sam's hand was on the doorknob, Ben's hand on top of his. "But they'll screw you any way they can, and I'm telling you that plain up and down. Do *you* in? Tell me, if you're so smart, what defense does a man my age have against the automatic workings of an economy that's endlessly inflating?" Ben laughed, angrily. "They won't do *me* in, either, do you hear? I'll make my own specials, damn them!"

"You do what you want, I'm getting out." Sam set his teeth. "You don't fool me."

Ben lifted Sam's hand from the doorknob. "Relax, Sam. With all the, you'll pardon the expression, *shvartzehs* they have to keep their eyes on, they never give an old man like me a second glance." Pulling Sam back into the room, he whispered: "How do you think we've been eating so well? Answer me that! Granted you chip in, but—well, if you calculated sometime, you would have seen, long ago—"

"Look, Ben—"

"Trouble budgeting, folks?" Ben said, his voice moving down, into its favorite register. "*Steal!* In these days of soaring costs and run-away inflation, we all do our best to make ends meet. Your money will go farther when you steal. Remember—"

"No," Sam said, and got to the door before Ben could stop him. "No. You don't fool me. Not for a minute. I don't need one of your routines." He stepped into the hallway and, hoping to wound his father, found something to say which he thought would do the trick. "I'm glad Andy's hurrying—that he sent for you. Sure. Inflation being what it is, what'll he be worth if he kicks off in a few years?" Sam laughed, felt the laughter, sharp, as it moved from his throat and across the threshold to his father.

"I—I don't understand," Ben said, sitting down at the table. "I think I get your drift, but, what I mean is, in exact terms, it doesn't make any *sense,* Sam—what you've just said."

3

Something was up. The Knicks had now won their ninth game in a row, Stallworth was playing well—coming in as their sixth man sometimes, ahead of Cazzie Russell—but when Sam had telephoned Mr. Sabatini to put something on their third game (as planned, he had not bet on the second game), Mr. Sabatini had, for the first time in six years, refused to take his bet. "I'm sorry, sweetheart," he had said. "I'd like to help you out, but the Knicks are off my board until further notice."

Sam had telephoned again, before each succeeding game, but the reply was always the same. Whatever was up—Sam's guess was that Sabatini couldn't farm out enough of the action to cover himself: the Knicks were not only winning, but they were having an easy time with the point spreads—Sam couldn't do anything about it. He figured that any other bookie who would handle bets of three hundred and less would be in the same boat as Sabatini; Sam would bide his time, then, and when the Knick window was open again, he'd be there. The season was long.

He leafed through the newspaper, from back to front, checking the results at Aqueduct, not for the horses, but to see what the previous day's number had been: the last three digits of the day's mutuel take gave you the Brooklyn number. Six, eight, and six. Double six. The numbers men wouldn't like that. It was trickier to figure the Manhattan number—you had to put together the payoff prices on the winning horses in the first three races to get the first digit—then the same with the fourth and fifth races for the second, then the sixth and seventh. Sam never bothered. Only suckers played the numbers anyway. He checked the point spreads on the pro football games, the pro basketball games, some college games. "Look, sweetheart," Sabatini had said the last time Sam had called, two days before, when the Knicks had been at home against the Celtics. "I'm not the Bank of Israel. Three of my colleagues went on unemployment last week because they handled the Knicks." That was rich, Sam thought—the Bank of Israel. A lot his father knew.

It was probably true about how many people bet the Knicks. The streak helped, of course—everybody loved a winner—but Sam figured the betting had been heavy even before the string began to develop. Guys in the city were that way: about the Knicks, the Mets, the Giants. When the Dodgers had gone to Los Angeles, Brooklyn had been like a funeral parlor.

On the subway, coming home from the game two nights before, he'd tried to remember as many other guys, like Stallworth, as he could. It picked him up, thinking of guys like Ben Hogan and Pete Reiser and Ray Berry—guys who'd had the deck stacked against them and had come back anyway. Hogan from a near-fatal auto crash, Reiser from running into the centerfield wall in Ebbets Field, Berry from polio as a kid. And what, he thought, about Ed Head, who'd been a top Dodger prospect before the war, had gone into the service, had had his right arm ruined by the Nazis, and then had come back, in 1945, to pitch a no-hitter with his left hand! A sportswriter in the *Post* had suggested that Stallworth hadn't had an actual heart attack in the first place, that, given the perfect reading of his EKG now, it might have been something else—some kind of clot—but Sam laughed at that. What difference did it make? The point was, any way you looked at it, that the guy had come back: he'd had to live with the thought that he was washed up at twenty-five, he'd had to fight with the doctors and the coaches to prove that he had a right to get out on the hardwood again. And even if it had been a mild heart attack, so what? A heart attack was a heart attack. Sure. You couldn't be a little bit pregnant.

Sam slipped into his trousers, put a shirt on over the T-shirt he'd slept in, buckled his belt. He'd call Sabatini later, put something down on the Milwaukee Bucks—the kid Alcindor, all seven-foot-three-and-a-quarter inches of him, was showing a lot of class, and you could still get a good point spread there. There were others: Monty Stratton—Jimmy Stewart played him in the movie—who'd shot his leg off in a hunting accident and had returned to pitch for the Indians, and Lou Brissie, who'd pitched hand grenades into Jap bunkers and had come back to pitch for the Red Sox with a leg made out of steel plate, and a guy named Bert Shepard, with a wooden leg, who'd pitched in one game for the Senators in 1945. And others: Herb Score, hit in the eye by a line drive; Eddie Waitkus, shot by a love-crazed girl in his hotel room; and the immortal Lou Gehrig, the Iron Man, playing his heart out, building the longest consecutive game-playing string in history, and knowing he had a fatal sickness all the time. His disease had been like muscular dystrophy, only different—Flo had given Sam the technical term several times. Ezzard Charles, the former heavyweight champion, had the same thing; Sam had seen him in a wheelchair, during last year's telethon.

"I consider myself the luckiest man on the face of the earth." That was what Gehrig had said when they'd given him a farewell at Yankee Stadium—Sam had heard it on a recording—and he would have given anything to have been alive then, to have been there, to have seen Lou and Babe Ruth hugging each other. There wasn't a dry eye in the stadium, since every fan had known just what Lou knew when he had said what he did. Sure. That was what it was all about.

Sam left the apartment. Down the corridor, on the other side of the banister, the door was cracked open and the little girl—Muriel—was staring at Sam with her large brown eyes. That was a bitch, being brought up by your grandmother. When he'd first moved in, before Muriel was born, Sam had said hello a few times to the grandmother, Mrs. Reardon, but she'd only grunted. Thin as a rail, bent over, one hand on her back, the other always hiding something, as if . . . Sam started down the stairs. He'd seen Muriel's mother coming in at two or three in the morning: a first-class floozy, with thick make-up, high heels four inches from the floor, a huge pair of knockers, orange-red hair. The word was that she was working steady now, living with a small-time gangster in the Pigtown section. Sure. Things were rough all over—even the subways were in a hole.

Okay, too: Ben had had it rough—he granted that—working his guts out for over thirty years, wearing out the seat of his pants driving a hack around Brooklyn and Queens. The guy had been made for better things, that was what Sam believed: with his voice, and his intelligence . . . and then, at the end, selling his medallion and sinking all his money into that stupid school. . . . Well, maybe it hadn't been stupid—Sam had honestly thought it might work out, a fifty-fifty chance. Ben had been able to get bit parts now and then on radio programs, and during the war he'd given his time free, announcing. As far as Sam could tell—he tried to be honest with himself about it—he never, even now, resented the money he'd put into the school: *Ace Broadcasting School, Ben Berman, Executive Director.* Even with the way things had worked out—Ben falling sick, and the hospital, and having to move out of the Linden Boulevard place, and the bankruptcy—his father had had a right—that was the word—he'd had a right to that school.

Only a madman could drive a hack in New York. His father had said something about mystery—*that,* in Sam's opinion, was the true mystery: how Ben had rung up fares for over thirty years without winding up in the funny house. Sure. Even though he'd had only eight months at the school before the ceiling fell in, Sam knew the eight months had meant a lot to his father.

When he'd gotten sick, he'd tried not to involve Sam. They hadn't been living together then—Ben was, so Sam had thought, still on Linden Boulevard, and Sam had had his own apartment on West 76th Street, off Amsterdam Avenue. They'd admitted Ben to Mount Sinai Hospital—Ben had called from his office at the school—and Ben had told them he had Blue Cross, Blue Shield, a Major Medical policy. Sam had received a call from the administrator two days later. . . .

Ben had offered again—that morning—to give him something before he left for California, and Sam had of course refused. The last thing he needed, when he was in a hole, was to have Ben looking down at him. He didn't blame the guy: if anything ever happened to him, he'd have done what he could not to have them cart him off to a city hospital. Kings County—a few blocks away—Sam knew what it was like there. He didn't need Ben's description: the lines in the lobbies, the smells, the foreign doctors, the drunks and deadbeats and addicts crawling all over the place. Ben had been scared they'd take the wrong thing out, the left lung instead of the right, and Sam had agreed with him. The brown-skinned doctors—students is what they were—how could they cure you if they couldn't even understand your language? If it had been a lung, Ben had joked, he would have applied for disability insurance; but it had been a kidney. His voice box stayed where it was. The guy in the hospital office had said he wanted to be of service to the family, he'd tried to reassure Sam about the competence of the doctors in city hospitals. Did Sam know that his father had been living in his office, on West 48th Street, at the time of his illness? The hospital, the man explained, even with its high rates, still worked at a deficit, relying on private contributions . . . how, he was obliged to ask, did Sam expect to pay for his father's fees?

"With money," Sam had replied. He liked that, remembering the sound of his own voice. Ben had appreciated the line, when he'd heard it. Sam opened the door, smiling—it picked him up to remember that, when his father had needed him, he'd come through.

Outside, it was colder than it had been the day before. Sam inhaled. He heard a tapping, on glass—Flo was smiling at him through the rummage shop window, motioning to him with her finger to come inside. He bet Flo would have adopted Muriel if it were possible. That was the kind of woman she was.

"How's tricks?" he asked, entering the store.

"Fine, dear—a cup of coffee?"

"I had already." The store was quiet—just one woman, toward the back of the front room, going through dresses.

"You haven't been stopping by as much as you used to," Flo said. "We miss you."

"I got things on my mind," Sam said.

"I'm sure you do." Flo sipped from her paper coffee cup, then spoke: "You must be upset about Ben's leaving."

Sam liked the fact that Flo came right out with things. "I don't blame the guy," he said. "I mean, at his age, and—well, why live here if you can live there?" Sam knew that Flo was sad about Ben's decision, maybe more than sad. When he and Ben had first moved in and Ben had begun helping in the store, Sam had often thought that Ben and Flo might get together, though in the end he'd figured it was best that they hadn't. Sometimes—he didn't push the theory—he'd thought that Flo would have done it because she worried about him. "Anyway, he said it was just for a visit—nothing's definite."

Flo looked at him. "You expect him to return, then?"

"No."

"I don't either." She paused. "We'll miss him."

"Sure," Sam said, and had an idea; he tried not to smile. "It'll be just like—like losing a member of the family."

Flo put her hand on his, then looked away, through the window, to the street. "It's quiet today," she said.

Sam's eyes followed hers. In the window, leaning against one wall, was a sign: BUY HERE! YOU SAVE MONEY—YOUR MONEY SAVES LIVES! He wondered if, after five years, Flo saw that there was no need to worry, if she understood that he'd get by, with or without Ben. He had a heart, sure, but good times or bad, he looked out for number one. He watched a bus go by, heard the noise its motor made, pumping away, and realized that he was comforted by the lack of talk between himself and Flo. Pete Gray! The name flashed across his mind—how could he have forgotten him? The one-armed outfielder who'd played for the St. Louis Browns during the war. Sam had read his life story in a comic book, how he'd lost his arm when he'd fallen off the back of a trolley car, hitching a ride as a kid, and had been run over by a truck. Or maybe he'd hitched on the truck. When he caught a fly ball in his glove, he'd toss the ball in the air, and, before the ball would fall, he'd pull his glove off under his bad arm—between the stump and the armpit—and then catch the ball and fire it to the infield with his bare hand. Sam had practiced doing it—there'd been no great trick; it was the speed that counted, though, and Gray had given away nothing. You didn't get to the major leagues on charity.

"You'll stay, though, won't you?"

"Oh sure," Sam said, quickly. "Where else would I go?" He laughed: "I mean, you ever see pictures of where his brother lives?"

"We'll miss him," Flo said again. She held his hand. "You keep promising to take me with you—to work."

"Sure," Sam said. He liked the way she used the word work.

"One of these first days." He looked down, shook his head. "You want to hear a good one: a few weeks ago—me and Ben were having what you'd call a"—he forced a laugh—"a father to son talk, and, get this, he said my grandfather would have thought I'd discovered the ideal profession." Sam rubbed his fingertips against the chair, between his legs. "That's a laugh, isn't it."

"Tell me about your grandfather." Her voice was insistent.

"He died when I was—before I was ten," Sam said. She was a queen all right, he thought, in charge of everything, but the truth was that she was the one people should worry about. He could feel what it must have taken for her to have kept going. Maybe, when it came to fading in and fading out, she was the one Ben had passed his gift on to. "I don't remember him much, except that he was always there—praying or reading a Jewish newspaper. Ask Ben if you're interested."

"I asked you," Flo said. "I don't think your father likes to talk about him. I think he's never gotten over—people are like that sometimes."

"You got it all wrong," Sam said. "He worshiped his old man. He's always quoting from him." He leaned forward, looking over his shoulder first, as if he were worried that somebody was listening. "Hey listen. I'll tell you what I remember most about my grandfather." He felt heat rising from his collar. "Ben wouldn't tell you this, because he used to make me take him downstairs. He'd say, 'Sammy, be a good boy and take Grandpa to the subway,' or to the bus. He was always going places. He was a little guy, maybe five-foot-one, and he always wore a vest under his jacket, and a tie, and he carried a cane, and a mesh-type shopping bag. He wore a hat—I remember that—and when he'd come in from outside, he'd take it off and put his *yamulka* on right away, so that his head was never uncovered. He wore one of those square ones, the old-fashioned kind. He still had most of his hair."

Sam could sense the eagerness in his voice, the response his story was registering on Flo's face. "I'd walk down the stairs with him—he never let me help him—and then—"

The door opened. A tall black guy, glassy-eyed, wearing a T-shirt, the fading orange and blue emblem of the New York Mets on it, swayed forward. He wore a gold earring in his left ear, a violet handkerchief wrapped tightly around his skull. He kept his palm to his mouth. "Help a guy out," he said, to Flo. Sam stood, slipped his right hand into his pocket. He could hear his heart pumping; the guy was out of it, though—if he tried anything he wouldn't stand a chance.

Flo stood, walked to the table by the opposite wall, and returned with two cans of food. "Oh baby, that ain't what I mean—that ain't the kind of bread I need, don't you know that?"

From the back of the store, the woman who had been going through the dresses came forward and snatched the guy—a head taller than she was—by the arm, pushing him to the door. A boy—Sam hadn't seen him—peeked out from the back room, a comic book in his hand. "You ought to be ashamed of yourself, Calvin—" the woman said. "You'll be the death of your mother, bless her soul, and of your own poor self too. You used to be such a good boy."

Calvin looked down, his head circling slowly. "Can't put a guy down for trying," he said. "I didn't mean nothing. I asked polite."

"You get on home. Here—" The woman took the two cans (corned beef hash, Sam saw) from Flo, gave them to him, and pushed him out the door. Through the window, Calvin seemed to be trying to doff an invisible hat to Flo, but he couldn't get coordinated. The woman came back in, reached into her purse.

"How much was that, Flo honey?"

"No, no," Flo said, and again, "no."

The woman accepted Flo's decision and walked to the back of the store. "Sure," Sam offered. "She's right—that takes real brains, getting strung out like that."

"You were telling me about your grandfather."

Her voice was cold again, like ice, yet there was something so direct in her coldness that Sam found he could respond to it. "When we'd get downstairs," he continued, "and I'd start to try to get him to the subway, or the trolley—it ran right out here, in front of the store—what he used to do—you got to give him credit—he'd shush me away. *'Gei, gei,* Samela,'—that's what he called me, Samela, and—the first time it happened my heart must of stopped, I got so scared—he walked right out into the traffic, and when a car stopped for a red light he'd tap on the window with his cane. Then, when whoever was inside would roll down the window, seeing this old guy, my grandfather would say: 'Are you going to New York please?'—or wherever it was he wanted to go. If the guy said yes, my grandfather would say 'Good' and just like that he'd open the car door and get in."

Sam leaned back, watched the reaction on Flo's face. From the way she laughed and said "No!" he knew she'd gotten the picture, but he also saw her eyes flick sideways, past him to the street. He was angry that the story had been interrupted, that his timing had been thrown off, that the words hadn't come out in the exact way he'd hoped they would.

"He was like that," Sam continued, looking down. "Nothing stopped him. Sometimes he'd take the trolley, but even then, if there was a long line, he'd cut in front of everybody else when the trolley came. 'I'm an old man,' he'd say, and get on." Sam looked up and saw that Flo was smiling at him. Her thoughts, though, he could tell, were elsewhere. "I used to think people stared at me because of what he did. Sure. Ben probably knew—why else would he have made me take the guy downstairs?"

"He was a religious man, wasn't he?" Flo said.

"Yeah," Sam replied. "I suppose. He prayed three times a day—mornings, afternoons, and at sundown." Sam laughed. "If we were away from home when it started getting dark—he took me for walks after school—he'd go into a phone booth, lift the receiver to make believe, and shuckle back and forth. I stood guard." Sam got up from the chair. "Look, I got things on my mind, so I'm gonna take off now, okay?" He knew he didn't have to ask permission, and Flo, with her eyes, indicated as much. "When I told Ben once, he asked me if his going into phone booths made me imagine he was Superman, but that didn't make sense to me then, I remember telling Ben: I mean, with the way the guy spoke and his beard and . . ." Sam moved to the door. "We'll talk some more sometime soon, okay? I promise." He considered, then spoke again: "One thing I meant to ask you before, though—did Tidewater say anything to you about having something for me—for after Ben goes?"

"No," Flo said. "Why?"

"Nothing," Sam said. "Ben said something screwy about—I was just curious is all."

He stopped. Flo stood, moved toward him. "I think he'll miss Ben more than any of us." She paused, as if pleased by what she had just said. "That's why Ben asked you to look after him. He told me." She held Sam's hand again. "Your father likes to make mysteries of things, but there's no need to be afraid of Mason. He—"

"I'm not," Sam said, quickly.

Flo waved his answer away. "I didn't mean afraid." She smiled. "I liked your story," she said then. "Try not to think about your father leaving. Take care of yourself."

"Sure," Sam said. He was annoyed, but he didn't want her to see his annoyance. She had enough to think about. How had she put it once?—the only time they'd had a long conversation about it: "I guess I'm what you'd call, in your line of work, a jinx." He remembered that clearly. "I left a trail of casualties, Sam." She'd offered it as a statement, but there had been a question in her voice. He'd tried to contradict her, but it had done no good—she'd apologized for bringing up the subject, and Sam had honored her wish: she didn't want to talk about it again. But it must have been . . . heavy was the word which occurred to him, to outlive your husband and your two kids. He wondered: had she known her husband had muscular dystrophy when she'd married him? How old had she been then? What had the man looked like? And at the end, in which direction had he gone—ballooning up, or wasting away? They called that atrophy—but it was still dystrophy. His hand was on the doorknob. "You don't worry, Flo. This boy is always looking out for number one."

His hands in his jacket pockets, he walked along Nostrand Avenue. Two women at the corner were talking with Nate, one of the local runners, giving him their numbers. The guy stood there every day until two o'clock, not making believe he was doing anything but what he was doing—he never wrote any of the numbers down and Sam thought that he would have liked to have played cards with him sometime. It interested him—not the numbers themselves, because he figured you could get better odds just throwing darts at a board—but the organization behind it all. People didn't know about these things—from the drops to the pick-up men to the controllers to the central pick-up locations to what was called the bank, with the bank supervisors and the lieutenants, and at the top, the big man, the bank owner. With all the security precautions, the alternate pick-ups, the signals when raids were coming, the payoffs to the cops, to the winners—it was, Sam thought, like its own government.

Harry Gross had been paying over one million dollars a year in protection money when they'd caught him. That told you a lot. Now, with the bookies pretty much closed down on off-track betting, they'd thought of new angles: a night number from the Yonkers track, a *bolito* on the first or last two digits, a payoff on the weekly lottery from Puerto Rico for the Puerto Ricans, and on the treasury reports from Italy for the Italians. Sam laughed. They showed you something too, with the business cards their banks gave out—"Not Responsible for Arrested Work" printed on them, meaning there would be no payoffs on numbers seized in a raid. Still, the odds were six hundred to one against you in pure arithmetic—and that didn't take into account that your chances didn't improve from one day to the next just because your number hadn't come in the day before. Sure. For a lark once in a while, maybe you took a chance and threw away a dollar—on your birthday or some other lucky time—but to stick with it, day after day, that took brains.

He gave them credit, though: nobody could know how many streams they had feeding into their runners and banks and drops. That took control. At the corner of Church Avenue, on his side of the street, Sam entered the candy store. At the soda fountain all seats were taken. He nodded to Steve, the owner, behind the counter.

"How's tricks, Sam?"

"Can't complain," Sam said.

He heard two black girls talking about a test they were studying for, in trigonometry. He stepped around the paperback book racks and slid into a phone booth. He smiled, remembering Flo's face—her reaction to the story about his grandfather. Maybe he should try to get Ben to tell some stories about the old guy before he left: what his life had been like in Europe, the ideas he'd had on things. . . . What he admired most—he had to swallow when he imagined the entire thing—was Flo's courage in having had the kids anyway, knowing by then that her husband had what he had, and knowing what the chances of inheriting the disease were. He pictured her with a full belly, her husband—faceless, Flo kept no photos—hobbling beside her. He saw her in the hospital, when the nurse handed her the baby in a soft white blanket, and he saw tears running down Flo's cheeks. The kid had been normal for the first two years, and then he'd begun having just a little bit of trouble, Flo said, when he tried to stand up. It was noticeable. The muscles in the calves were tight, she'd probably had a physical therapist come in and massage them, but when it started that young, there wasn't much hope. Guys like her husband—if it came when they were already an adult—they had a fifty-fifty chance to live out their lives.

And then—Sam wanted to drive his fist through the wall of the phone booth—she'd tried again: she'd had a girl the second time. Sam wondered—how could he ask?—if the girl had come before or after the son had died. Sam imagined Flo in the hospital again, the huge belly under a sheet. The choice of kings—he'd heard that somewhere: what they called it when you were lucky enough to have one boy and one girl, instead of two or three of the same. Sure. Flo had had the choice of kings. That, he thought, lifting the receiver from its hook, was really rich.

A man's voice answered. "Yes?"

"This is Mr. Benjamin here," Sam said, giving his code name.

"Yes, Mr. Benjamin. This is Mr. Sabatini—what can I do for you today?"

"You can pay somebody to throw a game for the Knicks so I can bet them again."

"Ah," Mr. Sabatini said, chuckling. "I like that. We all have to keep up our sense of humor in times like these. It's bad times, sweetheart."

"You don't have to tell me," Sam said.

"What can I do for you?" Mr. Sabatini asked.

"Look, I'll take the Bucks tonight. The papers said six and a half points over the Hawks."

"No," Mr. Sabatini said. "Here. I'm checking. I can only give you four and a half."

"I'll take it anyway, for two singles."

"Good. A regular customer like you—with the drought on our own beloved Knickerbockers—I'd like to see—" Sam heard the man breathing, the slight wheeze he always recognized. Sam saw his grandfather's face, saw him asleep in the corner of the old green sofa, on Linden Boulevard, his legs dangling above the carpet. "Look, I'll tell you what I'll do for a good customer like yourself—with the Knicks, I'd be willing to take something modest if, instead of points, you'll take one-to-two odds. That's the best we can do for you here at the Bank of Israel—"

Sam almost spat into the phone. "One to two!" He exhaled, feeling warm, and snapped on the ventilator fan. "You got the wrong baby. You're out of—"

"Shh, shh. Don't get upset, sweetheart. It was only a suggestion. You're the one who—" He stopped suddenly, became businesslike. "We're talking too long. We shouldn't support the telephone company. So. The Bank of Israel bids you *shalom.*"

Yeah, Sam thought, hanging up: guns for the Arabs, sneakers for the Jews. He shook his head to clear it, pulled the folding door toward him, checked the coin return box, but there was nothing there. The old schoolyard cry—whatever it had meant, Sam liked it: guns for the Arabs, sneakers for the Jews.

He sat at the counter, in the middle. "I'll take a toasted English," he said to Steve, "and a glass of milk."

Steve nodded. Sam folded his hands on the counter, like a schoolboy, and wondered what he could do: Ben didn't know it, but Sam's reserve was slipping away fast, even with the small amount he needed to live on: rent, chipping in for food, carfare, a haircut once a month, a movie now and then, a snack here and there. He didn't need much. If Ben didn't move his ass out soon, though, he'd have to take off himself. Mooning around, trying to scrounge up a card game, waiting for Sabatini, betting on things he had no business going near . . . Sabatini had let him have credit the week before, sure, but Sam knew where that led. He'd seen what they did to guys who didn't pay off, he knew how they'd try to suck you into working your debt off—running bets, trying to pick up some of your own clients, giving half of everything to the big man, plus interest. But this waiting around for Ben to leave, for Andy to die, for a game, for action on the Knicks—for *something;* he was leaving himself wide open this way, he knew—a sitting duck—and it was time to do something about it.

Sure. You're a sitting duck, Sam Berman Junior, he repeated, and again he took the words literally: he saw himself in the middle of a pond, flapping arms that were heavy with feathers, squawking in pain because his mouth and nose had been pressed together into a hard flat beak.

"How do you like the way the Knicks are going?" Steve offered, bringing Sam his muffin.

Sam spread grape jelly on one half. "Yeah," he said. "They'll go all the way this year—I said so before the season started."

"That's right," Steve said. "I remember." He left, served some other customers. Sam looked straight ahead. Steve returned and Sam focused his eyes on Steve's white apron. "Listen," Steve said, leaning closer, "you must be sitting pretty, huh, Sam? I mean—"

Sam wiped the moustache of milk from his upper lip. "Something's up," he said. "The bank is closed. Sabatini won't touch the Knicks with a ten-foot pole."

"Oh yeah?" Steve said, surprised. "I hadn't heard."

"That's the size of it," Sam said. He wanted to relax. "How's your old man doing?" he offered.

"Pretty good," Steve said. Steve's father, Mr. Krichmar, who had had the store before Steve—when Sam had been growing up and he and Steve had been going to school together—had had his heart attack in the store, while (the way the story had been told) making an egg salad sandwich. "He likes it there—they got everything he needs, and the weather, it's good for his heart."

"California, right?"

"No, Florida—West Palm Beach—he bought into a cooperative —a condominium they call it. He and my old lady, they like it swell. He'll live till a hundred."

Sam started on his second piece of toasted English. "Did I tell you? My old man, he's thinking of leaving too—to one of those same places, only in California. A senior citizen city they call it."

"It makes sense," Steve said, collecting some glasses and sloshing them up and down on the soapy brushes. Sam always liked to watch the way Steve worked. He was no genius, sure, but still—it took a certain kind of talent to keep track of all the things you had to keep track of in a store like this: the counter and ordering all the supplies in advance and remembering when the eggs or grilled cheese sandwiches were done; and the junk—the paperbacks and magazines and school supplies and greeting cards and toys and cigarettes and candy . . . "Me and Barbara, when the time comes—that's what we plan to do." He looked left and right. "Maybe get out before even, if you know what I mean—the way things are—well, changing . . ."

"I been to Florida," Sam said. "It's nice there."

"Oh yeah?"

"For spring training, at Vero Beach—me and Dutch went—oh maybe twelve-thirteen years ago." Sam drank the last of his milk. "Sure. They got a lot to offer you there. We knew some of the players too. When the Dodgers were still there, Labine—he used to leave passes for us at the box office during the week sometimes. Not weekends. But during the week."

"I remember," Steve said. "Labine, he was terrific."

Sam gestured with his index finger. "He had a break here—in the first digit, you know? That's what did the trick—it made all his stuff sink down and away, naturally."

"They always had good relief pitchers," Steve said. "Hugh Casey, Clyde King, and then Joe Black, Larry Sherry, Eddie Roebuck . . ." Sam watched Steve spread pieces of roast beef on rye bread. He was, unlike his father, generous with the meat. "Hey listen, when you were there—in Florida—you play the horses?"

"Oh sure," Sam said, and smiled. "You know me."

"Be back in a minute." Steve smiled, and the smile changed something in Sam, made him feel good again. What did it cost him, since he had the time, to come in like this, pass the time of day with an old—he couldn't call him a real friend—but a guy he knew. It meant something, just seeing a guy regularly after so many years, even if you weren't asshole buddies. Sam thought of Ben and Tidewater: he remembered when, before they'd moved into the apartment over the store, Sam had seen them meet for the first time after all those years—the looks of disbelief on their faces, the way they'd smiled, as if it was the happiest moment of their lives. They had embraced, on the sidewalk in front of the store, Tidewater lifting Ben up, and Sam had to laugh, remembering how Ben's feet had dangled above the pavement. Sure, Sam thought, with the way things were, in Steve's own words, changing, it must pick him up for me to come in here. All the years they'd known one another— they counted for something.

The annoyance he'd felt after he'd told Flo the story was now gone. Miami Beach, the Keys, Hialeah, the dogs, jai alai, all the old

Jews baking their asses under the sun—Pioneer Estates would be the same. California and Florida, Sam thought, if you switched them around one night when nobody was looking, who'd know the difference?

To his right, somebody sat down. Steve's father had been held up twice, conked on the head once, but Steve hadn't had his initiation yet. Well. That would come too.

"How've you been feeling, Sam?"

Sam's eyes shifted, took him in. The guy was smiling at him from bloodshot eyes. Sam felt something grip his heart, but he tried to show nothing. "I ain't interested," he said. Was that what it had been like with Stallworth, Sam wondered—only more severe? As if a great hand had reached down, inside his chest, and grabbed his heart in its fist.

The guy rested his elbows on the counter. "Relax. I'm not selling that stuff anymore," he said. His voice was tired. "You don't have to worry." He looked down the counter. "A cup of coffee here, Steve—"

"Coming up."

"How've you been feeling, Sam?" the guy asked again. There was nothing oily or holy about him now, in the daylight; sure—just another deadbeat, Sam figured. Like the guys in his last poker game. "Listen, that night—you just forget about it, all right? I go through that kind of thing every now and then and you have to learn to ignore it." The guy laughed. "Basically, I'm just a good backsliding country boy come to the big city. . . ."

"I'll see you around," Sam said to Steve, putting two quarters down on the counter, next to his plate, and standing up.

The guy's hand was on his sleeve. "How do you like our boy Stallworth?" he asked. His eyes started to shine again, Sam saw, even behind the bleariness, inside the dark circles. "I mean—you're doing all right, aren't you? You're getting your share—right, brother?"

Sam yanked his arm away with such force that his elbow, swinging back from the man's grip, crashed into a rack behind him. Greeting cards floated to the floor. "I'll get them," he said in Steve's direction, and felt himself blush. "I don't know what your game is, and I don't care," Sam hissed, bending over. "But you stay out of my—my life." He put the cards back on the rack, restrained his right hand from reaching into the pocket, from showing the knife.

"Sure, whatever you say, Sam," the man said softly, as Steve brought him his cup of coffee. "Everybody has his periods, right? I know how it is—I just saw you in here so I thought I'd—" He put his hand out, leaning from his stool, balancing himself by holding onto the counter with his left hand. "No hard feelings, okay? I won't pull . . ." Sam walked away, not looking back. "No hard feelings," the guy repeated.

Sam turned, glared, and, unable to stop himself—how he hated his lack of control—he said, in a voice he hoped afterward had not, in the general chattering, been noticed by anybody else, "And lay off with that Christ bit, hear? For your information, I'm a Jew."

Sure, he thought outside, in the air: guns for the Arabs, sneakers for the Jews. He stalked across Nostrand Avenue, heading toward Flatbush, his head burning. The two of them, his Bible man and Tidewater, they should go live in the desert together. He saw the guy's pasty face under an Arab headdress, and the headdress made him see his father, in the white and black *talis* . . . he wondered what they'd looked like as boys, one tall and thin, the other short and stocky. He walked faster, passing the Bel-Air supermarket, trying to think of the depressions his feet made in the sidewalk, trying to stop the chain of pictures that was starting to march across the screen inside his head. He heard the sound of money jingling. Shit, he thought to himself, it was too late to cross over. He should have remembered. In front of the Granada Theater, rolling himself into Sam's path on a wooden dolly, was another one of the regulars—the new regulars, since the neighborhood had started changing. Sam tossed a dime into the guy's cup without looking into his face. The dog yipped at Sam, its tail wagging furiously. He suspected that they'd pinned the guy's legs up in some way, to his ass, the way they did to actors in the movies when they played one-legged soldiers returning home—but the dog was real enough, rocking back and forth on its belly like a seal, pulled forward on its own small dolly by a rope attached to its owner's set of wheels. The guy pushed off, shoving his hand—his knuckles—against the sidewalk, propelling himself back under the arcade. Had the dog been born that way? Or—anything was possible—in the hope that it was just what his act needed, had the guy . . . Christ! he thought.

You are really heading for deep waters, thinking up that kind of picture.

Still, he had the feeling things were happening on purpose somehow. Those were the words which occurred to him. Sure. If he'd crossed over, he bet to himself, the guy probably would have been waiting for him in another spot anyway. Sam knew something about the way streaks worked, after all, and it wasn't luck—at least not in the way most guys used that word—which made the difference.

4

"Who's there?" Sam asked.

"Mason Tidewater."

"Yeah," Sam said. "Just a second. He placed the sheets of paper on which he'd been figuring things inside the *Post*, put the *Post* back in the rack. The ideal profession—that was really rich. His grandfather had, from the grave, become a joker too.

Sam opened the door. Tidewater stood there, a mop in one hand, a manila envelope in the other, a bucket next to him on the floor. Muriel looked at the two of them from between two posts of the balcony which separated the landing from the stairwell. "Your father is downstairs at the moment, but I carry my—the tools of my trade, as it were—as a precaution." He licked his narrow lips. His tongue was orange. "I'd like to have a word with you. I asked Ben to tell you—"

"Sure," Sam said, remembering what Flo had said. "Come on in."

Tidewater leaned the mop against the wall, placed the bucket to the side of the door, then entered, carrying the envelope. "Sit down," Sam offered, gesturing to the couch. He thought of Steve and the conversation they'd had—and he remembered, in Steve's store, having thought of Tidewater and his father. "You want some coffee or something?"

Sam saw that Tidewater's eyes were taking in the apartment; it might, he realized, have been his first time inside—Sam didn't know what went on when he was gone and Ben was alone. Maybe Ben had thought things out in the same way, about being friendly with the guy: what did it cost you, after all, if you had the time? Tidewater took one step into the room and stood to the side of the door, stiffly. He seemed taller than usual. Most people would have taken him for six-three or six-three-and-a-half, even though he was probably six-two. The thinness of the man's cheeks, the length of his neck, the way his arms hung almost to the tops of his kneecaps, and those long slender fingers—like a musician's—things like that could give the illusion of extra height. Sam sat down in the easy chair. "It's about your father," Tidewater said. "He's worried about you."

"What?" Sam looked away.

"Can I help in any way?"

"I look out for myself," Sam said. Tidewater didn't move. "Look—if you want to talk, sit down." His eyes on the manila envelope, Sam thought of asking Tidewater if his inheritance was in it. "It makes me nervous, you guarding the door there. Nobody's gonna steal anything."

"This is important," Tidewater said, and his voice was cool. He moved forward, noiselessly, pulled a chair from the table, and sat. "There was a time," he said, "though you might not believe it, when I could have been of some use to you. Perhaps Ben has—"

"He said something once," Sam said.

Tidewater's eyes closed, and Sam's own eyes widened, watching the man's face—it was as if, he thought, there were two huge marbles under the eyelids. Holy rollers, you might call them, he thought, but the joke only annoyed him. Inside his mouth, he ran his tongue over his gums. "You're worried about your father," Tidewater stated. "That—"

"Ben can take care of himself."

"That you might not see him again if he leaves for California," Tidewater continued. The man's voice was strong, and Sam didn't like it. "We all hope, of course, that he'll have many years ahead of him. Still—"

"Cut the gas," Sam said. "I got things to do. What's on your mind? I mean, like I said before, Ben told me you wanted to see me."

"You're right," Tidewater said, and Sam saw the man smile slightly, pleased to hear that his message had been delivered. "He's worried about you and I thought you should know. It might affect—well, I thought you should know. That's all."

"Now I know," Sam said, standing.

"He's making a mistake, of course. He should stay here—with you, with all of us."

Sam tried to get the wheels to spin faster inside his head, to figure what the guy was after. So Ben was worried about him. Flo too. And the Bible man, and now Tidewater. The whole world was out to save Sam Berman's ass. That and twenty cents . . . "He's his own man," Sam said. "It's all the same to me."

"He's making a mistake. You're staying on, which means that you must know it's a mistake. That is why I'm here, you see—we have something in common now, Sam." Tidewater looked up, his eyes large, and then he laughed suddenly, with a bitterness that surprised Sam. "You're my farewell gift from him, don't you see?"

Sam moved backwards. "Listen, I don't have the time for this. I get enough of it from—"

"That's just where the words came from," Tidewater said, and he leaned back in the chair. "From your father. There's no reason not to tell him my feelings: that I wanted him to stay—he knows what our friendship means to me, what discovering one another again, after all the years . . ." Tidewater's voice trailed off, and Sam relaxed, made himself concentrate on the fact that Tidewater was, like Ben, just another old man. "But what he does not—and will not—know, is that you are my farewell gift to him."

Sam drew a deep breath. Maybe this was how the two of them had passed all those hours in Tidewater's room, below the rummage shop, trading words and riddles. Maybe things like that happened when you got to Ben's age, he thought. It was no skin off his back. Maybe, one morning, he'd even find Tidewater in the living room, wrapping black straps around his pale arms. Sam blew through his lips, sideways. That would be rich.

"Here," Tidewater said, and held the envelope toward Sam. The man's voice was soft again. He seemed hesitant, embarrassed. "I'd planned to share this with your father, but he has forfeited his chance. 'My son,' he said to me, 'will take my place.' If you have the time, then, I'd like . . ."

He set the envelope down, on the kitchen table. "It's something I've been working on which I hope you'll read. It has to do with baseball."

"Yeah," Sam said. He tried to figure, quickly, which would be the easy way out. "Ben said something once, about when you were young. He looks up to you."

"Ben knows much of what is in here—I've shown him sections from time to time. Perhaps, after he leaves, you'll come to my apartment sometime, and we can talk."

"Sure," Sam said, and sighed. "One of these first days."

Tidewater stood and approached Sam, his eyes bulging forward, revealing his anger. "Do not talk to me like that. I told you before: your father is worried about you. I'd like to help. He's making a mistake." Sam watched the man's tongue, how it flicked his lips, his teeth. He saw a streak of darker skin inside Tidewater's mouth— he'd seen it before: the man with the two-toned tongue, he'd called him. Tidewater's breath, sweet like honey, washed over Sam's face, but Sam stood his ground, looked straight into the man's eyes. It was relaxing him—a surprise—simply to see the guy get carried away, out of control. The envelope was in front of Sam's chin, held forward, and Sam tried to imagine what would happen between them, after Ben was gone, if he refused to read it. There was Flo to think about too; she might feel sorry for the guy. "It's important to me that you read it, that you know. When you're done, you do not have to say anything if you don't want to, though I would welcome your reaction. Please? I—"

"Sure," Sam said, and he took the envelope. What would it cost him, except a few hours, and once it was out of the way, maybe the guy would let him be. "I'll take a look at it." There was no point in saying anything about Ben's leaving—but he could understand that too: how upset the guy might be, and how Flo might take his side.

"It is the story, not of my life, but of one part of my life—the part that was most crucial for me. I hope—"

"You don't have to explain," Sam said. "I said I'd take a look."

Tidewater was sitting again, his head back, as if dreaming. Maybe Ben had had this figured too, Sam thought—maybe it was just another favor he needed from Sam, one which, with his ways, he couldn't have asked for directly. Sam wondered if Ben had told the hospital story to Tidewater, and if that was the reason the guy seemed to trust Sam so much. Then too, Ben might have bragged about Sam's knowledge of sports—he was a father, after all. Sam held the envelope and listened. . .

"My earliest memory—or what I remember as being my earliest memory," Tidewater was saying, "is connected with your father, you see. It is of a game we played on the weed-grown lawn of an old wood house situated across the road from our own houses—did he tell you that we lived, for several years, side by side?—and behind the houses and gardens of our neighbors." He stopped. "Has Ben—or Andy—ever told you about their house, the one—"

"No," Sam said, and unfastened the metal clasp on the envelope.

"Not the house they lived in—but the house we played in: it was the last one before the open fields and all the neighborhood children used it for their games. Ben remembers. The game he and I would play had to do with one of us standing on the porch at twilight and trying to discern the movements of the other—who would be creeping through the grass and weeds toward the front porch. I remember that I would keep my back turned, my eyes resting on my forearm, until the shout would come from him—'Ready!' I remember also the great joy when one of us would discover the other, and I remember most of all the feeling of crawling on my stomach, through the grass, over stones and debris, of creeping closer and closer to the front porch without being detected, and of seeing, my head raised inches from the dirt, Ben's socks rolled down over his shoe tops, and his scabbed knees."

Tidewater coughed lightly, the back of his hand to his mouth. Sam was sitting on the couch. It was the first time he'd ever heard the guy go on at such length, yet he found that he was not surprised. If Tidewater had known Ben that far back, then, Sam reasoned, he had known Sam's grandfather too. Sam lifted the sheaf of papers part of the way from the envelope. "It is a feeling," Tidewater continued, "—the crawling forward at twilight—before which I can find no memory." Sam was, he admitted, curious now about what the guy had written, but he said nothing: when things were moving like this—in ways you hadn't foreseen—the best thing was to keep your mouth shut and let the other guy show his hand. "Of what should have been a significant event—the birth of my younger sister Elizabeth—I have no recollection; I remember her only from the time she was walking and talking, which means that the game with Ben must have preceded this memory, and so, I reason, all others until then.

"Ben knows this," Tidewater said, his voice suddenly sharp. "What he does not know, however, is that, after he moved from our section—to East New York, where only Jews lived—the house we played in was torn down and the land cleared. I remember watching the process with daily sadness, thinking of him, and when a secret chamber was found in the cellar of the building, and bones in the chamber, I did not find the discovery strange. There was no other evidence—neither clothing nor papers, nor shoes, nor eating utensils—but the conclusion in the neighborhood was that the bones had been those of a runaway slave, hiding out on his way to Canada and freedom. My chief thought at the time, though, was of Ben, and I ached for some way to share the good news with him—the news that our house had been a haunted house, and that we had, creeping through the grass at twilight, been braver than we had ever imagined."

Tidewater stood suddenly. "There is more, but you will read what I have written." The man filled his chest with air, reached out with his long arm, and opened the door. "You'll forgive me, of course. I'm grateful for your time." He picked up his bucket. "I had wanted to tell your father what I have just told you, but there is more—the story has had, here, a new ending, and Ben will not know what it is." The man's eyes shone, happier than at any moment since the day Sam had first seen him meet Ben. Sure. Sam had to give himself credit. He was replacing his father already. Sam moved into the doorway. The line of Tidewater's frail back curved slightly, and Sam was reminded again of the man's age. "I know," Tidewater said, very gently, and he sighed, sounding like Ben. "You're worried about him also. Who would not see it, after all—that you care. I'm grateful."

Muriel had not moved from her position between the wooden posts. She stared at the two men; then, her hands gripping the posts, she pulled herself to a standing position and leaned over the railing to watch Tidewater descend. Sam did not hear the man's shoes. On the ground floor, Tidewater disappeared around the bend, under the staircase. Muriel looked at Sam. "How's tricks, kid?" he asked. She said nothing, stuck her middle finger into her mouth, at the side, so that Sam could see it wiggling against the inside of her cheek. In another ten years, would she, he wondered, have breasts like her mother's? There was a streak of something dark—dirt? chocolate?—under her chin. The color of her lips seemed paler than the color of her cheeks. Her hair fell in sandy-colored curls, to her shoulders.

Sam pulled the pages from the envelope, riffled their edges with his thumb. He thought of his account with Sabatini, and reminded himself to tear up the sheet of paper on which he'd been figuring his finances, so that Ben wouldn't find it. Don't bet what you don't have—the first rule, and he'd gone against it. It showed you how smart he was getting. Ben knew what he was doing, giving him away now.

Sam didn't smile at his own joke. He didn't mind letting Tidewater think he'd replaced his own father; but that, in some way, Tidewater felt that he was going to take care of Sam now, that he too was taking Ben's place—it didn't make any sense. The door to Muriel's apartment creaked. "Sure," he said, and turned to walk back into his apartment before the grandmother could see him. "Never take candy from a stranger, you hear?"

MY LIFE AND DEATH
IN THE NEGRO AMERICAN
BASEBALL LEAGUE

A SLAVE NARRATIVE

CHAPTER ONE

I consider the high point of my life to have been that moment on the fifteenth day of February, 1928, in the city of Havana, Cuba, when, after I had pitched and hit my team, the Brooklyn Royal Dodgers, to a 1 to 0 triumph over a team composed of players from the New York Yankees, George Herman "Babe" Ruth mocked me again for having chosen the life that was mine, calling me a "make-believe nigger," whereupon I slammed my fist into the pasty flesh of his dark face and struck him down; it was a blow I should have struck long before that day, and one which, filling me momentarily with joy, would lead, on that same afternoon, to my own death as a player in the Negro American Baseball League.

I was known by another name then, and was often called, for my abilities (though never to my face), "the Black Babe"; if things had been otherwise, however, he might have been named for me, and he often admitted as much in the privacy of our friendship. He called me a fool on that day, though, for he knew what was common knowledge at the time—that if I had chosen to hide my origins (as, I should note, others did, including two—an outfielder and a second baseman—whose bronze busts reside in the Cooperstown, New York, Hall of Fame), I could easily have done so, and I could thereby, as he put it, have had it all.

But what will seem now to have been a then unfashionable pride in my origins, and what might seem here a too fashionable retelling of history, is really neither. The facts of the time, and of my life, were simpler. As anyone could know who would bother to investigate, it was common, in post-season games, for teams of blacks—raggedy and ill-trained and part-time as we often were—to defeat the best of the white major leaguers. In after-season barnstorming, men like Bruce Petway threw out Ty Cobb regularly; pitchers such as José Mendez and Smokey Joe Williams beat Plank, Coombs, and Mathewson, Alexander, Marquard, and Bush; and teams such as the Indianapolis ABC's, the Birmingham Black Barons, the Bacharach Giants, and the All Nations regularly defeated those men popularly called World Champions. It was often our pleasure, against white teams, when the game was put away, to whip the ball around the infield before getting the batter out at first base.

I was "the Black Babe"; they called John Henry Lloyd "the Black Wagner"; the great Andrew "Rube" Foster received his nickname for defeating Rube Waddell 2 to 1 in a nineteen-inning pitcher's duel. And yet, I wonder if the irony of stealing the names of those players who (though defeated by us) remained synonymous with greatness to the general public did not, even then, turn ultimately in our favor. Would it have changed what we were, and what they knew they were, had they been forced to take on our names, had Ty Cobb been named for "Cool Papa" Bell, or Lou Gehrig for "Rap" Dixon? Would it change the feel of the hardball in my hand, or the earth under my spikes, or the endless conversations (in which I did not join) that went on in the back seat of Jack Henry's old Buick, as we made our way from town to town, making four games on a good Sunday, during the years 1923 to 1928.

We were called the Brooklyn Royal Dodgers then, yet I was the only player who had been born and raised in Brooklyn, and of my birth and parentage I will say a few words, for riding in the back seat of Jack Henry's car, I was, as I had been since my earliest memory, a pale face among dark faces.

My father, whose family name I give here as Tidewater, was exceptionally intelligent and talented, a light cocoa-colored man born in 1856, who had been a house servant on a large plantation in Garley, South Carolina, and who, in 1882, upon the death of his master (with whom he had stayed, even after the war), was given passage money, references, and sent north with an introduction to a man in Brooklyn, Mr. Christopher Tanner, who found employment for him as a carpenter and furniture maker.

Mr. Tanner lived in a large wood house, in the section of Brooklyn now known as East Flatbush, but known to me when I was a boy as the Dutch Highlands, and I recall with great vividness the soft velvets and brilliant leathers of his sitting room, where several times a year we would be invited for tea, after which my father—who had a fine voice, and could read Latin with ease—would recite the poems of Horace, Ovid, and Catullus, and each of us, my father's children, would recite a poem we had learned by rote. I can still, if required, recite the simpler love poems of Catullus, and, in the slowest of cadences, that poem of Ovid's (stolen by Marlowe and embellished by him with unnecessary repetition) which contains the slow and beautiful line *O lente currite noctis equi.*

My father was, like myself, a tall man in his time, standing straight at what must have been six feet two inches. His head was long, his hair, which I inherited, soft and straight, and his lips (again my inheritance), wide and narrow—a gift through his mother, of his master's father, from whom I received my original name.

My mother, whom my father met during his second week in Brooklyn (she was a cook for the first family to which he was referred for work), came originally from the West Indies, and could, except for the deep black oiliness of her hair, have passed for white. She played the piano beautifully, and, reading music herself, taught all of us to play, and also gave lessons in our house to whites and blacks alike. In our presence she always called my father ''Mister Tidewater.''

If you were to see a photo of my family, while we were all together, you would notice at once my white boy's face, long and narrow, staring at you from among brown and mulatto faces, and it was, I now believe, this lack of color which endeared me to my mother, and which, at the same time, made me alien to my father. I was the youngest of his sons (though not the youngest child, having had a sister, Elizabeth, born two and one half years after me). Thus, what I have indicated may seem to have been a then unfashionable pride in my racial origins, had, as I have said, a simple—a literally childlike explanation: my family was my world in those years, and though my father did not attempt to teach us either to be proud or ashamed of our birthright, I wanted, as a child would, to be like the others, and I resented whatever unseen force it was that had removed from my skin the pigment that my father had given, through his blood, to my brothers and sister. I believed, as a child, that he did not consider me his son, and though I see now that this was untrue (he could be as cruel to my brothers as he was to my mother and to me), it was a reality I lived with. We construct our universe on the model of our immediate world; mine was black, and I, dependent on it, felt as if I were its white victim. It was, I believed, for this reason that my mother singled me out for extra affection, calling me her "White Star," her "Hope and Deliverance," and though I willingly accepted her physical attentions to me, it must—to judge from what I know today—have been my father's love that I coveted.

"For whosoever shall keep the whole law, and yet offend in one point, he is guilty of all." This, from the Book of James (2:10), was my father's guiding light, repeated to us countless times, and holding for me always an obviously special meaning. For my mother too, whom my father accused of an attraction to Mr. Tanner, the adjuration contained a deadly force, and it amazes me to think that, before I was nine, I realized fully not only that we were, my mother and I, allies against him (our love made strong by what we understood as his condemnation of us), but that we found in each other the love which, since he was too cold a man to possess, he could not really have given to us even if we had not felt ourselves cut off from him.

But my childhood within this family, myself among my brothers and my sister, our family among our neighbors, and all of us (on two sides of us there were white families) living in an area of Dutch estates which had, sometime in the seventies, been broken up into small farms, and which was, during my childhood, being further divided into lots for one- and two-family dwellings such as our own—our life there, our friends, our schooling, our play, our churchgoing, our leaving home are not, here, my subject, for if I began to slide down the trail of memories which leads to and from that house, I would certainly become lost forever, and though I might, after some time, give shape and particularity to my own timeless childhood, I would not, I believe, find the end of the trail, and I would not—the important thing—have the time to set down what I have vowed now that I will set down.

I cannot remember a time when I was not, as a boy, playing baseball, though I retain no specific memory of the first time I held a bat, or of the first time I played in a game. I do recall that my older brothers were proud to take me with them to their games, and to have me show off my skills to their friends—and I was immensely happy to be able to please my brothers. My eldest brother, Tucker, played on Sundays for the Brooklyn Remsens, a semi-professional team which could, on a given day, hold its own with any team in the Negro Leagues, and I accompanied him, thus, as the team's mascot and bat boy, enjoying my first taste of fame. I was seven years old at the time, but I could, already, play in games with boys of ten and eleven. I became part of the pre-game entertainment, standing at home-plate in a baggy Remsens uniform, and taking a turn in batting practice.

Professional baseball was prohibited on Sundays in New York during those years, so the crowd would be admitted free, and after the game had begun I would go around the stands with some of the players (who were waiting their turns at bat) and collect money for the programs we sold: fifty cents for programs in the grandstand, and twenty-five cents in the bleachers. Tucker's team played their games in Dexter Park, and some of the players filled my ears, in the dugout, with stories of the places they had been to, and the things they had seen. They were forever debating the merits of various players, and bragging of their exploits with women. The player whose name I recall most from those years was Oliver Marcelle, a man of Creole origin who had been nick-named "The Ghost," and who, by the time I had begun playing in games for money (at the age of fourteen) had already disappeared, although he would still have been a young man himself. What had driven him from baseball was the fact that, in a fight he and Frank Warfield had during a game somewhere in Cuba, Warfield had bit Marcelle's nose off. Marcelle had been, according to my brother's team-mates, tall and handsome, and had fancied himself a lady's man; after the fight, he tried wearing a black patch across his nose, but within a year became so distraught that he could not play baseball anymore.

I told the story to my mother, but the result was for her to chastise my brother for allowing me to hear such stories. She seemed to feel that I was, somehow, afraid for my own face, and though I protested, she insisted on comforting me, and on telling me how handsome I would be. She did not, however, dispute the truth of the story.

When my father died in 1914, Tucker stopped playing on Sundays since he could not earn as much money from the game as he could from carpentry, a trade he had learned from my father. My brother Paul, who was still in high school, took Tucker's place, however, and I continued to spend my Sundays in Dexter Park. By the age of twelve I was pitching batting practice and was occasionally being sent in as a pinch runner. In the games I played with friends from school, in the the fields already mentioned, I was miles ahead of the others. I remember nothing in particular about any game during these years, except that, while they were in progress, I thought of nothing except the games themselves.

Whatever else may have nagged at me—my brothers, my sister, my work at school, my chores at home, my mother's state of being, my battle not to ruin permanently what Tucker had taught me was "the temple of the body," my broodings concerning my color—these were gone, not in any ecstasy, but in the simple act of playing, in the attention required to see through every seemingly leisurely detail of any game, short or long. I remember specific feelings, of course—and can see myself now, as if I am one of the old men who would stand in the high grass, on the third base side of our makeshift playing field, clucking over us: I was tall for my age—six feet by the age of thirteen—and though everyone in our section (which was all black by this time) knew me and never thought but that I was one of them, still there must have been something striking in watching this slender, fair-skinned boy, in overalls and flannel shirt (the sleeve slit into strips with a razor blade, as Tucker's teammate Bill Stacey had taught me, so that, in the follow-through, the ball would fly at the batter from a background of fluttering white), rearing back, striding forward, and firing bullets.

I had, from this age, a natural hop to my fast ball, so that it seemed to be a fiery white line moving from my hand to the plate, heading downward, breaking some fifteen or twenty feet from the plate, soaring toward the catcher's glove at an angle identical to that at which it had been moving down. That is to say, I picture it now not as a ball in flight, but as one long hard white line, and when I threw it, if I thought at all, I thought of it this way also: as if there were a transparent piece of tubing (narrowly larger than a baseball) on a line from my hand to the plate, through which, without touching the sides, my ball would spin. I threw no curves, no sinkers, no changes of pace, and did not—a source of pride at the time—have need to throw the various kinds of spitballs that others relied on (the most popular being the cut-ball spitball, in which the ball, where the spit was to be applied, would be nicked with a bottle cap). Unlike most fastball pitchers, I had also—my greatest strength ultimately, and the talent which would have seen me through for the long pull—little trouble with control; I was able, from the beginning, to tell the ball where I wanted it to go.

In 1919, at the age of fourteen, I pitched my first game for the Brooklyn Remsens, defeating the Brooklyn Atlantics 6 to 2, with my brother Paul catching me. The enthusiasm of my brothers for my pitching performance was infectious, and I soon found myself something of a hero in our neighborhood, to the children and the old men; my mother fussed over me also—had she not told me that I was her White Star, her Hope and Deliverance?

I started games every Sunday after that, from March through October, and during the years 1919 through 1923 I rarely lost. By that time Paul was working with Tucker (they opened their own store in the Bushwick section, featuring custom-made furniture); George was attending Columbia, on his way to the New England Conservatory, and it was agreed upon by all that I too would attend a university; thus I stayed in school and did not accompany the Remsens when they traveled away from Brooklyn. Even during July and August, when school was out, I did not go against my family's wishes; I stayed home, reading books, giving piano lessons (thereby making my contribution to the family's expenses), helping Tucker and Paul in their store, and waiting for Sundays.

Despite my brothers' pride in my reputation (for I was known throughout Brooklyn), and their knowledge of exactly how good I was, my family began, I know, to fear my abilities, for the idea that I might want to make a career of baseball was odious and impossible. Riding around in broken-down cars, playing in games that were preceded and followed by minstrel shows, being teammates with men who were generally of little or no education—this was not, in brief, the life that had been envisioned for me, the life of a gentleman.

As for myself, I did not think much about it one way or the other. Traveling around the country—seeing far-off cities and living the life that Tucker's teammates had described so graphically for me—this held no particular appeal. I was happy at home, in Brooklyn, pitching on Sundays; what I wanted, simply, was to be able to play more often and (I admitted this at the time) to play in front of larger crowds. More than this, I began, after the first time Mr. McGraw came to Dexter Park to watch me play (in 1923), to nurture the most foolish of my private dreams: that I would, one day, play in Yankee Stadium (which had opened that year), for a team of blacks, before a crowd of whites and blacks, and that I would, in the name of my people, defeat the enemy.

The vision lacked specifics: I do not recall if I saw myself pitching for a team that was all black, yet part of the Major Leagues; if my team were part of a separate league which played in an annual World Series against the white champions; or if I saw the team as, somehow, of mixed races—like the All Nations Club (but with the blacks as regulars and the whites as substitutes). I knew only that I wanted to be there, proving to the public what all baseball men knew in private. What I dreamt of, then, was that I might someday have the best of both worlds: to be the champion of my own people, loved and honored as one of them (as the best of them)—and, at the same time, to have my abilities (and thus, the abilities of all my brothers) acknowledged as superior by those whose color skin I possessed.

I did not, however, think things through in this manner. I knew only, when Mr. McGraw came up to me after the game, and when he shook my hand and told me that he wished to speak with me in private, that—though I gave him my coldest manner, my most indifferent air—I saw, not the dream that was soon to burn in my own head, but the light in the eyes of my teammates, the slight breathing in of satisfaction by Paul and Tucker and George, the deferential way in which all those friends and fans who had come down from the stands to shake my hand began to back away; so that I was left alone with Mr. McGraw at a time when, truly, I wanted the warmth of those other bodies around me. I must have known, of course, that I would say no to whatever offer he might have made, and if, as I accepted his praise and his good wishes, as I watched his ruddy hands gesticulate, I sensed what was to come, then I must have sensed also where this left me—I sensed, that is, not only that I could never have the best of that world I was about to begin dreaming of, but that I would no longer be able to have, unthinkingly and fully, the world which had until then given me such pleasure.

The alternatives were clearer then, though I can perhaps *name* them more convincingly now; no matter which road I chose, I saw that I would lose. Therefore, I chose no road, but stayed where I was. "I grew up in a fighting baseball school, young man," McGraw told me. "And I will fight for you, if you're willing. You're well-known in Brooklyn, but you're only seventeen years old. Your body will change—if you drop from sight for one or two seasons, people will forget. I'd like to have you play for the New York Giants, and I believe, taking on a new name at the age of, say, nineteen, that this can be. I've seen the best of the best, and you can be one of them." I said nothing. "It has long been my hope, as you may know, to bring people of your race into the Major Leagues, and I believe—if you will play the ballgame as I have outlined it—that, after you are established, we will be able to reveal your true identity. Once the breaking of the color bar is a fact, I know that we will have no trouble. Judge Landis, the Commissioner of Baseball, will support me in this—he already knows, in fact, why I have come here today. If you say yes, you will be doing a fine thing, for yourself, for baseball, and for your race.''

I did not, of course, hesitate—nor did I give him any reasons; what reasons, after all, even to myself—and more, to all my teammates, my brothers, the fans who loved me—would have seemed adequate? I would, to be sure, have been a fool, by their lights, to have refused, and yet, if I had accepted, I would have proven to them the very thing I longed to disprove—that I was one of them. If I had been the instrument for the success of Mr. McGraw's plot, I would have only cast greater doubt on who I was; I would have succeeded, that is, not for those things which made me one with my brothers, but for those very things which set me apart from them, and this included, not merely my outward appearance, but those God-given skills which made me special, and which were destined, over and above the reality of my origins, to give my life its special providence.

This then must be something like what entered into the sentence I gave Mr. McGraw without prethought, with a shrug of my lean shoulders, and with a smile which must have shown some kind of embarrassed appreciation for his having gone to the trouble of approaching me: ''I'm a colored boy, Mr. McGraw,'' I said, and I said it without any particular pride, without deference or shame, and without the rage which would come later.

Was I being merely selfish?

This is, of course, the question which came to haunt me when it was all over—and it is a question for which I have never had an adequate reply. I had to choose, and to choose irrevocably, and I have never doubted the choice I made, since I have never believed that I had a choice. What I have doubted, though—and the distinction may, to one who has not lived with it, seem more foolish than fine—is my belief, my faith *in* that decision. I have not considered that interview with McGraw to be one of the high points of my life for the very reason that I do not—and did not—feel it to be a moment of decision; yet all of my life, and its events, have clearly flowed from what passed on that day.

I knew, first of all, that I could not have accepted his offer and have remained the player he courted; to put it most simply, how could I, disguising myself as a white man, have retained the speed of my fast ball, and the superb control I had of that speed? I knew, as soon as he had presented the possibility of another life to me, that I could only, during games in such a life, have become, literally, a self-conscious man. And if, on the mound, I had begun thinking at all, then I surely would have been lost.

Still, though I could not have done otherwise, I must wonder, now more than then, if an opposite decision would not have led to early opportunities for others, and if, despite the (to me) deceptive foundation these opportunities would have been based upon, they would have been, nonetheless, opportunities. If I reflect, however, and see that my excessive pride may have kept me from doing what Mr. McGraw thought I could do for my people, then I must also see that it was this very pride which had made me who I was; if I had lacked an ounce of it, I would not have been the man Mr. McGraw would have chosen to approach. What the world calls selfishness or self-interest was necessarily a part of that pride, and it made me the man and player I was; and yet, if I could not have done otherwise, and if I do not, after all the years which have passed, doubt my decision, why is it that my faith in that decision seems always so weak, crumbling now more than ever?

That summer I went on the road with the Remsens—as far west as Harrisburg, Pennsylvania, and as far south as Washington, D.C.—and when the fall came, I had to tell my mother what her fears had already confirmed: that I had decided to try to make my way as a ballplayer in the Negro Leagues. I sat at her feet, my head on her lap, and, as I had expected, she did not protest; my brothers, for their part, tried to persuade me to go to college first, to play baseball on Sundays and during summers, but I think they were—certainly this was so with Paul and George—secretly glad of my decision; they assured me that they would, as always, see to my mother's needs; I vowed that I would be home as often as possible during the season, and would continue to live at home during the winter months. Listening to my mother humming, I dreamt of her standing in the crowd at Yankee Stadium, in a box behind third base, wearing an orchid corsage. I tried—swelling with my own pride—to imagine the mother's pride she would feel in my moment of glory, and I thought, at the time, that there was no other gift I could have given her which would have made her life as full.

My imagination, clearly, was even more foolish and self-serving than my life could possibly have been.

There had been, up to this time, and not counting the days before the color bar, some half-dozen major attempts to organize a successful Negro League, but they had all, for one reason or another, ended in failure. I had heard the stories and the reasons: dishonest booking agents, the competition of the white leagues, failures in leadership, the lack of capital and backing (genteel Negroes looked down, of course, on educated men who played in these leagues)—it would not take a genius, surely, to imagine what, given the general conditions in which we lived during the early years of this century, the problems would have been. Still, by 1920, when Rube Foster had taken the Negro American Baseball League in hand, and had fought and defeated the power of Nat Strong, the major New York booking agent, we were holding our own. The cooperative plan, as it was called (this meant, simply, that players lived from game to game, dividing the percentage of the gate receipts their team was given) had been replaced, in 1920, by a guaranteed annual salary; and though this salary was generally small, a man could— with the additional money earned from barnstorming against white teams after the regular season ended, get by. The big stars, of course, always did well, and even under Foster they were allowed to hire themselves out to teams other than their own for major games and exhibitions. Men such as Foster and Buck O'Neal and Bullet Rogan and Rap Dixon earned as much, some years, as any of the white stars.

Several teams made me offers, and in the summer of 1923, shortly after a second visit from Mr. McGraw, I left the Brooklyn Remsens for the Brooklyn Royal Dodgers. My salary was to be six thousand dollars for my first full season, plus bonuses which were to depend upon gate receipts and the number of my victories. The offer was not the best I received (this came from the Pittsburgh Crawfords), but it was close enough so that I could see my way to accepting it. I was happy, thus, to be able to remain in Brooklyn.

I was seventeen and one-half years old, and though many men had sung my praises to me, I knew that I was not yet the best of the best, and this is what I vowed, putting on a Dodger uniform for the first time in late August, that I would become. Having chosen my path, having relinquished the opportunity that could *not* have led to the fulfillment of the dream that drove me, I developed—on and off the field—a special hatred for the men who were my daily opponents, and

I set myself the task of defeating them as badly as I could, of outdoing their finest achievements, of driving myself to every possible success in their league; why I felt this way is by now clear, but that I might have wanted to be the best of the blacks in order, once again, that I might be a man set apart from them—this is a thought which did not occur to me, as self-evident as it is, until I had begun to set down this narrative.

On August 28, 1923, a Sunday, at Ebbets Field, I took the mound for the Brooklyn Royal Dodgers for the first time, in a game against the Indianapolis ABC's, and, pitching against the great Bullet Rogan, my brief career in the Negro American Baseball League began.

If, haunted by a dream which I knew could never be realized, I drove myself to a hatred for other black men, it remains true that this hatred was, like the dream, intangible and general. It was, of course, my own self against whom I struggled most; it was my own self-hatred which needed an external object, and the turning outward of this passion enabled me to survive, and to survive by subduing those whose love I wanted most dearly, but wanted in a world which—thus my dream—had been ordered otherwise.

I wanted to be the best of the best, and the intensity with which I wanted this was gone only during those actual moments of action, when, as I have indicated, the ball was in motion, the world was timeless, and my body moved, with strength and grace, of its own accord. I fought against opposing teams, and I fought against my own team: for I could only do so much—once I had put the ball where I wanted, if I did not strike out the batter, and if he hit the ball—even if he hit it where I had planned to have him hit it should he not swing and miss—I could not control what those behind me did when the ball came to them. To put it in simplest terms, it bothered me that my teammates where there, it bothered me—and I was aware of how unreal the grounds of my feeling were—that there had to be eight other men with me, that I could not do what had to be done alone. I did not, in truth, think of it at the time in the terms I give here. I knew only that I preferred to keep to myself, and to win. It was as if, at the age of seventeen and a half, from the time of my first game, I was already some older version of myself; or rather, as if, while I was in motion on the field, I was in fact that young man whom others cheered and admired and talked about, and, at the same time—and whenever the ball was not in flight, whenever I was obliged to be with others—I was a man who had already lived through it all and had passed to the other side; it was as if this other self were there, glaring at me, mercilessly judging my every action.

But just as the dream which drove me had its counterpart in actuality (my brief career, here described), so my hatred had its counterpart, though not among the white men with whom, in the Major Leagues, I knew I would never play, nor among the white men who kept me from playing. The first man I hated after I had joined the Brooklyn Royal Dodgers, and the man who returned this hate with an easy scorn I was never to match, was the pitcher whose place I took, a mean and shrewd black man, then forty-three years old, named Amos "Brick" Johnson. For while it is true that all black men are brothers, yet some are less brotherly than others.

I was young and fair; he was old and dark. I was not yet in my prime; he had seen his better years. I had been raised in the city and trained to be a gentleman; his origins lay in some anonymous country village, and he could not sign his name. The oppositions—in our history and nature—were endless, only our rivalry uniting us, and it must have appealed to me that the basis of our opposition had such classic proportions.

Until my arrival Johnson had been, despite his age, the mainstay of the Dodgers' pitching staff. During a career which spanned at least thirty years, he claimed to have won over eight hundred games, and to have lost fewer than two hundred. He had begun playing before the turn of the century, and had played with dozens of teams, including Rube Foster's great Leland Giants (of 1910), the Birmingham Black Barons, the Nashville Elite Giants, the Celeron Chocolates, the Genuine Cuban Giants, and the Brooklyn Brown Bombers. He could still command fifty dollars for an important game when he rented himself out to a semi-pro team not in our league. He had never been considered the best of the black pitchers, but he had sometimes been called the fastest —and the meanest.

I had, as a boy of ten or eleven, seen him pitch against the Brooklyn Remsens several times, and had tried to imitate his pitching motion— a high kick and big overarm delivery which had, as we said then, a lot of show on it. But the big motion, even when I first saw him, was already being used sparingly; by the time we became teammates, it had given way to a variety of less awesome pitches: an assortment of cross-fires and sidearmers and submariners—a hesitation pitch and a quick pitch, an emery ball and a burred spitball. Like many before and after him, he had, for some years, been getting by on savvy. He saved what was left of his fast ball, most often, for soaking batters—and he did not, as lesser pitchers did, aim for the chin or the shoulder: he fired, using a submarine delivery, for the temple. Old Brick, the players said, he *means* to be mean.

Before the day I first pitched for the Brooklyn Royal Dodgers, I did not, however, know how much I would hate him. When, shortly before game time, Jack Henry, our manager, informed me that I and not Johnson would be the pitcher against Bullet Rogan, I allowed the innocence I still carried with me to be exposed to the man. I went to him and informed him that I had seen him pitch when I was a boy and that I had once modeled myself after him.

He studied my face, then laughed. "Hey then, you got real brains, fair ass," he said. Our teammates did not hear the exchange between us, but they did hear his laughter—a rumbling and coughing growl that overpowered me, and though I set my eyes upon his, and vowed never to give him another chance at me, I could feel my heart shrink, and my body, like a twig, bend in humiliation, as if the weight of his barrel-chested torso were upon me, crushing me. I blushed and turned away. He had seen too much, of course: he had seen that the boy who had worshiped and imitated was still alive in me, and that, from his point of view, my superior abilities could, therefore, be dismissed. I was struck also—frozen to the spot, as it were—to sense something about him that I had never previously understood was possible: he did not care about baseball.

Nor did he really care about me. Baseball was, quite simply, the way he earned a living, and my presence meant that he would, in time, have to be occupied with the bother of looking for another way to earn his keep. I was his enemy because I had taken his place, and though he found a special language to deal with me—one which amused him and —the expression is too accurate—got under my skin as nothing before had—I think now that he would have acted in a similar way toward any young pitcher joining the team.

But I was not any young pitcher, and it was, I think, the indifferent quality of his hatred—his refusal to regard me as special—which most infuriated me. That, given my age and abilities, I would win was foregone; that I would replace him and surpass him was apparent to both of us—yet there was, I saw at once, nothing in him capable of being touched by my victory—of acknowledging or understanding what it was in me that wanted so dearly to win. ("It is no victory," says Claudian, "unless the vanquished foe admits your mastery.") It was this diffidence, then, crueler than indifference, which I found unbearable, and against which I set myself.

Or so it seems now. Why it is that the generality of the world's injustice, as it came home to me at that time, should have been embodied for me in this particular man is not, of course, given the simple twistings of my young mind, difficult to understand. Would it have been easier for me to have refused McGraw, and later, to have left the Negro American Baseball League, if I had been able to wear Johnson's dark skin, his indifferent scowl? Once, I recall, during that first summer with the Dodgers, Little Johnny Jones, our third baseman, asked him about his mother. I expected Johnson to laugh at Jones as he had laughed at me, but instead he grabbed Jones by the front of his uniform, slamming him against a locker. "You think any woman could give birth to Brick Johnson? You want to mind your business—you want to keep your damned questions up your ass, hear? Your life ain't nothing to me."

At the time I suspected that he had said this for my benefit, that he watched my face, and not Jones's, for a reaction. And yet, I knew that this could hardly be true, since the source of my own anger was not that he desired to provoke me, but that he did not. Was he so shrewd, then, that he could invent anger within himself, in my presence, so that I would wish the force of this anger directed against me? I cannot say. His black perforated face, in my mind, reveals no answers now, as it revealed none then.

But such are, of course, the ruminations of an old man, and they do not correspond to the glory I did feel on that day almost fifty years ago when I took the field for the first time, wearing the uniform of the Brooklyn Royal Dodgers. It was a broiling August day, without wind, and in my hand the new ball felt as cool and hard as the sun overhead was hot and molten. There were no shadows across the green lawns when I warmed up, and when I threw there was no web of speculations in my head, nothing which could impede or diminish the speed of that fiery white line between myself and the dark hole in the catcher's glove. If, before the game had begun, I wanted to win in order to extinguish what had passed between Johnson and myself, in order, in some way, to defeat him—to fire the ball with such speed that it would become an invisible white pellet—it remains true that, once I did wind up, kick, and stride toward home plate, his face and voice were gone, and the hatred which had inspired my determination was transformed into something resembling pure forgetfulness and joy. I might, fingering the red stitching on the ball, vow to show him—and the world—who I was, but once I had begun my motion, even while warming up, the truest thing is that I released all thought before I released the ball.

Without wind, the flags above the grandstands and scoreboard were still. Despite the heat, the crowd was good: fourteen thousand fans, more than Wilbert Robinson's white Dodgers would draw on an average Saturday when they were at home. My three brothers sat together behind the third base dugout, and Mr. Tanner, still alive and in his senses at ninety-two, was with them. I can feel again the fiery ball moving slowly and steadily above me in the heavens; I can see my brothers' proud faces; I can feel the sweat washing down my neck and back and chest, soaking my uniform; I can see the spectators holding their paper fans, painted with tiny flowers, moving like inverted pendulums in the grandstands—cooling my admirers' unmoving faces on that windless day; I can feel blood coursing through me as I moved, in a world that defied entrance, from action to waiting, from pride to anger, and back again; I can taste the ice that was hacked from the slabs, which, wrapped in burlap, vendors carried on their backs from row to row in the stands. But I knew that the only escape from the heat lay, not in fanning a small breeze, nor in sucking on chips of ice, but in playing hard—in heating the body through work, in trying to equal the day's heat; and yet, though my body did defy the sun's strength, my defiance seems now the most obvious instance of the futility of all that energy—how little, after all, it mattered that I rose on my right leg, kicked, whipped my arm over, and sent a round piece of white leather across some sixty feet of earth! I wonder, then: was it, on that broiling day, some flickering sense of my insignificance which was, after all, the truest inspiration for my fury and will?

I was at the center, standing in the small circle of dirt at the mound; around the dirt was a diamond of emerald green-grass, ninety feet square, and around the grass was the basepath, another diamond—clay-colored, some fifteen feet deep, oval-shaped at its outer rim. Bingo Rouillard, my catcher, squatted behind home plate, in his own ring of dirt. The infield (Rap Dixon, Jack Henry, Olen "Junior" Barton, and Little Johnny Jones) was poised within the clay behind me, bent over low to the ground; beyond them, in the acres of grass which stretched away to the far corners of the field, my outfielders (Johnson, Galen "Gunboat" Kelly, Rose Kinnard) played straightaway, their hands on their thighs, bent over, but not so low as the infielders. At their backs, the fences rose, squaring off the field, and the rows of seats, one behind the other, capable of holding some thirty-one thousand fans, moved away and up at an easy angle, all around the park (except for right field and right-center, where there were no stands, and an eighty-foot wall containing the scoreboard separated us from Bedford Avenue). Within these stands, the fans sat immobile on the sloping steps, their eyes fixed on me—a thin and pale boy, tiny when seen from the height of the grandstands and bleachers and upper decks—trapped in the circle within the diamond, the diamond within the oval-shaped square, the square within the larger green diamond of the field, the field within the square of dirt that separated it from the people, the people themselves trapped in the steel and concrete stands. And yet, with the warm-ups completed, and the national anthem played, my players and fans ready, I felt, as I dug out a bit of dirt in front of the mound with the heel of my spikes, that things were somehow inverted —or is this memory speaking?—that, since I commanded it, I also contained, within my small ring of earth, the entire arena. I felt, in brief, as if I were untouchable. Then, since we were the home team, I wound up, and, in my glory at last, fired the first pitch of the game.

It was a strike, knee-high, that whistled past the batter. Bingo returned the ball to me without rising from his haunches. I threw two more strikes, to the same spot, and the batter remained, like the fans, immobile. Only their mouths moved, letting loose a cheer which echoed from the steel girders and told me that I had pleased them. I wiped the sweat from my forehead, using the back of my glove, and fired three more times, striking out the second batter, and Bingo Rouillard, loud enough for those in the dugouts and in the boxes along the first and third base lines, asked me if I would prefer to have him call in the outfield for the third batter. I smiled, wiped my fingers along my thighs to dry them, and watched the great Oscar Charleston bend over, rub some dirt into his palms, and step into the batter's box. His fame and power, however, were nothing to me, and I reared back and let fly with my fast ball and it found the hole in Bingo's glove before Oscar could move the bat from his shoulder. "You got 'em all, honey," Little Johnny Jones called to me from third base. "Oscar's posin' for pictures there—you got 'em all, honey." I fired again and Charleston swung, late, missing a low outside pitch. "I feel the breeze," Jones called to the plate. "Oh I do feel the breeze."

Bingo showed me his glove, just outside the plate, and I threw it there, hoping to have Charleston swing and miss on a bad pitch, but he left his bat on his shoulder, and I was obliged to throw again. I threw inside this time, letter-high, where Bingo showed me, and Charleston stumbled away, on his heels, but did not fall. With the count two and two, Bingo showed me the heart of the plate, knee-high, and I sent the ball there, lower than the spot I was aiming for, so that, rising somewhat past the halfway point, it cut upward and Charleston—his bat stationary on his shoulder—muttered something and walked away, knowing he was out before the umpire had told him so.

I walked from the mound, the roar of the crowd raining down on me, my own teammates running by, slapping me on the back. Johnson ambled in, the last to reach the dugout. "It's hot today," he said. "You want to pace yourself, boy." I sat by myself at the end of the bench, wanting my own men, I realized, to make out quickly, so that I could return to the mound. Bullet Rogan, pitching against us, accommodated me. A man of average height for an athlete—perhaps five-foot-ten—and of average build, Rogan had begun his career as a catcher for the Pullman Colts of Kansas City and had first earned fame as a pitcher during the First World War with the Negro 25th Infantry team in Honolulu. He was very fast—not as fast as I was, nor as fast as Johnson had been, but he threw what we called a heavy fast ball. Coming at you, it seemed larger than it should have been, and you strained to try to hit it solidly. In addition, unlike most fast-ball pitchers then, he had a fine curve ball. I watched him work, getting Barton to hit out in front of a curve ball, thereby tapping it to second for an easy out. He blew two high hard ones past Rose Kinnard, then caught him looking with an easy inside curve. Johnson, batting in third position, swung on the first pitch—a low fast ball—and lined it to third. Rogan had thrown only six pitches, but that was all right too. I was back on the mound that much sooner.

I forgot about Johnson, and I forgot about Rogan. I smoothed over the spot on the mound Rogan had dug out, and went to work, oblivious of the heat, the crowd, the "book" we had on each hitter. I left the spots to Bingo, who had been around for as long as Johnson had, though he himself had never been a star, merely a journeyman catcher who knew how to handle pitchers, and—his one distinction—could, until he quit (at the age of forty-seven, a year after my departure), rifle the ball to second base and catch a runner stealing without having to rise from his squat position. His right forearm seemed twice the width of my own.

Batting first in the second inning, Mule Suttles, the ABC's clean-up man, ticked a foul ball into the first base stands, but he was the only man to touch the ball. I gave him two balls before striking him out, ran the count to three and two on Anderson, who followed him and went down swinging, and then struck out Rogan, batting sixth, on three straight pitches, all low and away.

Johnson sat next to me between innings. "You want to pace yourself, boy," he said again. "You'll melt that arm, a day like this. You want to pace yourself." Sweat dripped down above my eyes and I tasted salt in my mouth. I looked at the field and said nothing. Jack Henry, the hot day making the light olive caste of his skin seem especially cool, sat on my other side, rubbing his hand across the D in Dodgers, thereby giving Dixon the sign to take until two strikes were against him. He nodded. "Sure," Brick said. "You listen to old Brick, who's been around. You want to pace yourself."

Jack Henry agreed. "It's a hot one. Rogan has his stuff, but if we make him throw a lot of balls, he might get tired seventh or eighth inning. You got to have luck against him."

I watched Rogan. He used his fast ball sparingly, varied his speeds, wanted us to hit the ball; he tempted us by making the first and second pitches his best ones, but Jack Henry made us wait him out, and, two strikes in the hole, our second three men all had to chop at bad pitches, where they didn't like them, and we were down again in the second, one-two-three. "You'll melt that arm, fair ass, a day like this," Johnson said as he passed me on the way to the outfield at the beginning of the third inning.

I could not reply. Instead, I threw hard. I stung Bingo's hand with my warm-up pitches and refused his advice to take it easy. There was nothing I wanted to do except to throw strikes, to make the ball move faster and faster, until it disappeared. My infielders chided the opposing team, but I no longer heard their sweet teasing words. I heard only Johnson's voice, telling me that I had brains. I mowed down the first man to face me, on three pitches. When he had swung and missed for the third time, and the ball made its way behind me, around the infield, Jack Henry, instead of tossing it to me, walked with it to the mound. I knew, from the way I felt, that my face must have been flushed. "You got to pace yourself some," Jack said. I blinked, aware of the sound of laughter. "You gone to put us out of jobs if you keep this up." The laughter grew and I tried to place it, to clear my head—though I did not want to; I wanted to get on with it, but Jack Henry held the ball, his glove slipped down along the underside of his left wrist so that he could rub the ball for me with both hands. He motioned behind me and I followed his glance to right field, where Johnson, lying on the grass, was feigning sleep, his cap over his face. I did not smile, for I knew, of course, that this alleged comic tribute to my strikeouts—a standard ploy of outfielders on all barnstorming teams—had its double-edge.

Bingo Rouillard joined us. "I been tryin' to get him to go slow, Jack," he said.

"All right," I said.

"Sure," Jack Henry said. "You get them to hit it a few times, first or second pitch, we'll handle the rest. You got to save yourself for the late innings. A day like this, you goin' to lose seven, maybe eight pounds from sweat—even a skinny boy like you. You want to pace yourself, save some of that juice for later on."

"All right," I said a second time, grudgingly, knowing that they were wrong, but lacking, in the dizziness my anger induced while I was not in motion, the confidence which could have made me forswear surrender.

Bingo squatted behind the plate. "You ain't goin' to even see this one," he told the batter, and I gave him my big motion, reared back and tried to take a little off the ball, aiming it low and outside. As soon as it was released, however, stumbling slightly to the right from the awkwardness of having pulled the string, of having arrested the fluidity of my motion, I saw my error—I saw the ball spinning lazily, high and outside, too slow, as large as a grapefruit. I saw the batter swing the instant I released the ball, anticipating my blazer—and I saw him smile—though I remember only that he did, and cannot now see that smile or remember that face—and catch his swing, hitch the bat as one never should, and then continue, whacking the ball with the meat of the bat, hitting it where it was pitched—shoulder high and on the outside corner—so that as soon as it left home plate there was no doubt but that it would land on the other side of the right field wall.

"That's all right now," Jack Henry said to me, handling the slightly roughed ball that was to replace the first. "Ain't but one run—you pitch to 'em."

I knew that, behind me, Johnson was smiling. I had pitched badly—taken too much off the ball, but even if I had pitched as I had wanted to, I knew, it would have been wrong. Rouillard and Barton were at the mound also, thinking they had to calm their young pitcher down, but I did not hear, or need to hear, their words of consolation and encouragement. I threw hard to the next batter—as hard as I had thrown to the men in the first two innings—and he lofted an easy fly to Kelly in left field. The man after him bunted, but I was on the ball at once as it skittered along the third base line, and I threw him out at first, with steps to spare. The inning was over, they had only one hit and one run, and yet I sensed that for me it was all over; the spell had been broken, and try as I might—throw as hard as any man had ever thrown, harder than I had thrown in innings one and two—I would never again match the perfection of those innings, I could never, I sensed, be satisfied. ("But fortune is glass," says Publilius Syrus, "it shatters when it shines."

There had been, I saw at once, no need to pace myself. I had more than enough energy to bear down on every pitch in every inning of every game. Why, then, had I listened?

"You took too much off that ball, boy," Johnson said to me, between innings.

I said nothing, for to reply would have been to acknowledge the difference he had made in my life; still, I vowed that I would never again, for as long as I played, let up on a batter. I vowed that I would begin every game with the will to pitch a perfect game—no hits, no runs, no walks, no man reaching first base—though I knew that no matter how mightily I pitched thereafter, I could now, in the language of the game, be reached.

I held them hitless and scoreless through the fourth and fifth innings. In our half of the fifth, we pushed a run across: I singled to left, Jones moved me to second with a bunt, and Jack Henry, batting left-handed, poked a long single down the right field line which enabled me to score. We touched Rogan for at least one hit in each inning after the third, yet we remained unable to score against him. As the day wore on, the crowd grew quieter, and it seems to me now, as I see them again, that—after the home run against me—they lost interest, grew languid, as if they were sleeping. We sucked on oranges between innings, and our bat boy fanned me with a newspaper. I did not bother to tell him to stop. Jack Henry took Johnson out of the game in the seventh inning, the hot day being brutal to a man his age, and, though Johnson did not request his own removal, surely it was not accidental that, in their half of the eighth inning, his replacement, a young boy named Virgil Whitaker, trying for a shoestring catch of a sinking line drive, missed the ball, so that, as it rolled into the rightfield corner—a hit and not an error—the two men I had allowed on base via a walk and a Texas League single both scored. Johnson sat on the bench, his head back, a wet towel around his neck, shaking his head. He would never have tried to catch a ball like that, he told us.

In the eighth and ninth innings Rogan pitched at the same pace he had employed in the first inning, mixing his fast ball and curve ball, getting us to hit in front of the ball when he would slow down, and to chop at balls that threatened to nick the corners of the plate. I struck out their side in the top of the ninth, but after Bingo Rouillard had popped out to the second baseman to start the bottom of the ninth, even I knew that the fans were right to begin moving toward the exits. We went down without seriously threatening, and I had lost my first game, 3 to 1, giving up a total of six hits to Rogan's ten.

My brothers came to the locker room and tried to console me, pointing out that the winning runs were not, in the true sense, earned, but they saw that I was beyond consolation. Mr. Tanner shook my hand and commended me in a Latin phrase I did not understand. "Don't you worry none," Johnson said to me, as I sat brooding in front of my locker. "It was a hot day and McGraw wasn't watching."

"I'm sorry," I said, without thinking.

Other players moved near. I could smell the piercing sweetness of oil of wintergreen, though it did not cut the thickness of the day's heat. "Sure," Johnson said, and his hand was on my shoulder. My brother Tucker sat on the bench next to me, his jacket and tie still on, his derby in his lap. "But let me ask you something: how many kids you got?"

"None," I replied, pulling my shoulder from under him. "I'm only seventeen—why should—?"

I broke off. He was laughing at me, satisfied with himself, and the other players who had gathered around laughed also, good-naturedly, I suppose, thinking Johnson was riding me properly, in the way a veteran should ride a rookie. "You mean you ain't got no children yet?" He walked away, chuckling to himself. Even now, I can hear the voice and be angered by the question he would come to take such pleasure in repeating. *You ain't got no children yet, fair ass?* He had not calculated the remark that first time, since in anything other than pitching, he calculated nothing, and yet he knew he had drawn blood, and he would, with the same off-handed manner, come to ask the question of me again and again, for no seeming reason, and at no particular time. My teammates never, I think, understood how deeply his remark went, yet they laughed nonetheless, as they had the first time, whenever he used it.

I was the last player to leave the locker room, and when my brothers and I and Mr. Tanner reached the outside of the field, along the Sullivan Place side, there were no fans waiting. Three young black people—a girl and two boys—stood at the corner of Bedford Avenue and Sullivan Place, however, holding placards which urged us not to play on Sunday, the Lord's Sabbath. They were all very handsome, and I must have thought that they had—with the crowd gone—been waiting especially for me. Their eyes were bright and clear and I envied them their simple faith. *And God blessed the Seventh Day and sanctified it: because that in it He had rested from all His work which God created and made.*

The girl looked at me with a frankness I found startling. She held an open Bible in her hands, and her face—a high yellow color—despite the day's heat and the proper black dress she wore, covering all but that face, seemed so very cool. "Father would have agreed," Paul said to me, as he ushered us into Mr. Tanner's carriage. I thought of Jack Henry, the third of eleven children, whose father, originally from Tennessee, had been a Baptist minister, and I felt sad, as I often would, because Jack himself had never married, and had had no children. I looked back, and the girl's eyes moved to mine: she carried herself beautifully, her back arched, shoulders straight, chin lifted. "Not the least of your troubles," Paul said to me, "is that you have defamed the Sabbath." He laughed, mimicking what was written on one placard, but I saw no reason to laugh with him. I think he was made too smart, at the time, by his revered college education, by the Mencken-loving dandy it brought out in him. I preferred him as he had been behind the plate at Dexter Park, rocking slowly and talking to the batter: "Li'l brother goin' to blow it by you, Cap'n. Li'l brother *throws* that ball!"

I was furious, and all the way home, in Mr. Tanner's elegant carriage, I fumed silently—against Johnson, against Whitaker, against Paul, against my father, against myself. I contained caverns of rage then, and though the anger in me would later become deeper, there was something wonderful about the ability of my young body to contain so much sheer rage. Then I acted; now I consider those actions—and while I do, hearing Johnson's laugh or Paul's voice, I can feel that younger body tighten again, and I find that I have no desire to deny the hunger I feel to be back in it. Our passions may grow more intense as we grow older, but this is so, at least in part, because we act upon them less and less.

My mother was not in her music room when I entered our home. Instead, I found her on the ground in back of the house, her skirt spread in a circle under her as she weeded her flowerbed. She looked at me, smiling, and seemed to know that I had lost and that I did not wish to talk about it. I kissed her on the lips and asked if I could bring her something cool to drink. Was the sun not too hot for her? My brothers took her by the arms and sat her down in a metal lawn chair, under the shade of a tall oak which grew to the left of the house. I thought of the girl holding the Bible and I would have been willing to have had my mother's arms around me, to have rested my hot head on her lap, even with my brothers there. Her eyes were most loving toward me—yet, with my brothers present she offered only those eyes. She had prepared something to refresh us, if I would get it from the ice box. She knew how hot and weary we would be. I went to the kitchen and brought the pitcher of lemonade, with glasses, back with me on a tray. My brothers had removed their hats and jackets and were laughing, though at what I never knew. I poured their drinks for them. My mother's eyes were closed, and she did not watch me. I had not, until I drank my first glass, realized how thirsty I had been, and when I had, unmindful of the others, downed two more glasses straightaway, I found that my family was staring at me, silently. Then they laughed, and mother went inside to prepare supper. "Flowers and lemonade," she said, smiling at me. "Oh Mason! Flowers and lemonade."

Feeling, as I write, the quiet of that garden again, I must wonder if I was mad to have felt the way I did feel when I was on the playing field. The peace of the Sabbath reigned in our home, yet it could do nothing for me. I allowed my mother to serve me, I allowed myself to rest, to think of nothing—still, the peace I felt as I threw a baseball was the peace I sought, and cherished.

I wonder: when was I more mad—then, when the phantoms of my mind drove me to love and to hate, to desire and to deny with a passion that was beyond words? Or now, when I find names for what passed then, when I try to fix with words those things which had no names, those events and feelings which never did have, or could have had, beginnings or ends?

II

Birds

Then I asked: "Does a firm perswasion that a thing is so, make it so?"

He replied: "All poets believe that it does, & in ages of imagination this firm perswasion removed mountains; but many are not capable of a firm perswasion of any thing."
—William Blake, *The Marriage of Heaven and Hell*

5

In a daze, Sam descended the staircase, walked around the first-floor landing, and entered the store. He heard the sound of his father's laughter. "Ah, Mason," he heard Ben say. Flo saw Sam, took his hand. In the front room, Ben and Mason sat on wooden chairs, facing one another, holding paper cups. Tidewater looked at Sam, steadily, and Sam returned the man's gaze.

"We were just talking about you," Ben said. "The three of us were planning a trip."

Sam's own eyes were steady, he knew, and Tidewater would sense nothing. Still, things were blurred—he felt the way he did sometimes, coming in from the snow to a warm room. Pinpoints of light, like stars, flickered in front of him.

"Will you come?" Flo asked, pressing his hand, and handing him a cup.

"We intend to visit—before your father leaves us—some childhood scenes. It was at my request," Tidewater said. "We'd like to see the houses we grew up in, the fields we played in."

"Sure," Sam said. "I've just been reading your story."

"Good," Ben said, and leaned forward, toward Tidewater. "Didn't I tell you, Mason? My son Sam Junior is the sports expert."

"Don't be like that," Flo said, sitting down between Tidewater and Ben. Sam saw Tidewater's eyes enlarge, in anger, and then close. In high school, Sam remembered, on his team jackets he'd

97

always had *Sam Jr.* stitched in. He remembered the jacket from their synagogue team: red and yellow, a satin material, with the initials of the synagogue on the back—CST—and, on the front, where the left breast pocket would have been, a Star of David embroidered over a felt emblem of a basketball. His name had been stitched in on the right side. Ben's middle name was Sam also—for Samson. His own Sam was for Samuel. They'd been named for different grandfathers, he for his mother's father, whom he'd never known, Ben for his father's father, plowed under somewhere in Poland. Benjamin Samson Berman. Samuel Paul Berman.

"Think of it this way," Ben had said, when Sam was a boy—it was a game they'd played. "We're both Sams, but I'm Samson."

"No," Sam would reply. "I'm Sam's son."

"Then you're my son, if you're Sam's son."

"But you're Samson. That makes you my son." And around and around they'd go, he recalled, like Abbott and Costello. At the Linden Theater, on Nostrand Avenue, when Ben had taken him to see *Abbott and Costello Meet Frankenstein,* Sam had been petrified, he'd tried to hide his face in his father's shoulder. Ben had laughed, stroked his son's head. "Some Samson," he had heard Ben whispering. "Who sheared your locks that you can't look at the screen? It's just an actor, my little Sam—like your father sometimes, on the radio—just an actor, a man with make-up on. . . ."

"A penny for your thoughts," Flo said to him.

"What odds?" Sam asked, and the others laughed. The store was quiet, without shoppers. Sam saw that Tidewater was staring at him, smiling. Now that he knew about the guy, he had no reason to doubt it. It had always interested him, in fact, about athletes: the difference between what they were as players, and what they were in their private lives. Some of them—like Namath or Stallworth— were the same on and off the field, but there was no rule that said it had to be that way. Some of the greatest players could be the biggest deadbeats; and some of the quietest guys, guys who didn't even look like athletes, had been the greatest players, the born leaders. In truth, the only thing that bothered him about Tidewater's story, now that he had it, was that he felt—especially with the guy's eyes fixed on him—that it had been written somehow for him. Sam sipped his coffee and kept his mouth shut. He could see, from the wrinkles at the corners of his father's eyes, that Ben was flying, enjoying himself.

"You will come with us," Ben said. "Won't you, sonny boy? You'll join our excursion?" Ben showed his left palm to the others. "I can still feel the sting, Mason—that one time I let you pitch to me." He sat back. "But I said nothing at the time. That was always my trouble, you see. I could take it, but I couldn't dish it out. That's why, with my wife, with the school, with . . ."

"Poor Ben," Flo said, and, with the others, Sam found himself laughing.

"All right, all right," Ben said. "But notice my son's silence. Has he answered my question?"

"Sure," Sam said, and he saw Tidewater smile. "I'll come."

"Tell Sam," Ben continued, as if his son had not spoken, "what you were telling us before—about your speed. Then he'll understand. Or"—Ben paused—"has Sam already read that story?"

"No," Tidewater said, and he seemed, suddenly, embarrassed. "But it's a story he might have heard before, assigned to another."

"Please," Flo said.

Sure, Sam thought, hearing the man begin to speak: Negro players had had it rough. Sam had seen Satchel Paige on television, talking about his barnstorming days, and he remembered what they'd done to Jackie Robinson when he'd been the first Negro player in the Major Leagues—siccing black cats after him, making him room by himself, making him promise that he'd never talk back to anybody, even when they called him nigger. But Tidewater, Sam thought, and laughed at the idea, had had two strikes against him before he'd started: the first, his being white, and the second, his being black.

"When it was said of me that my fast ball moved so fast that you could not see it," Tidewater was saying, "the figurative expression became literal. Sometimes, in the late innings of a game, with darkness descending, I would call my catcher to the mound, prolonging the game as visibility decreased; I would slip the ball to him, return to the mound without it, then go through the motions of firing an invisible ball—my catcher would crack the pocket of his glove with his fist, the batter would swing at nothing, and the catcher would return the ball, which he had hidden, all the while, under his chest protector."

"Ah," Ben sighed, leaning back, his small eyes closed. Then his finger pointed at his son and his voice rose. "Do you see now, Sam, why I . . ." But he seemed, all at once, to lose energy. He sighed again. "It's a parable," he said. "I've always considered it a parable."

Flo nodded. The bell above the front door jingled, and a Negro woman, one of the regulars, carrying a bundle in her arms—a small baby, Sam saw—entered. "Sometimes," Flo said, "life can go by so fast that—"

"But as a story—as a story first," Ben said, interrupting Flo. He shifted, and his eyes twinkled. "What I mean to say is, it's incom-parable."

"Ah Ben," Tidewater said, pleased. "I should have seen it coming. You're too quick for me."

Ben stood, placed a hand on Sam's shoulder. He spoke softly, his head lowered. Sam watched Flo, looking at the woman's baby. "I'd like to pay you back," Ben said. "You know that, Sam. It meant—it still means—a good deal to me. Especially now."

"Forget it," Sam said. Flo was holding the baby in front of Sam. Was she, he wondered, thinking of what she had once told him? If it had been him, he knew that every time he saw a baby—any baby—he would have thought of the children he hadn't had—or rather, of those he'd had and then had had taken away.

"Isn't he beautiful?" Flo asked.

"Sure," Sam said. "He's an ace."

"Don't put me on, son," the woman said. "But put a kiss on his cheek, for good luck."

Flo nodded and Sam did what she wanted; he bent over, felt the blood rush to his head, and touched his lips to the baby's skin, on the forehead. "You have a good boy there," the woman said to Ben. "Like my oldest. Most of them now, they run off and leave you first chance."

"He's a good boy," Ben said.

Flo carried the baby to Ben, and then to Tidewater, and they each kissed it. Mrs. Scofield—Sam remembered her name, she was one of Flo's favorites—sat on a chair, and Flo returned the baby to her. She laughed at something Ben said, and talked about what had happened in the hospital. Was the new baby her seventh? eighth?

her ninth? Sam couldn't keep count. She would bring the entire family in with her sometimes, to outfit them, as she put it. Her oldest son played basketball for Erasmus and would be going somewhere in the Midwest on a scholarship the following year. She did okay—he didn't know the exact figure—but the checks she got from the city for all the kids, from the government for her first husband (killed in Korea) . . . Even with the money rolling in, though, having an armful of kids was no picnic. Sam thought of all the diapers, filled with mush—and if the kid hurt somewhere and started bawling and you couldn't figure out where he hurt . . .

Mrs. Scofield laughed and, without interrupting her story, she slipped the baby's head under her blouse and put his mouth onto her breast. Sam watched the baby's mouth, swallowing the nipple. It seemed impossible that he could take so much in. The breast was enormous. "So then, seeing how this young doctor knew I'd been through this eight times before, I reached over and took his hand in mine and I said to him, 'Honey, don't you worry none, don't you be nervous—why you just open your two little hands and I'll drop it right down in!' "

She leaned back then, laughing, and the baby went with her, lifted across her chest, sucking away. "I got to get going," Sam said, and he looked at Tidewater, as if, he realized, he were asking for permission.

"I'm glad you'll come with us on our little trip," Ben said. "To see where your father grew up, where he and Mason . . ."

"I got the picture," Sam said, and walked out. He felt Tidewater's eyes on his back, and it bothered him, not the way the guy looked at him, but that, there was no reason to deny it, he felt something for the guy now. To have been an ace, to have had it all in your hands, and then to have had it taken away: Sam could understand that that was something in life that could hurt. He walked along Linden Boulevard, his head down, against the cold.

That was why, when he thought about it, he himself had never gone after the big kill. If you did, the way Sam saw things work out in this life, you always lost. Sam had never had any dreams, night or day. He figured that dreams were the things that wore people down. Sometimes he wondered, as he did now, where dreams came from in the people who had them. Maybe, he thought, if you had a

bundle of talent, you could consider yourself chosen, the way
Tidewater had—you could make yourself think you'd had some
kind of calling—but the only time Sam figured he would believe
he'd been called was when he was holding three of a kind, or more.

At the corner of Linden and Rogers Avenue, he stopped in the
grocery store. The cold air, all the words in his head—they were
making his stomach talk to him. A black man and his wife owned
the store now and there were crates on the floor: beans and
vegetables. Behind the counter, in the glass case, were strange-
looking meats. Sam picked up a package of Drake's Devil's Food
Cakes, and thought of the white cream center, then sucked away
the small pool of saliva from under his tongue. A black girl, in
pigtails, was ahead of him: "My mother wants two quarts of milk, a
loaf of Silvercup white bread, a pound of rice, and fifty cents on
number three eighty-eight."

Sam watched the grocer write something down. What he could
do, he thought, was to give Ben back some of his own—the word
fitted—medicine: tell him he didn't want the money back, just what
he would have lost during the five years from inflation. The grocer
handed the girl her food, then took Sam's dollar bill. "And how are
you today?" he asked, with enthusiasm. He spoke very clearly, very
politely. His smile revealed a set of perfectly even teeth.

"Fine," Sam said.

"Yes," the man said. "It's been a lovely fall season this year."

"Sure," Sam said, pocketing his change.

"Thank you, and come back again, young man."

The guy was too much, Sam thought; he preferred, in his
memory, old Mr. Bender—a bastard if ever there was one, always
on the lookout to make sure you weren't tucking away candy bars
under your jacket.

When he got to Garfield's, his payoff man was waiting for him at
a table in the back. Sam took a large glass of milk and two
cinnamon buns, then joined the man at the table, under the
stairwell which led to the toilets. The guy was called Willie the
Lump and Sam didn't have the foggiest idea why, since he was, like
the grocer, the kind of black man who, in Ivy League clothes, could
have walked down Madison Avenue without making you look at
him twice. But when you had looked closely, you saw that Willie
the Lump had one eye that never moved, made of glass, Sam

imagined, and when he spoke at all, he lisped. Sam looked at him, drank some milk, measured his words.

"I guess," he offered, "you don't have an envelope for me this week."

Willie the Lump nodded. He lifted his coffee cup, his small finger sticking out. He had rings on six of his ten fingers. Willie the Lump moved mechanically, following prescribed procedures: he pushed a copy of the *Daily News* across the table, for Sam to use for his envelope. "Did you see this item in today's paper?" he asked, the "th" reminding Sam—he cursed the connection—of Tidewater's precise manner of pronunciation.

"Yeah," Sam said. "Well, look, Willie—I've been good to you, right? I mean, I always treat you good when I'm on, right?"

Willie nodded. "Did you see this item in today's paper?" he asked again. His brown finger pointed to a photo of Lew Alcindor stuffing an opponent's shot, Alcindor's huge hand appearing to be larger than the ball.

"Yeah," Sam said. "Well, you tell Mr. Sabatini that I'd like to speak to him, he should put this on my account."

Willie the Lump drank from his coffee cup, focused on Sam's face with his good eye. "This is the third time," Willie said.

"Yeah, well I got something in the works—I'll speak to Sabatini about it. Say *shalom* to him for me, okay?" Sam paused, saw that Willie was going to leave. "I wish I could give you your usual—tell me: did I ever stiff you when I was going good? Tell me that, Willie. Didn't I always give you your cut? So how come"—Sam tried to surprise the guy with his question—"how come nobody will touch the Knicks? What's up, Willie? Come on—"

"You always treated me fine, Mr. Benjamin," Willie the Lump said. He reached across and—for the first time in Sam's memory— shook Sam's hand. "I hope you have better luck, Mr. Benjamin. I truly do. You always treated me fine."

"But the Knicks?" Sam asked, as Willie started to move away. "What's up, Willie?" Sam let his cinnamon bun drop to his plate, and held onto Willie's jacket, but lightly. Willie stopped. "What's up?"

Willie shrugged, lowered his good eye to the floor. "He was the one said to tell you this is the third time if you didn't. It weren't my idea."

Then he walked away, leaving Sam alone. You too, Sam Berman Junior, he thought: put your money where your mouth is. Words were for the birds. Sure. Sam the Lamb, that's who he was. He left his second cinnamon bun on his plate, uneaten, and walked to the cashier's desk: an elderly white woman in platinum-colored hair, red lipstick that was caking off, took his check, punched his change into the tin cup. There were a lot of high school kids in Garfield's at this hour, but Sam didn't look them over. Even if he saw a girl, where could he take her? That would be one good thing when Ben was gone—he could get something going for himself again; according to the old saying, his luck should be running at an all-time high in that department, although, with his brain, he'd probably wind up with jailbait.

"H-how's things, Sam?" Milt asked.

"Slow, Milt. Slow," Sam answered.

"Did you say hello to your f-father for me?"

"Oh sure," Sam said. "He said he'd try to come by to say good-bye to you. He's going to California, to live in an old people's home. . . ." Sam tried to see Milt's eyes behind the thick lenses.

"Is he s-sick?"

"No, no," Sam said. He sighed. "Not a home really—a kind of retirement city. A resort-retirement community is what it is."

Milt nodded. "I see," he said. "Well, you tell him I wish him well and the b-best of success in his new v-venture."

"Sure," Sam said. "I'll do that. You got this week's line from Jimmy the Greek?"

"T-tomorrow," Milt said. "I sincerely hope your luck changes, Sam, but you're young and healthy, and that's the important thing. I believe that. Tell your father that he should be well and that Milt said so." Milt looked around, then whispered: *"Zei gezunt,* if you know what I mean."

Sam had never heard such a long speech from the man. "Yeah," he said. "I'll tell him."

He crossed the street, went into the phone booth, watched the kids sitting on the steps of the Dutch Reformed Church, pigeons around their feet. He knew what some of them were smoking: they said it wasn't habit-forming, that it relaxed you—but Sam wasn't fooled: they'd start you there, and before you knew it, feeling relaxed all the time, you wouldn't care about keeping in shape. He dropped a dime in the slot. Still, he knew that they said that

Namath and most of the boys on the New York Jets were on stuff even more powerful—even when they'd been out there slogging it in the Super Bowl. It didn't figure, from what he knew, but maybe when you were in their class, things changed.

"Yes?"

"It's Mr. Benjamin here."

"This is Mr. Sabatini, Mr. Benjamin, what can I do for you today?"

"Look," Sam said, rejecting the apologies that he had heard himself giving. "Can you trust me for another week or so?"

"Trust you?" Mr. Sabatini said, and Sam thought he could see the man smiling at him with a mouthful of yellow teeth. "We *love* you, sweetheart."

"Sure," Sam said. "I got something in the works."

"Of course," Mr. Sabatini said. "All things can be arranged."

"But one thing else," Sam said. "If you happen to hear of anybody looking for a game—poker—you keep me in mind, okay?"

Sam listened to the silence. Then: "I don't usually let myself get involved in something like that, of course. . . ."

"I just thought—if you heard, that's all. It's not serious."

"But for a good customer like you—a nice Jewish boy—!" Mr. Sabatini howled with laughter at that, and Sam jerked the receiver away from his ear. "I'll see what I can arrange, all right? No promises, sweetheart, but the *Kinesset* will be thinking of you." His voice descended again. "Still, there's a terrible credit squeeze on, you know—everybody's feeling the pinch. Don't feel—if you understand me—isolated."

"Yeah. Well, thanks."

Sam heard the click at Mr. Sabatini's end. He pulled the doors toward him, stepped out. A black guy, about Sam's height, carrying a pile of schoolbooks under one arm, moved into Sam's path. "How about a smoke, chief?"

"Don't smoke," Sam said.

The guy's eyes were glazed, he looked away, his body swayed. "How 'bout some bread, then, okay? I'll pay you back—I seen you around."

"Sorry," Sam said, and walked away. The guy held Sam's jacket-sleeve. Sam whirled around. "Chuck off, Farley, you hear?" he said.

The guy blinked, then smiled, his eyes suddenly clear. "Hey, that's good, man. I like that. Chuck off, Farley—ain't heard that one before."

"He bothering you, mister?" Sam turned. A cop—about Sam's age, perhaps a few years older—was speaking to him. "You don't have to be scared, mister—I know this kid."

"No," Sam said. "It was nothing. He just asked for a smoke is all."

The cop kept his eyes on Sam, but talked to the kid. "Okay. Take off. You're lucky. Know who your friends are from now on."

"See you, Chief," the kid said, and winked at Sam—then ran across the street, dodging cars.

"You got to keep your eyes open. They give you the soft talk, see—but they know what they're doing. They're not dumb, I'll tell you that."

"Yeah," Sam said. "Well—I appreciate your interest."

"Okay, Mr. Benjamin," the cop said, and turned away, walking off in the direction of the Kenmore Theater.

Sam's brain spun. He clenched his fists. Sure. Watch your ass, he told himself. He crossed the street, in front of Garfield's again, then moved on down Flatbush Avenue—past Martense Street, where the New Yorker Café was (the high-class hookers worked from it). At Linden Boulevard he turned right, passed in front of the library, continued to Bedford Avenue. The apartment houses were set far back from the street here—there was no street, in fact—and, as now, for as long as Sam could remember, there'd been the triangle of free space, where Caton Avenue branched off from Linden Boulevard, marked out by white paint and poles set in concrete. Some kids were playing slapball, but Sam didn't stop to watch. Instead, he turned back, and walked to the library. There was no need to return to the apartment, to have Ben asking him questions, to see Tidewater's eyes. He didn't doubt the guy; still, he figured he'd check a few things out, to be sure. He looked in the card catalogue under Negro Baseball and found—other than the names of stars: Robinson and Paige, Campanella and Gibson and Howard and Mays and the rest—only one book that looked as if it would have what he wanted, the title: *Only the Ball Was White.* He went to the shelf, found the book, sat down at a desk, took his coat off, and began to read.

The facts were all there, about the history of Negro leagues and players going back before 1900, but Sam discovered that, though he tried to concentrate, his mind kept wandering: the trouble was, everytime he read something that wasn't just a fact about where and when some guy had been born, he found himself thinking of something in Tidewater's story. And as soon as he thought of Tidewater's story, he found that the guy's words pushed all other words and pictures out of his head. Sam looked in the index, under Marcelle; that part was true; there had actually been a man by that name who'd been a player in the Negro Leagues and had had his nose bitten off. He wondered if, reading through the entire book, he'd be able to figure out which, if any, of the players had been Tidewater, before the guy had changed his name.

He grew drowsy. The library was cooler than the rummage shop, and the fluorescent lighting, when he glanced up, made him squint—but he felt sleepy nonetheless. He saw no reason to keep reading, and so he closed the book, and put his coat back on. He'd go outside to wake up. He remembered what Tidewater had said about wanting the ball to go so fast it would disappear. That, Sam thought, and found himself smiling, would really be out of sight.

It picked him up, thinking of a line like that. He walked down the steps, remembering what Tidewater had said about being bothered by having to depend on eight other men. Sam could understand that. Sure. He had to give the guy credit for being able to tell a good story—no matter what name Ben gave to it. What he wondered about, however, was why, since it was out of sight, it wasn't out of mind. He didn't press the question, though. If reading Tidewater's life story was the price he had to pay for getting Ben off his back, he figured he was getting away cheap.

6

Sam stood at the living room window, watching the snow fall: everything was white and beautiful now, but by nine o'clock the next morning, he knew, after people had made their way to the subway, to go to work, it would be brown and slushy, slippery underneath. Directly below, he saw Tidewater and Flo helping someone out of a taxi—a girl, in a wheelchair. The girl wore a purple scarf on her head, and Sam saw light glisten from gold threads that were woven into it. He could hear the music—old rock-and-roll records—coming from below. Tidewater pushed the wheelchair forward across the snow while Flo held an umbrella over the girl's head. It was night. There were circles of luminescent green, like rings around the moon, surrounding the lights of the lamp posts along Nostrand Avenue. At the moment there were no cars or buses passing. Sam could see fresh footprints on the sidewalk.

Someone was banging on the pipes. Sam listened. The banging stopped, then started again: three times. It was Ben's signal. Sam touched his fingertips: they tingled. He wondered if, on a night like this, the others would show up. Ben had offered Sam money, again, but Sam had taken his loan—five hundred—from Sabatini. Willie the Lump had passed the envelope to him that afternoon, at

Garfield's, and Sam was supposed to return it—plus one hundred interest—the next day. It was, Mr. Sabatini had assured him, a favor, a way of helping out a good customer in time of need. "Remember," he heard the man saying, "in the thirties, Mr. Sabatini sold apples."

Sam checked his wallet, touched his sidepocket, then slipped his rubbers on over his shoes, took a sports jacket out of the closet—a brown tweed that must have cost a hundred dollars new, but which Flo had put aside for him three years before, for eight dollars—then his raincoat. He reached for his wallet, counted out six fifty-dollar bills, folded them, and put them in his sidepocket, next to his knife. Sabatini would play it straight with him, he felt certain, but with low stakes—half-dollar–dollar—you were bound to be in with deadbeats. He locked the door.

Muriel sat on the first step, holding a rubber doll. "You see the snow?" Sam asked her. Muriel looked up at him, without smiling, and said nothing. She had on a clean dress—pink—and black patent leather shoes. Flo, he figured, must have given them to her. Sam reached down, to smooth the girl's curls, and, to his surprise, she didn't flinch. "You like the music, huh?" he said. She looked at him with her large brown eyes. "You wanna come downstairs and dance?" Muriel stood and walked around the landing to her own apartment. He picked up her doll, which she had left on the top stair, and started toward her. "Hey, you left—"

She pushed, and her door opened. Sam stood there, offering the doll to the empty corridor. He put it down, then went below, his raincoat draped over his shoulder. He walked around the staircase, to the back, knocked on the door. The music was fierce—much too loud—nobody would hear him. He turned the doorknob and the sound from the phonograph, scratchy, struck his face like waves crashing toward shore. The back room was packed solid with furniture, tables moved in from the front room. Ben, standing at the opening between the two rooms, saw his son, motioned to him with a finger. Sam pushed a chair aside, squeezed past some furniture.

"Flo wanted to speak with you before you went out," Ben said.

Sam nodded. Directly in front of him five wheelchairs were lined up, side by side, their backs to him, and in the wheelchairs five bodies were bobbing up and down, to the music. The racks of clothing were pushed to the sides, and in the middle of the floor,

Sam saw the heads of several couples moving, stiffly. He kept his eyes away from them. The record—Little Richard screaming his lungs out—changed; another one fell in its place: Johnny Ace singing "Pledging My Love." Sam could remember dancing to it, at a Jewish center after a basketball game; he could feel his leg wedged between the legs of a girl wearing a cashmere sweater, his erection pressed against the inside of her thigh.

"I'm glad you hadn't left yet," Flo said. "Come—I want to introduce you to somebody—"

"I can't stay long," Sam said. "I got something on tonight."

"Please," she said, and took his hand. He moved around the outside, between racks of coats, next to the groups of parents who were talking with each other. Marion was serving—pouring punch from a big pitcher into paper cups. Johnny Ace, Sam remembered, had killed himself backstage, playing Russian roulette. The song, coming out after his death, had been his biggest hit. Sure. That told you a lot. Sam kept his eyes away from the couples in the middle of the floor. Marion smiled at him. Tidewater stood at the door, dressed in a jacket and tie, watching the snow.

"This," Flo was saying, "is Stella."

Sam nodded, looked down. "Pleased to meet you," he said, began to put out his hand, realized what he was doing, and stuck it into his sidepocket. He blinked. The girl's face was beautiful: she wore the purple scarf around her back, and her hair—jet black—fell straight to her shoulders. She sat very straight in her wheelchair, and smiled at him. Her lips were full, her teeth a yellowish white—and her smile, like Flo's, made Sam feel warm, made him want to smile back. From his angle, he could see the fillings in her bottom teeth. She kept her arms on the handles of the wheelchair. She wore a white blouse, and her breasts, Sam could see, were large. Under the purple scarf, around her shoulders, a tan sweater was pressed against the back of her chair. She wore black slacks, and her shoes touched the floor.

"Flo's told me all about you—you're Sam the Gambler, right?" she said.

Sam looked at Flo. "I guess," he said.

Flo reached down and gave Stella a hug. "She's like my own daughter," Flo said.

"Two mothers beat one, right Sam?" the girl said.

Sam could feel the heat rising from his collar. "I guess," he said.

Stella laughed. "I'm sorry," she said, and looked down. "I'm embarrassing you, right? I shouldn't—"

"Excuse me," Flo said. "There's a car." She came close to Sam, kissed him on the cheek. "If I don't see you before you leave, good luck tonight—"

"You have a game on?" Stella asked. Sam watched Flo walk outside, Tidewater next to her.

"Yeah," Sam answered.

"Poker?"

"That's it."

"Well—five'll get you ten, right?"

Sam blinked. "What?" He shook his head, as if to clear it. "I'm sorry," he said, then looked at the girl. "I mean, with—my head's full, that's all. My head's full."

The girl nodded. Sam felt an urge to touch her hair, the way he'd touched Muriel's—but then he thought of the girl's legs, of how she probably had to be hoisted in and out of bed, and he felt himself tighten. "You don't have to say anything," Stella said, not looking at him. "It's like—well, going for a no-hit game, right? You don't want to say anything or you jinx it."

"Something like that," Sam said.

"We could dance," Stella said, "but we can't." She moved her shoulders sideways and her left hand fell from the arm of the chair, into her lap. She left it there. "You have nice eyes." Sam looked into her face. "Don't mind me," she said then. "I just talk sometimes. We could dance but we can't—that was a great line, don't you think?" She sighed, closed her eyes. Sam saw that she used no make-up on her eyes, and he noticed—for the first time—that she wore no lipstick. She strained, managed to lift her left hand, to let it fall on the arm of the chair. "I only came because Flo insisted." She laughed. "What I mean is, Sam the Gambler, you shouldn't mind me. If you have—business, right?—you go on ahead. You don't have to be polite." She tapped with her fingers on the arm of the chair. "I was thinking—with a machine like this, you could really, like they say, wheel and deal—"

Sam found himself laughing with her. "I'll have to tell that one to Ben," he said. "He likes to play with words."

"And you—?"

"Wheel and deal, that's pretty good. You got to have a sense of humor, right?"

"Your eyes are nice when you laugh. Flo said they were. She notices things."

The music blasted toward them, Sam Cooke singing "Bring Your Sweet Loving to Me." "What'd you say?" Sam said, leaning over, close to her. He could smell perfume—light, sweet.

"They killed him—Sam Cooke—they shot him dead with three bullets in 1964 in a Hollywood hotel—do you remember?"

"Baseball's healthier," Sam said.

"That's good," Stella said. "Flo said that too—about your way of putting things."

"You live around here?" Sam asked, then covered the first question with a second. "I mean, what do you do—? You work—?"

"Is that your father there—the little man talking with Marion?"

Sam nodded. "What do you think of her?" Stella asked. "I mean, how do you figure it? Two sisters like that—"

Sam shrugged, watched Ben, behind the row of wheelchairs, moving his mouth. "It takes all kinds," Sam said.

Stella gestured with her head, backward. "My sweater's falling, could you fix it?" She leaned forward, and Sam reached behind, lifted her sweater from where it had become crumpled. "Lift the scarf first." Sam lifted the scarf, placed the sweater around Stella's shoulders. His fingers touched her blouse, and he could feel her warm skin beneath. He glanced at her face, saw that her eyes were closed. Great, he thought to himself. Sam Berman Junior scores again. Stella leaned back. "Thanks," she said. "I live down by Flatbush Avenue, on Clarkson, and—don't ask me how—I work too—as a commercial artist."

Sam rubbed his thumb across his fingertips. He remembered, at Hebrew School once, when he'd been ten or eleven years old, being called into the Rabbi's office. It was a small room, smaller than Ben's bedroom, and Sam could see the desk, overflowing with papers and letters and Jewish newspapers; he could see the UJA tree plaques and certificates on all the walls. The Rabbi had heard the other boys calling him Sam Junior. Was Sam aware that Jews did not name sons after fathers? Sam had explained to the Rabbi—had given him the whole routine—but the Rabbi had not laughed. "All right," he could hear the man saying, waving a hand, dismissing him. "I'll believe you this time."

Sam clenched his fists. Marion stood in front of him, offering some punch. Sam shook his head. "How about you, Stella?" Marion asked.

"Sure," she said.

"Here," Marion said, and Sam took a paper cup from her left hand, and held it while Marion poured. "Are you enjoying yourself?" Marion asked. "I know the others are much younger, but—"

"You don't have to say anything," Stella said. Marion looked down, smiled weakly, and walked off.

"Why do people always have to say things is what I want to know," Stella said. Sam saw something angry in the girl's eyes, something that drew him toward her. "Look—if you don't mind, you'll have to feed me that stuff—but if you mind, drink it yourself. Believe me, coming here, I could use something stronger."

"I don't mind," Sam said, and held the paper cup to her lips. Her chin touched the backs of his fingers, and he was amazed—confused—at how soft she was. More than that—he felt his heart tighten—he knew that, despite everything, he was, below, being aroused. "Then I got to go," he added.

"Listen," she said. "Flo gets an idea sometimes, I wouldn't make too much of it. You concentrate on your game. I'll be okay here."

"You want some more?" Sam asked. He saw her lick the drops of punch from above her upper lip.

"You're a real gentleman, Sam the Gambler. You can come calling if you want. Sure—come see my etchings." She laughed again, but there was something almost mean, Sam felt, in her laugh. "Go on. I've kept you too long already—and your old man is giving us the eye. I'd offer you my hand, but . . ."

"It's been . . ." Sam couldn't find a word.

"If you pull three ladies, think of me, okay?"

"Sure," Sam said to her, but he hadn't moved. He heard Sabatini, emphasizing the special low interest rate he'd given Sam: "I'm no loan shark, Mr. Benjamin." That was true enough, Sam figured, because—when he'd been a kid he had thought that was what it meant—he knew who the lone shark was. "I get the picture," he added.

"I mean," she said, and whispered so that he had to bend closer. "Where's it get you in the end is what I want to know, right Sam?" She swayed to the right; then, with a great effort, she lifted her left hand and let it fall, her palm slapping against the leather cushion on the arm of the chair. "Oh damn! Just get out of here—I never should have come, you should leave me, I'm sorry. I'm sorry and we know all the rest, right? Don't mind me, Sam the Gambler. Good-bye and good luck. You be real bad tonight—"

She turned her head away, toward the window, and Sam followed the direction of her eyes; Tidewater was glaring at him—it was as if, he felt, lines of white light were moving across the room, through the music and noise; he felt something physical enter his own eyes, and then Tidewater looked away, at Ben.

"We'll see you around," Sam said to Stella. His eyes searched the room once more, for Flo, for Ben—but he saw neither of them. Marion smiled at him. He figured he knew what she'd like from him. Sure. If he wanted, he could be a real winner. Ben had the right idea—get out while you could. Sam put one arm into the sleeve of his raincoat, at the door, and found that Tidewater, silently, had taken his raincoat and was holding it for him. "Be careful," Tidewater whispered. "Be careful tonight." Sam slipped his arm into the other sleeve. Across the street, next to Mrs. Cameron's building, through the falling snow, Sam saw a cop frisking somebody. If he found some hard stuff on the guy, he'd probably sell it, Sam figured.

He waited, for a few seconds, in the doorway of the rummage shop, trying to relax, to forget Tidewater's voice. It was a relief, just being away from the sound of the music. He'd asked Stella where she lived, when she'd said what she had about Sam Cooke, because the only baseball player he could think of who'd died that way had been Hugh Casey, the Dodgers' great relief pitcher when Sam had been a boy; Casey had shot himself in the head just a few blocks away, in the back room of his bar and grill, on Flatbush Avenue. The bar and grill still had his name on it, near where they'd torn down the Patio movie theater. The policeman's back was turned to Sam. Maybe he wouldn't sell the stuff—if he found anything— maybe he'd use it for himself. Sure. There were a lot of them who'd had the brains to try it for themselves and who were strung out good by now. People didn't think about such things, with cops, but if you thought about it, it figured. Sam lifted the collar of his raincoat, walked out into the snow.

The door to his building opened. "Sam—" Sam stopped. Ben was standing in the doorway, in his black overcoat. "Wait a minute. I'll walk with you—if you're heading for Church Avenue."

"It's freezing out—you'll catch cold."

"Come," Ben said, and put his arm into Sam's. "I told Flo I'd get some more refreshments—they're running out."

"What's Tidewater get paid for?" Sam asked, but he kept walking, his father beside him.

"I don't mind the snow," Ben said. "It may be the last one I'll see."

They crossed Martense Street, Ben's small body pressed against his son's, his head down, to keep the snow out of his eyes. "You should have worn a hat," Sam said.

"You know what?" Ben replied, then waited. "You're right."

"This way," Sam said, and they crossed Nostrand. The lights in the laundromat and the liquor store were still on. In front of the TV repair shop a man was fixing a piece of cardboard on his windshield, under the windshield wipers.

"Also," Ben said. "I wanted to see if you needed anything for tonight."

"I told you before: I'm okay. You worry about yourself."

Sam thought he heard Ben sigh, but it might, he realized, have been the wind. It was getting colder. "There are some things we should talk about," Ben said. "When you have the time." He paused. "I had a letter from your mother today."

At the corner of Nostrand and Church Avenues, Sam saw an old woman, a bundle of scarves wrapped around her head, tilting a litter basket—it was almost her height—toward her, picking through it with bare hands. "Look," Sam said. "I got things on my mind. If you have something to say to me, just say it, okay?"

Ben nodded. "I'm sorry. You're right. Come—" The light changed, and they crossed the street, arm in arm. The sound of a police siren wailed in the distance. In front of the Bel-Air supermarket, its lights seeming extra bright through the snow, a boy was waiting to help people carry packages home. He jogged up and down, trying to keep his feet warm. "Come inside for a minute, while I get what I have to—unless you're late."

They passed through the electric-eye door. Ben took a shopping cart, pushed it around the checkout registers. The store was quiet, almost empty; the music—all violins—seemed particularly sweet to Sam. "So?" he said to his father.

"That's all. She asked about you—she wondered if you would be in Florida this year, to visit her. Next year, she said, she hoped to be in Cuba—her husband, you know, had a large villa and property there, and your mother expects to spend her sunset years enjoying them." Ben's voice shifted. " 'That man down there will have to open up to tourists again sometime, won't he? Irving says he likes baseball, after all, that he used to be a pitcher.' "

"So?"

"That's all. It's the way she reasons."

"She's a bird," Sam said, aloud.

"A what—?"

"Nothing."

"I'm sorry about that too—but you know that. She shouldn't have cut you off the way she did." Ben took a giant bag of potato chips and dropped it into the shopping cart. "But I'll give her credit: she knew herself. She wasn't cut out to be a mother. When she said to me, twenty years ago, that I would do a better job, she wasn't being a joker. Maybe if my father had not been living with us, if I hadn't insisted—"

"Look," Sam said. "I said before, I got things on my mind—no cat and mouse, okay? You said you had things to talk about. I've been through the rest before."

Ben took two bottles of store-brand soda, and dropped them into the shopping cart, then he took two more. "As long as we're here, can you think of anything we need?"

"No."

"Also, before I forget—you're invited to a farewell dinner for Benjamin Samson Berman, tendered to him—that would be your mother's word, yes?—by his neighbors. A week from Friday night—after we go on our trip. Mason and Flo offered it—and we'll have it in our apartment. It's simpler for everybody that way."

"I'll be there. What else—? I don't have all night."

"Come here a second—closer." Sam saw an old woman wheel by at the far end of the aisle. "Which can of nuts do you think we should bring back?"

Ben lifted a can of Planter's Peanuts with his left hand, then put it back on the shelf. "Closer," he commanded, and Sam drew near. He saw his father's other hand move quickly—something dropped into the left-hand pocket of Ben's coat. "There! Ah, you've been of great service, Sam Junior—I knew we could work as a team—"

"You're bats," Sam said, and turned away. Ben grabbed the sleeve of his son's raincoat. Sam felt hot. "You just leave off. You don't fool me."

"Samela," Ben said, quietly. "Calm yourself. You shouldn't take things so seriously. I told you, there's no danger. Who would press charges against a nice old man from the neighborhood? Use your head."

"Just lay off is all." Sam shook his father's hand off.

"But you will come Friday night, yes?" Ben said. "And on our little trip. I'm pleased about that."

"Excuse me—" A black woman, with purple-black hair that covered her forehead in ringlets, held out a piece of paper to Sam. She spoke very clearly, as if she were a schoolteacher. "I was wondering if you could help me, young man. I seem to have left my eye-glasses at home. Could you be so kind as to read this coupon for me?"

She held her head high, leaning back, as if she were farsighted. "Sure," Sam said. " 'If you will try our new delicious cream of turkey soup, Campbell's will send you a coupon, good for one box of Nabisco Saltine crackers. Simply cut the labels from two—' "

"Yes, thank you," she said, putting her hand out. "That's what I thought. You've been very kind indeed."

She turned and walked away. He knew the routine. He heard the sound of Ben's cart, jangling behind him. "Don't be an idiot your whole life," he heard Ben saying, in a stage whisper. "Do you hear? Use your head for once. Take, Sam. Take! Believe me, if you let them—"

Sam stopped, faced his father. "I know all about what a rough life you had, but you don't fool me anyway. I got a game on tonight, and you want to get my mind off it, right? You'd like to see me sink way down into a hole so you could be the one to pull me out, right?" Sam laughed at Ben, felt good again. "I can figure some things out, and the thing I figured out is that the sooner you get out, the better for everybody."

"I don't understand," Ben said, and Sam saw that his father's eyes were watering. "Of course—I wouldn't deny it—of course it will be, let us say, difficult not living with you. I'm used to having you around, naturally. What you did for me . . . But you have your own life to lead, and—"

"Enough," Sam said. He heard Stella's voice, and it reassured him. "Sure. Why do people always have to say things is what I want to know."

"Shh—you're making a scene." Ben's eyes flicked sideways.

"I'll see you tomorrow—don't wait up."

"But—what I wanted to talk to you about—the most important thing—forget the money, and some arrangements that we have to take care of—but what I want to know is this, Samela—" His father's tiny eyes were dry now, and Sam tried to get ready for him, for the words. "When I'm gone, and you're left, what, of me, will you pass on?"

Sam found himself laughing in his father's face. "That's rich," he said, and left his father standing there. At the checkout register he showed his hands to the girl, palms up, to indicate that he'd bought nothing. The kid who'd been standing outside was inside now, at the exit, and Sam saw water dripping from his sneakers. "You got a fag on you?" the kid asked, then looked up, sneered. "Nah—you're the guy who says he don't smoke. I know all about it."

Sam laughed, reached into his pocket, tossed the kid a quarter. "Get yourself a cup of coffee," he said, and walked outside. He felt better. In front of Ben, he felt sometimes—like the Negro woman—ashamed of what he didn't know. But not this time. The snow hit his face, and a flake stuck to his upper lip. Sam licked it off. He headed toward Flatbush Avenue. If he'd wanted, he knew, he could have said more: he'd figured it out all by himself, Ben hadn't surprised him—he knew how his old man's head worked sometimes. But if he'd said the stuff out loud, Ben would have found something—some detail—to confuse him with.

I figured it out myself, without your help, he heard himself saying. If I die, then you die too. No more Ben, no more Berman, no more wooden dolls. Sam wiped snow from his eyebrows. Dolls? Ben would have asked. Sam felt good: he'd been right not to have said anything—he had other things on his mind, and if a word like that had slipped out, he would have been finished. This time Ben could stew. Everybody was always acting as if they were so worried about saving Sam Berman's ass, he thought, but when it came down to it, they were all pumping away for number one, the way Ben had just proved.

It was, already, Sam could tell, well below freezing. He stuffed his hands deep into his pockets; the tips of his fingers felt frozen. Across the street, the marquee of the Granada Theater was dark. Sam wondered where the guy with the dog stayed on a night like this. He crossed Rogers Avenue, his bare head down. How he had forgotten to take his gloves was beyond him. With his head full—all of Ben's words, about the loan and leaving for Andy—and with Tidewater's story taking up space, he wasn't concentrating the way he had to.

The city seemed especially quiet—no cars, no people out walking, no lights on in the stores—and the stillness comforted Sam. His arms locked to his sides, his shoulders hunched up at the neck, he began to feel warm, to enjoy walking against the snow. He stayed in shape, and that counted for a lot; if the others showed up, he'd have an edge there. Through the thick downfall of white flakes, the clock on the tower of Holy Cross Church was barely visible, but it looked, to Sam, as if it were almost nine o'clock. The game was scheduled for nine-thirty. If he kept up the pace, he'd make it easily. He imagined Ben walking along Nostrand Avenue, a shopping bag at his chest, cradled in his arms. Sure. It would be Sam's luck to have his father catch cold and postpone the trip. The way things worked out in this life, Andy would probably be the one to sit *shivah* for Ben, and not the other way around.

Sam bent his head down, lower, strained with his forearm, and brushed away the flakes from his eyebrows and eyelashes. It was a question he hadn't obsessed about, but he wondered now what he would do when Ben kicked off—if he would go to synagogue every day for a year, the way Ben had done for his father. Maybe that, with his ways, was one of the things Ben had really wanted to talk about—he had intended to give Sam his wishes on things like that. Okay. If Ben wanted him to do it, he'd do it. He got up early anyway, and he could understand—even if Ben didn't believe—how at a time like this it might reassure him, to know that Sam would think of him that way afterward, the way Ben had done for his father. But if Ben was his other self, and made some sarcastic remark, that would be fine with Sam too.

His nose was dripping, and he sniffed in, then wiped it against his shoulder. In the schoolyard next to Holy Cross, there was a ring of snow—perfect—on each basketball hoop, an inch and a half or two inches high. Sam wondered if, with the wind, the rings would last until morning. The lights in the apartment house, on the other side of the street, were dim, blue-white, from the reflections of televison tubes. There was, he knew, only one way to describe the weather on a night like this—the way the guys had always talked about this kind of weather: cold as a witch's tit.

Sam crossed the street. It was crazy, and he cursed himself for seeing things this way, but he could feel his fingers moving a black gown aside, playing with the lace, the meshlike material, and, despite the flames which surrounded him on all sides, scorching hot, the woman's chest, when he touched it, was stiff and cold. He thought of Stella, of how warm he had felt when he had adjusted her sweater and his fingers had grazed her chin. He'd thought about that too, sometimes—why it was he felt so much about guys like Stallworth and Pete Gray, why he felt the way he did about Flo. Sure. His eyes could tear for Stallworth—hundreds of feet below— and for Flo's children, whom he'd never seen—but, though he did what Flo asked him to, he knew that he recoiled when he actually had to lift one of the muscular dystrophy kids. It wasn't so hard to figure out.

The snow was deeper, and Sam's legs felt heavy; a trickle of sweat slipped down his back, under his T-shirt. To his left, Erasmus was closed. Next to it, the Yeshiva (when he had been at Erasmus, the building had been used for delinquents, the last stop before reform school) seemed to glow slightly, its red bricks wet, its window sills and fire escapes lined with even borders of white. It was really a bitch out—but if he'd called Sabatini and canceled, where would he have been then? He'd had no choice.

Being an only child—an only son—had, in his mind, always had something to do with it. If he'd had brothers, at a time like this, with Ben leaving, they'd have taken some of the heat off him. Maybe—it was a connection he'd made before—that was why he'd felt so much for players who'd had careers cut short by injuries and disease: without any brothers or sisters coming after him, he'd always felt somehow as if he were incomplete—as if, it was crazy, Ben hadn't finished making him. It wasn't a theory, or an idea he'd tried to trace back—Ben could really have flown, if he'd gotten hold of it—but it was something, as now, which he sometimes felt.

He passed in front of the Biltmore Caterers, and Joe Spinella's bowling alley. Above, behind the snow, the neon lights, in circles, lit up a bowling ball which moved down the alley—a series of bowling balls which Sam watched light up, one after the other, in a greenish yellow color—until the neon ten-pins at the end of the alley blinked and fell.

What he didn't understand, though—it was a question that had occurred to him before—was what he had done to deserve this. It wasn't a question he'd put to somebody like Ben, but it was a question he asked himself, and a question whose answer, though he would have liked to deny it, had something to do with the Knicks' winning streak. But that, he knew, was crazy too: sure, he rooted for the Knicks, he always had—and sure too, he had predicted that they'd go all the way this year; but Sam knew that he was nobody to them, that, if you asked the question you had to ask—where was the control—you saw of course that he'd had nothing to do with their streak.

Luigi's was closed. They didn't deliver and nobody was out walking tonight. It made sense. But the bank closing on the Knicks, his debt to Sabatini, no games and now this: freezing his ass off to play for stakes he would have laughed at a year or two before. It didn't figure, not at all, and to try to figure out why it was all happening—that was the quick way to hit the bottom of the hole. If you put your mind there, you could forget it all. Like trying to figure out if a guy was bluffing or not: it didn't matter. You had to keep your mind on your own cards and forget the rest. Play what's there, don't bet on air. . . .

The snow was falling more heavily, and Sam could not see the clock at the top of the Dutch Reformed Church. Milt's newsstand, at the corner of Flatbush and Church, was closed, a mound of snow. There were lights on in Garfield's, filtering through the snowfall, but Sam didn't have time to stop, to warm himself. The exercise was enough; his fingertips were numb, but his body—his chest, his neck, his legs—felt warm, almost sleepy. Snow did that to you. He'd have to be careful, coming in from the cold, to keep his head the way he wanted it.

He crossed the street, making tracks in the fresh snow, and

stopped under the marquee of the Kenmore Theater. He left his
hands in his pockets, shook himself so that the loose snow fell from
his head and shoulders, his sleeves and cuffs. The city would be
paralyzed by morning, he knew. Only the subways would be
running, underground—they were bound, with the temperature
below freezing, to have trouble on the elevated lines. The theater
was closed for the night, no sign on the cashier's booth. Sam wiped
his nose with his sleeve, set out again, and saw, directly in front of
him, the shape of a man, under snow, lying on the ground, propped
up next to the wall of a store. The man's head, uncovered, was at
his chest, and there was barely a space the snow had not covered.

Sam went to the man without hesitating, bent over, lifted his own
hands from his pockets. The snow got into his eyes, hung from his
lashes, magnifying things. Squinting, he saw the geometric shapes
of individual flakes. "Hey—you okay?" he asked. There was no
reply. This was, he thought to himself, really what he needed, but
he had no choice: you never knew, and on a night like this the guy
might be totally covered by morning. Sam grabbed the body
through a layer of snow, at the shoulders, and shook it. "Hey—
wake up. Wake up there!"

The snow on the man's face, from Sam's shaking, slipped away,
like pieces of a jigsaw puzzle, and dripped down. Sam held the
man's shoulders, stayed down at his level, in a deep knee bend
position, and saw—it made his heart catch—that the man's eyes
were shining, that his mouth was turned into the side of his face,
smiling at Sam. Snow fell lightly between the two men, and Sam
could feel the warm air of the man's breath.

"I thought you'd be coming this way," the man said. "I waited
for you. Listen—"

Sam flung the man against the wall, heard a soft thud. "You lay
off!" he said.

With a gloved hand, the man held onto Sam's trousers. "Don't
worry," he said. "I'm dressed warmly. I don't take chances
anymore. I just wanted to warn you. Be careful. Be careful
tonight."

All the snow had slipped from the man's face, and the flush of his
skin—bright pink—made Sam see him as he had been when they'd
both been clapping their hearts out, that first time. Sam's jaw
trembled, but there was a small river of sweat now, running down

his spine, and he felt hot. He spoke the only words which occurred to him: "I don't believe you."

"Listen," the man said, and his voice, like silk, had something comforting in it, something that made Sam's eyelids, for a split second, close, that made his mind look toward the end of an endless corridor, the way it would sometimes in the subway, if he was about to nod off. "I can understand that, with the spiel I gave you. Sure. But I wanted to tell you, when I had a chance, that you were right the first time—I work for Sabatini." Sam saw the man's gloved hand—a gray glove—slice through the snow, toward him, gesturing. "But I work for the Lord too." The man's eyes looked up again, happy. "It comes and goes though, part-time." He laughed, and the laugh hurt Sam's ears as it echoed under the marquee. He looked beyond Sam, up, above Sam's head. "Working for Him, that's just moonlighting, if you know what I mean."

"Lay off," Sam hissed. "I'm warning you."

"Sure," the guy said, easily. "With Sabatini—that's temporary too—but you know how it is, having to work off a debt. I keep my eye on a few guys for him, pick up a few bets. If you didn't have your own man you've been using all this time . . ."

Sam stood and turned, but the man's hand held him by the sleeve. "No hard feelings, brother, all right? That's how come I waited for you tonight—to warn you." He chuckled under his breath. "Christ teaches us that death is the wages of sin, but I never put much stock in that—you and me, the *wagers* of sin is what we have to worry about, right?" The man's left hand held him, while his right hand—in the gray glove—was in front of Sam again, for Sam to clasp in a handshake. "No hard feelings, right, brother?"

Sam pulled away, then—he couldn't help himself—he kicked savagely with his foot, heard the man groan even before he felt his toe collide. The shock—inside his shoe his toes tingled—made him vibrate all through his body, and he had to flail at the air, the snow, for a second, to maintain his balance. That really took brains, he told himself at once, turning and moving away.

He was burning—furious with himself for having shown his anger. At Ocean Avenue, he turned right, walked a block and a half—fast, to make up for the time he'd lost—and found the building, number 275. But what if it had been some old man who'd slipped and cracked his skull? Sam wanted an answer to that question. He walked into the lobby, and the thick warmth, hitting him like air in a steam room, made him dizzy. He took off his raincoat, blew into his cupped hands. He would let the sweat dry—he wouldn't wipe it off—and that would cool his body down. The light in the lobby was pale orange, and it reminded Sam of the lobby in his old building on Linden Boulevard. The sweat was cold between his thighs. He remembered seeing his grandfather coming home from synagogue on a Friday night, a night like this, his large hooked nose bright red, dripping. He remembered that he'd been afraid for the man, had followed him to the bathroom, watched him as he washed his hands, spat into the toilet bowl, blew his nose, urinated. Sam could hear his grandfather wheezing, he saw the thin lips—like Ben's—mumbling a prayer. For eating, for washing, even for pissing—they had one for everything in life. Sam sniffed. If you sneezed, the thing to watch out for was your tongue—not to bite it.

An elderly woman, her hair dyed silver, came down the staircase, stopped when she saw Sam. She carried a plate with pieces of cake on it, and she wore a yellow flowered housecoat. Sam didn't move. He wondered if his mother would take one of her trips again—across the ocean—to a place in Europe where they packed you in a special kind of black mud, to restore the quality of your skin. She'd explained it all to him once.

The woman descended to the bottom of the staircase, her eyes on Sam, her plate of cake wobbling. Sam rubbed his hands together and the woman turned, clacked down the hallway in her high heels, her wide bottom bumping up and down. Sam laughed, imagining the expression on her face had he taken a step toward her and shown her his knife. He worked on his fingertips, crossing his arms, against his chest, under his jacket, rubbing his hands beneath his arms, where it was warm. He'd have to be careful—it had been a while, and, even at half-dollar–dollar, if the ante built up and there were a few big hands, you could be in trouble fast. He could hear Ben, laughing, making some remark about Sam having the bathroom to himself now, but he would fool Ben there: he'd use the bathroom, sure, but he'd sleep where he'd been sleeping. With the kitchen there, and the phone, it was more practical. If he didn't use the other room, he wouldn't use it, that was all. At fifty-six dollars a month he could afford to waste space. Sam Berman was a real sport, right?

He laughed, heard his laughter echo in the lobby, and wondered if the woman was looking out at him from a keyhole. He felt—from the cold, he figured—the way he sometimes felt during the middle of a game, his mind unattached, so far ahead of him, spinning so fast, that it was as if he were watching himself playing. Playing cards—he had the feeling that it was just what he was doing to pass the time, as it were, while he . . . while he what? He'd figured that out too, once, that if you were passing time it meant just that: you were going by it, watching yourself in a dry run, a practice game, while you figured out how you would play the cards when the real game began. He shivered. It wasn't the kind of thing he needed to be reminded of, the feeling he had of being there and not there at the same time, but it was what he saw: himself watching himself playing cards, as if—the sensation was so strong he felt he could touch it—it wasn't his own life, as if what you were doing was just to get the lay of the land so you could figure out what to do with your life the next time around. He heard Tidewater describing the feeling he'd had when he was on the mound, and he pressed his eyes closed, tried to sweep away the picture of the guy, behind him, holding his raincoat, whispering to him. He saw Stella, watching them both. He'd be careful, all right. He took his hands from under his jacket, wiped his nose with the back of one, then opened the door to the elevator. The numbness was leaving. He stepped into the elevator, and the outside door creaked.

Sam pressed a button for the fourth floor, but nothing happened. He looked around, saw the sign—IN EMERGENCY, PRESS HERE—in large lettering; he studied the compartment—it was no more than three feet square. He looked up, saw the trap door, the screws you'd have to take off if you wanted to get out. He was in shape, though—he could fit through the small opening: good luck to anybody—all his old buddies—with a pot belly. He pressed the button again, and, still, nothing happened. Sabatini didn't fool Sam, either—one player was sure to be one of his henchmen, sizing Sam up, seeing if they wanted to move him up in class, like a thoroughbred, to bigger games. Sam saw himself at once, draped in bright silks; he could feel his stomach straining as somebody's legs straddled his back. Shit! He slammed his palm against the control board, the buttons, heard something in the compartment rattle, then realized his error: it was the old-fashioned kind of elevator.

He'd forgotten to draw the iron gate closed. A sitting duck, out of luck, that's who he was. Sam the Lamb. He measured things, drew the gate closed, slowly, watched the iron latticework expand. Something above clicked, whirred, the elevator bumped, then started upward.

They'd have their eye on him tonight, but it wasn't that that was bothering him—he'd play his game, no matter who was watching— but the business about moving up in class. That was when the smart money bet on a horse, the first time it moved up or down—but seeing himself in silks, his feet turning to hooves, that was really great, that took brains. His mind was slightly high, the way it should be before a game—but the rhymes and pictures, the pictures and voices, words conjuring up images, images sending him voices, and himself going nowhere fast—he didn't need any of it. He closed his eyes, tried to imagine the feel of the cards against the sides of his fingers. When he was in shape, playing regularly, his fingers did the counting for him: he could gauge things that way, especially with a fresh deck; he could lift it to any number of cards he wanted, feel for the slightest nick in the side of a card. The elevator stopped, he got out, sniffed in—his left nostril was still stuffed—and rubbed his hands against the sides of his pants, to dry the perspiration.

He found apartment 4G—no name on the door—and pressed the buzzer.

"Who's there?"

"Mr. Benjamin," he said.

The door opened, and a hand—dry and cool—was thrust into his own. "Simon's the name. Simon Schwartz. Glad you could come—it's a real bitch out tonight."

Sam passed the guy, smelled something sweet, like roses. The guy was an inch or so shorter than Sam, about the same age, had dark black hair slicked back, a wave in front, and he wore a maroon-colored silk smoking jacket, tied at the waist with a sash. His eyes were clear, alert; he looked, Sam thought, as if he'd just come back from a holiday—clean-shaven, sun-tanned, relaxed. "Come on," Simon said. "You must need a drink on a night like this—what'll it be? Scotch? Bourbon?"

Sam said nothing, followed the man down the hallway. Simon took Sam's raincoat, hung it in the closet. Sam waited, then followed again. The living room, sunken, had a card table set up in the middle, chips already stacked on the table. To one side, liquor bottles and glasses were lined up on a silver-rimmed cart. Simon wheeled the cart to the center of the living room, next to the card table. The carpeting, fire-engine red, was thick and soft, and the room was diffused in a purple light, through silk lampshades. Simon smiled at Sam, lifted a stopper from a crystal decanter and poured two drinks. His teeth were too white, Sam thought, as if they'd been capped, the way movie stars and old women had them done. Sam saw that there were only two folding chairs set up at the table.

"Here," Simon said, handing Sam a glass. "This should warm you up." The man's voice was light, young. Sam thought he looked familiar—like somebody he'd known from high school, somebody he'd played basketball with in the schoolyard. "I saw you looking at the table—you're right: the other guys called and chickened out—a night like this, I'll tell you the truth, I didn't really expect anybody to show." The guy kept his eyes on Sam, sipped from his glass, toasting to Sam first. "I wouldn't have blamed you." He motioned to the card table. "Look, whatever you say—I mean, if you want to play anyway, one-on-one, I'm ready—"

Sam almost laughed out loud, the guy was so obvious, but he'd save his laughs. You never knew, until later, why a guy put something up front at the beginning. There was an ice cube in Sam's glass, floating in a red liquid. Sam didn't drink. "And I appreciate your coming . . ." Simon said. "Ahead of time too, but if you'd waited another half-hour you probably couldn't have made it. It's freezing fast—I could tell from looking at the fire escape."

"Ahead of time?" Sam asked.

Simon pushed back the cuff of his smoking jacket. "It's only five after nine—they told you nine-thirty, right?"

Sam thought of the clock on the Holy Cross tower; he tried to show nothing, to return Simon's look, but he saw the drink move, in his own hand, so that some of it almost sloshed over the side. He kept himself from looking at his own watch. He tried to inhale slowly, to get his breath back. It didn't matter, even if the guy worked for Sabatini—or, anything was possible, if Sabatini worked for the guy; Sam could smell it, and it wasn't roses. Sure. Something was up, and he'd been the last to get the word.

"I mean, whatever you say," Simon said. "We could wait till nine-thirty, you get a chance to warm up that way. I know what it's like just coming in from the cold."

"No," Sam said. He felt dizzy—Tidewater's warning, Ben's

games, Flo making him meet Stella—he wanted his life to go more slowly. He felt himself swaying forward, as if he might faint: too much was happening too fast, and Sam saw no point in trying to figure it out. Don't bet what you don't know. Sure. He needed time to get his bearings, to figure why they were shifting the odds on him. In the meantime, the best thing was to follow his own rule: when you don't know, lay low. "No," he said again.

"No what?"

"No."

"Whatever you say, Sam," the guy said, and put his drink down, on an end table. "But drink up first—warm yourself before you head back home. I'll tell you the truth, it's probably just as well—if we got into a good game, by the time we were done, how would you get home? Even the taxis won't come get you on a night like this."

Sam put his drink down. "No."

The guy rushed by Sam, bent over. "I didn't mean to press you before—" He seemed too apologetic. Sam walked from the living room. "Whatever you say—like I said." Simon opened the closet, took Sam's coat off a hanger, held it for him. "Some other time, right?"

Sam said nothing, walked to the door. Simon bustled alongside him, reached the door first, unlocked a series of three locks, one above the other. The guy, his eyes looking down, seemed much older to Sam suddenly. "I mean," Simon said. "You know who to get in touch with—and, let's face it, I can say it to a guy like you, it's not so easy to get games anymore. Times are really changing."

"Yeah," Sam said, softly, unable to sustain the anger he'd felt a few minutes before. Outside, he pressed the button for the elevator, turned his eyes away, heard Simon's door close. Sabatini had been testing him in some way—Sam was sure of it—but it didn't matter. He'd done what he had to. He'd had to decide quickly, and he hadn't hesitated. There were a few things Sam knew, without anybody's help, and one of them was how to tell when somebody else was playing you for a sucker; even in a two hundred dollar silk robe, a deadbeat was a deadbeat. The guy's eyes had seemed, in the darkness, as Sam had glanced back from the outside hallway, to be wet. Sure, Sam thought, descending: It was rough all over. Even the dogs were bitching.

7

In a world of birds, Sam thought, Tidewater would be king. Sam liked that idea, and as he walked along Flatbush Avenue, toward Dutch's street, he laughed out loud. Tidewater had spoken to him that morning, promising to give him the second part of his story before Ben left, but Sam wasn't sure he wanted it. What he would have wanted, if not for the fact that he knew where it could have led, was to put a question to the guy: why was it that none of the Negro teams he'd talked about, and none that Sam had heard of, or read of in the library book, had named themselves after birds, the way white teams did. There were the St. Louis Cardinals, the Baltimore Orioles, the Philadelphia Eagles, the Hawks, the Redbirds—even the Brooklyn Dodgers, Sam knew, had at one time been called the Brooklyn Robins.

Still, Sam reasoned, the guy was in a class by himself; you had to give him credit. Sam turned right, walked down Lenox Road, toward Bedford Avenue. Compared to Tidewater, all the other birds in the world were pigeons—and as soon as the thought had occurred to Sam, he saw himself, one of them, on the top shelf of Sabatini's shooting gallery. Sure. There were clay pigeons and stool pigeons, sitting ducks and dead ducks, mockingbirds and jailbirds. Sam knew all about it. He remembered the jokes, from high school: there were guys with wood peckers, guys with two in the bush and your bird in her hand, and his own father, he realized, smiling, and seeing him aboard an airplane, was the original Jewbird. Sam laughed again, at that idea; he was really—the word was there— flying, thinking this way, because when it came down to it, he wasn't a bird at all; he was Sam the Lamb, and he knew it.

He crossed the street, went into the lobby of Dutch's apartment house. Stella had been on his mind, too, and he didn't like it—especially now, having to be with Dutch, having to see the old crowd. A lot of the athletes who'd become sick, like Campanella and Stallworth, had been divorced by their wives, even though the newspapers didn't go into that part of things too much. Sure. It was one thing to love a crippled kid in a TV telethon, or an athlete in a wheelchair; but if you had to touch them all the time . . .

Sam buzzed. "Who's there?" Mrs. Cohen asked, through the intercom.

"It's me—Sam." He spoke into the grating.

"Come on up, darling. Dutch isn't ready yet."

Sam walked into the lobby—the checkered floor, made of huge squares of marble, green and cream-colored, and the walls—a yellow-orange stucco—seemed especially cool to him. He thought of Simon's lobby. A doorman, sitting in a corner, was asleep on a wooden chair, his head to his chest. Sam took the elevator to the third floor, got out, walked down the corridor. There was no point in going into that—how they'd tried to set him up—with Dutch. He'd keep his mouth shut and listen, and the time until Ben's take-off would be that much shorter. He buzzed again, heard clicking sounds (Mrs. Cohen was looking through the hole, he knew—a one-way mirror, in the center of the door), then the sounds of locks turning.

When Sam had entered, he watched her fasten the locks again. She kissed him on the cheek, sighed: "You can't be too careful these days. Mrs. Lebowitz, on the fifth floor, was mugged last week right in front of her door. They took her diamond ring—which came from her grandmother; who knows how valuable it was . . ." She led Sam through the dark foyer, into the living room. "But I say, thank God they took the rings and left her fingers!"

Mrs. Cohen sat down in an easy chair, and motioned to Sam to sit across from her. "Dutch—Sam is here!" she called. The living room was large and there was a baby grand piano in the far corner of the room. Dutch had been the pianist for the school orchestra

when they'd been at Erasmus together—and he'd put himself
through a year of college by playing at weddings and bar mitzvahs.
"Tell me how you've been," Mrs. Cohen said. "You've been hiding
yourself from us lately. I said so to Dutch."

"I've been fine, Mrs. Cohen," Sam said. "My father's moving to
California soon—to visit his brother Andy. I think he's gonna stay
out there."

It amazed Sam, when he thought about it, that such a little
woman could exercise such control over Dutch. But she made him
feel uncomfortable too, and he wasn't even her son; he always had
the feeling, sitting there, that they were both thinking of Dutch's
father; as if the man had died so recently that you couldn't bring
the subject up. Mrs. Cohen never mentioned him; the man had
kicked off before Sam and Dutch had even known one another.
Still, it was what he felt whenever he sat there, looking down,
watching the gold and blue birds swirl around the corners of the
oriental rug. Sure. As if Mrs. Cohen, who never left the apartment
—Dutch still did all the shopping and errands—was . . . was what?
Sam stopped. He didn't owe her anything, either, he told himself.

"I knew your uncle Andy," she said. "He was a very handsome
man in his youth. Your father's very lucky—to be getting out." She
sighed. "I wish I could . . ."

"They got one-room apartments in some of the places—in
Florida, too," Sam said, and he touched the moisture in his palms
with his fingertips. "They're not too expensive."

"I've looked into them. Dutch—!" she called again, raising her
voice suddenly. "But I'm still rent-controlled here, and you have to
make a substantial down payment. . . . Maybe when my child gets
on his—well, his feet again." She was whispering: "Your friendship
has meant a lot to him, Sam. Why don't you go—leave me
here—you go into his room. You know where it is. I don't know
why he keeps . . ." She broke off.

"Yeah," Sam said, and rose immediately, went back into the
foyer, around and through the kitchen, and knocked on Dutch's
door. He and Dutch, when they'd first become best friends, they'd
had that in common—Dutch with no father, Sam with no mother.
He didn't remember what they'd said to each other, if anything—
but it had been a bond that the other guys had appreciated.

"Come on in, Ace—"

Sam entered. Dutch was sitting on his bed, his legs crossed under him, Indian-style, dealing out a hand of cards. "The witch get her fangs into you?"

"I told her about Ben's leaving for California."

"Good thinking. Maybe she'll take the hint." Dutch didn't look up at Sam. "Like you say, she's a real bird."

"She's just an old woman," Sam said. "There should be places for them."

"A lot you know," Dutch said, and looked up for the first time. "I'll tell you the truth—I don't much feel like seeing the guys now, if you know what I mean."

"I know," Sam said.

"Watch," Dutch said, motioning to the cards. He dealt out two hands of five cards each, looked at each hand, threw in two cards from his own, three from his imaginary opponent's, dealt the new cards, showed Sam the results. "I win. Jacks to nines. I let him keep a lady for luck." He pulled a piece of paper from under him. "Of course, I'm not figuring on the betting—just to show the over-all percentages—but here: since I started, it's six thousand two hundred and eighty-nine to six thousand and seven. Would you believe it could be that close?" Sam said nothing. Dutch shrugged, put the cards together, gave them a quick shuffle, and got off the bed. Dutch was two inches shorter than Sam—still, if he wanted to get mileage from it, he was the kind of good-looking guy girls went for, with his dark black hair and deep-set eyes, the full lips, the slight cleft in his chin. Mrs. Cohen said he looked like a Russian prince, and Sam guessed that there was some truth to that. "I'm waiting to see if—at particular junctures—three-three-three-three, seven-seven-seven-seven, for example—things—well, happen."

"You're bats," Sam said. "Come on, let's get our asses out of here. I checked. We got to catch a train at six forty-eight, which gets us out there just before eight. If we miss the six forty-eight, we got to wait another hour."

Dutch went to his closet, stripped off his sweatshirt. His body, Sam noticed, was still in shape. That was something. "How come you've been making yourself so scarce these days?" Dutch asked.

Sam sat down at Dutch's desk, looked across, at the tropical fish tank on the window sill. "I got things on my mind," Sam replied.

"Don't be so tight with me, Ace—like what things do you have on your mind? Your old man leaving?"

"No," Sam said, watching Dutch wipe a deodorant-stick across his underarm. "I don't blame the guy. You know that. I mean, he's okay—he never bugs me the way you'd think—but I'll be happy when he goes."

"Then what?" Dutch picked a shirt out from his drawer—a button-down, blue dress shirt. He slipped his arms into the sleeves, looked at Sam with his blue eyes. "I'm sorry, Ace. I really am. You know that."

"I told you to forget it."

"Well," Dutch began, the story Sam had heard before—what he'd heard every time for the past half-year, no more than five minutes after they were together. "Until I split from you—I mean, when we were both in it—you did okay. And now that I've given it up, your luck has changed. What else can I think, Sam?"

"Get off my back with that line, okay?" Sam said. "Just lay off and let's get out of here."

"Sure, Sam. I understand. I just—the truth—it's just not like old times is all."

"The sun goes down every day."

"I see what you mean," Dutch said, slapping Sam on the back.

Dutch led the way from his bedroom, back into the living room. He kissed his mother good-bye. "You be careful," she said. "Don't separate. They have very clever ways." She looked at Sam, then kissed him too. "I mean, they even—I heard this only a few days ago—they hire nice young boys like yourselves to show their faces into the cameras in the lobbies, so that the person doesn't suspect and buzzes for the downstairs door to open. Then the other—"

"That takes brains," Sam said, and Dutch laughed.

"I'll lock the door well. You remember to have a good time. Tell the boys how lucky they are to be living on Long Island." Dutch pushed Sam toward the door, Mrs. Cohen following. "And give my best regards to your father, Sam. Tell him he's making the smartest move of his life. . . ."

"I don't listen to her half the time," Dutch said, in the elevator. "You know what she gets a kick out of, though—? I gave up all my fish except for the black mollies, and I had to give her a reason, so I quoted to her what you said Ben is always saying, about living in a neighborhood in transition." The elevator bumped, the doors slid open. Dutch put his arm around Sam's shoulder. "If, God forbid, they should ever come in, I said to her, you can show them my fish tank as an indication of—"

"Why'd you get rid of the others?" Sam asked.

They walked outside, headed toward Flatbush Avenue. "I don't know. Okay. Maybe it reminded me too much of high school, if you know what I mean. Everytime she looked at my zebras and angel fishes and the rest she was thinking of what I could have been. You know. All that stuff about what an ace I was in high school."

Sam nodded. In their senior year, Dutch had been a runner-up in the National Westinghouse Science Contest, for an experiment he'd run: banging tuning forks against the sides of tanks. Sam had never understood it all, but there had been some definite difference in the way the fish had responded to different notes running through the water, and Dutch had written it all down.

"Sounds fishy to me," Sam said, and they both laughed.

At Flatbush Avenue, they got on the bus, walked to the back. Sam had told Dutch—long before—about what his grandfather used to do, when Ben had made Sam take him outside. Would they, Sam wondered, allow men like his grandfather where Andy was? The bus moved along Flatbush Avenue, past Parkside, where the entrance to Prospect Park was, then to Empire Boulevard, where, years before, they'd always gotten off together to go to Ebbets Field. Dutch raised his eyebrows. "Yeah," he said. "It still gets you—just a bunch of apartment houses now."

The bus moved out from the curb, past the entrance to the botanical gardens. Sam supposed Dutch's mother wasn't all that bats—he'd read in the papers that they'd had to begin chaining new trees they planted down to the ground, sinking weights below the root levels. They passed the zoo, on the other side of the street, then came to Grand Army Plaza, where the main branch of the Brooklyn Public Library was, set back from the street. "Look," Dutch said. "I know you said to lay off, but give a guy a break, okay? Let me tell you what's been happening."

Sam didn't look into Dutch's eyes. "Sure," he said, relenting. "Sure, Dutch."

The bus circled around the huge triumphal arch, a war memorial.

"It hasn't happened again yet," Dutch said, his voice low. The drivers—they protected them now too—with walkie-talkies, with exact fares required to cut down robberies . . . he couldn't blame Ben. "A couple of straight flushes—three, to be exact, one for me, two for him—but it hasn't happened again, like before."

"That figures," Sam said, wanting to be kind. "I mean, if it would happen even once in a lifetime that would seem like—"

Dutch pressed Sam's arm with his fingertips. "That's just it, Sam. That's just it!" He lowered his voice. "I jinxed you, Ace. It's pure and simple. I jinxed you, having luck like that."

Sam said nothing. He saw the marquee for the Brooklyn Fox ahead of them, stood, caught onto a metal strap, above his head. "C'mon," he said. "We get off here."

They walked across the street, then entered the Atlantic Avenue station. This was where, Sam remembered, O'Malley had asked for a new Ebbets Field, in downtown Brooklyn. But the bastard had known all along the city would never give it to him—he'd had the Los Angeles contract in his pocket the whole time. Sam moved ahead of Dutch, down steps; he'd been here before, to get the train to go out to the races: Belmont and Roosevelt Raceway. In the Long Island Railroad rotunda, they bought their tickets, round-trip to Westbury, then searched, found their way to the right track. "Made it by seven minutes," Sam said. "I told you we had to hurry."

"You're a genius," Dutch said.

Over the public address system, somebody was reading off the names of the towns the trains would stop at. Sam thought he could see Tidewater in the back seat of Jack Henry's car. A few stops in Brooklyn, then a change at Jamaica, in Queens, and then the crazy-sounding names of all the places: Printing Press Road, Floral Park, New Hyde Park, Rockville Centre, Garden City, Roslyn, Manhasset, Neponset, Oyster Bay, Plainview, Patchogue, Babylon, Syosset, Mineola—and Sam's favorite: Hicksville. He laughed to himself—you spend your whole life saving your money to buy a house in a place with a name like that. That took brains.

Sam and Dutch entered a double-decker car, one of the old ones—two sets of seats facing each other in a pit below, and two more sets of seats above. Sam ducked his head, slipped down, sat. The rocking of the train, while the motor warmed up, made him sleepy. "You can flip a penny in the air a hundred times," Dutch was saying, "and most times you'll get fifty heads, fifty tails—approximately. Fifty-six and forty-four, something like that. But it happens, Sam—you can get one hundred heads in a row." Dutch sat across from him and leaned forward, his hands spread apart, his palms up. Seeing Dutch's hands, Sam thought of Tidewater, who'd played the piano also. He watched the shadows along Dutch's face, under the cheekbones. "Listen: I explained before how there's a theory in physics which says that everything in a room—all the particles—can suddenly collect in one corner: *everything*—chairs and tables and mirrors and the rest." Sam nodded, looked out the window, saw somebody's shoes running by. Maybe, since he liked speculating on things so much, he should suggest to Tidewater that he sell his theories to Dutch. Sure. Let them take their trip with each other, instead of through his head. "Okay, so anything's possible. Who knows better than you? Okay, so I pull a royal straight flush—like you say, it can happen once in a lifetime. And okay too, I pull a second royal straight flush—two in a row—after all those years, the thousands of hands, let's say it's like the theory in physics. Anything's possible, right?"

The train was moving now, chugging along slowly, away from the lights of the station. It picked up speed, entered a tunnel, went around a curve. Nobody sat above them. Dutch's blue eyes were shining. "It wasn't getting the two hands which made me decide, can't you see? I thought maybe you thought that when I got two hands like that it—well, spooked me." Dutch put a hand on Sam's knee, tapped with his knuckles, then shook his head. "But that wasn't it, Sam—it wasn't anything like that. All the theories and explanations—I was covering up something simpler."

Dutch was flying now, Sam thought. Poor Dutch. He could say what he wanted, but he'd never be the same. There were, Sam imagined, a few things like that that could happen—he thought of Stallworth—and then everything was different afterward, forever. He could understand that. There were moments in every person's life when things could happen that way—as if the whole universe would stop for just an instant, the part of a second you couldn't even measure; it would stand still because of you somehow. Ben could say what he wanted, but Sam believed it. Things happened sometimes and you didn't always ask why. That was the difference.

"But the basic fact isn't that I drew two hands like that, in a row—and that"—he licked his lips; Sam watched the shadow, deep black, in the cleft below his nose—"nobody bet against me." He paused, the tip of his tongue moving across his lower lip. "Right or wrong, Ace? When a guy in our business draws even once like that, and can't get any mileage out of it, then it's time to get out. As simple as that—"

Sam waved him off. "You're bats," he said. "You got to play the cards, that's all. If you pulled six deuces and lost a nickel on it, it wouldn't mean dick." He looked out the window. The train was riding an el now, along Fulton Street, and Sam looked at the buildings below—old, red brick, empty junk-filled lots between them. "You got to play the cards, that's all. I've folded with power, lots of times. Sure. I told you about the guy, in Virginia Beach, kept asking me when the Dodgers were gonna move back to Brooklyn, cause that was when I would win." Sam found himself laughing, at Dutch. "I pulled four jacks once, he never knew it, but I reamed the bastard's ass good anyway."

Dutch shook his head. "You just don't understand," he said. "I had my good years too; I have my bundle stashed away, till I . . ." He grabbed Sam's knee between his thumb and forefinger, and put pressure on. "Listen: I drew the two hands, one after the other, nobody went in with me, and I said to myself, Dutch Gabriel Cohen, with luck like that, you don't need enemies—it's time to switch to something else. As simple as that, Sam."

"You're—you're . . ." Sam couldn't find a word. "Fuck it. Just lay off, okay? You believe what you want, I'll believe what I want, and we'll all live happily ever after. I told you. I got things on my mind."

Dutch whistled. "You're in a great mood, I see. I'm really glad—I mean, it's good to share things with a buddy at times like this."

Dave Stallworth took the ball in bounds from Dick Barnett, and began dribbling upcourt. Suddenly, two men converged on him— his head bobbed, and, moving past half-court at full speed, he slipped between them, his silver medallion swinging from around his neck. Without looking to either side, he shot a pass to his left.

Bill Bradley took it, and a second later, under the basket, Stallworth had the ball back from Bradley. He faked right, spun around left, his head directly under the net, flicked the ball upward with his right hand, and the ball spun off the glass backboard and dropped through the hoop. Stallworth wound up on the floor, a whistle blew, and the referee—Mendy Rudolph—pointed an accusing finger at the guilty ballplayer, Gus Johnson. The crowd roared, Stallworth smiled, flipped his medallion under his uniform shirt; he took a helping hand from Barnett, stood, and walked to the foul line.

"They hacked the guy to death!" Herbie said. "But did you see that shot? Did you see it? That guy is something, isn't he, Sam?"

Sam lay across the bed in Herbie's bedroom, his head on pillows. Herbie sat up next to him, his back against the headboard, a huge piece of openwork black wood, carved in the form of two giant Japanese letters. Above Sam's head, a round white ball—a Japanese lantern, Herbie had explained—was suspended from the ceiling, giving off a frosted yellow-white light. To the right, Dutch and Shimmy sat next to each other, on chairs, and at the foot of the bed the other guys—Nate, Max, Sid—were leaning forward, their eyes fixed on the color television set. "Yeah," Sam said, "he's an ace."

Shimmy, a round, balding man who had, Sam knew, been in and out of a half-dozen ventures during the last few years, and was now, so it seemed, making a fortune in real estate, leaned forward, chewing on the skin around his nails. His face was pock-marked, he lifted a can of beer to his lips. Sam reached to his left, to the night table, and took another cashew nut. "C'mon, Davela baby," Shimmy said. "Come home now."

The camera zoomed in for a close-up of Stallworth's face. Despite the brilliance of the color, you couldn't tell, Sam realized, that his gold tooth was capped in the shape of a five-pointed star. Stallworth breathed in, balanced the ball on his fingertips and flicked it up and away. Swish! The guys cheered, and Sam felt his heart pump. "That's it! That's it!" Max yelled, sitting at the foot of the bed. "They're gonna do it. Sixteen in a row! One to go for the record. C'mon you Knicks!"

"Knicks, dicks," Shimmy said, glancing toward Max. "C'mon you beautiful greenbacks!"

"How much you got riding on the game?" Herbie asked.

"Enough," Shimmy said. "Enough."

The Baltimore Bullets brought the ball upcourt—Earl "The Pearl" Monroe getting away from Barnett with a fancy behind-the-back dribble, but he was immediately caught in a trap—Bradley and Stallworth surrounding him, their arms waving furiously, and when Monroe tried to flip the ball away, Stallworth got a hand on it. The ball rolled along the floor, Bradley scooped it up, flipped it ahead of him, and Barnett was there, ready, taking the ball and going in alone for a layup.

"Oo-eee!" Shimmy cried, sucking on his lips. "Ain't that sweet!"

"They are really good," Max stated. "I mean—they are really good. It's their defense, don't you think, Sam?"

"Sure," Sam said. "They'll go all the way this year."

"You get to a lot of games, don't you?" Sid said to Sam, but Sam kept his eyes on the TV set. The camera pulled back for a long view and Sam picked out Stallworth. He ate another cashew nut—he couldn't stop—and he wondered if, when he got up, the sweat from his back would show against the bedspread. Under his rear-end, on the red silk bedspread, was part of a huge monogram—Herbie and Ruth's initials, Japanese-style, in black raised lettering. Nate Mandel, who'd been a starter on the Erasmus team when they'd all been seniors there together, sat in front of Sam, not saying anything. Why didn't they ask Nate questions, if he was the star. Sam had played J. V. one year, and that was all. He didn't like it—hearing the guys going on and on about how great the Knicks were, seeing Shimmy biting his nails over his six-point spread (the Knicks were up by thirteen now, with less than a minute left), feeling himself rooting for Stallworth—pulling for each of the Knicks individually—with one part of him, yet with another . . .

"I been to a few—the opening game, and a couple since. It's rough to get tickets this year," Sam said.

Shimmy leaned back, assured of a victory now, and lit up a cigar. "That's what I like to see," he said. "They are a beautiful team. Simply beautiful!"

Sam remembered when Shimmy—Simon Stein—had run for president of Erasmus. Now, watching the fat man puff on his cigar, Sam was glad Shimmy had been beaten, and mad at himself for thinking this way. Each guy that he looked at he saw at some point fifteen years ago—all these pot-bellied, balding married men—he saw them as they had been when . . . "But look," Sam heard Dutch say. "Did you ever think of this—Barnett there, he's the only guy who's older than us. Think of that for a second."

Sam slid backward on the silk bedspread, until his rear-end came to the pillow and he was sitting. Between his legs, above the H and R, he saw no stain on the spread. "So what?" he said, challenging Dutch.

"Turn it off, turn it off," Herbie said to Sid. "They have it locked up." The television screen showed a close-up of the clock—the bulbs lighting up the remaining seconds, the shot of the clock superimposed over a long view of the entire arena. Sam saw people moving toward the exits. He watched the top of Stallworth's head.

"So nothing," Dutch said. "Christ, you're touchy tonight, Ace— just that these guys we root for all the time—they're all younger than us now." He shrugged. "It makes you think, that's all."

"He's got a point," Herbie said. "I mean, I can remember when we were all rooting for Harry Gallatin and Sweetwater Clifton and that Knick team—and those guys were *twice* our age!"

Max stood in front of the TV set. He was an accountant now, and worked for a big firm in midtown Manhattan. He lived on Long Island also—all the guys except for Shimmy, who lived over the Bridge in Teaneck, New Jersey, lived somewhere on the Island. "Remember—like this—how he'd shoot the ball from his goddamned waist!" Max demonstrated and the other guys shook their heads, in admiration. "He had the biggest goddamned hands!"

"That was their last great team," Nate said. Sam realized he liked Nate best of all, at the moment, simply because, being the best ballplayer, he said the least about basketball. Sure. Words were for the birds. Guys like Shimmy and Dutch and Max had to showboat, but if you really had the goods . . .

"You're a hundred per cent right," Shimmy said. He stood also, took a place next to Max. "Okay—who's this?" He leaned back, lifted his right knee into the air, as if he were marching, raised his right hand above his shoulder, an invisible basketball in his palm.

"Carl Braun," Sid said, just as Shimmy lost his balance. Max reached out, caught Shimmy around the waist. Shimmy grabbed his cigar in his fist, pointed to his belly. Then he smiled, looked straight at Sam, and rapped his knuckles against the side of his head. "Brain over brawn," he said. "Brain over brawn."

Everybody groaned, and Sam could see Shimmy falling backward into the TV set, the tube splattering into a million pieces. Herbie nudged Sam with his elbow; the other guys were naming names to each other, old ballplayers they remembered from their high school days: pro ballplayers, college stars, high school players—"Easy Ed" McCauley, Johnny Groll, Bobby Wanzer, Ernie Vandeweghe, Chuck Cooper, Mike Parenti, Johnny Lee, Max Zaslofsky . . . "Hey," Herbie was saying to him. "You and Dutch, you didn't get the tour yet—of the house. I mean, we all had so much to say to each other—Jesus, it's been a long time—and then the game. Come on—I'll show you around. The other guys have seen it all."

Sam remembered, their second year in high school, when he'd nominated Herbie for vice-president of their home-room class. They hadn't known one another well before that, but they'd played on the same three-man basketball team in gym one day, and had won seven games in a row, until the bell rang ending the period. Sam thought of his father and Tidewater, playing in the grass together. Herbie, a buyer for Bloomingdale's now, had been a good ballplayer; he'd played J. V. with Sam—a hustler, a scrapper. If he'd had two or three more inches—he was, at most, five-foot-six, though he'd always claimed to have been five-foot-eight—he would have made the team. "Mousie" had been his nickname—for the way his ears stuck out and his mouth puckered in above his tiny chin—but he'd been sensitive; nobody had ever used the nickname to his face. "Sure," Sam said, and swung his feet to the floor. The carpeting felt good under his socked feet. "C'mon, Dutch."

"Hey, Sam," Dutch asked, "who was the guy who played first base for the Dodgers—just after the war—and played pro basketball too?"

"Schultz," Sam said.

"Sure," Dutch said. "I knew you'd know—Howie 'Steeple' Schultz." The other guys nodded, remembering. Dutch leaned over, while Sam laced his shoes up, and put his hand on Sam's knee. "If I had his memory, guys, I'll tell you the truth—I wouldn't have given it up, despite what happened. What I told you before."

"You know," Sid said, rubbing his chin, "it's very interesting—
your whole story, Dutch. The connections between things. I had a
boy at school recently—he was referred to me for the usual:
mischief, hooky . . ."

Shimmy nodded, looked at Sam. "It's terrific, Sammy, terrific—
the way you remember things."

"That's what my father says," Sam said.

Sid had risen from the bed, taken Shimmy's chair, straddling it,
backward. He faced Dutch. "Let me tell you about this kid. It
turned out that . . ."

"Why you could have been anything," Shimmy went on, smiling
slightly. "Anything at all, with your memory. Even an elephant."

"A Jewish elephant!" Max cried. "It speaks in Yiddish—tusk,
tusk, tusk. . . ."

"Dick Groat," Herbie said, standing at the door. "And there was
Gene Conley and Bob Gibson. Guys who played two pro sports—"

Sam saw Sid bent over, talking intensely to Dutch. Better him
than me, Sam thought. Sam remembered an entire afternoon at
Sid's house on Clarkson Avenue, Sid lying on the bed, the
telephone to his ear, talking to one guy after the other—the phone
never stopped ringing—while Sam sat there, lamenting the fact that
they were never going to get to the schoolyard. Sid had been like
that—everybody had always gone to him with their problems. He
was, everybody had agreed, a sweet guy. And yet—Sam smiled at
the thought, at the connection—Sid had never had a steady girl,
he'd never seemed much interested. He'd dated, he'd gone to
dances—but Sam never remembered hearing Sid talk about the size
of a girl's breasts, or how far he'd gone. Sure. Now Sid was a
guidance counselor at some fancy Long Island high school. It
figured.

"Don't forget," Shimmy was saying. He was next to Sam,
whispering so that nobody else could hear. "I want to talk with
you—about Brooklyn."

"I got nothing to say."

Shimmy put his arm around Sam's shoulder, led him to a corner
of the room. Sam fixed his eyes on the Japanese lantern, hanging
over the bed. He heard more names: Tony Jackson, Bobby Davies,
Heshy Weiss, "Zeke" Zawoluk, "Zeke" Sinicola . . . "Listen,"
Shimmy said. "Don't be such a shithead your whole life. Things get

rough sometimes. Believe me, I know how it is. I've had my ups and my downs too. You shouldn't resist me so much. I'm in the neighborhood now and then—we'll have lunch, we'll talk. I could use a man like you in my operation, Sammy boy. Why should I take in a stranger? With your brain—your memory—and the way you know Brooklyn. I could use somebody with your style."

"Forget it."

Shimmy pressed him. "Look, could you use a few hundred? Just tell me—just say the word, Sammy boy, and it's yours. How about three singles?" He reached into his pocket for his wallet, but Sam didn't react. He watched Sid's puckered face, looked beyond, saw Dutch's blue eyes, shining, Dutch's hands, moving, explaining. What bothered him most of all was not so much that he thought about Tidewater and his story—he could live with that—but that he caught himself sometimes, as he did now, seeing if he could put himself in the guy's place. "Why should I lie, tell you business isn't so good, it isn't so bad. I'm rolling in the green stuff now and what am I gonna do with it all? Sure, me and Barbara, we go on trips, we have the new house, we put something away for the kids for college, but there's plenty for a smart guy like you also." He smiled at Sam, and Sam saw him in "the chapel"—the Erasmus auditorium—on the stage, giving his speech when he ran for president. Sam had, of course, worn one of Shimmy's tags on his loose-leaf book: STEIN IS FINE FOR YOUR G.O. "Right now, I'll tell you the truth, there's too much to keep track of for one man. My brother-in-law, I took him in also—it keeps the peace—but, between you and me, he's as much use as a fart in a salami factory."

"Forget it," Sam said again. "Just tell me one thing: who's taking your money for the Knicks?"

Shimmy eyed him, then laughed. "That's good, Sammy boy," he said. "That's really good, you asking me a question like that." He smiled with his mouth closed. "You're terrific, like I say. Just terrific. That's what I mean by style, if you get me. That's just why . . ." He sighed, closed his eyes. "I have to be down at City Hall so fucking much—I'll tell you the whole thing when we have lunch together, agreed? Say yes, Sammy you old shithead, for your old schoolyard buddy. Picking up most of the property for back taxes—and there are other ways—believe me, there's a lot of palms I have to grease, a lot of *shtipping* to be done. It won't last forever, either. The government will move in soon with its own kind of renewal, and after that . . . you see? While I'm taking care of the business end, I need somebody in the field I can rely on." He paused. "We're made for each other, Sammy. You—you need the money, you can't deny it; you know the area like the palm of your hand; and you—you have the style. The *shvoogies* trust you. I know it."

"I appreciate your offer, Shimmy, I really do, but I'll keep playing it my way, okay?" He found himself patting Shimmy on the shoulder, and although he was certain Shimmy didn't notice, he knew he had a worried expression on his own face when the next sentence slipped out. "No hard feelings, okay?"

"Of course not." Shimmy walked back toward the bed with Sam. "You think I give up this easily? I'll be seeing you, anyway." Shimmy's voice rose, for the benefit of the others: "We see each other too little, don't we, guys? We should all get together more often. Sid, Max, Nate, Herbie—you're near each other out here, but Dutch and Sam, and me in Jersey—we all get into the city, right?"

"We should go to a game together," Nate offered.

"Great! Great!" Max said. "Look—through my firm—I can get us some tickets. We got a season . . ."

"C'mon," Herbie said, taking Sam by the arm. "But there first—you see the way Ruthie did up the bathroom?" He giggled, and Sam looked in, over Dutch's shoulder, at gold racks and oriental lettering. The floor was carpeted in a deep avocado green. "There—" Herbie said, and pointed to the wastebaskets, carpeted also. "From Fortunoff's. They have everything you want. Leave it to Ruthie . . ."

Herbie led them from the bedroom, along a dark corridor. A red and yellow tricycle was parked next to a door. Herbie opened the door quietly, putting his finger to his mouth. Sam glanced behind. Sid was there, smiling at him. He patted Sam on the shoulder, ate from a palmful of peanuts. Herbie motioned to Sam and Dutch. They looked in. "This is Mark's bedroom—see—he's got pictures from *Sport* magazine on all the walls, but we—Ruthie's idea—we use burlap for wallpaper. It's terrific. The thumbtacks don't leave any marks."

"That's good," Dutch said. "No marks from Mark."

"You've seen it all," Herbie said to Sid. "But come anyway."

"It's terrific, what you've done here," Sid said. "Terrific. Susie gets most of her ideas from Ruthie, you know."

Herbie led them along the corridor. Framed pictures of Walt Disney characters—Mickey Mouse, Donald Duck, Goofy—hung on the walls. They were originals, Herbie explained, from the Disney studios. He opened another door, showed them Katherine's room. Sam saw powder blue and pink. The little girl was on her back, her nightgown gathered around her waist, her legs sticking out from rubber pants, a thumb in her mouth. She had deep black curls across her cheek. Sam thought of Muriel.

"They grow up so quickly!" Sid said.

"This is an extra room," Herbie explained, opening a door at the end of the corridor. The room was small, there was a bed in it. "For a sleep-in maid if we have one, or another child—we'll see. . . ."

The four men turned around, looked into the children's bathroom, then walked back along the corridor. Dutch stayed next to Sam. Sam heard Herbie explaining, to Sid, about the way you could get sleep-in maids from Jamaica, in the West Indies—not from Queens, he joked; Ruth's parents would handle it. The maids from the West Indies, Sid agreed, were dependable. "What do you think?" Dutch asked Sam, softly. "Would Barbara still put out for me?"

"Come on," Sam said. "Cut it—"

"She gave me the eye before, when we first came in—Shimmy, with all his hotshot operations now, he's probably forgotten what she has between her legs." Dutch rolled his eyes. "She still has the body! I wouldn't mind. . . ."

Herbie opened a door, next to the bedroom, flicked a light switch. Sid lagged behind, and Sam knew he was waiting to speak with him. Sam remembered, when he was a boy, going around his own apartment on Linden Boulevard with his grandfather—Sam had held a candle, and his grandfather had held a wooden spoon, a rag, and a feather. He remembered it very clearly, his grandfather telling him to come closer, closer—it had been the night before Passover, and his grandfather had placed scraps of bread on window sills, under cushions of couches, in the desk of the breakfront; Sam walked around with him in the darkness, a lit

candle in his hand, and watched him sweep the crusts into the cloth
with the feather and spoon. Had Ben been with them? Sam couldn't
remember.

"The basement is only three-quarters finished since you saw it,
Sid—it's gonna be a game room for the kids—and a guest room
maybe."

"How've things been?" Sid asked, his arm on Sam's shoulder.
They walked down the steps. Sam saw copper pipes running along
the walls. He remembered, afterward, following his grandfather
down to the basement of their apartment house. It had terrified
him—the shadows, the barking of the super's German police
dog—and when his grandfather had opened the iron door of the
furnace and Sam had seen the fire—white light leaping on top of
the burning coals—he had wanted to cry. Burning the *chumitz*, it
had been called. Sam remembered. His grandfather had pushed
him close to the furnace door and Sam could still feel the heat on
his face, the weakness in his thighs. The crumbs were in the bowl of
the wooden spoon, the feather and candle on top, the rag wrapped
around, tied in a knot. "Give a throw, Samela," his grandfather had
said, and when Sam had thrown it in, and seen the package burst
into flame, his grandfather had bent over—slightly, for Sam was
almost his height by then—and kissed him on each cheek. His
grandfather had, for some reason, been crying, and Sam had been
proud of himself—glad that he had held back his own tears. His
grandfather had pulled him close—Sam remembered the man's
smell: rancid, like clothes which had been waiting too long to be
washed—but he had not moved, he had kept his body rigid. His
grandfather had said—had sung—something in Yiddish, and
though he had not understood a word of it, he had been sure that
his grandfather had been thinking of his wife, and of his two older
sons, Ben's brothers, who had never crossed the sea and come to
America.

"I got no kicks," Sam said, to Sid.

"This is the hot water boiler," Herbie said, opening a door,
revealing two large tanks. "And that's the furnace." He spoke to
Sid. "We use forced air heat—that way, with the ducts already
there, we can have central air conditioning hooked right in some
day if we want."

Sid nodded. The basement ran for the full length of the

house—thirty or forty feet—and the walls were covered in a wood-grain material. The ceiling was made of white perforated squares. There was a bench along one side of the wall, an old TV console, shelves filled with games and toys. There were cartons and several old pieces of furniture—a dresser, end tables, chairs, a Formica kitchen table. The floor was made of red and white squares, alternating in a checkerboard pattern. The fluorescent lighting, overhead, was too bright for Sam's eyes. He had never liked fluorescent lighting. Screw Sid, he thought. He won't get anything from me. Herbie opened another door, halfway down the length of the room, revealing a bare concrete floor, more pipes, concrete walls. The room, he explained, could be made into either a guest room or an at-home office for himself. If he did the latter, he would get a tax break. Sid nodded. He did some private counseling and testing now, and took off something every year for the room he used at home.

"So?" Herbie asked, facing them. "What do you think?"

"Great stuff," Dutch said. "You got it made, Herbie. The life of Riley—"

"It's something," Sam offered, when Herbie's eyes caught his, and he could see, in front of him, ten couples—all past sixty-five years of age—arms on one another's shoulders, the women's hair done up, their wrinkles hidden under creams and powders. *You may dance the buckles off your shoes, whatever your dance is. . . .*

Herbie moved off, Dutch kidding him about married life, about his pot belly, but Sid detained Sam by stepping slightly in front of him. "Listen, Sammy, you look like—if you don't mind my saying so—as if something's bothering you."

"I got things on my mind," Sam said. He heard Stella's voice, speaking to Sid, and it made him smile. *Why do people always have to say things is what I want to know. . . .*

The still photo from the brochure—a white-haired woman in the foreground with diamond earrings and a diamond necklace above her low-cut pink gown—suddenly came to life, the way pictures did sometimes at the beginnings of movies. Sam saw the old people dancing around Herbie's basement. "Look, Sam—I'll tell you the truth, with old friends like us, we shouldn't stand on ceremonies. I won't press you, but . . ." Sam thought that Sid's eyes were watering. "If I can do anything—if you want to talk about it—well—just know that I'm available, any time, night or day, okay?"

"Sure," Sam said. "That's white of you, Sid. I mean—"

Sid put up a hand, to stop Sam. "None of that shit with me, you jerk—but, like my wife's girl says, 'anything I can do to resist you, Mr. Adlerstein, you let know.' "

Sam smiled. He wanted to let Sid know that he appreciated the offer, that he knew—the truth—that any of the guys would have given the shirts off their backs for him if he'd asked them. Sure. Sam felt his Adam's apple bob. He saw Sid lying back on the bed in his T-shirt, the telephone receiver cradled between his shoulder and his ear; he remembered listening afterward while Sid told him all about what one of the other guys—Sid wouldn't say which one—had been telling him about what had happened, something between the guy and his sister. "I'll let you know, Sid," he said, and felt Sid's fingers tighten along his arm-muscle. "Sure. You'd be the first."

Sid patted Sam on the stomach. "I don't know how you do it, Ace—how you keep in shape." Sid motioned with his head, and the two of them walked, toward the staircase.

Sam glanced at the room with the boiler and the furnace. He wondered if Sid ever thought about his own grandfather, he wondered what Sid would make of his thoughts—of the business of the wooden dolls, of how he sometimes saw himself, Ben, and his grandfather in reverse order. . . . "Flo said to say hello," he said.

"Flo. Flo—she's terrific," Sid said, as they made their way up the staircase. "Flo. That girl is terrific—still running a store in a neighborhood like that. She has a lot of what we call ego-strength."

Sam flicked the light switch. "In here!" he heard Herbie calling. "It's eating time, Sam, Sid—in the dining room."

Sid looked into Sam's eyes. "I have a good life, Sam," he said. "I really do." Sam looked down at Sid's balding head, at the dark spots along his cheeks, where the bristles of hair were beginning to come back in. "Sometimes, of course, I envy guys like you and Dutch—the freedom you have, the girls you can *shtup*—but I have a good life." Sam didn't know why Sid was talking this way, and yet, when he thought about it, it was the way Sid had always been; it had been, he thought, this way of sharing his life—this sincerity—which had made everybody love him so much, which had made him, as others put it, such a sweet guy. "I love my work—and I'm good at it. Believe me, Sammy, I've helped a lot of youngsters get out of some tough jams. You wouldn't believe the things they do nowadays—it's nothing like when we were growing up. But they're terrific youngsters. And my wife—Susie—you should see her with our kids. She's a terrific wife. . . ." Sam found that he couldn't listen to Sid. Sure. He imagined that Sid would probably have found the library book more interesting than Tidewater's story.

There were, Sam knew, exactly sixteen major league baseball players earning over a hundred grand a year now—it was a fact he found himself wanting to offer Sid, for conversation, but he knew that Sid might have found it strange, Sam simply introducing a subject like that. It made you think, though. Things changed. Sam remembered when he'd thought being a pro ballplayer would be a great life because there was a minimum yearly salary of five grand. Now, in addition to the sixteen, there were close to a hundred ballplayers earning over fifty thousand a year. Sid's arm was around Sam's shoulder. They entered the dining room, from the hallway, and Sam saw that the other guys were already seated around the table. The girls, as always, had eaten first. Ruth had put out the usual spread: plates of lox and pickled herring and cream cheese and butter, baskets of bagels and rolls and bialys, smoked white fish and matjes herring, carp and sliced tomatoes, platters of cookies and *rugelech* and egg salad. "But you know something I realized," Sid said, as they sat down, next to each other, between Shimmy and Dutch. "There's something missing out here—our kids have a terrific life, but they don't have what we had: for example, I can't send Elliott to the corner to get anything. Do you see what I mean? The kids out here, in developments like ours, they grow up without ever knowing what it is to run down to the corner for an *errand.*"

"I see what you mean," Sam said, and he thought of a guy he'd seen walking along Church Avenue a few days before, sporting a mink jump suit. He remembered the twin El Dorados. He saw all the guys sitting around a table in Garfield's: Cohen, Stein, Mandel, Adlerstein, Zelenko, Gotbaum, and Berman. Strange how, when they'd been younger, they'd called one another by their last names or nicknames—he'd always been Berman, or Sam the Man, or Sam

Junior—and now, in their thirties, they'd taken to using first names. Sid reached in front of Sam for a seeded roll, split it with his hands, began spreading cream cheese on it. Sam took a piece of rye bread and watched the others work, buttering their toasted bagels, laying the pieces of lox on their rolls, filling their mouths. He laughed to himself. That was the quick way to get out of shape. Sure. He'd still be wheeling and dealing long after the rest of them were in their graves.

All eyes were on Max, who was telling one of his jokes: ". . . so Rastus lies there in the gutter, poor Rastus, his lip torn, blood streaming from his ears, his face a pulp, his knife in his hand—while Rufus staggers off, heading up to the second floor where Ella Mae, who they've fought over, is looking out her window, her eyes rolling, her bazookas dancing up and down—and all the *shvartzehs* look down at Rastus, poor Rastus, wondering why he has such a huge grin across his beaten face . . ." Was this the guy, Sam wondered, who had been the best dancer in their high school? Sam saw Max, a crowd of guys and girls around him while he moved his feet wildly, beautifully. And yet—the crazy thing—with all his rhythm, with the endlessly subtle moves of his body and feet and hands, he'd been a lousy athlete, totally uncoordinated. ". . . 'Because,' Rastus said, looking up at the crowd from the gutter, showing them his knife. 'Wait till he get upstairs with Ella Mae—I got that mother's balls right here in my back pocket—!' "

Shimmy laughed, gagged on a piece of his sandwich, and Sam saw the seeds from a sliced tomato trickle down his chin. The other guys roared with laughter. Max was working them up. Sam watched their mouths. "You know what nine out of ten Cadillac owners say?" Max asked. Shimmy rubbed the tears from his eyes. The other guys were still laughing, eating, rocking back and forth. Max lowered his voice. "De Cadillac am de best car on de road."

"You told that fifteen years ago," Nate said, and he didn't laugh.

"And the tenth one," Max went on, wrinkling his nose, eyes and mouth together, giving his best Yiddish inflection: "Hit's ha very good car. . . ."

Shimmy waved him off, and swayed against Sam's shoulder. "Say dere, Kingfish," he said, pointing a piece of bagel at Max. It was like old times, Sam thought, Shimmy and Max trading jokes. "Did you hear about the homosexual who had a hysterectomy?"

"Stop!" Max cried. "You're getting personal."

"They took out all his teeth," Shimmy said. There was a moment of silence and then the laughter exploded again. Sam found himself laughing also, but he wasn't sure if it was at the joke, or at the sight of the other six guys' faces, at their laughter.

"I'm *plotzing* already!" Herbie cried, trying to get into the act. "Wait till I tell Ruthie that one—"

The jokes continued, Ruthie came in and put down a lemon meringue pie, a coffee cake, a platter of butter cookies, and a pot of coffee. Herbie pinched her, the guys laughed. She wore black toreador stretch pants—all the wives seemed to be wearing slacks, Sam noticed, except for Lillian, Max's wife, who wore a mini-skirt. That figured. Sam remembered her, in high school, with her cone-shaped brassieres. He'd gotten what he'd wanted off her, he told himself. He took a slice of lemon meringue pie. She'd always had the hots for him. If he'd dry-humped her once, he'd dry-humped her a hundred times. Max could have his private house and his fancy sports clothes and his filthy jokes; Sam knew—and Max knew too—which one of them had taken sloppy seconds. When Max had been social chairman of their club, Sam remembered, driving out to Belle Harbor and Manhattan Beach to get them socials with the rich Jewish girls, he'd called himself Jonathan Avant the Third.

Sam saw Lillian in the doorway to the kitchen, helping Ruth. With all the make-up she wore now, and the frosted hair—part silver and part a fake red color—you wouldn't even know who you were doing it with. Sam looked at Dutch. Dutch glanced toward Lillian, back at Sam, then winked. Sam smiled. Sure. Dutch was okay. In the train, coming out, he shouldn't have been so hard on the guy. Maybe, with time, Dutch would come around—the two of them could ride the rails together again. If anything ever opened up, that was.

"Watch this," Max said, then called into the kitchen. "Lillian— tell the guys—who's Cazzie Russell?"

Lillian looked in, smiled. "Oh Max," she sighed. "He's the seventh man on the Knicks." She saw the guys smiling at her, and handed them the punch line. "Everybody knows that."

The guys laughed. Sam looked at the gold chains hanging from her neck in bunches, past her navel. A gold safety pin held her skirt together at the side. "And—watch this—what makes them so tough this year?" Max asked.

"Their defense, sweetie—Red Holzman has worked miracles with them."

Max beamed. "Get this," he said, to the table. "And who's Sandy Koufax?"

Lillian waved him off. "Silly—everybody knows that—he's a nice Jewish boy from Brooklyn."

She winked, opened her mouth, wide—in imitation, Sam supposed, of Marilyn Monroe—and turned around, shaking her butt back into the kitchen. "Terrific," Shimmy said. "You got a terrific girl there, Max." He paused. "You still have fifty-one per cent of the shares, right?"

"Tell me," Max asked Shimmy, "for a hobby, do you still sniff bicycle seats?"

The guys groaned. Sid touched Sam on the arm. "Do you play the market?" he asked. Max and Shimmy continued to rank one another out.

"No," Sam said.

"Well, if you did, now's the time to buy," Sid said. "You can get some good prices on solid stocks."

"I don't agree," Herbie said. "It looks bad to me. With money tight, everybody I know is crying. Thank God, me and Ruthie, we don't have to sell—we can wait till the market comes back up—but a lot of people are getting hurt."

"Of course," Sid said. "If you live over your head. But I look at the market as an investment—not as a gamble." He turned to Sam. "I know that goes against your grain, Sammy, but I'll tell you something, every morning when I pick up the *Times* and turn to the stock page and look at mine, I get a genuine thrill—just like following a team, if you know what I mean."

"Well, without us pricks," Shimmy was saying to Max. "Where would you cocksuckers be—?"

"Keeping your savings in the bank," Sid said. "What with inflation—you have to have your head examined—"

Sam began laughing at that, and Shimmy patted him on the back. "You're terrific, Sammy—and you too, Dutch—don't you think, guys, we should give them medals for staying behind in Brooklyn and guarding the schoolyard!"

"Cut it out," Dutch said.

"But I'll bet they pick up a lot of"—Max paused—"of local color."

"I'm serious," Shimmy said. "I mean, I have to go back there now, for business. I know. It takes a kind of—bravery, I'd call it—not to move out." The table was quiet. "Sure," Shimmy continued, seriously. "All of us—we do okay, but we run away from the problems. Dutch and Sammy, they're sticking it out—"

"A lot you know," Sam said, and stood up.

"Sure," Nate said. "I'm in midtown a lot. They think they own the city now. They're always bumping into you, daring you to say something. And believe me, I tell them where to get off." Sam was surprised; Nate rarely spoke so much. "Sure," Nate went on. "You know how I'd take care of the problem—with one big bomb, that's how."

Shimmy shrugged, spread his hands, palms up. "Nathan," he said, admonishing his friend. "And what would that do to *my* property?"

"I get your point," Nate said. "Yeah. You got the right idea, Shimmy—take what you can from them, and run. Because that's just what they'd do to us. Ask Sam—I'll bet he knows."

Sam shrugged. "They leave me alone," he said.

"Sam's father—Ben—he calls it a neighborhood in transition," Dutch offered.

Sam glared at Dutch, turned, left the room. "If they're so undernourished," he heard Max saying, "then how come they grow so big is what I want to know—"

Sam walked down the corridor, into the bedroom, went into the bathroom. He'd eaten more than he'd wanted to. As he shook himself off, he watched his face in the mirror of the medicine chest. Carpeted wastebaskets—that took brains!

He stepped back, zipped his fly, unlocked the door. "I thought I saw you come this way." Susie was sitting on the bed. Her slacks, bell-bottomed, were made out of a gold mesh material. Sid had met her at college, out of town, at Syracuse University, but she was from Brooklyn too, he knew—had gone to Tilden High School.

"How's tricks?" Sam asked.

"Listen," she said, standing, drawing in on a filter-tipped cigarette and letting the smoke trail upward, toward the hanging lantern. "I didn't want Sid to know . . ." She looked straight into Sam's eyes, and Sam returned the look. She wasn't a world-beater, but she was all right. Sam didn't mind plain girls. She had a sweet smile and a good body. Her ass was a little heavy, but that, as they said, came in handy sometimes. "Would you take a number of a girl—a friend—if I gave it to you?"

"Sure," Sam said.

Susie laughed, touched Sam's forearm with her hand. The room seemed to be glowing, in a soft red color, from the bedspread. "I know you'd take it, but would you *use* it?"

Sam shrugged. "I got things on my mind now. I couldn't promise, Susie. Why not try Dutch?"

"He's your friend, isn't he?" She rubbed her cigarette out in a black ashtray, next to the bed. "I mean, your best friend."

"I guess," Sam said.

"How can I put it so that you won't—" She licked her upper lip. "From what Sid says, Dutch has his—well, his ups and his downs."

"Things are rough all over," Sam said, and looked toward the door.

"Here," Susie said, and, from under the wide black leather belt that held her tunic tight at her waist, she pulled a folded piece of paper, and handed it to Sam. He slipped it into his shirt pocket without looking at it. "I'll leave it to you. One thing you should know, though—then come, we wouldn't want to be caught here, or everyone would start asking why—is that Gail, she was a friend from college, was married. In fact, her divorce has gone through recently. I thought you should know."

"Sure," Sam said. "I can understand something like that."

"She's a tough girl, though," Susie said. "And cute." She took Sam's arm. The sleeve of her tunic, made of a flimsy silk material, with a sheen to it, slid sideways against the muscle of his arm. "I think you two would hit it off. I have a feeling . . ."

Sam smelled Susie's perfume. He wondered how often Sid gave it to her. Her hair, at least, was its natural color: a kind of auburn. "You got to take some chances," Sam said.

Susie stopped, just outside the doorway, and looked up at him, her eyes sparkling. "That's what you do, isn't it?" she asked. The corridor was dark. Sam heard voices—the guys laughing, their wives chattering. "I mean, it must be an exciting life." Here we go again, Sam thought. Sure. All these bitches, hustling their asses through high school and college to marry dentists and doctors and guys like Shimmy and Herbie, and then they still creamed all over you because they thought you weren't like that. A lot they knew. He should introduce them all to Willie the Lump.

"Call me, all right? Tell me how it goes. Promise me that . . ." He felt the points of her breasts graze his chest. He needed air. "You'll like Gail—"

"I didn't promise anything," Sam said. Sam the Lamb, he thought, that was his real name. "You shouldn't sell Dutch short," he added.

"I didn't mean to—" Susie stepped back.

"It's okay," Sam said, and walked away, feeling better. "Don't sweat it, right? Take care of your kids."

He heard her laughter, soft. She probably thought that was rich too, the way he talked. Sure. Sam Berman Jr., king of the jock-sniffers. He sat down at the dining room table, watched the guys drinking their coffee. Nate's face was red. Sid was talking softly, explaining things about Negroes, about a Negro girl from his school whom he had helped. Sure, Sam thought, but while you're out dripping tears all over the ghettos, you'd better keep a lock on your bedroom. Nate was getting angrier and angrier. Sid sat in his chair, cradling a pipe in the palm of his hand. "I'll tell you this," Nate said, pointing a finger. The guy, Sam could tell, still had plenty of power; under his shirt, above his pot belly, Sam could see that his chest was broad. Sam looked at Nate's neck. It was still wide, coming down directly from under his ears, without any indentation. The guy had been a *bulvan*—third-team All-City, and that on sheer hustle; there were a lot of guys with better shots and moves, but Nate would have gone through a brick wall if the coach had asked him to. Sam gave him credit. "My aunts and uncles—my mother's brothers and sisters—they didn't die in Hitler's gas chambers so that a bunch of dumb *shvartzehs* could knife my wife in the park, do you hear?"

Sid sighed. "Nate—try to calm down. You're not making any sense."

"He makes a lot of sense to me," Max said.

"But try to think of what you're saying," Sid said. "Try to put yourself in the other guy's place. You don't make sense, Nate."

Nate laughed, and waved a hand at Sid. "You want sense, Sid? I'll give you sense. Did it make sense for six million Jews to die in the ovens—answer me that!"

Sid knocked ashes from his pipe. "Look, Nate, first of all, you're confusing your personal emotions with—"

Nate sat back, shook his head sideways. "No, Sid. I don't buy it—you don't fool me with your fancy talk. Personal? Tell me, if you're so bighearted—did our mothers and fathers sweat their guts out in Brooklyn so that some day a dumb boogie could knock up your daughter? Does that make sense? Tell me that!"

"I understand how you feel," Sid said, leaning across the table, tapping his pipe on an ashtray. "Believe me, I really do. But—if you could try to get a little distance on yourself—if you could try to see how the other guy feels—"

"The only distance I want is between my family and them," Nate said. "We suffered enough." He lifted his left arm and showed it to everybody. "I still put *tephillin* on every morning—do you understand what that means, with all your high-faluting theories, do you?"

Herbie put his hand on Nate's arm. "Relax, relax—Sid's not attacking you, Nate. We all know about your aunts and uncles— and Sid's not defending what the *shvartzehs* do, either—are you, Sid?"

"Of course not," Sid said, quickly. "But there are reasons sometimes . . ."

Sam remembered sitting in the balcony of the Granada Theater with Ben, just after the war, and seeing a newsreel of skeletonlike bodies that were supposed to be people. Ben said they were Jews. A bulldozer picked up bundles of them. Nate was like that, on the court: a bulldozer. The words separated suddenly, and Sam was confused. Like a bull—that made sense, but why, if it had so much power, like a *sleeping* bull? Sam wondered if Nate had ever seen pictures of them, near the end. Since high school, Nate had worked with his father; they owned a small plant in Queens—Woodside— that manufactured buttons. "Did you hear about the *shvartzeh* who went into the drugstore to order some film—and beat up the druggist?" Shimmy asked.

Sid turned at once toward Shimmy—relieved, Sam could see. Nate didn't seem interested. "Why'd you all beat up that druggist-man?" Max asked.

Shimmy turned on the accent: "Why dat man—he had de nerve to ask me what size box mah Brownie had!"

Everybody laughed. "Terrific," Sid said to Shimmy. "I don't know where you get them all. Terrific." Herbie turned to Nate, who was still scowling, and Sid shifted in his chair, spoke to Sam: "Tell me," he said. "How's your father been—still driving his cab?"

"Where've you been hiding?" Sam asked. "He gave that up six–seven years ago."

"That's right—of course." Sam saw that Sid's hand was trembling. Well, he supposed he'd have been shaken up also if he'd gotten into that kind of fight with Nate. Not a fight, really—but it made you feel responsible somehow just to have the subject brought up. Not that anybody could have done anything for Nate, and not that you couldn't understand the way he felt. It was as if somehow you'd invaded his life. Sam understood that. There were things you had that you didn't want anybody stepping on, that was all. If Nate wanted to put on *tephillin* every day—if it meant something to him—that was his business and nobody had a right to take it away from him. "He had that school, didn't he, and then—"

"He lives on social security now," Sam said. "He gets by." He considered, decided: let it out this way, he figured, and be done with it. "But he'll be moving out soon—to a senior citizen place in California, to live with his brother Andy."

"You know," Shimmy said. "I could have given you a lift tonight—I was in Brooklyn. I didn't think."

Herbie was standing, in the doorway to the kitchen. He held something in his hand. "My parents—they've bought into a condominium in Florida," Sid said. "They won't go there for another few years—till my dad retires—but I think it's a wise move. We'll miss them, of course—the kids are terribly devoted—but with the weather, and the way their neighborhood is changing—"

"In transition?" Dutch asked.

"I could have given you a lift," Shimmy said. "I didn't think."

Sam saw the deck of cards in Herbie's hand. I'm Lady Luck, Stella had said to him, when she'd telephoned and he'd told her that the game hadn't come off, the night it snowed. He looked at Dutch, and saw that Dutch had seen the cards also. Sam stood. "We better get going," he said, looking at his watch. "With the way the trains run, we won't get back to Brooklyn till early morning."

"You don't want to be walking the streets alone there," Max

said. "When you get to Atlantic Avenue, take a taxi. Don't wait around on the corner for the bus."

"We were just going to start a card game," Herbie said. "Nickel-dime—"

"I'm sorry," Dutch said, standing also, and joining Sam at the doorway to the corridor. "I told you guys about what happened." Sam felt Dutch's shoulder touching his own.

Sam shook his head. "I—we never play for money with friends. You know that."

Ruth and Marge cleared the table. Marge, Nate's wife, was, by far, the best-looking of all the wives, a tall hefty blonde—*zaftig*—who'd done part-time modeling when she'd been in high school.

"You forget," Shimmy said, to himself. "All those games we used to have in Sid's basement—"

"That was fifteen years ago," Sam said.

"Before he turned pro," Dutch added, and the guys nodded their heads. Sam saw each of them looking at him. That was something, he supposed: that his old buddies all thought he led a special life. He bet that they bragged about him to guys they worked with, to their neighbors on Long Island. Sure. What they didn't know didn't hurt them.

"Why don't I take you down, then," Herbie said. "There's a train in about fifteen minutes—the next one after that is an hour later." He put the deck of cards on the table. "You guys can start without me."

"I could have given you a lift, coming out," Shimmy said, taking out his wallet, and putting some bills on the table. "But we head straight over the bridges going back: Throgs Neck and then the George Washington. I could drop you off at the IRT stop near the George Washington if—"

"It's quicker this way," Herbie explained. "I'll just run them down. I don't mind."

"I'm glad to hear about your father," Sid said, shaking Sam's hand. "I think it's the best move—for him, and for you too, Ace."

He chipped Sam on the shoulder with his fist. Sam heard the women in the kitchen, discussing their children. Marge's older daughter, in the second grade now, still had a urinary problem she would have to have a series of operations for. A girl from the sixth grade—a neighbor's child—came for her at school, every hour, to take her to the bathroom. Sam heard Ruth ask about the kind of sack Marge's daughter had to use, about how it was attached, and then he heard the sound of the dishwasher. He heard Nate and Max discussing their baby sitters.

The guys told Sam and Dutch how great it had been seeing them again. Shimmy stood, took Sam around the shoulder and said they'd be seeing one another, Sam should wait, he shouldn't be obstinate, he should listen to Shimmy's offer. Dutch was saying something to Sid about his mother. Nate and Max shook hands with them. To his old buddies, he supposed, he was still Sam the Man. They were still proud of him, of the way his life had turned out. Damn that Sabatini, though: if only he didn't have to play the teams, if only he could get some decent card games. He walked into the living room, said good-bye to the women. Susie winked at him, Lillian played it cool, Dutch made a wisecrack that had the girls laughing, but Sam didn't catch it. They thanked Susie for the food. Sure. One game a night for just one year and he'd be on easy street forever . . . he and Dutch could retire, get themselves a fancy bachelor flat down in Florida somewhere, where the baseball teams came for spring training, where there was always a supply of long-legged chicks.

In the car, Herbie spoke about each of the guys in turn, about how well they were all doing, and about himself, about a trip to Paris he and Ruthie would get to take the following winter at company expense: a buying trip for the store. "I'd go in with Shimmy if I were you," Herbie said. "It's a chance in a lifetime. Nobody knows how much he's raking in, but it's in six figures easily. Even with a few good tips on the market, none of us is ever gonna see that kind of money."

Dutch turned around, faced Sam. "What's this about?" he asked.

"Five'll get you ten," Sam replied.

Dutch rolled his eyes. "I see what you mean," he said.

"There," Herbie said, pointing to the right. "That's the big shopping center—Roosevelt Field—Ruthie gets her stuff there, for decorating. 'I'm fortunate with Fortunoff's,' that's what she says."

"I guess Shimmy's really what you'd call—well, prospering," Dutch said.

Sam flinched at the word. He heard the silk voice: *He that covereth his sins shall not prosper.* He watched the lights along Old

Country Road, the diners and gas stations and motels, and laughed to himself. "What's up?" Dutch asked.

"I thought of something good," Sam said.

"You know," Herbie said, "There's a plaque in the middle of the shopping center, to show you where Lindbergh took off from on his trip to Paris. It used to all be an airfield."

"We've been here before," Dutch said. "To come to the track."

They arrived at the station in Westbury five minutes before the train was scheduled to arrive. Herbie parked in front of the Westbury Animal Hospital, across from the elevated tracks; he reached behind, took Sam's hand in both of his. "It's been great, Ace—we'll get together again soon." Sam unlocked the doors of the station wagon. Herbie was shaking Dutch's hand. "You guys are looking terrific—in top shape. Give my regards to Garfield's."

Sam and Dutch walked across the street. Herbie honked the horn of his car, then drove off. Sam and Dutch walked inside the station and up the steps. In a corner of the waiting room, a girl with long brown hair was necking with a man. Sam couldn't see what the guy looked like. Most of the people in the waiting room were, to Sam's surprise, blacks. It figured. They were going to have their problems on Long Island too, before long. No matter how much they paid for their houses.

"I need some air," Dutch said, opening the door. They walked a little way down the platform, then leaned back against the railing, waiting for their train to come. They didn't say anything to each other for a minute or so, and then Dutch asked Sam what it was he'd been laughing about, in the back seat.

Sam nodded, to himself. He'd been thinking of Sid, just then, when Dutch had asked him the question. "All these guys playing the stock market," Sam said, and he clicked with his tongue. "I got one question for you, right?" He saw Dutch smiling broadly. In the dim light of the lamp posts on the platform, Dutch looked handsomer than ever. Sam bet that the wives had talked about him, and that, if their husbands had the energy left to give it to them when they got home, it would be Dutch's face the wives would see, when their eyes were closed and they were moaning. "Tell me this," Sam said. "What the fuck are pork belly futures anyway?"

8

They were lost, Sam knew, and had been lost for some time. Flo's arm, linked in his, pressed against his side. Several steps in front of them, Ben and Tidewater were walking arm in arm, Ben having to take three steps to Tidewater's two. They had been walking all morning, in Ben's and Tidewater's old neighborhood, but they had yet to find anything familiar—not their houses nor their playing fields nor the schools they'd gone to. It didn't matter to Sam, though. He believed in nothing now. He spoke when he was spoken to, as he had all morning, but he wasn't, the way he figured things, obligated to believe in any of it. He watched them, he listened to them, but what they did and what they said, and the reasons they gave—it was all the same to him.

"I'm cold," Flo said as they passed the entrance to a live poultry market. "Ben—" she called ahead.

Ben stopped and waited. Sam saw water tearing from his father's eyes, behind his glasses. Tidewater stood straight, his pale skin revealing, in the cold air, the lavender veins beneath. A scarlet muffler was wrapped around his throat, and though Sam had to look up at him slightly, to see the guy's eyes, he realized that the man did, in the street—away from the rummage shop—seem to be what he was: just another old man, not even an especially tall one.

"I'm cold and hungry," Flo said.

"Soon," Ben said. "We'll stop and eat. I promise."

"Mason will catch cold," Flo insisted. She shivered. Along sides of the street, store front windows were boarded up. On the sidewalk, behind Tidewater, a rusting fender lay in a pool of oil. Sam saw an old woman sitting at a window, two stories above them, in a building in which all the other windows were gone. Her wrinkled face, watching them, reminded him of the face of the green-stamp woman.

"Maybe it was a foolish idea, wanting to return," Mason said. "It's all so changed, so—"

"We'll find it," Ben insisted. "You'll see—just a little farther. We're bound to stumble upon some landmark."

"It's all so changed," Mason repeated, to himself.

Ben clung to Mason's arm, for warmth, and looked around. At the corner, a man was stuffing his garbage into a mailbox. In the alcove of an abandoned store, two men, their legs and hands wrapped in monstrous balls of rags, huddled close to one another, a bottle of Thunderbird at the lips of one. Ben laughed. "This," he declared, "is what I would call—" and he paused, for effect "—a neighborhood which has already transished."

"Come," Flo said, pulling on Sam's arm. "We shouldn't stand in one place. We'll stay warm if we keep moving."

They walked again, following Ben's lead, and Sam didn't protest. He could, he thought, have made a list of the things people expected you to believe: Ben's reasons for leaving, Dutch's reasons for having stopped gambling, his Bible man's story, Simon's lies, Mr. Sabatini's line about selling apples. He had felt, in fact, ever since the night of the snowstorm, not so much as if he were passing time, but as if he were marking it; it pleased him, the feeling that he was there, walking, speaking when he was spoken to, even feeling sad about Ben's departure, and that it was the others now who were merely going through the motions. If they couldn't fool him, they couldn't touch him.

"Stella will be there," Flo said, "when we return."

Sam said nothing. There were some stores left on the street they walked along now: a laundromat, a grocery, a used furniture store. A black woman, one leg swollen with elephantiasis, limped to the curb and sat down, to wait for a bus. Since they had gotten off the train two and a half hours before, Sam had not, he realized, seen a single white face. Ben stopped again. "This is familiar," he declared. "I remember something about this street."

Sam looked around. In an empty lot, across from them, a group of old men were huddled around a chimney. The chimney—it had once been, Sam realized, a fireplace in a home, but the home was gone—rose for several stories, a line of smoke trailing from it. "They're cooking in it," Flo commented.

"You might say," Ben said, his eyes wandering the length of the red brick chimney, "that things are stacked against them."

"Ah Ben," Tidewater said, and color returned to his cheeks.

"Unlucky in cards, lucky in love," Flo whispered to Sam. "Isn't that the way it goes?"

"Our house sat on a lot like that," Tidewater said. "With an enormous fireplace, on the first floor. My father's greatest pleasure in life, while we lived there, came at what he referred to as our Sunday *soirées*, during which we would recite the Latin poems we had memorized during the week—he would not teach us grammar; we learned sounds only, and some meanings. Then we would play the pieces we were learning, and, when this was done, my mother would sit down and ask him what his request was. Severe and classic as he thought himself, his favorite pieces were Schumann's romantic *Scènes d'Enfance*." They stood in a circle, their breath steaming in clouds. "The fire would be blazing, my brothers and Elizabeth would—" He broke off, looked down at Ben. "It was worth the journey, to remember that."

At the far corner, where an oil truck was double-parked, a man ran across the street, a pistol raised above his head. Sam pushed Flo and his father away from the curb and toward the building. Two boys—about thirteen years old—ran across the vacant lot, swinging a portable television set between them. The old men at the chimney looked their way, but did nothing.

"Inventory shrinkage," Ben said.

"What?" Sam asked, and he remembered what he had thought in the supermarket, looking at Ben's nose and ears.

"It's what they write off stolen goods to," Ben said. "Many of our finest department stores and best-run supermarkets are having trouble these days with inventory shrinkage. The cautious client . . ."

"Come on," Sam said. "Save it. Flo said she's cold."

"It's appropriate, though," Ben said to Tidewater. "Living when we do with so many people using psychologists and psychiatrists—you might say that we live in a shrink-age."

Tidewater groaned, but he was, Sam saw, pleased. Sam jerked his arm forward, and saw Flo glance at him. Damn! He didn't want her to see his annoyance, but the walking and the cold were getting to him. He shouldn't have agreed to come, he knew, but he hadn't really had a choice—if he wanted to keep Ben from bugging him. "There—!" Ben declared suddenly, and he pointed down the street. "There!"

The evening with the guys had made a difference, Sam admitted to himself. If, from now on, he saw them once a year, that would be plenty, despite what they had all said. He could understand why Tidewater seemed pleased by Ben's attentions to him, his word games. Sure. Sometimes you wanted to hold on to what was left, even if what was left was only a memory. Sam wouldn't—he laughed at the word—tax his own memory. It wouldn't do much good, the deficit he was working at. But with his money about gone, Ben finally leaving, his friends living their new lives outside Brooklyn, and Dutch flying off on his theories again—there wouldn't be much left for him to believe in, except Sabatini's voice and Tidewater's words, and he knew how much they were worth.

"It's my *shul*—the synagogue I went to, with my father—your grandfather, Samela." Ben's voice was suddenly high-pitched, like a boy's. "I told you I'd find something. Come. We'll ask directions. We'll stop for a minute and get warm."

They crossed the street, Ben, excited, pulling Tidewater along. The synagogue—Congregation Shaare Shamayim—was a small brown brick building, wedged between two abandoned apartment houses. Sam mounted the steps to the entrance, behind his father and Tidewater. Above the iron doors, in stained glass, he saw lions and Jewish stars. Flo held tight to his arm.

Ben reached forward to pull the handle of the door, but before he could it had opened, and a man stood there, smiling. Sam stopped. "We're . . ." Ben began, stepping backward. "We're lost."

The man was no more than five feet tall, dressed in black: a squarish black *yamulka* on his head, a long black coat, black pants, black shoes. His dark beard swirled about his cheeks and fell in curls to his waist. Only his eyes—greenish-brown—had color, and they sparkled as he laughed. "And I'm not?" he said.

Sam watched Ben's mouth. It hung open, in astonishment. "You're Rabbi Katimsky!" Ben exclaimed, and his hand groped for Tidewater's arm. He steadied himself. "I remember you from when I was a child. But—"

"I am Rabbi Katimsky," the man said, and his eyes laughed again. He emerged from the doorway and stepped down to the landing where Ben and Tidewater stood.

"You must be the son," Ben said. He turned to Sam and Flo. "He looks just like his father. If I didn't know—" Ben broke off, breathing hard. "You must be your father's—Rabbi Katimsky's son."

The Rabbi smiled. "I am Rabbi Katimsky," he said again. "May I help you?"

Ben shrugged. "We're lost," he said, and Sam saw his father look down, unsure. "What I mean to say is, I once lived here—I was bar mitzvahed in this *shul,* my father prayed here." Ben waited, but the Rabbi said nothing. "We were looking for the house I grew up in." He gestured to Tidewater. "Where *we* grew up—my friend is from the neighborhood too—when I spotted your *shul.*"

The Rabbi smiled. "Yes?" he said, as if he expected Ben to say more.

"We were thinking you might give us directions—it's why we stopped."

The Rabbi was, Sam saw, enjoying himself. "They tell me that's my job—to give directions in life."

"Look," Sam said. "We're cold. We don't have time for—"

"Yes?" the Rabbi asked.

"I mean they're older than I am," Sam added, indicating the others.

The Rabbi closed his eyes, let his chin drop to his chest, as if he had made a decision. "Are you Jewish?" he asked, speaking to Tidewater.

"No," Tidewater said.

Ben forced a laugh. "Look, Rabbi Katimsky—being friends with me for so many years, growing up here—he might just as well have been." Ben paused, saw that the Rabbi found no humor in the remark. "What I mean is, if you knew about his life, you'd—"

"Then we still wouldn't have a *minyan*," the Rabbi said. He spoke to Tidewater, wearily, as if lecturing a child. "In our faith, you see, we need to have ten adult Jewish males, above the age of thirteen, in order to hold a service. If you were Jewish, along with the other two—the father and son, yes?—we would have ten, but without you we have only nine. There's no point in telephoning the others. I'm sorry. Believe me."

"Come on," Sam said. "Let's get out of here. I didn't pay to listen to this kind of—"

"One minute," Ben said to Sam. He spoke louder: "Howard Street," he stated.

"Yes?"

"It's the street we lived on, when we were boys together."

"Maybe it's there, maybe it's gone," the Rabbi said. "I don't get out much anymore." He chuckled to himself, then pointed to either side, to the street. "You see what things are like, but I'll tell you the truth, I don't mind—it gives me all my time to devote to Torah. My pulpit, as we say in the trade, is a scholar's dream." He sniffed in and his head dipped backward, his eyes closing. He hummed to himself in the way Sam remembered his grandfather humming. Then his eyes opened and they flashed pale green light in Sam's direction. "Listen to this, as long as you stopped: in the *midrash* I was studying when you interrupted me, the rabbis are telling a story of two men who are wandering in the desert when they discover that they have seven days of traveling left with enough food and water for only one man for seven days. It is an absolute certainty that, if they share the food and water, neither of them will reach their destination alive. What, the rabbis ask, is the man who possesses the food and water to do? Should he continue to share it with his companion, knowing that, if he does, neither of them will make it, or must he take the food and water for himself and let his fellow man die?"

"Take it himself." Sam heard the words and knew that he had spoken them.

"No!" Flo cried, her fingers digging into his muscle, through layers of clothes.

"Samela," his father said, as if reproaching him. Ben's eyes, behind his glasses, were watering. Sam would not look into Tidewater's face.

"Forget it," Sam said. "It was just what came into my head, when you asked. That's all."

The Rabbi's voice was stronger, "But you are right, my son. The rabbis conclude, reluctantly, that the man with the food has the obligation—the duty before the Almighty—to keep the food and water for himself, and thereby to survive, and live." Inside, Sam groaned, and cursed himself for having let the words out. "For life itself, according to our teachings, is the highest good—the *summum bonum*—and we must learn to serve it." His head dropped, and he glanced at Tidewater. "We Jews believe in this world," he said. "Let the *goyim* believe in the next."

"Howard Street," Ben said again, an edge to his voice—angry, Sam thought, for the way the Rabbi had addressed Tidewater.

"I'm sorry," Rabbi Katimsky said, his voice suddenly soft and weak. "I wish I could help you, but I don't get out much anymore." He put his palms to his cheeks and rolled his head from one side to the other. "Forgive me! I rant and I rave and—but when do I have a congregation, how often do I . . . ?" He put his hands out, taking one of Ben's gloved hands in his own. "I'm glad you came back. God bless you." He kissed Ben's hand with his lips and Sam moved down a step. "Others forget. You don't mind, do you—that I spoke to you of what I was reading, that I gave you one little parable?" He shuffled backward. "I hope you find what you are looking for—but be careful." He stood inside the synagogue, and his gentle laughter sounded suddenly sweet. "Why, after all, be a rabbi if you can't speak in riddles from time to time, yes? If you want to send a contribution it will be gratefully accepted."

The iron door closed, noiselessly. "Come," Flo said. "I'm getting dizzy from hunger."

"I'm sorry," Ben said to Tidewater.

"Am I wrong," Tidewater said to Ben, "or didn't he look something like your own father—?"

"I didn't like him," Flo said in Sam's ear. Ben and Tidewater were in front of them again, walking arm in arm, away from the synagogue. "What he made you say."

"I look out for number one," Sam said. "You worry about yourself." His eyes moved down, and he saw how red Flo's nose was. He heard Ben and Tidewater talking about Sam's grandfather, and Sam remembered the man's eyes, when he would sit in the living room, hour after hour, doing nothing. In truth, the eyes had never seemed sad to Sam. "I mean, living by yourself like that, with all those books, it can do things to a guy—"

"I'm glad you'll be staying—when Ben leaves. It means a lot to Mason, to have somebody to share things with."

"Sure," Sam said, and he wondered, remembering how he'd felt when he was in Herbie's house, unable, really, to say much to any of the guys, why it was that fifty years of knowing one another would bind Ben and Tidewater so tightly. He could understand that it would, of course—if he never saw Herbie or Shimmy or Sid or the others until the day they were covered up, he knew he'd still feel for them as if he'd known them every day for a lifetime—but he didn't understand, exactly, why things worked out that way. Especially since—he couldn't dispute the Rabbi there—he believed what he did about giving anything away, when it was a question of you or them.

They walked for a few minutes, and then Ben announced that he and Tidewater had decided to give up. It was too cold, they'd been out too long, they were hungry. On the next street, they went inside a small luncheonette, ordered sandwiches and tea, and warmed themselves; Ben and Tidewater seemed, as they talked and laughed about their adventure, more relaxed with each other than they had been for a long time, and Sam found that he enjoyed listening to them. They talked about their homes, their families, their schools, and they named the things they shared: their age, their place of birth, their youth together; the fame they had both sought, the talents they had possessed, the lost years during which they had not seen one another. "Your father was wonderful," Tidewater said to Sam as they were drinking tea. "I remember, in class, how I admired him—how I wished I could trade all my athletic abilities for his voice, for his way with words." Tidewater laughed easily and loosened the scarf from around his thin neck. "Do you remember the time in our first year of high school—it is, in my memory, your finest moment—when, for your mischief, Dr. Rabinowitz tried to humiliate you before the rest of us?" Ben smiled, sipped his tea. " 'You brat,' he declared. 'You bum, Berman. You ungrateful lout. You scum of the earth.' " The two men laughed together and Sam found himself smiling. "And then your father, from the back of the classroom, rose from his seat—all five foot two inches of him—and, his face red with rage, a red which I must believe now was forced, an actor's red—pointing to Dr. Rabinowtiz, whom we hated above all others, as much for his fancy airs as for his meanness, your father, as if sputtering with helplessness, declared: 'You—you *pedagogue!*' "

Ben feigned humility, as if accepting applause. "Time wounds all heels," he said in explanation.

They laughed again. Sam laughed with them, looked out through the luncheonette window at a mailman across the street, walking side by side with a policeman. The mailman probably had the welfare checks, Sam thought, or the social security checks. "He's talking about you," Flo whispered, nudging Sam.

"I wasn't daydreaming," Sam said. "Just looking at—"

"Of course not," Ben said with affection. "That's just my point. I was telling Mason how you followed in my footsteps, in your own way—how they called me down to school because they couldn't figure you out." Sam wanted to stop his father, to tell him to stick to his own life, but, with Ben in form the way he was, he knew he wouldn't stand a chance, trying to use words against him. "When you were in the eighth grade, remember?—they called me down. What they couldn't fathom, they said, were your lapses. How you could, at times, seem to have the most remarkable memory—the best powers of concentration of any student in the school, and then—you'd have what the guidance counselor called lapses: you wouldn't understand the simplest things. They said you were—your own words just now—too much of a daydreamer."

"That's a laugh," Sam said, but saw confusion in Flo's eyes. "I mean, I never dream at all is what—"

"But what then, when you were gazing out windows, or not paying attention to teachers, was going on in your head?"

"Nothing," Sam said.

"Of course," Ben said to the others. "It's what you said then—but were we fooled? They wanted me to seek professional help for you—but I refused. 'We need men of vision,' I told them. Isn't that—"

"Can it," Sam said, annoyed. "Nobody's interested in your—your—" He broke off. "I see what's there, that's all." He looked uneasily at Tidewater, and found that he was wondering what was going on in the guy's head, which part of his story he was trying to transfer into Sam's head at that moment. "If you're finished, let's go."

Sam stood, went to the coat rack. He heard Ben talking about his gift to him, about fading in and fading out, but he saw no reason to listen to him. If he'd wanted to, he could have seen the entire day—the journey—as Ben's way of getting around to this, and of doing it in front of Tidewater and Flo, but he didn't, he knew, have to take things that far. And he didn't, he warned himself, have to let himself get worked up. Ben played that way, saving things up, and Sam knew where it had gotten him. He put a dollar bill next to his father's cup. "Like the rabbi says, we each . . ." But he couldn't find a way of finishing. "I'll wait outside. Take your time."

On the street again, he found that he wasn't even angry with Ben. If they wanted to stay there forever, sipping tea and reliving every minute they'd ever spent together—like Max and Shimmy and Dutch, he thought, always acting as if nothing had changed when the truth was, everything had changed—it was all the same to him. Men of vision—that was really rich, except that, Sam recalled, at the time he'd connected his father's phrase with his own eyesight— with his ability to read the titles on records as they spun around. But one way or the other, Ben had helped him—he admitted that; after Ben had come to school that one time, they'd never bothered him again. Maybe, he thought, he should send Ben to speak with Sabatini.

Later, when they emerged from the IRT subway at Church Avenue, Ben asked Sam to go with him to the supermarket: they could buy some of the things for Ben's farewell party, they could get some cold cuts and all have supper together. In front of Flo and Tidewater, Sam saw no way to refuse.

They walked down the aisles, Ben pushing a cart, dropping items in the basket. Ben seemed calm, and Sam was in truth glad now, despite everything, that he had agreed to go with his father on the trip. It would have been worse, he knew, if Ben had gone without him and he'd had to listen to the story afterward. "The Rabbi," Ben said quietly. "He looked so much like the Rabbi Katimsky I remember . . ."

The store was crowded, noisy. Sam let his mind drift. "Your grandfather was a Zionist," Ben said, "but when I tried to tell him once that Theodor Herzl himself, the founder of Zionism, had been willing to settle Jews in Argentina or Central Africa, he refused to listen to me. He came to America dreaming of Palestine." Their cart half-full, Sam nudged his father aside and did the pushing. "What I'm getting at is this: why shouldn't the Jews buy a section of California—or Florida—and never worry about Arabs and hijacking again?"

"I don't blame you for going," Sam said. "I told you before."

"I was imagining it this morning—Katimsky telling me that he was living in Africa already, but . . ." Ben held Sam's arm. "I shouldn't try so hard, should I? But I'd like—" His voice was low, intense. "I'd like to give you things you could remember—it's why I asked you to come with us this morning, why I try to be clever, with theories and—"

Sam heard a wild screech. In front of the meat department he saw packages fly in the air. "Forgive me," Ben was still saying. "I'm happy that—" Sam saw an old woman in a long gray coat, her nails in the face of one of the butchers, blood under her fingers. The butcher tried to cover his face. Sam pulled hard—Ben's grip had become stronger—and in a few steps he was there, grabbing the woman's arms. Packages of ground beef were scattered on the floor, shopping carts converged on them. "Him! Him! . . . It's him! Him! Him! . . ." the woman cried. Her voice rose, her nails tore strips from the man's face.

"Please," the butcher whimpered. "Please." Sam pried at the woman's wrists, but she was hanging on for life. Her eyes protruded from great hollow sockets, her jaw trembled. "Him! It's him!"

Sam let go of one wrist, used both hands on the woman's other one. He knew what adrenaline could do, when a person was excited. He heard another old lady shriek. "Murder!" she cried. Two of the store managers, in white shirts and striped ties, were on the woman's other arm. A short man—not Ben—his own wife's arms around his waist, was tugging at the woman from the middle. The other woman wept. "*Gottenyu*! Stop, darling . . . *Genug* . . . Ethel, darling . . . Ethel . . . somebody stop her please!" The old woman hung on, tears streaming down her face, her mouth open so wide that Sam could see the back of her throat.

"Him! . . . Him . . . him . . ." She seemed frozen. "From the camp—!" she blurted, and with this, her grip loosened. Sam pried one hand off, and when the woman tried to move forward again, he held her.

The butcher backed away, and Sam saw the red splotches on his apron. The man's hands stayed across his eyes. "Are you all right, William?" one of the store managers asked. The old woman wailed, and when her friend threw her arms around her, Sam let go. The two women sobbed, their bodies pumping in great bursts.

"Thanks, mister," a voice said to Sam.

The old woman's friend tried to explain: "She says he was there, in an office, checking suitcases—"

The butcher walked off, led by one of the managers. Blood trickled from under his fingers. "She's crazy—I didn't do nothing. She's crazy. I work hard."

"It's all a mistake, folks," the manager said. "She must be mistaken. He's been with us for years—a fine man, with—"

"It's him . . ." the woman sobbed. "Oh! Him . . . him." Then she broke down again, mumbling in Yiddish. Sam pushed through the crowd. Some of the women—black and white—were crying, handkerchiefs at their eyes. Above full shopping carts, old men nodded their heads sadly.

Sam looked for Ben, but he wasn't in the meat department. He heard the manager saying that he could prove things, that he'd call for a doctor. "It's him," the woman repeated. Sam was breathing hard—he saw a hand, and realized that Ben was, at a checkout register, waving to him.

Sam stood at his father's side while a boy rang their groceries up, then packed them in two shopping bags. "You take that one, sonny boy—with cans—and I'll take the light one." He smiled. "Everybody left to see what the excitement was."

Outside, people were going the other way, through the entrance, to see what had happened. Ben patted his coat pockets. His voice was low, confident. "While the attention of the crowd was turned to the attack on Bel-Air's ace butcher, Ben Berman saw his chance at once, and—"

"No," Sam said, sharply. "No."

"But I've explained," Ben said. "And I did it more for you—how will I ever use all this up in a week? You bring me luck, Sam Junior. You—"

But Sam walked fast, the bag cradled in his arm, forgetting his father, thinking of the wish he'd made in Simon's apartment: for his life to go more slowly. He crossed against the light, between cars, cans jiggling against his chest. When he arrived at the store, Flo opened the door for him. Sam saw women shopping, Tidewater pushing a piece of furniture across the back room. "She's here," Flo said, her cheeks flushed. Sam stepped inside, keeping the shopping bag in his arm. He looked out the window, but couldn't see Ben. "I asked her to come while I was away."

Sam looked down, saw Stella's face, smiling at him. She sat in a regular chair—not a wheelchair—and her hands were resting on the checkout table. Sam wondered why he hadn't seen her from outside, or when he'd come in. He felt the anger inside him rise again. "Somebody had to watch the store," Flo said.

"Sure," Sam said, and he nodded to Stella. "I mean, it's good to see you again, but I got to get upstairs and—"

"Of course you do," Flo said. "I see Ben coming now. You go on."

Stella could, he knew, tell that he was confused, uncomfortable. He was glad at least that she said nothing—that she hadn't been the one to give out the old line about somebody watching the store. But it didn't mean that he was obliged to hang around, to have Ben start in on everything that had happened. "I'll see that Stella gets home all right," Flo said, "and then Mason and I will be up to—"

"We bought the food," Sam said, and felt foolish. Flo led him to the door. He looked at Stella and smiled weakly, gesturing with his shoulders—as if explaining to her that there was nothing more to say.

"Sure," she said, and laughed. "Good-bye and good luck, Sam."

Her laugh made something in him relax. "Sure," he repeated, without wondering about what was going on in Flo's head. "Good-bye and good luck."

The following morning, alone in the apartment, Sam thought of Stella. Outside, he knew, if he'd wanted to look, the line of shoppers probably stretched to the corner. She had been prettier than he'd remembered her. But it was, of course, easy to see himself with a

girl like that: like trying to imagine what guys like Gehrig or
Campanella or Stallworth had felt when things had been darkest.
Tidewater too, Sam told himself, and as the man's pale face—as
pale as the Rabbi's—fixed itself in his mind, he recognized the
knock at the door.

"How's tricks?" he asked, letting him in; it was almost as if, he
thought, he had summoned the guy to him simply by thinking of
him.

"Good," Tidewater replied. He held a manila envelope in his
right hand, and again he seemed shy and embarrassed. "I'm not
interrupting anything, I hope. Things are going smoothly below
and—"

"Sure," Sam said, motioning Tidewater into the easy chair. "I
was just getting ready to call my stock broker. Sit down and take a
load off your mind."

"Are you feeling all right?"

"Sure," Sam said.

"You look flushed."

Sam shrugged. "I take care of myself."

"Perhaps all that walking yesterday, in the cold—"

Sam laughed, remembering, then spoke sharply: "What's on your
mind?"

"This," Tidewater said. "I'd like you to read it sometime before
your father leaves. It's the second part. You needn't say anything
when you're done—just that you've read it. I promised Ben . . ."

Sam heard the edge of bitterness slip into the man's voice. "Just
leave it," he said. "I told you I'd read whatever you wanted me to,
right?"

Tidewater placed the envelope on the kitchen table and backed
to the door. His long face bothered Sam. "I mean, I told you that
before." He could tell that the guy needed him, that he had the
upper hand, but the knowledge didn't please him. The difference—
between the guy now and the guy then—made Sam uncomfortable.
When it came down to it, he didn't really understand how a man
could be just like any other man in every way—could be less than
other men—and, in a uniform on a playing field, be so much more
than other men. He didn't doubt the guy's story, but he wondered
what the exact difference was: between the guy's life and the story
of his life. "I like sports stories," he offered.

"Ah," Tidewater said, breathing out and smiling. He stepped away from the door, back toward Sam. "If you have any questions—if there is something on your mind—" The whites of his eyes grew large. "They won't harm you," he stated. "I promise that."

"There was a Negro kid I went to public school with named Barton," Sam said. "But he wasn't a good athlete."

Tidewater held Sam's hand in his long fingers. Sam's head was blank. "It means a lot to me, your reading this—your taking over for your father."

Sam winced, and walked to the sink. "You don't have to watch over me, like—" Like Ben was what he was going to say, but he stopped himself. Tidewater too, he was certain, had made the connection: that if they were both taking Ben's place, then somebody—to use the guy's own words, about Brick Johnson—was getting into somebody else's skin. "If you're gonna run your mouth, how about some coffee?"

"No thank you," Tidewater said. "My Barton was not a great athlete either—though he was the fastest man on the team, a superb fielder who could move equally well to his right and left." Sam put water on to boil. "I used to think of Barton and Jones as twins, though Barton was short and dark, a deep nut brown color, while Jones was tall and light. But they both had scars, do you see?"

"Sure," Sam said, and while Tidewater talked on, he thought of himself and Dutch, playing baseball together at the Parade Grounds.

"Jones was our talker. He had, perhaps, even less talent than Barton, but he loved the game more than any man I knew. His lanky body was always moving, and his tongue, as he would have been the first to admit, was more restless than his body." Tidewater's finger moved swiftly across his forehead. "He had a scar three inches long—here, above his left eye—the result of sitting up too quickly one cold morning, having forgotten that, as was often the case, he and some teammates were sleeping for the night under their car." Tidewater laughed bitterly. "He felt blessed to be with us after his experiences in the southern leagues, and he kept his bankbook with him at all times, even when playing."

Sam sighed and sat down to listen. The guy's voice did, at least, replace other things in his head. "Like Jones, Barton had played from the age of fifteen in the southern leagues—he was forever expressing his gratitude for the chance given to him to play with us. Off the field he stayed so close to Jones that Johnson called him 'Little Johnny's sister.' His shins were covered with scars that seemed to fold in and reach to the bones, from what childhood illness, I never discovered." Tidewater's color in his cheeks faded, even as Sam watched him. "I never recall having had a conversation with him."

"Look," Sam said. "If you got things to take care of, I'll take a look at the story you left. You don't got to—"

Tidewater opened the door. "I'm grateful," he said. "If you have any other questions—"

Sam thought of saying that he hadn't asked one in the first place, but didn't. "Hang loose," he said, and closed the door behind the man, listened to the quiet footsteps disappear down the stairs. Sam supposed the guy was—the expression was rich—making book on him.

Sam laughed, took the sheaf of papers out of the envelope and sat in the corner of his couch, leaning his elbow on the arm rest. Sometimes, when he'd thought about being in deep with Sabatini's henchmen, he'd been comforted by the picture of their astonished faces when Ben would say things to them: the big voice from the little man. While they were working him over, for as long as the pain would last (he had always imagined it taking place in the apartment), Ben would have been there, booming sentences at them. But Tidewater's eyes were even better protection. If—Sam liked the way things balanced—the local guys had left him alone until now because they knew he'd be protected by Sabatini, maybe Sabatini would have to leave him alone now because he'd be protected by the local guys. He had nothing to worry about. Sure, he laughed, not fooling himself: he could still do what he wanted—watch TV, take in a movie, or a game at the Garden, or go for a walk in the neighborhood, talk with Steve or Flo, or, as he would do right now, he could afford to settle back and relax on a Saturday morning with a good book.

MY LIFE AND DEATH
IN THE NEGRO AMERICAN
BASEBALL LEAGUE

A SLAVE NARRATIVE

CHAPTER TWO

As maggots make their homes in the open wounds and sores of ele-
phants, and with their deadly secretions cure these beasts, so Johnson's
remarks made their home in my skin, and gave strength to my young
right arm. After my first game, and loss, I won my nine remaining
starts during the 1923 season, and, through the spring and early summer of 1924, pitching three and sometimes four games in succession,
and on occasion pitching both games of Sunday doubleheaders, I won
twenty-six games while losing only two. I was now eighteen years old
—the golden boy of our league—and my pitching feats had become so
talked about on the Negro baseball circuit that, whenever we were to
play in the big cities—Cleveland, Chicago, Washington, Pittsburgh—
Jack Henry would have to promise, for the sake of the gate, that his
young star would be on the mound. The people always love a star, and,
for more reasons than I could ever recount or know, I was glad to be
that star, I wanted to shine for them, to burn brighter than any man
who had preceded me or would come after.

I might have been as good a pitcher as I was had Brick Johnson not
been there—the fires within me were probably sufficient—but his presence made certain that these fires never diminished. His eyes and his
voice found me often during that life I lived when I was not in motion
on the mound, and, piercing me as they did, I must believe that they

177

released within me those venomous juices which gave life to my passions and health to my body. And yet, remembering now how I felt then, and seeing the smallness of what it was that I was doing (I was only a boy throwing a ball), I fear that those passions which I believed were burning with such force may only, like thorns under a pot, have been crackling. For as the crackling of thorns under a pot, so, the Bible reminds us, is the laughter of the fool; this also is vanity.

"You want to take a day off now and again," Johnson would say, when I had pitched for the second or third day in a row. "You'll burn yourself out before you get hair on your chin. You'll melt that arm, fair ass."

I had nothing to say to him, of course, and my victories—and growing fame—seemed still to make him speak to me as if I was not there. When it happened, then, in the summer of 1924, that he informed me of something about which I had previously been ignorant, what he said drove like a poisoned arrow straight into my heart, releasing within me a power at bat which, given my narrow body, I had never suspected was there. Although what he told me (in an off-hand manner), about George Herman "Babe" Ruth was common knowledge, and might have been told to me by any of a thousand players or fans, that it was he, and not another who did tell me, mattered.

The occasion was a non-league game we played in Rensselaer, New York (outside Albany), against a touring team known as the Ethiopian Clowns— a team which played most of its games in Canada and which, though it performed shameless pre-game exhibitions in grass skirts, was as good a team as most in our league, and had often defeated teams of white major leaguers.

During those years our teams would often mingle non-league opponents with league opponents: the trips between cities were long and difficult, and though we were playing for guaranteed annual salaries and had (some of our teams) our own ballparks, we did whatever we had to to earn our way. When (this was so in every major baseball city that had both white and black teams) it happened that the white major league team was in town, and idle, and that a black team was in town, and idle, the two teams would meet, and all would know it, though for legal reasons the white players would assume fictitious names and play as part of a semi-pro team already in existence. Thus, even before the end of my first season, in Dexter Park on a Tuesday afternoon in late fall, I had pitched against, and defeated, by a score of 9 to 1, a semi-professional team known as the Flatbush Falcons, but which team, in fact, was composed at seven of nine positions of members of the (white) Brooklyn Dodgers. Burleigh Grimes was my opponent on that afternoon, and my teammates made easy work of his famed spitter.

By the summer of 1924, and the day of which I am here speaking, we had already played some ten games against non-league teams—defeating white major league teams twice, losing to them once, and winning our other games against semi-pro white and black teams. The Ethiopian Clowns, due to their assorted exhibitions and tricks, could draw good crowds wherever they played, even against the weakest of local teams. Our own teams in the Negro American Baseball League, finding that our schedules put us in their vicinity, would sometimes vie with one another in order to get a game against them. In this way, the Clowns were often able to get our teams to accept less than our usual ten per cent of the gate. In our own team's case, Jack Henry outbid the Pittsburgh Crawfords, who were on an eastern swing, not by agreeing to a smaller percentage of the gate, but by giving his word that I would —in both games of a doubleheader—be the pitcher.

"You can rest your arm next winter," Jack Henry said to me, thereby referring to the fact that, at the end of the first season, I had not traveled south with the Dodgers on their post-season barnstorming tour. They had done well without me—Johnson defeating Pennock and Shawkey of the so-called World Champion Yankees—but when they could not get games against touring white stars, and had had to take what they could get playing against local teams and ragtag collections of other Negro barnstormers, Kinnard, Dixon, and Kelly had jumped the club and played the rest of the winter in Cuba. (If I had had to make the choice again, though, I would have done the same: my mother needed constant attention that winter, which attention none of my brothers, nor my sister Elizabeth, could give, since they all worked a full week—but it was not, as Jack Henry probably thought, from any feeling of guilt that I did not object to pitching as often as he asked me to. As tired as I might be immediately following a game—I sweated profusely and would, though all of me weighed but one hundred and sixty-five pounds, lose more than ten pounds when I pitched on a hot day—once I was in uniform and on the mound, and once my fingers gripped the seams of the ball, my fatigue disappeared and I could reach into myself for all the energy I needed.)

We arrived in Rensselaer early on the morning of July 23—after riding all night long in Jack's Buick (seven of us cramped in his car while the six others rode in Rap Dixon's Ford) from Darby, Pennsylvania, where I had been obliged to pitch league games on the two preceding days (defeating the Hilldale Club, our closest rival for the eastern championship, 3 to 0 and 6 to 2)—and we saw, from the signs pasted to buildings, that our coming, and my appearance, had been amply heralded.

In *Colored Baseball at Its Best, The Ethiopian Clowns* would, in addition to their *World Famous African Repertoire, with Laughs and Chuckles for All,* challenge, in two baseball contests on the same afternoon, *The Brooklyn Royal Dodgers,* of *The Negro American Baseball League,* which team featured its *Young Golden Boy*—myself—*The New Sensation of the Colored Nation,* who would pitch in both contests. The information was flanked by silhouettes of baboon-lipped men, wearing grass skirts and baseball caps, and wielding bats as if they were warclubs.

Because we were not going to stay in Rensselaer overnight, having to be on the road that evening in order to arrive in Cleveland on Monday for the start of a series against the Elites, we did not check in at a hotel. Instead, we found our way to the ballpark, and, since it was still empty, we lay down on the grass next to our dugout and slept. When, shortly before noon, the Clowns arrived, and with them the first fans, we changed into our uniforms, ate sandwiches, and began to warm up. Fortunately it was a hot day, and the sun helped as we shagged flies and ran through infield practice, to loosen our stiff muscles. While we were practicing, members of the Clowns, in their skirts, went around the stands, selling box lunches and pleasing their fans with various shrieks and calls they sent to one another across the park. I warmed up along the first base side, throwing to Bingo and trying to ignore them, but it was soon evident that this would be impossible: due to my featured role in the day's activities—and not less, I would guess, to the fairness of my skin—I found at one point that they had installed a huge iron pot nearby, under which a fire had been lit, and that several of them were dancing in a circle around me—rolling their eyes and licking their lips. I stopped pitching, naturally, and saw that—as one of the Clowns lifted my right arm to examine its weight and tenderness —even my own teammates were laughing. I did not become angry; I do not believe that I felt much of anything, in fact, except, as always, a desire to be done with it, so that the game could begin and I could be pitching.

At the last minute, they changed into their playing uniforms, and, before a good crowd of some twelve thousand—including, I would estimate, some four to five thousand whites—I took the mound and mowed down those unfortunate sons of Africa 3 to 0 and 8 to 1, allowing them a total of seven hits in the two games. Their second baseman, I recall, was a muscular man with quick hands and tremendous speed. He was called ''Tarzan'' and was required to cry mightily from his throat whenever the Clowns scored a run. That I limited his opportunities to one made him, in the late innings of the second game, when many of the fans had already left and my fast ball seemed, in the dusk, faster than ever, approach me menacingly on several occasions, so that my own teammates—coached by his—would, as part of the act, hurry to the mound to protect me. In his eyes, though, I saw something which told me that he was not merely acting—and the laughter of the fans only inflamed his murderous intent. While he allowed himself to be bullied from the field by my teammates, his mouth hung open—soundlessly—and, forced as he was to keep his cry locked inside him, he seemed to me to be in physical pain.

''You hear what they call that crazy man?'' Rose Kinnard asked, as we sat on the bench between innings.

''Sure,'' Johnson said from the corner of the dugout. He spat tobacco juice. ''They call him nigger.''

''Hey—'' Rose said, objecting—piping his reply as our teammates laughed.

Johnson spat again and patted Rose on the back. ''That's okay,'' he said. ''They call the big boy that too—Ruth—back in Baltimore everyone calls him nigger.''

My heart stopped. It was only when I found that Johnson was staring at me—his own puzzled frown bringing me back to life—that I realized I had been gaping. I closed my mouth and leaned back, rubbing my right shoulder with my left hand, to keep it warm. ''Sure,'' Johnson continued. ''Ruth ain't no Tarzan, but he's probably more of a nigger than our golden boy here.'' His dull eyes laughed as he stood to take his place in the on-deck circle. ''Everybody knows that,'' he added, for my benefit.

''Oh, yeah,'' Rose piped. ''I heard of that a lot. I seen him in the summer too—this time of year—and he's blacker than me, that man is. He loves the sun, that man.''

My head swirled, and Johnson, swinging three bats in the on-deck circle, kept his eyes on me, not accusingly—he did not act as if he had discovered any secret about me—but mockingly, as if he did not believe that any man could be so young and ignorant.

I kept my eyes on Rose, and I found myself hating him too. He had, after myself, the fairest skin of my teammates—a pale high yellow complexion which, even in summer, made him seem slightly jaundiced. The skin on his left cheek and the left side of his lips was rose colored, as if he had been burned when a child, but his name, he insisted, had been given to him at birth. "He's darker than you and me, fair ass, the Babe is!" Rose cried (trying to please Johnson, whom he fawned after, despite the fact that he himself, a six-foot two-hundred-pound boy of nineteen, was the finest all around player on our team), and could not contain his laughter. My teammates talked on, elaborating on Johnson's news, trading anecdotes, but I did not listen to what they said.

When I took the mound in the Clowns' half of the inning, my stomach was unsettled. I bent over to pick up the rosin bag in order to dry my fingertips, and the earth rose to meet me, my head spinning wildly; the world tipped first to one side and then to the other. I saw, in my mind's eye, photos of George Herman "Babe" Ruth, and I felt—despite the fact that dusk was upon us and the heat of the day had already given way to an evening chill—as if I needed air, as if the earth which had risen to meet my face was now moving in upon me from all sides. I could do nothing but hurry—I reared back and fired the ball, and as always this made things right. "They ain't got no time," Jones yelled from third base. "You're too fast, too fast, honey."

But I could not catch my breath. I saw, between pitches, only those features, so familiar and beloved to millions of American schoolboys, so evident in a thousand photos: the moon face, the broad flat nose and wide nostrils, the almond-shaped eyes that turned down at the outside corners, the heavy lower lip. I felt as if, between pitches, my only chance for survival—for not fainting—lay, and the very thought made my heart sicken even more, in embracing that man whose image was the cause of my sickness. I needed to support my body upon his, to have that moon face tell me that everything would be all right. "You feelin' badly, son?" Jack Henry asked, taking a place next to me in the dugout. "You've gone sixteen innings straight—Johnson can finish up for you, if you want. It doesn't matter now."

I shook my head. To either side of me my teammates were still talking about him, although Johnson no longer joined in the conversation.

They sang his praises, telling one another what a great pitcher he had been for the Red Sox before he had switched to the outfield. I heard Jack Henry say that he would not have been as great a home run hitter as Oscar Charleston or Christobel Torrienti if he had played in our league, but this opinion was disputed by Kelly. Nobody would claim that he actually had colored blood in him, but there were rumors. . . .

I let their remarks, their debates, flow through me and around me, and I closed my eyes—pretending to rest—and prayed that my strength would last until it was time again to take the mound. I heard Rap Dixon say that he had seen him play in Yankee Stadium—already called "The House That Ruth Built," though but two years old—and Dixon sneered at the short right field line, only two hundred and ninety-six feet from home plate. I myself recalled when he had pitched twenty-nine and two-thirds consecutive scoreless innings in the 1916 World Series against the (white) Brooklyn Dodgers—a fact that my brothers had, in their enthusiasm, impressed upon me, and a record which, coming first, was to endure longer than his more famed one of sixty home runs.

"You want to ride that ball now, fair ass," Johnson said, poking me in the side to tell me that it was my turn at bat. "Give yourself some insurance."

There were two men on base—Barton and Kelly dancing off first and third. I had not—pitcher's courtesy—had to wait my turn in the on-deck circle. I tapped some dirt from my spikes, trying to steady myself, and stepped into the batter's box. Ruth's smiling face hung before me, suspended in the air halfway to the pitcher's mound. I was afraid that I might faint but the opposite happened: as I raised my bat to my shoulder I felt my weakness begin to disappear, to slip from my body. I tightened my fingers on the handle of the bat, and unexpected power surged through me, winding itself tight, like a spring coiling. Dixon, coaching at third now (Jack Henry rested in the dugout, before his turn at bat), hollered that I was on my own, and I filled my lungs with air and cocked the bat behind my shoulder, tightening my grip on its handle. The pitcher threw two balls and I did not move. I kept my eyes on him, on the spot above his right shoulder from which the ball would come. The third pitch was a fast curve, starting for my left shoulder, but I watched it carefully—as if my eyes, by fixing intently enough upon the ball, could stop it—and when, twenty or so feet from the plate, it began to break, to fall off the table, as we put it, I lunged forward—striding a half-foot with my left leg and delivering the full weight of my lean body against the bat: the crack of bat against ball was deep and solid and I did not, as I snapped my wrists, turned them over, and followed through, need to look. The sound —of the bat against ball, and then, a split-second later, of the crowd's gasp—its intake of breath and then its cheer—told me that the ball was gone. My body uncoiled, as strong as it had been, and I saw the infielders turning around, their hands on their hips, to watch the ball travel in a line, disappearing—while still rising—beyond the left-center field fence and into the pastures beyond.

"Oh you rode that one!" Jones said, shaking my hand as I crossed home plate. "They got their money's worth, honey, coming out to see you today."

Each of my teammates came to see me in the dugout, congratulating me—and Kinnard said what they must all have been thinking: "Didn't think you had that kind of power in you. You must be all leather and bones."

I was breathing more easily now; my fingers and palms tingled, alive in a way they had never been before. "She ain't come down yet," Jones said, standing outside the dugout and peering off into the distance, into the pale light beyond the center field fence.

I did not get to hit again that day, but the next afternoon, in Cleveland, I found that—before the game had begun—I was thinking only of my batting, of holding the wood in my hands; I was imagining the feeling that would flow through me when I would drive the ball far and straight, and I was wondering how it could be that I had not, through all the years I had played baseball, concerned myself much with hitting. I had always been, throughout my childhood—on the fields near our home, and at Dexter Park—a good batsman: a line drive hitter who could be depended upon in the clutch. But like everything else that occurred between those moments when I was alone on the mound, hitting seemed unreal somehow—something which filled the time, as it were, between those moments in which I was alive. I took my stance, I studied the pitchers, I tried my hardest, and I was good enough—on days I did not pitch—to be used occasionally as a pinch hitter. I had good reflexes, strong wrists, and—the quality which, in the end, was most important—exceptional vision. I could see the ball longer than others did, and I could time the break in a curve ball, and even a spitter, so that I was rarely off balance when I swung. Still, I had never found within myself what was suddenly there: a desire which can be expressed most simply in the commonplace players' phrase which had long been familiar to me: I wanted to murder the ball.

When I took my turn in batting practice and found that, instead of hitting solid line drives over the infield, I was driving the ball to the far corners of the outfield, my wonder increased. My teammates watched me, but they neither praised my hitting nor commented upon it, and when Jack Henry told Johnson that he would be pitching, so as to give me a day's rest, I resented the decision. I sat on the bench all afternoon—we won handily, 5 to 2, and I was never needed, as a relief pitcher or pinch hitter—and each time the ball spun toward home plate, I was there, timing my swing.

When, the following afternoon, Jack Henry gave me another day's rest, pitching Jacknife Tompkins, the kind of pitcher we called, for what reason I cannot say, a sockamayock—meaning a pitcher you kept on your roster as a utility ballplayer, but one you would never have used in an important league game—I grew angrier. In practice, moreover, batting against Tompkins, who admittedly did not put much on the ball, I supplied my own power and consistently drilled the ball into the stands, thus angering Jack Henry and Aaron Baussy, the manager of the Elites, for there was always the danger that some young boy would keep the ball and run off with it. The Elites defeated us that afternoon, 7 to 1, and again Jack Henry did not use me.

On the third day of our series with the Elites, I was the pitcher. I set them down in order during the first two innings, hurrying my pitches so that my own turn at bat—I was, as usual, ninth in the order —would come sooner. The Elite pitcher that day was a man named Harcourt Simmons, a crossfire pitcher with good speed and fine control. In our half of the third, I came to bat. Simmons wound up for the first pitch, stepped to his right, and whipped his arm across his body, waist high, so that the ball sped at me as if it were coming from third base, rising slightly, as if it intended to bury itself in my ear. I could not restrain myself. I stepped forward and met the ball, inside, in front of the plate, my hands vibrating from the shock. I heard the third baseman grunt, and, from the corner of my eye—I had just had time to drop the bat—I saw him, sitting in the dirt, hold up his glove, the ball wedged in the pocket. I returned to the dugout, cursing myself silently. I expected Johnson, or Jack Henry, to say something, but they did not—nor did Jones tease me, as he usually did.

Their silence irritated me; and my irritation increased when, in my second and third at-bats of the day, I was deprived of the opportunity to swing away, receiving a base on balls one time up and being required to make a sacrifice bunt the other. When I came to bat in our half of the eighth inning, we were already leading 5 to 0 (I had allowed the Elites but three hits), and Simmons had been replaced by a young southpaw, a sixteen-year-old stringbean of a player named Tennessee Bray, who was as wild as the wind. He had already soaked Henry and Rouillard, and on his first pitch to me I had to drop my bat and fall to the ground to avoid catching the ball in my cheek. His second pitch hit the dirt some twenty-five feet in front of home plate and bounced past the catcher, allowing Jones, who was at second, to move to third. The third pitch came toward the plate, below the knees. I forced myself to wait an instant—in order not to be ahead of the ball, as I had been my first time at bat. I could hear the ball whistling and knew that, as I stepped forward—a longer stride to compensate for the lowness of the pitch—I was smiling. My body strained and I felt the pressure which had been building in me for three days release itself with my swing: my anger flowed into my hands and shoulders, and from them into the bat. I drove the ball straight at the pitcher—who threw up a gloved hand in self-defense and then fell sideways from the mound—and the ball continued on a line, directly over second base, at eye-level; the center fielder began to set himself for it, but the ball continued to rise, whistling through the air as the pitch had whistled toward the plate, and the centerfielder had a look of pure stupefaction on his face as his neck dropped and he watched the ball, some twenty feet above his head, sail past.

I was, as I rounded the bases, happy; I felt satisfied in a way I had never felt from any pitching success, and I saw—as I expected I would —an image of the man whose slugging prowess I knew I could now challenge: it waited for me as I rounded third base, and it smiled at me as I crossed home plate. I could breathe again.

I took my place on the bench, beside my teammates, and accepted their congratulations. Though I had only jogged in rounding the bases, I was panting. I looked right and left, willing to hear more—to have my teammates go on, as they always did with one another when a home run had been hit, but they addressed their remarks to the Elite pitcher, advising him of the benefits a cold shower could bring. They said nothing to me, and I scanned their faces, as hurt as I was surprised. Surely they were aware of the power I had suddenly unleashed, and surely they were happy for me!—and yet, as soon as these thoughts had crossed my mind, I realized my error. What I saw in their faces was suspicion, and something more than suspicion—I had, I knew, hurt them in some way; I had again, by my success—by making myself more whole as a player and us more powerful as a team—only repeated the old pattern; I had only succeeded in separating myself that much more from them.

They were—I saw this clearly in the weeks which followed, when I continued to hit well, and for distance—wary. They did not, I am certain, connect the change in me to the conversation that had taken place during our game against the Ethiopian Clowns, but they were not pleased that, like the white star they so admired, who had been a pitcher first and a slugger later, I too was changing. In a series against the Dayton Marcos, I blasted four home runs in three games; in a double-header against the Indianapolis ABC's, I went six for nine, including two doubles and a triple; and against the Kansas City Monarchs, while pitching my second no-hitter of the season, I hit my longest home run, far beyond the four-forty mark of their left-center field wall, thereby winning my own game 1 to 0.

Although I found that I was—at least in the minutes which immediately followed—happy after I had delivered a long blow, I did not, as when pitching, feel in any way transported—rather the opposite: hearing the crack of bat against ball, and seeing the white sphere rocket across the infield, I felt as if I had never been more firmly rooted to earth. My spirits soared, yet my body seemed more substantial than ever.

That my teammates remained suspicious is understandable. Previously, it would not have occurred to any of them, as it had not occurred to me, to have asked why it was that I was a great pitcher yet an ordinary hitter. Still, it occurs to me now that, until then, my want of excellence at the plate must have been something which had made me acceptable to them, something, that is, which had made them assume that I was what one part of me wanted to believe: merely an imperfect man, like any of them.

Once, however, I had tasted the thrill that could come from hitting, I could not, as with all things in my life, get enough. I wanted still to be with them, one of them—yet I knew that my desire to surpass them, in that which had previously been their domain, ensured that I would again move farther from them. Outwardly, nothing changed. Jack

Henry played me as before—pitching me as often as he had to, and my
teammates left me alone—appreciating my contributions to our efforts
(we had, before the end of August, clinched the eastern circuit championship, thus ensuring ourselves a place in the World Series and a
share of the money that that would bring in), respecting my silence,
but acting—off the field—as if I were what I had, in truth, done everything to encourage them to believe. I was, simply, a man apart—and,
except for the ritual laughter which accompanied Johnson's barbs,
there was nothing they showed which indicated that they wished things
to be otherwise.

I was to my team, then, what Booker T. Washington—in a statement
my father had regarded with the same piety he reserved for the Bible—
had claimed my race should be to the white race. "In all things that
are purely social we can be as separate as the fingers," Washington
had said in 1895, "yet one as the hand in all things essential to mutual
progress." The words still seem, residing with me as they have through
some fifty years, to carry force, to signify my particular condition with
the Brooklyn Royal Dodgers during the years 1923 to 1928. Although
I did not try to be but what I was—although I continued to drive myself, to pursue perfection with a rabid passion in that league which had
no white men—it must be clear that, far from releasing me from any
bondage, my efforts were the truest evidence that (aware even then that
I may never have had choice in any of these matters) I did have choice
in my feelings about them, and I did, with every act, sustain that slavery which was mine, and which, alas, I must have loved. ("Slavery
holds but few," says Seneca. "Many hold fast to slavery.")

How else can I explain my decision, made before the end of the season, to accompany our team on their post-season barnstorming tour?
For I knew, even as I informed Jack Henry, that my reasons had little
to do with pleasing him or my teammates, and less to do with anything
concerning my mother and family. I was thinking of one thing only:
of the possibility that our team would, while on tour, come up against—
as they had the winter before—a team composed largely of members of
the New York Yankees.

Jack Henry did not question my decision, nor did he, as I had hoped
he would, greet it with enthusiasm. "That's good," was all he said.
"You'll help bring in the money."

My hand moved then, involuntarily, to my thigh, as if to hide what
was there: for, though I had no basis for believing so, I felt that he

knew that I carried, concealed in my wallet, a piece of folded newspaper which was the source of my decision, bearing as it did a photo of that man I dreamt of meeting, and of defeating. I had gazed at it often—the body twisted in a follow-through, the bat straight up and down but tipped back slightly above the right shoulder, the narrow eyes and bulbous nose shaded by the visor of his cap, the mouth parted in a half-smile—and I had, concentrating on the image, seen it come to life; I had watched the man swing and miss again and again and again as I threw the ball past him with such speed that he was forced—mystified and broken—to admit that I had taken from him those alliterative titles, King of Clout and Sultan of Swat, an ignorant public had bestowed upon him. I did not, of course, care about having such foolish titles applied to myself. I knew that, even if I should defeat him as a pitcher and outhit him as a batter, the word would go out among baseball men only that we had met and that I had carried the day; so that when I thought of playing against him, I did not, in truth, think of the acclaim a victory would bring; I thought—and this was, facing Jack Henry, what made me lower my eyes and cover my sidepocket—only of the way the man's eyes might look at me when he had faced me and lost.

Sometimes I believe that that image of him—ripped from a newspaper one morning in what I thought was a fit of jealousy—was, during those months which preceded our first meeting, more real to me than the man would ever become. For if I did not want to take from him those banal titles, and if I had resigned myself to the fact that my first decision had been irrevocable (as, with my first game of the previous season, it had become), why was I so jealous of his fame?—and if I knew that I could not, by defeating him on the playing field, put on his power and his glory—and if I believed that I had no need to—why, in the privacy of my room at home and in hotel rooms on the road, did I continue to fix my eyes upon his image?

As my first complete season with the Dodgers wore on through late August and September, I continued to win as a pitcher and to excel as a hitter. By the end of September, when we were preparing to meet Rube Foster's Giants, winner of the western circuit crown, for the World Series, I had hit twenty-four home runs; I had won thirty-nine games while losing seven, had pitched three no-hitters (though no perfect game), four one-hitters, and an even dozen shutouts; I had also begun—on the days Johnson or Tompkins or Kelly (coming in from left field—born in Cinq Hommes, Louisiana, he was called "Gunboat" from the fact that his father had been a gun runner to Cuba during the Spanish-American War) were pitching—to play in the outfield. During the month of September, with the pennant already clinched, I pitched only every third or fourth day, and I knew that my presence in the outfield on the days I did not pitch, and the length of my home runs, though they did not yet draw the fans to the ballpark, had begun to be talked about.

Through August and September, I played as well and as hard as I ever had, yet I felt all the while as if I were merely going through the motions, as if this boy whom others claimed could throw like lightning and hit like thunder was somebody I myself was observing. Only when I would, at times for hours on end, take the photo from my wallet and gaze at it, did I seem to wake—I grew warmer, imagining the details of the encounter I hoped would come, and though the numbed feeling would leave me then, I knew, of course, that the essence of these moments was their very unreality, and they became, therefore, the most vivid example to me of how foolishly in dreams my life was led.

The first official World Series in our league took place in 1924, and since the (white) Brooklyn Dodgers had finished in second place in the National League, we were able to rent Ebbets Field for the opening three-game series against Foster's Chicago American Giants. We held two days of workouts at Ebbets Field, and for the first time since late July, my teammates seemed to want to approach me, to offer me their friendship. The instant I left the pitching mound, one of them would run to me with a jacket, to cover my right arm and keep it warm; when I took my place in the batter's box for the first time, I found that Rose Kinnard had climbed the left-center field wall and was playing for me in the bleachers; and when I drilled the ball consistently into the seats, the players wailed and moaned, mocking the fate of Rube Foster's pitchers.

"You want to give them your purpose pitch," Jones said. "You let Johnson learn it to you."

"What's a purpose pitch?" Barton asked.

"A purpose pitch," Jones explained, "is where the purpose of the pitch is to separate the batter's head from his shoulders."

They were on edge, riding high, as excited as a bunch of schoolboys. I *wanted* to care about the series as they did—it should, I knew, have

been the high point of my life until then—and I bore down and concentrated as hard as I could; still I felt, the instant I was not in motion,
as if I were only half-there. When I see Jones's skinny arms flapping
away as he runs for Barton, to embrace him after Barton has made a
superb diving catch of a low liner, or when I see the easy way Rose
Kinnard would drape his long arm around Kelly's shoulder, consoling
him after I had struck him out, my heart stops: though I wish that I
might have cared enough to have been one with my teammates during
those autumn days, I know, now as then, that I wished for other things
more.

Even when, on the afternoon of October 5 of that year, a Tuesday
(the day after John McGraw's Giants had opened their World Series
in Washington, where Nehf defeated the great Walter Johnson, who, at
the age of thirty-seven, was pitching in his first and only World
Series), I took the mound before a crowd of over twenty thousand, and
checked the flagpole atop the scoreboard to see if the wind had shifted,
my mind was elsewhere. The roar of the crowd was for me, but when I
raised my eyes and, squinting, looked into their happy faces so far
from me, I found that I felt almost nothing.

I wanted to be pleased by their cheers, yet as I reared back and fired
the first ball of the game at the Giants' second baseman for a called
strike, and thus made the crowd roar again, I found that the only thing
I really felt was annoyance. I wanted to be done with it. I wanted to
leave the ballpark as quickly as possible. I wanted the series to be over,
and I tried in vain to stop myself from imagining what might happen
when it was.

I pitched quickly, striking out the first three men on eleven pitches,
and all the while my teammates' chattering filled my ears. "I feel the
breeze," Jones called, as he always did. "Oh I do feel the breeze!"

I returned to the bench, my teammates telling me how good I
was, and I discovered that my hands itched terribly, wanting to
hold a bat, to slam the ball low and hard at Johnson, at Jones, at the
others—I leaned forward, controlling myself, as if studying the play
on the field, and as I did I saw from the corner of my eye that
Rube Foster, the Giants' manager, was sitting at one end of his bench,
watching me. I wondered if he suspected. He was dressed in a business-
man's gray pin-stripe suit, with vest, a wool cap set to one side of his
large head. He was taller than me by two inches, weighed some two
hundred and sixty pounds (thirty more than he had when a player),

and his thick neck, bulging from his starched collar, made him seem even larger than he was. Less than a dozen years before, in his prime, he had been considered the greatest pitcher our leagues had ever known. He sucked on his pipe, one leg crossed over the other, and his eyes regarded me without expression. The World Series, like the league itself, had been his idea, and it was difficult, sitting there with sweat pouring from me, to remember that I had, coming into the league but a year and a half before, wanted to model myself after him, wanted to be so good that my name would, someday, have replaced his when baseball men argued about who was the greatest of the black ballplayers.

I would not, I reminded myself, have been the first black man to outplay George Herman "Babe" Ruth in an exhibition game—Foster himself, among others, when he was long past his prime, had been able to handcuff the man on a given day and if I did it too, I knew that this would prove nothing, and change nothing. I watched the field half-dreaming; I felt Johnson's eyes mocking me; I heard Jones chattering in my ear; I thought of the scars on Kelly's back—three horizontal lines which, he claimed, came not from the time he had spent in prison for armed robbery, but from the brothers at St. Thomas Catholic orphanage in Baton Rouge, and then my teammates were running by me again, beginning to talk it up, to send their promises across the grass.

I opened the second inning by throwing three strikes past the fourth man in the Giants' lineup, their leading home run hitter, Christobel Torrienti, a light-skinned Cuban who, the players said, could have been a star in the white leagues had his hair been slightly less kinky. (There were, in fact, two other Cubans, Armando Marsans and Rafael Almeida, who had played for the Cincinnati Reds in the white Major Leagues a decade before, but not counting those others, Spanish and black, who had made it by disguising their true identities, Marsans and Almeida had been the last.)

Their first baseman, "Mule" Suttles, second to bat in the second, flied out to Kinnard, and against their catcher and leading hitter, John Beckwith, Bingo held on to a foul-tipped third strike. Their half of the inning was over on eight pitches, and I was in our dugout again, listening to the fans rain their praise on me, trying not to hear my teammates' words, trying to ignore Jones's arm, which was around my shoulder as his sweet voice told me that he personally guaranteed me the runs I needed.

We made out as quickly as the Giants had in the bottom of the second, yet the game seemed to me to be moving with excruciating slowness. Even now, remembering those innings, being able to see each movement of each play, my eyes begin to close, and drowsiness seeps through my body; I feel again as if I am perpetually on the verge of dropping away into a sweet and comforting sleep. Although nothing in my outward appearance would have indicated it, I felt as if I were in some kind of distracted trance, as if I were observing a sleepwalker who bore my likeness.

In their half of the third, "Cool Papa" Bell, not as fast any longer as his legend would have had him, but fast nonetheless, led off by beating out a grounder to third; he taunted me by taking a long lead. Bingo called for a pitchout, and then "Cool Papa" was flying behind me; Bingo's throw was low, bouncing off Jack Henry's chest, and Bell was safe at second. Annoyed that the game had thus been lengthened, I bore down and, shaking off Bingo's signs and pitching only fast balls, retired the next three men on two strike outs and a pop-up to Jack Henry.

I came to bat in our half of the third with the bases empty and, on the second pitch, I hammered the ball high into the upper deck in left field, giving myself the only run I knew I would need. I took small pleasure from the hit, however, or from the crowd's applause. I worked as hard and as quickly as I could, setting down the Giants in order for the next four innings, while, silently, I urged my own teammates to hurry, to swing at first pitches, to make out so that I could return to the mound.

When, in the top of the eighth, with Jones and Barton on base, Rose Kinnard hit a home run into the lower left-center field stands, putting us ahead 4 to 0, Jack Henry told Johnson that he would be the starting pitcher on the following day, and that he was, in order to give him some rest, removing him for a pinch hitter. Johnson left the dugout at once; he did not look my way but I believed that he was smiling, and I burned; for though in truth I thought that I cared about the outcome of the game as little as he did, I felt that he knew that I wished I could care.

In the last innings I remained as distracted between pitches as I had been at the outset, and when, at the game's close, the fans poured down from the stands to the field and surrounded me, I felt still as if I were not there. They hugged me and kissed me, danced around me and tore swatches from my uniform, and though Jack Henry and some others intervened, escorting me to the dugout by pushing our way through the crowd of joyous faces, I felt nothing, neither fear nor elation. Now as then, I can feel their physical presence—the space around me dense with bodies, my own skin being touched by theirs, my sweat making their hands slide as some of them try to grip me, to show their gratitude—and yet I lift my eyes and search, among their black faces, for the face I know I will not see. I am not repulsed by their show of affection, yet neither am I thrilled. My body is tired, and I do not even draw my shoulders up protectively, as I see my teammates do in front of me.

In the locker room, they tease me about what has happened. Johnson has vanished. They tell me there will be girls waiting for me outside, and ask if I will share the fruits of my success with them. They do not throw water on me, as they do to one another, and they do not provoke me to harmless wrestling matches; but, in the flush of our victory, they seem, for the moment, to have abandoned their suspicion. I am, more than ever, in a trance, and yet, as they celebrate my greatness, and proclaim their own acts of heroism to one another, they see only my silence, and assume therefore that I am the same man I have always been.

If I could have danced with them, I would have. If I could have hugged them and wrestled with them and enjoyed—if but for the moment—the kind of happiness they were feeling then . . . Was there not one of them who would not now call me a fool—or worse—for wishing that I could have changed places with any of them, so that I might, for once in my life, have known what it was like to have felt this ordinary release grown men seem to feel when they have fought together and won.

It would never have occurred to me then, in my vanity, that to envy them was only, once again, to treat them as beings apart—to envy in them those things which have always been used to master them. Yet this was what I was doing, and it accounts for the fact that, in that year and the three which followed, I never did know each of them as they must have known one another.

III

Farewell!
Farewell!

The rabbi of Kobryn said: "We paid no attention to the miracles our teachers worked, and when sometimes a miracle did not come to pass, he gained in our eyes."
—Martin Buber, *Tales of the Hasidim*, "The Later Masters"

9

The room was almost dark. Light flickered from two candles, removed to the window sill so that Flo could serve, but even in this atmosphere, Tidewater seemed harmless to Sam. The guy's story was in his head, taking up space, it was true, but since Ben would be gone in less than twenty-four hours, Sam figured he would have extra room there. Stella's face and voice bothered him more—because, he had to admit, they made him feel easy about things, they made him feel that he was right not to believe in things such as his account with Sabatini—and he was glad that Flo had not invited her. He would have been the one who would have had to feed her, and he didn't need to have Ben, on their last night together, see him in that position.

Flo asked him if he wanted another slice of roast beef, or some more potatoes, but he said no, that he was satisfied. He had been able, truly, to enjoy the meal. While he had been out during the afternoon, searching for a present for Ben, Flo had been in the apartment with Tidewater, cooking. Ben and Marion had taken care of the store. Marion, sitting next to Sam, had not opened her mouth since the meal had begun, but Sam saw that she was putting it away, glass by glass. They had all been drinking, slowly and steadily, since late afternoon. At the sink, Flo stacked dishes.

Sam could, with his eyes open, see her smiling at him just before she had covered her face with her hands to recite the prayer over the *shabbos* candles. It had been—her lighting the candles—Ben's request, and Sam had looked straight back into his father's eyes while Flo was praying. It was all the same to him. The tears that were in his father's eyes when Ben had raised the glass of wine and recited the *kiddush*, the silence of the others, the picture Sam saw—the one he knew Ben wanted him to see—of Ben's father doing the same in the apartment on Linden Boulevard: Sam could take it all in without having to believe in it, and he could even, seeing things this way, understand that it was—a word he liked—normal for Ben to feel this way at a time like this. Ben had passed the glass around and each of them had sipped from it. Then Ben had gone to the sink, washed his hands, returned to the table, motioned everyone into their seats, and, above the slices of *challah* on his plate, covered with a white cloth napkin, he had recited a prayer and made a cutting motion, three times, with the bread knife. Sam had smiled at him, taken the piece of soft yellowish bread that Ben gave to each of them, and Ben had misread the smile, and smiled himself.

What could any of it mean, Sam could have asked if he'd wanted to; not just because his father claimed he didn't believe, which was an old story, but because the last time it had occurred to Ben to go through all the Friday night rituals had been at least twenty years before, and Sam couldn't remember what the occasion had been then. Sam said nothing, though; he let his father go through the routine. What did it cost him, after all?

At the head of the small table, his back to the front door, Ben was leaning on his elbow, sideways, his head close to Tidewater. His eyes, small and sleepy from too much wine, were almost closed. "Tell me, Mason," he was saying, "what kind of privacy, do you suppose, is peripheral?"

Tidewater leaned back, his chair rocking on two legs. "Ah Ben," he said. "I see what you mean—exactly what you mean."

"When I'm gone, my son will be here."

"I mean to speak with him," Tidewater said, but he did not look Sam's way.

"His silence," Ben said, and switched to his other elbow, breathing on Sam. "What do you make of it? Is it because—" Ben stopped, seemingly confused; he touched a napkin to his forehead, blotting, and sat back. "My desire, as I prepare to leave you? What it has always been: to die in my sleep at the age of ninety-eight, with my grandchildren and great grandchildren standing around me and weeping." He wiped his hand across his face, from the forehead down. "I might have considered remarrying, my son, and providing you with a mother," his eyes looked straight at Flo, "but I was afraid, you see, that I might catch the disease also, and be—" He looked around. "Wine does this to me," he said, then smiled at Sam. "I'm entitled to lapses also, don't you think?" Then his voice shifted, and his eyes, avoiding Tidewater's, fixed on Marion: "She may look like your sister, but she has V. D."

Flo was behind Ben's chair. "You cut that out, Ben, do you hear?" she said. In the darkness, Sam could see anger in her eyes. Marion looked at the table.

"No, no," Ben said. "I was just remembering—my most famous line. I recorded it for Armed Forces Radio, shortly after V. E. Day. To protect our boys." Ben turned his head upward, looking into Flo's face. She caressed his cheek with her hand.

"Ben," she said, softly. "Benjamin."

"She may look like your sister, but she has V. D."

Sam felt warm, watching Flo bend down and rest her arms on his father's shoulders. Muscular dystrophy was not, of course, contagious, yet Sam felt there was something to what Ben had said, though he wouldn't have admitted it aloud, even for a joke. "I had a friend in college," Flo was saying, "who always told me how lucky I was, to know I would marry a Jewish man. Poor Irene. She had a theory that Jewish men were more considerate because, as children, they'd been trained to worship their mothers."

As always when he listened to Flo's voice, Sam felt himself relaxing, growing sleepy. But Ben's voice was harsh. "And why do you tell us this tonight?" he asked.

Flo put her cheek next to Ben's head, on Sam's side of the table. "Why don't you stay, Ben? Why don't you cancel your trip—at the least, why don't you wait until Andy—"

"He's lingering," Ben said, and laughed sharply. "Those are his own words. 'I'm lingering, Ben. I'm lingering.'" Ben paused, looked at Sam. "No. I'll go now. It will be better for everybody."

"Not for me," Flo said.

"Nor me," Tidewater added, and moved his head so that Sam thought the man was going to press his face against Ben's other cheek. "But you know that."

"And you, Marion?" Ben asked.

"Yes," Marion said. "I'd like you to stay."

"But notice," Ben said, drawing away from Flo and raising a teaspoon in his hand, pointing the handle at Sam, "how silent my son remains. Our children are our immortality, yes?—and mine is like stone. If I'd had four sons, he would have been the fourth—do you know what I mean? In the *Haggadah* for Passover . . ."

Flo stepped back, looked at Sam. "You shouldn't," she said to Ben. She came around, behind Sam's chair, and Sam felt her hands, tightening on his arms. "You have no right."

Ben turned to Tidewater. "You agree, don't you?"

Tidewater looked across the table at Sam, a reflection from the candlelight flashing from a corner of his left eye, then lowered his head. Sam felt Flo's fingers on his shoulders. Would she sense the slight tightening there? Tidewater looked up, his nostrils flaring. "We have a rare thing in this building, and you are a fool to throw it away, Ben Berman. That we are here—you and Sam, and Flo and Marion, and myself for reasons too—too what—?" He stopped suddenly, winced—Sam could feel the blow that had just struck the man—and, his eyes pressed closed, he reached across and grabbed Ben's hand in his own. "That we found one another after all the years apart. You are the only man who knew me before—" His voice was suddenly passionate, bitter: "It is all so stupid, Ben. Don't you see that? Don't you see that you should stay here?" He looked up at the others, embarrassed, and drew his hand from Ben's. "I do not mean to offend, but we have a rare thing, all of us living and working in one place, all—" Tidewater closed his eyes, unable to continue.

"A neighborhood in transition is what I call it," Ben offered, smiling.

Sam felt Flo's fingernails dig into his shoulder muscles. "Stop!" she said. "Oh stop!"

Ben hesitated, looked at Tidewater's face, then spoke. "I'm sorry," he said. "There were four sons: one was wise, one was wicked, one was simple, and one was too young to—as the translation goes—have the ability to inquire." Sam could feel, as Tidewater's eyes opened, looking nowhere, what his father must have been remembering, and he knew he didn't need it. But Ben's voice was dry, he recited the story without drama, and though he looked at Sam with affection, when he came to the simple son's question, as to—the words were perfect—what it was all about, it was the wicked son Sam had always remembered: the son who asks what *you* signify by all these things, and thus, by the use of the word "you" excludes himself from the community.

When Ben was done, Flo sat down, next to Tidewater. "Would you, tonight, tell us about your father?" she asked Ben. "Then— your presents. We each have something for you."

"There's nothing to tell," Ben said. "Ask Samela here. He, at least, made my father smile. My father was a funny man, yes? His advice to my son: 'If you drink a malted every day for ninety-six years, you'll live to be very old.' "

Sam remembered, but he didn't laugh. "Please," Flo said. "Be serious at last. You owe us at least that, don't you? To be serious. If it weren't—I wouldn't press you so."

"It's nothing," Ben said, rubbing his eyes.

"Tell her the story," Tidewater said, and his voice was forceful, commanding. "You have nothing to be ashamed of. I've told you."

"Ashamed?" Ben lifted his head and laughed. "It was his decision, not mine." Ben drank some wine, looked around the table. "But all right. Why not?" He kept his eyes on Sam. "Sunshine and hot competition, yes?" He laughed to himself, and then began: "My father's dream, of course, was to bring all his sons to America. He arrived here in 1909 with myself and Andy, who was already old enough to go to work, and did. My father worked as a baker, for a distant uncle, leaving Andy to watch me when Poppa would leave for work at midnight." He blinked. "I don't remember much. Your grandmother he never spoke of. Andy knows nothing either. It was a forbidden subject. Maybe my other two brothers knew something, but by this time—they were older than Andy—they have doubtless taken whatever story was there to sleep with them."

Sam looked past his father, at the candles burning down in the window, at the windows across the street; he thought of people walking outside, below, where the melted snow had now turned to deadly layers of rippled ice. He didn't need to be out on a night like this. Sam expected nothing. That was his number one rule now—and if, in whatever his father would tell, there were some truth about Ben, and about Ben's father, then he figured he'd be ahead of the game. He was curious—he admitted that to himself—and there was something now in Ben's tone which made him less suspicious than he would have been ordinarily. The sarcasm, for one thing, was gone—and the deep tones were softer, more mellow.

"All right. It's nothing more than this, as Mason knows. Andy went to work in the garment district, as a cutter; he saved, he had a few ideas, he found a man with money to back him—you know the rest. I worked for him in a haberdashery store on Lexington Avenue. In those days, there were still wealthy Jews living in Harlem." Tidewater nodded. "Poppa and Andy wanted me—planned for me—to go to law school, and Andy had it arranged, but it wasn't for me. Like my son, I wanted a kind of freedom, yes? I didn't want to be bound to—" Ben waved his hands, in small circles, helplessly. "To what, after all?" He nodded several times, to himself. "A job, I suppose. A boss. I thought, with my voice, that I wanted to be an actor, and Andy had contacts in the Yiddish theater, which was thriving then, but I couldn't, you see, speak Yiddish. Poppa had seen to that. He wanted us to be Americans and so, though he spoke to us in Yiddish, we were forbidden to reply to him in that language. I could, then, understand the language, but when I went to see the man Andy had spoken to, and he gave me something to read, I was of course lost.

"I tried hanging around theatrical agents' offices. I went to Atlantic City—but for the American stage, well—it's obvious, isn't it?—I had the voice of a leading man, and the body, even before I was twenty—the small body of an old Shylock. Radio was nowhere at the time; it was only later, after Roosevelt, that I saw its possibilities for me, but by then . . ." His voice was firm, and he stopped, started again, without any shift in tone. "That is, of course, all beside the point. Here. The story that Mason refers to: my father's dream to bring his elder sons to America—Simon and Reuben—and the determination he brought to this dream. He put all his savings to that purpose, and he must have worked very hard. The war came, and after the war, the immigration laws changed, there were people who had to be paid off here, and now there were problems on the other side. Their village, which was in Galicia, where I was born, became part of Russia, a town near the Polish border named Riminov, and—after the war and the revolution— there were problems on their side too. Not all letters came through, my father spent his time seeing people, he found a man in New York named Harry Epstein, a flashy lawyer who had international connections and who said, for a price, that he could arrange things at both ends.

"We had been in America fourteen years before my father had the money together. Fourteen years . . . What does that signify, fourteen years?" Ben nodded to himself. "He refused to take from Andy, and he refused to take from me. I was, by then, to tide me over only, I thought, driving a taxi, and it had cost enough of Andy's money to pay off the right people there also. Andy knew some of the big Jewish gangsters. Things were arranged, I did all right, and I too had offered to give my father the money. But he said no and he went off, night after night, to bake his bread and twist his *challahs*. We were to save our money to buy ourselves houses, and for our marriages."

Ben stopped, looked at Tidewater. "It made me think sometimes, during those years of waiting and saving, that he didn't love me as much as he loved Simon and Reuben. One of my earliest memories, in fact—this I can tell—is of wishing I could take a boat back to Europe, so that it would be me he was working for and dreaming of day after day. Does that sound strange?" He stopped. "Does it?"

Nobody answered. "Then one morning," Ben continued, "he came home before I had left for the day—usually we missed each other—and he handed me an envelope. 'Here is the money in dollars.' Those were his words. I was not to open the envelope, I was not to take any passengers until I had delivered the money to Harry Epstein. 'Be careful, Benya,' he said to me, and I went out.

"I didn't look in the envelope, but I didn't go right to Harry Epstein either. I telephoned Andy who through his contacts had long before established that Harry Epstein was a fraud of frauds—a bastard of bastards whom the worms should feast on eternally!" Ben rose up in his chair, his eyes wide, and he slammed his hand on the table, palm down, rattling the glasses. He leaned forward. "But tell me, Samela, what could I have done? Andy had tried to reason

with Poppa, and had met—like you—a stone wall. Ha! Go talk to
the wall! That is an expression in Yiddish. So tell me, what was I to
do? You know about odds, you are an expert—for every ten people
trying to get to America, perhaps two made it on their own, or
perhaps even, give the man his due, Harry Epstein did what anyone
could have done. Those are percentages, no? Answer me that."

Sam said nothing, and Ben sighed, waved off any commentary.
"We were four brothers," he said, "but the wise one must have been
one of the two left on the other side.

"I drove to Andy's place of business and showed him the
envelope. I wanted proof. 'Have you heard of Lipsky?' he asked,
and I nodded. 'All right,' he said. 'Come with me.'

"Andy telephoned first, and then we got into my taxi. I met the
man Lipsky then who was supposed to be involved with Murder
Incorporated, which did him so much good that during a private
pogrom two years later he was killed by another Jewish gangster, a
cousin of his named Feigenbaum. 'At least they kept it in the
family,' Andy said to me at the time. He was always a joker." Ben
looked up. "All right. In those days Lipsky was the biggest of the
biggest. I spare you the theatrics. Men with guns under their
armpits escorted us into his apartment on Park Avenue, a girl who
looked like Clara Bow and was dressed for horseback riding sat
there sipping something from a glass, and Lipsky himself sat in a
big easy chair like a sultan, with somebody manicuring his
fingernails. His walls were covered with books.

" 'First tell me, young man,' I can still hear him saying. 'What do
you think of Spinoza?' I did not know who he was talking about—a
rival gangster? I wondered—and he was disappointed." Ben
stopped, closed his eyes. "The few details are for Sam, so he can
know how they used to, as Mason would say, order things, yes?"
Ben laughed, then leaned forward. Sam was glad that the room was
dark. "Andy started to make a big thing about how grateful he was
to the great Lipsky, but Lipsky told him 'shush,' and asked him
what his business was. 'For my brother,' Andy says. 'He has my
father's money, to get our two older brothers over here from
Galicia—in Russia now. He's supposed to give it to Harry Epstein.
Tell him—'

"Lipsky looked at his fingernails. 'Epstein? Epstein is a crumb. A
shonde,' Lipsky declared. 'See?' Andy said to me. Lipsky thought

for a minute. 'You seem like good boys. You love your father, and that is the most important thing in the world. *Chavayd es ahavicha v'es amechah.* The fifth commandment and the most important one. I will give you boys a tip. If you can get someone to take your money—it's not my line of business—the Yankees will win the pennant again. Forget about your brothers. Nobody can do anything now. But if I hear that things have changed, you will hear from me. Now boys, good-bye.'

"It was, of course, as if God had spoken. I could not doubt Lipsky's word on Epstein, and what were we to do with Poppa's money? We couldn't return it to him, and Andy could never have let Poppa know that he had contacts, for his business, with a man like Lipsky, who my father would have said was a curse on the Jews. We drove to a fancy restaurant whose name I don't remember, where they had to loan me a jacket and tie, and when Andy asked me what I thought of Lipsky's tip, I said, 'It sounds good to me.' The year was 1924."

Ben looked at Sam, and Sam felt his heart clench. Ben knew he would know, but, at the least, Sam would not give him the satisfaction of saying anything out loud. He waited; he saw, from the corner of his eye, that Tidewater was smiling knowingly, and that, next to him, Flo's face was grief-stricken, her color, even in the dark room, gray.

"As Sam could tell you as well as I—and Mason better than us both—the Yankees won pennants, consecutively, from 1921 to 1923, and again, from 1926 through 1928." Ben wiped the back of his hand across his eyes. "Happily, Mr. Epstein was found dead a year and a half later, in the trunk of his car." Ben's eyes narrowed. "And my father—your grandfather, Sam—he told me then the words I leave with you: 'Take, Benya! Take!' " Ben sat back, his mouth open, as if he were laughing, but with no sound coming out. "He cursed Epstein for having been murdered, and he cursed my mother, and my mother's father, and he walked downstairs, with me following him, and in the hot sun—it was then August—he spat seven times—I counted. Then, 'America,' he said.

"He sent me back upstairs and he himself went to synagogue. It was not, I imagine, for Epstein that he said *kaddish.*" Ben smiled, let his voice drop lower. "The moral of the story, my friends? My father never went to work again. Never. Not for a single hour. If we wanted to, he said, Andy and I could support him." Ben's smile was very broad. "All right?" he asked Flo.

"The story changes nothing," she said. "You should stay here. You have nothing to be ashamed of."

"Don't use that word!" Ben's voice rose. "I said before, it was his decision, don't you see?"

"Exactly," Tidewater said. "We see exactly. That's why—"

"You see then," Ben went on, his voice cool, "why Poppa admired Sam so much. He knew something—he knew that Sam would maintain family tradition, that—"

"You are a fool sometimes," Flo said. She stood. "I'll bring the presents. May I put the lights on?"

"It's Friday night," Ben said. "No work, no lights. On Howard Street, on Friday nights, there were no lights. On Howard Street . . ."

"Then you should not," Tidewater declared angrily, "mock what is happening here, where things have happened—before you were born—which command respect." Tidewater looked at Sam. "When you are gone, I will share that story with your son. You, Ben Berman, have forfeited your chance and when, from your son, you—"

Ben waved a hand at Tidewater. "This side of you I can do without," he said. "I've told you before. If you want your secrets, fine—but if you want them, why advertise them?"

"You should not mock what is happening here. You're a fool to leave us. When you're there, you'll see, you'll regret having gone away. What we have here is rare, what you will have there is nothing. Think: you mock it before you even know it—your resort-retirement community—doesn't that tell you enough?" Sam watched the man's narrow body, the long neck stretched forward toward his father. "Where you are going to is a place people pass through, from one death to another, as it were—the graveyard before the graveyard; where we are staying is a place that has substance. You do not kill great cities. In transition? There is more truth than irony in what you say."

"All right," Ben said. His eyes twinkled. "I'm sorry, yes? Let's say it was—well, just a phrase I was going through."

Tidewater's body relaxed at once, seemed to dance, sitting there. "Ah Ben," he said, smiling so happily that Sam felt his own stomach tighten.

Flo handed Ben a small package and he unwrapped it. "So that you'll write to us," she said, as Ben showed the silver pen and pencil set to the others.

"Thank you," Ben said. "From the gift wrapping I assume the proceeds did not go for muscular dystrophy."

"No," Flo said.

"Well," Ben said. "I appreciate it."

Flo kissed him on the forehead. Ben accepted a small package from Marion and untied the paper ribbon. Inside the wrapping paper was a box and inside the box was a leather travel kit: comb, brush, mirror, razor, toothbrush. Ben nodded a thank you to Marion.

"I hope you like it," she said.

"No kiss?" Ben asked.

Marion's chair scraped the floor. Flo stepped away, took her seat again, and Marion went to Ben, kissed him on the cheek. He reached up, held her hand, seemed emotional suddenly. "You do forgive me, don't you? For—"

"Things happen," Marion said, and sat down again.

Ben looked at Tidewater. "You go before me," Tidewater said to Sam, and Sam obeyed; he stood, went to the closet, next to the kitchenette, and took out the valise, brought it to his father. He'd returned four hundred of the five hundred to Willie the Lump, and had spent three-quarters of the hundred he'd kept on the valise, but it was the kind of thing he wanted to give his father: a genuine leather valise, with Ben's initials embossed in gold, next to the handle. It was the kind of valise he'd wanted to have himself, when he'd been traveling. He'd always bought quality stuff, but never anything as expensive as this, and it was, he realized, something he now regretted. "Here," he said.

"It's very—" Ben hesitated, wrinkled his forehead. "It's very handsome, Sam. Very appropriate."

Sam sat down. "It has your initials on it—on the top," he said.

Ben nodded. " 'S' is for Samson. I'm Samson," Ben said dreamily, but before there could even have been time for Sam to pick up his cue, Ben went on: "But—with your situation—where did you get such money? This must have—"

"Don't," Flo commanded. "Please don't, Ben."

Ben looked at the others. "What my son did for me—I'd like to make it up to him. I've told you all the story."

"That's right," Tidewater said. "We don't need it."

"All right," Ben said, caressing the coffee-colored leather. He rubbed a hand across his forehead, then brushed his hair. "I'll be like the man who lamented the coming of baldness—hair today and gone tomorrow—"

The others groaned, then smiled, but Sam saw nothing to laugh about. He was glad that he'd done the right thing—he hadn't wanted to get Ben something the others would have looked down upon—but the money it cost did hurt, it did put him that much deeper into Sabatini's—the word made him laugh out loud—grip. Sure. Sam knew how far playing with words could get you.

"You like that?" Ben was saying to him, he realized. "Hair today . . ."

"Sure," Sam laughed. "It's terrific, Ben," and, using the word—thinking at once of his buddies in their houses on Long Island, of Herbie's carpeted wastebaskets and Japanese lanterns—Sam found that he couldn't stop laughing. He felt tears rolling down his cheeks, he heard the others laughing with him, enjoying themselves.

"I see what you mean," Tidewater said to Sam.

"I'll say one thing for him," Sam said, feeling giddy now. He wiped his eyes. "Sure. He's been a terrific father. Terrific!"

Sam howled at this, and to his surprise found that the others, Ben included, were laughing with him. Marion, her hand against his shoulder, was telling Sam to stop.

"See?" Ben said, calming down. "Do you see what I mean, Mason?"

"Ah Ben," Tidewater said.

Ben stood. " 'Call me a cab,' the man said." Ben flicked his fingers into Marion's face. " 'Poof,' I said. 'You're a cab.' "

Sam's laughing stopped abruptly. "That's an old one," he said, aloud.

"Like your father," Ben said, and continued to laugh. "Tell him," he said to Flo. "Tell him—"

"When you're old," Flo said, reaching across for Sam's hand. "Ah, when you're old, Sam, the whole world is Jewish."

"Good," Tidewater said, his hand on Flo's arm. "That's very good," he said.

Sam looked away, did not take Flo's hand. "It's all the same to me," he said. "I'll put the valise away if you want—"

"No, no," Ben said, still chuckling. "Leave it beside me. It comforts me. You couldn't have given me anything more—appropriate."

"You said that before," Sam said.

"I remember things," Ben said. "I found a valise in my cab once, and the girl who called it to my attention—she was very beautiful. Do you know what was in the valise?" Ben waited, looked around. "I am certain, to this day, that the girl wanted me to know that the valise had been hers, though we both pretended it had not been hers. This was before your mother, Sam." Ben waited, then shook his head. "No. I won't tell."

"Please," Flo said.

"No," Ben said. "I shouldn't have mentioned it. I could have given other stories. My life as a taxi driver by Benjamin Berman— one would think, here in New York, that it was the king of professions—yet it was, in truth, dull and boring. Oh so boring. There were no interesting passengers, no back-seat births, no horde of people telling you just to drive around please. I watched the road, they watched the meter. The high point, in truth, was picking up by chance somebody you already knew—a relative, an old friend. . . . Famous people? They told you who they were before you'd recognized them." Ben sighed, swayed slightly from side to side, but his eyes twinkled. "It was, in short, the kind of life a man had to be driven to—"

Sam didn't mind hearing the others laugh. He remembered Stella talking about wheeling and dealing. He could add something to that, with Ben: sure, they were a regular team, with their professions—one wheeled, the other dealed.

"Except for Sam," Tidewater was saying, "we've passed the halfway point, and do you know what? I prefer it that way. Until a certain point, one lives with one's friends, one does things together—as we do every day, downstairs. And yet, one doesn't, after all. When one is with friends, I discover, one begins to spend much of the time reminiscing about the things one has done together previously—the way we might share tonight in time to come. The talking becomes the doing, don't you see? At a given moment in time, the reminiscing becomes more than half and the doing less than half. Things move in opposite directions until, near the end, we become almost all memory. Thus, you see, Ben, my gift to you tonight is the story I have already begun giving to Sam."

Ben sighed. "Didn't I tell you?" he said. "My son will take my place."

Tidewater's hand was resting on the handle of the leather valise. Sam nodded to himself: they could say what they wanted, about friendship or memories or dying or anything else, but they would never be able to deny that the valise was there.

"People worry about mugging," Ben said, performing. "How best to deal with muggers? It's simple: hypnotism." He looked around, smiled, but saw that nobody was smiling with him. "Schools of hypnotism. The world's finest hypnotists will train you to—" He lifted his glass of wine. "We couldn't have evening classes, though, could we, Samela?—people are so afraid to go out at night these days. . . ."

"It is your leaving, Ben," Tidewater stated, calmly, "now a certainty, which has—the good coming from the bad? the honey in the dead lion's carcass?—pushed me into putting my story into something resembling a narrative. Our talks, in my room, are over."

"Of course," Ben said. "But tell me one thing, what I asked you before: what do you want to *do* with your story, once it is on paper?"

"Do with it?" Tidewater asked. "Nothing, of course. It is enough to set it down."

"Ah," Ben said, seeing an opening. "But of what *use* will it be?"

Then Tidewater smiled, his eyes on Sam's face. "What use? Don't you know the answer to that, Ben?" Sam looked away and saw that Flo was sitting stiffly, her back straight, her hands at her sides, as if frozen in her chair. "To save your son's soul."

Then the two men were laughing together, and though their laughter was soft, even gentle, Sam didn't like it. "My son, my son," Ben hummed.

"You," Tidewater said, when he had stopped laughing. "You, Ben, are the only friend—with one exception—I have ever seen again. Any person I knew before 1928 I was obliged never—" He turned to Sam: "Your son should not be so foolish as to regard my life, and the writing down of this part of it, as anything exotic or unusual. There were thousands of us who played baseball in the Negro Leagues, and there were thousands of us—some as light-skinned as myself—who, in the half-century following the Civil

War, set down their life stories, often by themselves, with great literacy, often dictated to others. Then as now there was a great demand for the personal lives, for the details, the *secret* ways of black folks!" Tidewater spat the words out, laughed a wild laugh, almost maniacal. "I am not exotic, I am not even—the beginning of my tale—black. As you see, I am merely an old man saying good-bye to another old man, yes?"

He looked at Sam. "You'll have more—of my story—soon. You may serve the coffee and cake now, Florence." Flo brought a plate from the kitchenette—a chocolate cake on it—then put water on to boil, brought cups and saucers, spoons, plates, and forks.

"Well," Ben said, cutting the silence. He touched Sam's hand. "Mason's gift—it's not the kind I could have gotten on special—"

"Exactly," Tidewater said, but he did not smile.

"Who," Ben asked, "was the other friend?"

Tidewater stared ahead, at nothing, and made no move to reply.

"My girlfriend Irene," Flo said, "despaired of a happy marriage because, when she was living with a young Jewish boy, who had come to New York from Chicago, and who later became a well-known novelist, she tried to fix up his apartment for him, in Greenwich Village, and, instead of saying that she needed to go to the store for a can of paint, she said she needed to leave for a pain of can't . . ."

"So?" Ben said.

"Nothing," Flo said. "The phrase has been in my head, before, and while Mason was speaking. That was all. She never got over it, she claimed, and she put much too much stock into it, into one slip of the tongue. Still . . ."

Flo was trembling. She reached between Ben and Marion, with a knife, and cut into the cake. "I hope you like it. I wasn't used to your oven." She served a piece of the cake to Ben. "I'm sorry I'm so distracted, so far away. Irene and I were classmates, closest friends in college—at Barnard—and I keep hearing her say it, seeing her eyes get rounder and rounder. I keep hearing her voice, so plaintive, so—what do you think, Ben?"

"It sounds like pure cant to me," he said.

Flo started to reply, but changed her mind. She served a piece of cake to Tidewater, then to Sam, then to Marion.

"Very good," Ben said. "Thank you. It's very good."

Sam took a piece in his hand and bit into it; he watched Tidewater's mouth, obscure in the dark room, and thought of the soft chocolate—thick and sweet, the consistency somewhere between that of fudge and brownies—melting on his two-toned tongue. "And I'm sorry for being ugly," Ben said to Flo. He caught a crumb, falling from his lip, then hummed, the way Sam remembered his grandfather humming, at the end of a meal. When he spoke again, Ben's voice seemed very sweet: "You look at me and you see a small ugly man, cruel to friends and children, yes? But I was not always like this. Ah no!" Ben's hands were clasped in front of him, his body rocking gently back and forth. "When I was young, in Galicia, I was a very beautiful child, but when I was young, I was put into the hands of a wicked nurse, who exchanged me for another . . . and that is why today, you see before you the man who—"

"All right," Tidewater said. "All right."

"A fool," Ben went on, "can throw a stone into the water which ten wise men cannot recover."

"Enough," Tidewater said. "I will speak of my other friend, of—"

"Of course," Ben said, easily. "But note my son's continuing silence. If I think of how far I might have gone in radio—consider Sam's potential, for the first thing I taught any student at the school—my famous opening lecture—was silence. The only actors and announcers who succeeded were those who mastered the uses of silence—when to pause, how long to pause, how to sustain the pause, how, coming into people's homes, to let the silence work for you. The lack of sound . . . do you recall the lecture, my son? Will you use your silence, when I am gone, to look for a job?"

Sam laughed. Look for a job—that was the best one yet. The room was quiet again, and the quiet reminded Sam of how dark it was. Sam didn't measure the time, but in a short while Flo came to the table, poured the coffee, gave out second pieces of cake to each of them. "I will speak of my friend," Tidewater said, and looked, his eyes troubled, at Ben. Ben sipped coffee from his cup, his chin down at the table's level. There were, Sam could tell, a lot of things Ben might have said to Tidewater, but in the end, following his own advice, he rejected them all, and merely nodded his assent.

"In the early summer of 1930," Tidewater began, "posing as a newspaper reporter, I visited Rube Foster—the friend—who, in 1927, at the age of forty-eight, had been committed to the state mental institution at Kankakee, Illinois. He had been, from the time I decided to make my way as a ballplayer—from the time you last saw me, Ben, when we were in school together—the man I had respected most. Born in Calvert, Texas, he had begun earning his own living as a baseball player before he had finished grade school. A minister's son, he never drank (though he did not, when a manager, require abstinence of his players), and he carried a loaded pistol with him always. He had been one of the great players during the first two decades of this century, a man with unlimited confidence in himself and his right arm, and he had become, when I first knew him, a superb field manager, and the organizer and first president of the league in which I played.

"It was Foster, you see, and not John McGraw, who had invented the hit-and-run play, and the squeeze bunt, and it was Foster who was, in his time, the admitted master of psychological warfare. In fact, McGraw would hire him, between seasons, as a coach. I will never forget coming into his home park in Chicago, in 1923, and seeing the row of metal files, for sharpening spikes, which he kept hanging from the nails outside the visiting team's dressing room. I laughed, of course, at the sheer transparency of such a ploy, and yet, coming to know the man's glowering black face, I eventually came to feel a slight chill whenever I saw the files hanging there.

"Foster told me, at the end of my first full season, when, in Chicago, I had defeated his team for the World Series championship, that I could have been the greatest of them all. He had seen all the greats, from Moses Fleetwood Walker to John Henry Lloyd, and the best of the whites, too, from Willie Keeler to Cobb and Ruth and Johnson, and he declared that if I could last—for there were lots of young boys who could have one or two seasons as good as any other man's—I could make them forget all the others, including himself.

"When we could, though I did not play for his team, we would travel together, and share a room. He would often recount for me the fact that the separation of the races into separate leagues had come about quite slowly, and he believed that the time before there had been separate leagues—a time just before he had begun playing—had been the Golden Age of Baseball. He did not believe that the races would ever mix again, in baseball or elsewhere, and, along with his Bible, he kept in his traveling bag a copy of Moses Walker's *Our Home Colony—A Treatise on the Past, Present, and Future of the Negro Race in America*, not because he believed in the back-to-Africa movement, but because Walker had been the last (acknowledged) black man to play on a white team."

"I'm sorry we couldn't find the field," Ben began. "My intentions—"

"When I visited Foster in 1930," Tidewater continued, as if Ben had not spoken, "though he showed no sign of recognizing me, he did once—I spent but an hour with him, in a room he shared with five others—look out the barred window, and, pointing, said: 'There's McGraw, boy.' For though he knew that McGraw had tried, as with me, to hire black players many times under many guises—most famously in the case of Charlie Grant, a fine second baseman whom he tried to pass off unsuccessfully as a full-blooded Indian named 'Tokohoma,' it was his knowledge of my encounter with McGraw, when I refused to pass, which, I believed, first drew Foster to me."

Tidewater stopped, and his head pivoted sideways, to Ben. "He was a man with whom you would have had nothing in common, Ben, except perhaps your obstinacy, or your shrewdness, and these were not, of course, things one could have shared." His eyes moved from Ben, and his voice softened. "Foster died on December 9, 1930, and it pleased me in my foolishness to think that, sixteen years later, where he was, he had received the good news that, here in Brooklyn, a pigeon-toed black man of twenty-seven years old, whom even Sam has seen, one Jackie Roosevelt Robinson, the son of a Georgia sharecropper, had run out onto the grass of Ebbets Field, inaugurating what Rube Foster would surely have called, lacking my skepticism, the New Golden Age.

" 'You win the ballgame in one or two innings,' he taught us. 'Now is the time,' he would say, when the moment had come for his players to extend themselves." Tidewater paused, and Sam listened to the others breathing. "Even so is it with my own life," he went on. "For now is the time in which, setting down this brief narrative, and thinking of the years which have passed, I prepare to join myself with Foster, and with those others, discovered recently in the very place in which I am writing my story—my brothers who came before me and who, setting out from bondage toward their star, fell also, ignominiously short."

Tidewater exhaled in a way that let the others know he had finished. "Fell what?" Ben asked, as if puzzled. Tidewater glared at him, but did not reply. "You should leave the riddles to Rabbi Katimsky," Ben commented. "It's not your—"

"Please," Flo said, and Sam watched his father's small head bob up and down several times.

Sam checked the Knick box score of the night before, and winced: they'd beaten the Royals, 106 to 105, for their eighteenth in a row, three past the all-time Laker record. Stallworth had pumped in twenty-three points, his high for the season. Sam put the paper down, picked up the phone, and dialed. There were guys who would try to get back even by doubling up, but he knew how they ended. "It's Mr. Benjamin here," he said.

"Ah, Mr. Benjamin. This is Mr. Sabatini—I was just thinking about you."

"Sure," Sam said. "Listen, I thought I'd check—anything new with the Knicks?"

"It so happens, I can accommodate you now. Times are changing. But you'll have to take seven and a half points."

"Give me three singles for tonight then."

"Of course, sweetheart. It's why I was thinking of you—I was just having my first cup of coffee and saying to myself . . . and then, at this hour, your voice speaks to me." Mr. Sabatini chuckled. "You know what they say about the early bird catching—"

"Sure," Sam said. "Three singles." He hung up, and he didn't laugh. He put the newspaper away, listened to his father humming in the bedroom, where he was packing, picked up a copy of *Sport* magazine. There was an article on Stallworth in it, but they hadn't even put the guy's picture or the title of the article on the cover; it showed you how fast people forgot. Sam had read the article twice, and it still got him, all the details about when the guy had been laid up for the twenty-seven days, about how he'd begun cheating— going to the schoolyard against doctor's orders, about how he'd felt when he'd been given the green light to play again. "I felt like I could jump over a building." When you'd read a lot of these articles you could tell things: the guy who'd written it had liked Stallworth, and at the end, asking Stallworth—not about his heart (the guy had never done that, and Sam gave him credit there), but about the future—the words rang true, and Sam liked them: "What I look forward to most is—well, I'd just like to be able to relax for a change. I just want to relax. You know what I mean? I just want to relax a little in this life."

Sure, Sam thought, but with all he'd been through, they'd gone and given top billing to a half-dozen other articles. And what about—Sam's right fist clenched, involuntarily—all the guys who had never come back? Campanella, the greatest catcher of them all, who'd played in the Negro Leagues until he was almost thirty years old, crippled now, in a wheelchair, with his wife leaving him. Gehrig, of course, dead at thirty-nine; Big Daddy Lipscomb, six feet six and three hundred twenty pounds, who used to pick runners off the ground as if they were children—dead of an overdose of heroin; little Robin Freeman, the great guard from Ohio State, with two fingers sawed off his shooting hand before his rookie season in the pros; Ernie Davis, of Syracuse, maybe as good a runner as Jim Brown, dead of leukemia at twenty-two; Ray Chapman, killed by a beanball; Herb Score, never the same after a line drive had nearly taken his eye out; Ken Hubbs, the Cubs' second baseman, killed in a car accident after he'd been named Rookie of the Year . . . When he thought about it, Sam wasn't surprised at what they'd done to the article on Stallworth. Sure. For every guy who came back, who knew how many dozens never made it. Sam thought of the colleges—there seemed to be one every other year or so lately— which lost entire football teams in plane crashes, and, picturing himself watching Ben's plane take off from the runway at Kennedy Airport, he shuddered.

"I hope things work out," Ben said to him. "You know that. I couldn't help but hear your telephone conversation." Ben put a suitcase down, next to the one Sam had given him as a gift. "Tonight you'll have privacy."

"Peripheral," Sam said. "Whatever that means."

"Whatever that means," Ben repeated, and laughed easily. "I'm almost done now—if you could come into the bedroom for a minute, I'd like to show you a few things."

Sam followed his father into the room. Under the window, to the right of the desk, a trunk was open, packed two-thirds of the way. It was filled with boxes, manila envelopes, old newspapers—Ben showed Sam the cartons that were packed, ready for shipping, if Ben decided not to return to Brooklyn. The trunk was to be sent also, Railway Express. Ben's *tephillin* bag, Sam saw, was lying on the bed, with a *siddur* next to it, but Sam didn't comment. He followed his father to the desk, where Ben showed him the piece of paper with his address—for forwarding mail—and the envelope of papers that might, someday, concern Sam. Sam remained silent. "The brochure is yours," Ben said. "I thought you might like to have it, to—"

He stopped, shrugged, gestured to Sam to follow him into the bathroom. Ben opened the medicine chest above the sink. "I'm leaving you a few things—specials—that it doesn't pay to take with me: toothpaste, shaving cream . . ." Neither of them laughed. Ben closed the medicine chest, walked from the bathroom. "Sit down," he said to Sam. "On the bed—please." Sam sat, away from the *tephillin* bag, and waited. "Forget the specials business—I know all about it: it would make a good one-liner for an old radio routine—stealing to keep up with inflation—but I have my reasons, and—" He broke off, approached Sam. "Before I leave, there is one thing I want to talk to you about—just an idea, maybe as cockeyed as the last one we went in together on, but I'd like to have you hear me out. When I had to sell my medallion and give up the taxi, I think this idea was there then." Ben sat on the bed, pushed some manila envelopes and some undershirts to one side. "The trouble you're in—whatever it is—I think I can take care of it. I'd like to square accounts, to—"

"Look," Sam said. "I told you before, I take care of myself. You—"

"No," Ben said, putting his hand on top of his son's. "You don't understand. It's not like that. This is a—a what?—a dream of mine, let's call it. But things won't be so tight for me, and I've been figuring. I'll stay with Andy, of course, while he needs me—but when he's gone, I can sell the apartment, don't you see? I won't have to stay there—and I won't have to come back here. I know this is in the future, and forget about what I say with my usual sarcasm now and then, but what would you think if, when the time comes, we take off together, you and me." Ben paused. "We could buy a housetrailer."

Sam had nothing to say. Ben waited two or three seconds, then stood. "It was just a thought," he said, and turned away from Sam, toward the window, then continued turning in a slow circle, until he was facing Sam again, looking past him. "But I hear how flat it sounds now that the words are out. And I shouldn't have built your hopes up—the money, to help you out, isn't mine until Andy is gone, and he insists on lingering. You'll take care of shipping the cartons if I write—there's not much. It's good weather there, and if I need more clothing—for the active social life, yes?—I can buy. Andy isn't my height, or I'd—" Ben's eyes moved downward, to Sam's feet, then traveled upward. "Tell me, Samela—where did you come from?"

Sam tensed: he wanted, suddenly, to ask about Ben's father, and he sensed that Ben knew it. Sam felt pressure behind his eyes. It was bright outside—the sun melting the snow—but it wasn't, Sam knew, the glare that was bothering his eyes. He didn't like mysteries, that was all; the questions didn't come often, and he didn't dwell on them, but when they were there, they nagged at him, and if it were possible—if it didn't cost too much—it always made life easier to know a few things while you had the chance. Once Ben was gone there were things Sam would never know: things his grandfather had said and done, things about the village in Europe they'd all come from, things about Ben's own childhood and about Andy, the business about the girl in the taxi and about Sam's mother. Sure, he thought, if you started thinking this way—Tidewater had been right about that—there'd be no end: you could spend forever trying to get people to tell you about what you were like during those times you didn't, yourself, remember clearly. Sam had his usual advantage here—he remembered more than he wanted to—but there were still some blurred passages, some blind spots. Maybe, he thought, Ben's schemes were the equivalent of his own lapses. Maybe they were what filled up . . . "What," he found himself asking, "was that business between you and Marion last night?"

"Business?"

"You once told me some story about her, but I wasn't paying

attention." Sam stood and walked past his father. "Forget it—I was just curious. If you need any help—"

"I'd forgotten," Ben said. He arranged things in the open trunk, lifted a stack of papers from his desk and placed them in the space he'd made. "But of all the possible—why should you want to know this?"

"I'm a bird," Sam said.

"Ah," Ben replied, and smiled at his son. "All right. I'll keep working, though, yes?" Sam nodded, and Ben continued, easily. "It's very simple—the kind of story that we could have kept going for our listeners for months. Marion's husband—she's still married, you know, but he's on the road, a salesman—it seems that, before their marriage, Marion became pregnant and—his career at the time, her indecision about marriage—they had the pregnancy terminated. Her word."

Ben stopped, as if the story were over. "So?" Sam said. "It happens."

Ben nodded, bent over his trunk, his head below the top part, so that suddenly Sam was frightened that it might fall, clamping on his father's neck. "But—and here is the soap opera part—a few years after they were married they decided that they wanted a child, and they have been trying ever since. With your imagination, I don't doubt that you can see what even a single month—the daily obsessions—would have been like." Ben lifted his head abruptly, nearly grazing it on the lid of the trunk, where the hasp was. "They've tried different things, with each other, with"—Ben looked his son in the eye, then went on quickly—"others . . . with doctors, with tests—the entire catalog. Sometimes they're—"

"I was just curious," Sam said.

"But why—out of the blue—why that question, Sam? Aren't there other things that you'd like to know?" Ben's voice became sharper. "Now that the time has come for us to part, aren't there, in your mysterious brain, some questions simmering—don't you, too, my son, have your magnificent obsession?"

"Sure," Sam said, surprised that he was ready for his father. "I was wondering when—I mean, I have your address, right? If your two other brothers show up in New York, I'll let you know."

Ben's eyes widened, and Sam felt himself laughing, even though he could hear no sound coming from his mouth. "I see what you mean," Ben said. Sam leaned against the doorway, smiling at his father. Ben's head bobbed up and down. "Our fathers wouldn't—Mason's and mine—teach us the languages we should have known. That he learned the Latin sentences by heart, without ever learning to read and translate . . . It's something which moves me, which—"

"Look," Sam said, annoyed, "if I can help, say so, otherwise I'm gonna go downstairs, stretch my legs. You need anything?"

Ben hesitated, and Sam could have predicted the possible wisecracks his father could have made, but he saw also that his father was wary now, that he would not be so foolish as to say what he knew Sam would know he was going to say. Sam was not surprised, then, when Ben turned back to his packing with the single word, "Nothing."

Sam put on his green mackinaw and left the apartment. The line of Saturday morning shoppers stretched almost to the corner. At the curb, the snow, black-edged, was piled high between cars, but the sidewalks were clear and dark—wet from the melting snow. Sam didn't look into the rummage shop. He turned left. Nate the Numbers Man was standing at the corner, wearing sunglasses, talking to two women. If he'd wanted to, he knew, he could have said something about Andy—about the guy needing Ben's money, but being too proud to ask for it straight out. That was the real reason for having Ben come out there, and it surprised Sam to realize that his father, as smart as he was, didn't suspect. Sure. Ben had his blind spots too.

Sam crossed the street, lifting his head slightly to take in more sun. There was something lovely about the neighborhood on a morning like this, he thought—when the sun was out, and the sidewalks were wet, and people were heading out, to do whatever they did. Some girls were jumping rope on Martense Street, a few feet in from the corner. On the left side of the street, the wood-frame houses, wet—red and green and gray, with borders of snow on their pitched roofs—looked as if they'd been freshly painted. A football fell at Sam's feet. He picked it up, looked down the street where a young black kid was waiting with open arms. Sam lifted the ball, to toss it back, but it was slick from the puddles it had rolled through, and he couldn't get a good grip.

The kid, Sam could see, was eyeing him now, wondering if he was going to run off with it. Sam liked that. He cradled the ball in his right palm, his hand a few inches above the street; he skipped forward, on his right foot, his back bent over, let the ball drop, and laid into it with the instep of his right shoe. He remembered not to look up, and from the deep-sounding thud of the ball against his foot, he knew he'd connected. Even with his mackinaw restraining him, his foot went high and almost touched his left hand, which was stretched forward, for balance, parallel to the ground, and when he'd stayed frozen for a split-second in his follow-through, and then had let his breath out and looked up, he saw the ball still moving, point up, in a perfect spiral, high in the air, higher than the wood-frame buildings. He stuffed his hands in his pockets and continued along Nostrand Avenue, the picture of the kids in his mind—circling between the cars as they waited for the ball to come down. He wouldn't have been surprised if one of them would come up to him someday to ask if he'd ever played pro ball. It paid to stay in shape.

At Church Avenue, he crossed the street again and went into Steve's candy store. Ben's story about Marion hadn't surprised him. Things like that could run in families, he knew, in ways you wouldn't always suspect. Flo having had her kids, Marion still—the word they'd always used in Hebrew School—barren; it was, if you stopped to think about it, really the same thing with the two of them, only from opposite directions.

"How's tricks, Sam?" Steve asked.

"Okay," Sam said, and took a seat at the counter. A black man, in a carpenter's blue and white striped overalls, was drinking a cup of coffee three stools to Sam's left. "Quiet at this hour, huh?"

"Oh yeah," Steve said, his hands moving under the counter, cutting open a pullman loaf of white bread, stacking the slices. "Up till eight o'clock—when they're on their way to work—you keep going pretty fast, but it quiets down till about ten, ten-thirty, when the kids come in. You have to keep your eye on them—I mean, it's not the money, if you want the truth. They can take a couple of pieces of candy or some comic books—we all did that—but it's something else." He winked. "Like, they were scared to death of my father, and I feel I—well, you know—they shouldn't figure his son was a patsy is all, so I growl at them."

"I'll have a glass of milk," Sam said, "and a chocolate doughnut."

"Sure," Steve said. He lifted a stainless steel lid, below counter level, and took a container of milk from inside. "You know what I mean, though?"

"But they got your old man a few times, didn't they?" Sam said. "Not the little kids, but—"

"Sure," Steve said. "My mother wouldn't let him work finally, even after he was given a clean bill of health." He gave Sam his glass of milk, and the doughnut on a plate. "I keep a gun."

Sam shook his head sideways. "It won't help—they know what they're gonna do and you don't. The advantage is always with the guy who makes the first move in a situation like that."

"But they know I have it," Steve said. "Anyway, I get along with the locals. Unless a guy was really in a fix, he'd go somewhere else first. Things are changing, sure, but when I add up what's happened—in a year's time, say—it's not that much. A day like this, the neighborhood doesn't even look as if it's too different since we were kids."

Sam nodded. "I'm not moving out," he said, then added quickly, "but Ben is. He flies to California tonight—we have to be at the airport about six. He'll get supper on the plane, I guess."

"Sure," Steve said. "For a guy his age, it's the smart thing—take the snow last week, for example—when a guy his age slips and breaks a bone, it's not the same as it is for us. He's putting years on his life, moving out there."

"He says it's just for a visit—to see his brother, who's been sick—but we both know he's going to stay."

"I wrote to my old man, you know, after the last time you were in, and told him about your father, but he hasn't answered yet." Steve walked along the counter, took the money the black man had left, cleared the table, lifted some cold cuts out of a compartment, and wiped a piece of butcher block with a towel. "Hey," he said, coming back. "I knew I had something on my mind for you. An old friend of yours—Stein, Shimmy Stein—was in here the other day, and he asked if I'd seen you."

"He knows where I live," Sam said.

"I told him you stop by now and then, that was all." Steve leaned on the counter, close to Sam. "He's making a pile, but it's not the kind of money I'd want in my pocket. I know some of the guys he has to deal with. He could be in bad trouble, if—"

"He offered me a deal," Sam said, "but I turned it down cold."

"A guy like that, even though we grew up here together," Steve said, "he thinks he can come in now and clean up." Steve stepped back, glanced to the right. Sam saw two black teenagers enter the store, both wearing black leather jackets. "I could tell, just from his coloring, that it's taking its toll already. You did the smart thing, Sam, for what my opinion's worth."

The two boys sat down and ordered Cokes. The guy next to Sam unzipped his jacket, and on his belt Sam saw that there was, where a pistol would be, a slide rule, sticking out of a tan leather case. Sam asked Steve what he owed him, then paid. "See you around," he said, pushing off from the stool.

"Yeah," Steve said. "Take it slow. And give your old man all my best wishes. Tell him my father sent his regards—I mean, I know my old boy will say something, when he writes next."

"And if Shimmy comes around asking for me again," Sam said, and he winked, feeling warm, "you tell him you think I might have moved out with Ben, on the early retirement plan, right?"

Steve laughed and waved to Sam as he put two Cokes on the counter. Outside, Sam buttoned his jacket and headed down Church Avenue, toward the Granada Theater. The next time—he didn't want to press things—maybe he'd wait a few weeks, but he thought he might invite Steve to come over one night, after he'd closed the store up: they could have a few beers, some sandwiches, watch a game. It was strange how after all these years you could suddenly feel close to a guy you'd always known but had never been close to—and the others—except for Dutch, of course—who'd been your buddies, who you'd done everything with—there was something missing there now that your lives had taken different paths. The man and his dog rolled out toward Sam, and he tossed them a quarter, but didn't look when he heard the coin hit the sidewalk.

What he really would have liked to have bought—for Ben, and for himself too—was a pair of handmade shoes. Sam remembered that Mr. Fiala, who'd had the shoemaker's shop on Rogers Avenue until two or two and a half years before, had known how to make a pair of shoes, complete, from beginning to end. You lived in your shoes fifteen–sixteen hours a day, for a year or two years with a good pair. But Mr. Fiala's store was gone now, and Sam felt a peculiar hollow in his stomach, knowing he'd missed his chance.

At the corner of Church and Rogers, Sam entered a phone booth. There was no point in waiting until Ben had gone to start making plans.

"Hello?"

"Hi, Mrs. Cohen. This is Sam. Is Dutch in?"

"Hello, Sam," Mrs. Cohen said. "Dutch is in *shul.*"

"Shul?"

"He's been going every Saturday the past few weeks, and Monday and Thursday mornings also, for the reading of the Torah."

Sam sighed. He could see Dutch's dark eyes laughing at him. He'd timed things just right, hadn't he? "Okay," Sam said.

"He explains it all to me, of course, and it sounds reasonable, but . . ." She paused, and Sam waited. "What do you think, Sam? You're his closest friend."

Sam could see Dutch, on the Long Island Railroad platform, and he heard him laughing. "I got things on my mind, Mrs. Cohen. Tell him I called. My old man leaves tonight, for California. I got to go now, okay?"

He hung up before she could reply. He should have been ready for something like this, with the way Ben had called him into the bedroom, leaving the *tephillin* bag where he had. He left the phone booth and started walking. The two of them wandering around the country together, dragging a trailer behind them—that was really rich.

He returned home at twelve-thirty, and he and Ben ate lunch together: cream of mushroom soup, and tuna fish sandwiches. Sam gave Ben the message from Steve's father, but he said nothing about Dutch or Shimmy, and he felt, coming in from the cold after a long walk, relaxed. Ben was quiet, and this was all right with Sam too. After lunch, Ben took a nap; the packing had fatigued him and he said that the change in time would tire him, after the plane flight. Sam did the dishes and then, feeling tired also, he lay down on his couch and was asleep immediately.

When he awoke, his head felt thick. Ben was sitting at the kitchen table, dressed in a brown suit, a white shirt and tie. "I could go myself, you know," he said, "if you have something to do. It's Saturday night—"

"Come on," Sam said, and waved him off. He stood, went to the kitchen sink, and rinsed his face, then shook the droplets off, dried himself. "Whenever you say."

"We'll go downstairs first, to say good-bye."

"Sure," Sam said. He put his shoes on, changed his shirt, then sat at the kitchen table and drank a cup of coffee Ben had poured for him. He was surprised at how black his sleep had been. That rarely happened in the middle of the day. Ben's eyes were closed, as if he were dreaming. Sam saw his grandfather, remembered Ben's story from the night before. "You didn't sleep, then?" Sam asked.

"Oh no," Ben said. "I slept. I know I slept because I remember dreaming."

"What'd you dream?"

Ben smiled, his eyes open now. "That I couldn't fall asleep."

Sam wiped his mouth, laughed. "You," he said. He picked up his mackinaw from the easy chair next to the breakfront, then took a suitcase in each hand. "I'll take these downstairs now."

Ben opened the door, and Sam walked onto the landing. The suitcases weren't too heavy. Ben had probably left all his books and papers in the trunk—clothing never weighed much. Muriel gazed at him from between the wooden posts, and Sam thought he saw her smile. Downstairs, he went out the front door—he didn't want to push through the shoppers, from the rear—and entered the rummage shop through the street entrance.

"How's tricks?" he said to Marion, at her desk. "You sleep okay after all that stuff last night?"

She nodded. "Just fine, Sam."

"These are Ben's," Sam said. "I'll leave them here—don't sell them, okay?" Marion smiled, and Sam put the suitcases behind her chair. The store was crowded. "Busy, huh?" he said.

A woman handed Marion a cardboard carton, filled with torn nylons. Marion took them out, one by one. "The usual," she said. "Mrs. Scofield was in this morning—she asked about you. You remember her, don't you?"

"Sure," Sam said. He wondered if that was why—what Ben had told him—he'd always had the feeling she was waiting for him. "I gotta get some more things."

He walked outside, went back into his building and up the stairs. Ben stood in the middle of the room, a raincoat over one arm, a briefcase in his other hand. "If you take that valise—the one you gave me—we can leave."

Sam was sweating. He took off his mackinaw and held it under one arm. Ben opened the door, handed Sam his key, glanced back briefly, then left. Sam locked the door. Ben kissed Muriel good-bye, on the forehead, then walked down the stairs, stiffly, Sam following. When they entered the rummage shop, Flo was there, next to Marion's desk.

"Mason?" Ben asked.

"He said to say good-bye—that you'd understand."

Ben put his raincoat down, on Marion's desk, and reached into his inside jacket pocket. "I had something for him—for all of you—it came this morning, from Andy. I know Mason would appreciate it—you give it to him later, all right? It's an item from the newspaper."

Marion was taking money from a customer. From the back of the store somebody called for Flo—asking the price on a desk and chair. Flo left them, touching Sam's hand as she went by, and Sam and Ben stood at the side of the door, leaving a passageway for shoppers. "I bought this suit here," Ben explained to Sam. "But this is only the second time I've worn it."

Flo returned, her glasses swinging from around her neck. "I'll go down to Church Avenue and get a taxi," Sam said. "It might take a while."

Ben held his son's arm. "You should see this also—it's nothing special, just Andy's sense of humor, but—" He handed it to Flo. "So that you see the world I'm entering, so that—"

Ben stopped. Flo held the small piece of newspaper in her hand, and Sam leaned over her shoulder, to read it:

> *Pioneer City, California* (UPI) Dec. 10. The flames of love never die, it seems, in the quiet senior citizen city of Pioneer Estates. Yesterday morning, before sunrise, this village of some five and a half thousand residents was awakened by an explosion in one of its two high-rise condominiums, and this morning a 78-year-old resident was apprehended for having caused the explosion by throwing a Molotov cocktail, made out of a prune juice

bottle, through the second story window of an apartment belonging to a man he claimed had stolen his girlfriend from him. There were no injuries, but damage was estimated at $15,000.

Above the item, in ink, Andy had written: "Prevues of Coming Attractions. (Ha ha)" Flo laughed easily, but Sam—though he too found the item funny—felt something inside him clench. He wanted to get going. "I am sorry," Ben said, "that I forfeited my chance—as Mason put it—by leaving."

Sam rolled his eyes, and found that he was seeing Tidewater and hearing what Tidewater had said to him about Ben being worried. "She was on her knees," Flo was saying, her mouth close to Ben's cheek, "with the tears streaming down her face, and she was praying. This morning"—Flo glanced at Sam—"her husband and sons had pulled it—the refrigerator—into the store on a dolly, and everybody had gathered around. I was embarrassed at first—but when I understood, I didn't laugh. She hadn't heard the motor when she'd plugged it in—the machine is almost new, and very silent—and had thought, therefore, that it didn't work. But when I explained to her that the motor made no noise—I showed her the ice beginning to form—she hadn't even looked inside—she dropped to her knees and cried and blessed me."

"You'll write," Ben said. "And we'll trade stories, yes? Maybe Sam can help out with the few things I did for you—telephoning, and—"

"Sure," Sam said. "I've got the time."

Flo smiled at him, and he felt pleased. "You'd better get the taxi now," she said.

Sam left the store. He walked, then stood in front of Steve's candy store and, to his surprise, was able to flag down a taxi on the opposite side of Church Avenue immediately. He crossed the street and got in. "We're going to the airport," Sam said. "Kennedy. But we got to pick up my father first. He's the one who's going. Back on Nostrand Avenue, between Martense and Linden."

"Right, mack," the driver said, and flipped the lever down to start his meter going. He made the first right turn he could, to be able to circle around, and Sam settled back, relieved to have found a taxi so soon. "Yeah," he said. "My old man's retiring. He's going to live in California, in a senior citizen place."

"Good for him," the driver said. His voice was friendly, sharp. "I got an older brother who moved into one of them places, near Miami, and his wife went and died on him the first year. There's a lot of action, you know—more than you'd think. My brother says there's even guys who phony up records to get in early, so they can get a piece of the action, if you know what I mean." Sam thought of Andy's newspaper item, and laughed. "He was the goodlooking one in the family, my brother—we were six brothers and three sisters—but he says he's never rolled in it the way he's doing now." The driver lifted the cigarette lighter from the dashboard and lit a half-smoked cigar. "And then there's all that sunshine, a couple of good race tracks, and the dogs, if you go for that stuff. With the way the city's been changing, if you know what I mean, you got to be crazy—like me—to stay here. I got another brother moving down there this spring, but the brother I was telling you about—" The taxi stopped for a red light, back again at Church Avenue. "You got a minute—? He was a plumber, see, and he's seen it all, let me tell you. This one time, he was on his back under a sink, wedged in like, working away and all of a sudden he felt this thing crawling up his leg. He nearly cracked his head open, sitting up—surprised—but he couldn't move and—get this—this chick was going down on him right there, half his age, with her baby crying in the bedroom somewhere."

The driver blew smoke toward the roof of the car. The light changed. "Next block—in front of the rummage shop," Sam said, then added: "My old man was a taxi driver too—for over thirty years."

"Oh yeah?" the driver said, and Sam didn't know why, but he felt pleased, sensing the sudden coldness in the man's voice. They pulled up in front of the store, and Sam got out, went inside. He took two suitcases, brought them to the car, and left them at the curb, for the driver to put into the trunk. Then he returned. Two women were screaming at each other, arguing over who had seen a dress first. Flo held onto Ben's hand while she called to the women, trying to calm them. "It's all right," Ben said, and kissed Flo on the cheek. "I'll be all right." Nobody seemed to notice when Ben bent down and kissed Marion, on the forehead. Sam looked around the store—Tidewater wasn't there. Flo had her hands on the shoulders of the two women, facing the rear of the store, and Sam was glad—he could imagine what she was probably thinking; he vowed that, in the next few weeks, he would give her a lot of attention.

Ben walked to the taxi and got in. Sam got in beside him and didn't look into his father's face. The driver turned right, along Linden Boulevard, and headed for the Belt Parkway—he said nothing, and Ben too sat silently, seeming smaller than usual to Sam, in his suit, his raincoat folded across his lap. The sun was bright, and farther along Linden Bulevard, when they were closer to the highway, Sam remembered having been driven there as a boy, so that his mother could show him that there were still farms in Brooklyn. He nodded to himself. That part of Tidewater's story had been true.

The traffic was light, and they arrived at the airport just after five-thirty. "I can manage—you go back with the driver," Ben said when they were in front of the TWA terminal.

"Forget it," Sam said, and handed the driver a ten dollar bill, waited for his change. The two men got out, and Sam let a redcap take the bags. "San Francisco," Sam said to the man, who tagged the suitcases and gave the receipts to Ben.

"They might be over. . . ." Ben said, referring to the weight of the suitcases.

"I'll take care of it," the man said, and he flashed a smile. "Don't you worry, sir." Sam gave him a dollar, and wondered if, seeing thousands of people come and go every day, he understood what kind of trip Ben was taking.

Inside, Sam waited behind as Ben checked in at the counter and selected his seat, midway—just behind the wing—a window seat. "I've never flown before," Ben said to the man behind the counter, but the man smiled perfunctorily and said nothing. Sam glared at him for a second, but he didn't bother to get angry. Sure. It didn't cost much to be nice, the way the redcap had been, to take a little bit of an interest in people, but Sam wasn't going to let himself get worked up over it. The guy, from the way his hair was slicked back, and the way he moved, as if he were sliding around instead of walking, probably went in through the back door anyway. Sam laughed, remembering the expression.

"Yes?" Ben said.

Sam took his father's arm, led him away from the counters and into the lounge, where the plush red seats were sunk down, below floor level. "You want a drink or something?" Sam asked.

"No," Ben said. "Just tell me why you—"

They sat, facing the enormous window which looked out on the runways. "On the night of their honeymoon, see, this guy gets in with his wife—she's all spiffed up in a fancy nightgown—and just before, he says he has something to tell her. She asks him what. He tells her that, before they met, he'd had—you know—relations with another man." Sam licked his lips, glanced around, but nobody was paying attention to him. On the other side of the pit, a little boy in a fancy coat, with a velvet collar, was lying on his back on the floor, screaming and thrashing with his feet. "So this poor girl, see—she didn't know which way to turn."

Ben laughed and put his hand on his son's knee. "That's good. I'll remember to tell it to Andy." Ben sighed then, and leaned back. "I'm nervous, you know. What do you think, Sam—should I take out insurance? Pave the way for your comeback, should anything go wrong."

"Come on," Sam said. "You'll give me the creeps with stories like that."

"I don't think people buy plane insurance the way they used to," Ben said. "I was out here before it was an airport, you know—just marshes—" He started to stand. "Come—I'll get a quarter's worth, or whatever it costs. I saw the machine before. You put the money in. Since you're here with me, I won't even need a postage stamp—"

Sam dug his fingers into his father's arm, forcing him down. "I said to cut it out. You and your sense of humor."

"If Mason asks you not to tell me about what he's written, you won't, yes?"

"Whatever you say," Sam said.

"You're restless, I can tell. Please—why don't you go ahead. It's less than fifteen minutes till I board—I can manage myself. I'll write to you when I get out there—and—I'm sorry to say it again, but I will try to even our accounts, as soon as I can. I think I can work something out. So go ahead now—"

"I'll stay," Sam said.

"All right," Ben said, and sighed again, sinking into the softness of the chair. His color, Sam saw, was terrible, and—if the plane had a rocky flight—would probably get much worse. Sam looked intently at his father's face, hoping to see something new, to notice some physical detail—some sign of aging—that he could use, that he could fix his mind upon later, but the face seemed the same to him as it had always been. Inevitably, though, he saw himself—as he looked through the window at a man with earmuffs, flagging an arriving jet in—as a boy, as smaller than his father, but he was used to this feeling. If he had wanted to, he knew, he could have put himself inside Ben's head—he could have tried to see what thoughts were occurring at such a time, but that too, he knew, would have proven nothing. He appreciated the absence of Ben's voice. Words—and pictures too—where did they get you? There wasn't enough time for anyone else ever to know what had passed between them, and to give things names didn't help either. Sam understood now why Flo kept no photographs, and hearing her explain, as she once had ("if one has a photo of a time and a place, of yourself or a friend—then one tends to exclude those times, all those times, when somebody was *not* there with a camera . . ."), Sam felt that he suddenly understood her better than he ever had. He'd been fooled, hadn't he, thinking she didn't keep photos of her husband and two children because it was too painful; he'd forgotten until now, and realizing why she didn't keep photos—the same reason he would not start trying to imagine the pictures Ben was seeing in his head at a time like this—he felt himself grow warm, he knew how much—more than he'd ever imagined—she must have loved her children.

When Ben's flight was announced, he rose, and Sam walked with him arm in arm through the long tubular walkway that led to the departure gate. Ben showed his ticket to the man at the counter, and then walked to the door. Sam bent down, kissed his father on the cheek, and held him, with his right arm, behind the shoulder. He felt Ben's lips on his own cheek. "Yes," Ben said, and turned away. Sam waited, watching Ben disappear into the collapsible tunnel that had been hooked up to the plane's door, but Ben didn't turn around.

Sam left the terminal immediately and—he was low in cash—waited for a bus which took him to the East Side Terminal in Manhattan. He walked the few blocks to Grand Central Station,

got the Lexington Avenue IRT to Brooklyn. At the Eastern
Parkway–Brooklyn Museum stop, after he'd changed to the Seventh Avenue Line (at Franklin Avenue), two Puerto Rican kids
came jitterbugging down the length of the car, dancing to the beat
of a bongo drum that a third guy was playing. They kept dancing,
moving wildly, keeping their balance even while the train was
barreling along, and the smaller Puerto Rican boy, whose eyes were
almost closed, as if he were drugged, finished by running halfway
down the car and flipping over, holding onto the bars in the center,
then resting on the floor, in a split. When the train stopped at
President Street, the guy who'd been playing the drums—he was
white, maybe thirteen years old—went around, holding out a beret.
Sam put some change in. The kids worked hard. "Take it easy,
champ," one of the Puerto Rican kids—not the drugged one—said
to him, as they got out onto the platform.

Sam had nothing to say to them. He saw Ben, in the airport
lounge, laughing, and he realized that the joke he'd told had been
one that Ben had once told to him, on their way to the radio school
one day, in the subway. Sam gave his father credit. He was glad he
hadn't remembered until now.

He got out at Church Avenue and walked home, his hand in his
pocket, on his knife. The store was already closed, Tidewater
below, and Sam was surprised, looking at his watch, to see that it
was past nine-thirty. The bus, caught in the traffic—all the crazy
people who'd moved out to Long Island heading back into the city
for Saturday night—had taken longer than he'd expected it would.
In the apartment, Sam turned on the radio and sat down on his
couch. He listened to some light music, and when the news came on
he was not surprised to hear that the Knicks' winning streak had
been broken; they had lost to the Detroit Pistons, 110 to 98, and,
hearing the score, Sam knew that there was nothing to do but
laugh, and so he rested his head against the back of the couch and
let himself go.

10

Sam had telephoned Mr. Sabatini on the day following Ben's departure and had bet on the Knicks again. He took five points; the Knicks won by four. On the following day he had telephoned and bet again, this time on the Los Angeles Lakers. The Lakers had lost. Sam was not surprised. In fact, if he'd wanted to, he could have told Sabatini that the way to make a bundle now was to lay your money against whatever Sam Berman was picking. He continued— every day for the first three weeks he was alone—to bet, and to lose, and to shrug off his losses. It was all the same to him; he wasn't, he knew, required to believe in any of it.

He did, still, believe in some things—in things such as Ben's absence and the fact that he'd read part of Tidewater's story; he believed in the cartons of clothing he opened for Flo; he believed in the line of shoppers that waited outside the rummage shop on Saturdays; he believed in his knife; and he believed in the contraptions in Stella's apartment—the pulleys and wheels that were rigged up to enable her to have use of her arms and hands for her work. She had telephoned him, on New Year's Eve, while he was watching the finals of the Holiday Festival on TV, and he had gone to her apartment for the first time the following afternoon, and had stopped by twice since then. She was, like Flo, direct with him: "If I wouldn't call on New Year's Eve, why should I call some other time—you know what I mean?" She lived in a two-room apartment, smaller than his place, and—despite the presence of all the special devices which enabled her, in her words, to cope—he felt comfortable when he was there.

"If I were you and you were me, I'd be fascinated by all these contraptions too, right?" she'd said, and had given Sam a tour of the apartment, moving her wheelchair by herself, ahead of him. Once she'd shown him how the pulleys worked (attached to wheels near the ceiling, they looked to Sam like elaborate versions of the wiring attached to dentist's drills), Sam could see that she was telling the truth when she said that it wasn't all that complicated or difficult. Still, he gave her credit. And he was, he admitted, fascinated by the machines—the silver cups she slipped under her elbows and forearms, the attachments she had to grab with her teeth, the way rollers and ballbearings had been installed in drawers and in kitchen and bathroom equipment—and he liked the easy way, once her arms had use of the pulleys, that she could handle things, in the kitchen, or at her desk. The system of pulleys and weights, she explained, enabled her arms to float freely, so that she needed to expend a minimum of energy—of muscle—to get things to move. Her arms, when they started working, looked to Sam like the arms of a marionette, flopping jerkily, and yet she showed Sam, at her desk, just how precisely she could work. She made a decent living, she explained, designing greeting cards and—Sam laughed with her when she showed him a sample of her other work—the backs of playing cards. "I knew we had something in common, Sam the Gambler," she'd said.

Next to her bed, beside her desk, at the stove, and next to the living room couch, she had buttons which connected her with two other apartments in her building: one buzz was for the apartment of a fourteen-year-old girl, Sandra, who helped her get dressed and undressed, morning and evening, and two buzzes were for the superintendent (who'd wired the system for her), if the girl wasn't home, or if Stella was ever in trouble. "My mother comes by too," Stella said. "Once a day. You try to stop her—I gave up."

Sam had questions, naturally, but he let them ride. For the time being it was enough that he had a place to go to when he felt like it, now that Dutch had flipped out on religion. He liked being with Stella, and he had, of course, asked himself why, but, since Ben had left, he also liked being around Tidewater. He hadn't been to the man's apartment yet, but when Tidewater sat in Sam's room and droaned on, explaining things—about parts of his story or growing up with Ben—Sam felt at ease. The man had a good touch with words, and even when Sam wasn't paying attention, he enjoyed having the sound of the voice in the room with him. Sometimes, he admitted, he figured things wrong—he had to force himself to remember that it had originally been the man's silence which had riled him.

Flo, too, had been very kind to him since Ben had left—and Sam had, as he'd promised himself, spent as much time with her as possible, listening to her talk with her clients, listening to her retell some of Ben's stories, listening to her tell him how pleased she was—he was glad she didn't stay closed-mouthed about it—about his new friendships with Stella and Tidewater.

Sam enjoyed hearing other people talk. He liked being alone at night, watching television or listening to talk shows on the radio. He liked keeping his windows open, if it wasn't too cold, and listening to the sounds from the street below. The noise of the city comforted him. Why live in a place like New York, he reasoned, if you didn't like having sound around you. Sam liked the sound of the crowd at a basketball game, he liked the jabbering of the women in the rummage shop, he liked the sound of air-hammers and generators in the street. When he passed building construction sites, he would rest for a minute or two at the openings, listening to the noises that echoed inside. He liked the sounds of cars and sirens, portable radios and garbage trucks, and he enjoyed the screeching and deep rumbling of the subway. If he wanted silence, he knew, he could always go into Ben's room, which he hadn't touched since Ben had left.

The brochure lay just where Ben had left it, on the desk, and Sam stopped to look at it sometimes on his way to or from the bathroom. He could hear Ben's voice reciting the blurbs, and he could also hear, always, Tidewater's thinner voice, telling Ben the truth: that he was going off to live in the graveyard before the graveyard. But Sam laughed; he figured Ben had probably used that line a dozen times by now, making it his own. His father would get by, there or here, and the fact that nobody—neither Sam, nor Flo, nor Tidewater—had heard from him yet didn't mean anything. What could Ben say, after all: *Having a wonderful time in the*

heartland of this famous California playground. Wish you were here.
All residents must be ambulatory. . . .

On Sunday morning, three weeks and one day after Ben's flight, Sam telephoned Mr. Sabatini, as he did every day.

"This is Mr. Benjamin here."

"Ah, Mr. Benjamin," Mr. Sabatini said, and there was, Sam could tell immediately, something different in Sabatini's tone. "I have some good news for you, sweetheart. You don't owe me anything anymore."

"Sure," Sam said.

"Yes. When you forgot your weekly appointment with my boy Willie yesterday, I decided it was time to let you off." Sabatini paused, but Sam said nothing. He had a good idea of what was coming. "From now on you owe some friends of mine the money you owed me, all right? I've transferred your account. You pay them five singles a week until you're back even, plus some interest—but they'll be in touch with you about details."

"You're a sport," Sam said.

"Believe me," Mr. Sabatini said, "I'd like to keep your account, don't you know that? You've been a good client for over six years—and I must say I've taken a personal interest in you. If it was up to me, Mr. Benjamin, I'd let you charge it, but my accountant says no. It's a very hard year, as I'm sure you've noticed. Money is tight."

"Thanks a lot," Sam said, and tried to make his voice sound light, easy.

"What I wanted to do was to use you as a business loss—but, again, my accountant wouldn't let me. In this line of work, if I let my heart be my guide, where do you think I would be today? Remember, Mr. Sabatini sold apples in the thirties. That's why—"

"You talk too much," Sam said. "Thanks for nothing."

"My friends will be seeing you. You're a good boy, I can tell that—please, be careful. Do what they say. Do you hear me? I wouldn't want to hear one day that . . ."

Sam thought he heard passion in the familiar voice, but it meant nothing to him. "I look out for number one," he said.

"And give my best to your father, in his new life," Mr. Sabatini said. "Good-bye and good luck—"

"Don't phone me again, you hear?" Sam heard his heart pumping; he hissed into the mouthpiece. "You goddamned—" Sam searched for a word.

"Telephone you? But sweetheart, *you* telephoned *me*—don't you know that? I never telephone anybody."

Sam hung up. Don't bet what you don't have—the first rule, and he'd gone against it. But if you don't believe in any of it, then why, he asked himself, are you so upset? Sure. Answer that and win a trip to California. He drank a glass of milk and sat on his couch, adding up, for the first time, the amount he owed. He was glad at least that he hadn't given Sabatini satisfaction there, by asking for the sum. There were the bets before Ben had left; there was the loan for Simon's card game and Ben's valise; there was the first three hundred on the Knicks the night Ben had left; and there were the bets every day since then for three weeks—Sam hadn't needed to write them down: he could remember each bet, the score of each game; and he could figure the total in his head, with the interest: it came, exactly, to six thousand six hundred.

Sam laughed. Six thousand six hundred dollars wasn't, after all, the kind of figure someone in his situation could—the word was rich—afford to believe in. Good news was right. Sabatini would be off his back; there'd be no more telephone calls. Sam knew all about the kinds of guys he'd been transferred to—the things they'd try to do to get their money; the way they'd draw the noose tight; he could have thought it all out if he'd wanted to, and envisioned everything—but there was no point in thinking about things ahead of time, he told himself. Let the cards fall, that was all.

He put his mackinaw on and left the apartment. Muriel stood in front of her door, as if she were guarding it. Sam put his keys in his pocket. "You wanna come with me?" he asked. "Maybe he's got a story for you too."

Muriel's eyes did not move. There was something in the soft way they stared at him that he liked—but those eyes had something of their mother's glance in them. You had to watch out, he knew. Some of the biggest bastards and goons in the world had once been cute kids. He started down the stairs and it was only when he had gone halfway that he realized she was following him. He turned and watched her; she had one hand on the banister, while the other clutched a rag doll. She stepped carefully. Sam walked back up. "You got to stay home, kid," he said. "It's cold out and you're not dressed."

She reached across her body with her right hand, squeezing her rag doll between two posts of the balcony, so that it waited on the landing of their floor; then she offered her free hand to Sam. He took it and tried to get her to walk upstairs with him, but she refused. Her grip was hard. "Look, I got to see a man about a—" He broke off, removed his hand. "You just stay here, see?" He walked down and away, quickly. "Hang loose," he called.

He turned to his right, at the bottom, around the staircase, and entered the dark part of the corridor, where the light did not reach.

"Hello, Sam." The back door to the rummage shop opened. "I heard your steps. Come in a minute, dear."

"Sure, Flo," Sam said, and entered behind her.

Flo ran a hand across her forehead. "I've been working a little—getting things back in order after yesterday." She smiled at him warmly. "Sundays are lonely for me."

"I'll bet," Sam said, then laughed with her at the figure of speech he had used.

"Ben used to visit me sometimes on Sundays—we'd take walks." She sat down, in an old red armchair. "I shouldn't sound so wistful. Nobody ever promised me anything, as they say. We knew he'd stay out there—and I think we knew we wouldn't hear from him." She looked past him. "I must be keeping you. You have your coat on."

"I'm going to Stella's," Sam said. "But I got to see Tidewater first."

Flo's eyes seemed to grow darker. "He's been very busy lately," she said. "I rarely see him anymore. He stays below."

"He's okay," Sam offered. "I mean—"

Flo waved her hand at him, to be quiet, and her eyeglasses, hanging around her neck, bounced slightly on her bosom. She closed her eyes and, as she did rarely, looked her true age. "I'm tired."

"It's the winter," Sam said. "It gets to you. I mean, you can't blame Ben for—"

Sam fingered some silverware on a yellow Formica table. He wondered if Flo were thinking about her two children and her husband, and then he wondered why it was that, whenever he was around her, he thought of what her life had been. He was warm, but he didn't want to take his coat off. He would just as soon have gone downstairs and gotten that over with, once and for all. It wasn't that he was afraid—as he might have thought he would have been, if he'd asked himself about it previously; it was simply that, having decided to visit the man's place after all the time they had been living in the building together, it might as well be sooner than later.

"I didn't ask you in simply to tell you I was tired," Flo said. "And I won't keep you. But I want to say something that's on my mind. It's important."

Her voice was cold. "Shoot," Sam said, smiling, hoping she would see that he was pleased to have her address him directly.

Flo leaned back in her chair. "I could preface what I'm going to say with a thousand qualifications, thoughts—but they would all come to the same thing." Sam had an urge to reach out, so that he could smooth her forehead, her hair. "Yes. I think you care about my opinion, Sam. And I think I have some sense of your turn of mind. Here, then: I'd like Stella to bear your child."

Sam felt something hammer on his chest. "*What*—?" He coughed, needing air. "Listen, are you—?"

Flo continued, ignoring his reaction. "Stella has said nothing to me, but I love her and know her too, and I'm sure she has, already, allowed herself to hope. You should say nothing to her, though, about what I've said." Flo's lips were touching Sam's forehead, and—he didn't know how—he found that he was sitting in a green chair, his hands at his sides. Flo's hands were on the back of his neck, touching him. "You see, Sam, I love you like a son. And—this has all come to me since the day we took the trip together, to Ben's and Mason's old neighborhood—it pains me to think of you living on here by yourself someday, without seeing anything of yourself that will live on when you are gone. Ben is gone. My children are gone. Stella has no brothers or sisters. This store will be gone."

Sam thought of moving, but he didn't. His head, sticking out from his mackinaw, felt cool, but his body, inside, felt hot. Flo's lips were smooth, like satin, and they moved against his forehead, above his eyes, touching his skin. "Of course I want this for myself—isn't that obvious?—but that doesn't mean that it shouldn't be right for you too. This has been on my mind. I came here today hoping you would pass so that I would, once I'd stopped you, alone, have to tell you." Despite what she was saying, her voice remained cooler than her lips. "You'll do what you want—what you have to—and if nothing happens, that will be no worse than if I'd said nothing." He felt her breath on his neck. "I think sometimes that I know your turn of mind, and yet I couldn't be sure the same thought had, or had not, occurred to you. Ben was right. In some things, you are a mystery, Sam. You should have a child. You're not too old. Stella can bear you a child. Think about it. You don't have to say anything."

Her voice moved away and Sam found himself at the door. "Sure," he said. "I mean, sometimes I think about what you must have gone through."

"This has been on my mind," Flo said. "I came here today hoping you would pass."

Sam sniffed through one nostril. Then, feeling weak, he said, "I don't get it." He paused, his hand on the doorknob. He wanted to say something clever—after all, he thought, it had taken a lot for her to have said something like that to him, as weird as it was—still, nothing occurred to him. "I don't get it," he said a second time, and was surprised to hear himself, with a boy's voice, say such a thing.

"Don't be afraid," Flo said, but when she came toward him, through the maze of cartons and used furniture, her hands slightly outstretched, palms up, he turned and slipped through the doorway, into the darkness of the corridor. He closed the door behind him. Above, in the light from his landing, he saw Muriel's feet hanging down, below the posts of the banister. As he opened the door under the staircase, he felt the weakness pass from him. He didn't, of course, have to believe Flo, but she didn't fool him either. He imagined Sid and Herbie and Max and Shimmy—even Nate—crowing over him, telling him how terrific his kid was, and the thought angered him. The birds were, Sam knew, switching on the light and heading down the wooden stairs to the cellar, everywhere, trying to make you—he laughed to himself, sweating, hearing his shoes bounce on wood, thinking of words—swallow anything. He remembered Sabatini—heard his voice—trying to make him quail, and he laughed aloud because he could have told him, or Flo—or anybody—that they were wasting their time: in poker or in life, Sam Berman couldn't be gulled.

The cellar was dry and warm, the light dim. The furnace, black and red, was to the left. Pipes ran along the ceiling, packed in white casing. The concrete floor, under Sam's shoes, had a thin layer of grit on it, so that Sam felt as if he were walking on sandpaper. There were wooden bins along one side of the room, with padlocks—Sam supposed that he and Ben were entitled to a bin, though they'd never used one. Along the back end, arranged more neatly than they were upstairs, furniture and cartons for the rummage shop were stored, perhaps five or six feet deep. Sam had to duck, stepping around a supporting pillar, in order not to hit his head against low-hanging copper pipes. Shovels and brooms and wooden poles were lined up against the side of one bin, and three garbage pails stood next to them. Sacks of special salt, for the sidewalks, were piled about ten high against the bare wall. Everything was in order. The basement was longer—perhaps forty feet in all—than Sam had imagined it would be, but then, he figured, it probably ran the full depth of the house. Sam saw stairs at the back end, which must have led outside to some small courtyard behind the building that Sam had never seen. He breathed in, wanting to compose himself before seeing Tidewater, and he was surprised at how light and thin the air seemed. He walked forward, his head bent down, toward the front of the building, and saw a door, a dull orange color, about five feet beyond the staircase, to the right of what must have been the water boiler. To the left of the door, meters were attached to the walls and Sam could see silver horizontal disks spinning in them. He knocked and waited.

"Ah, Sam," Tidewater said, opening the door and stepping aside. "Please. I was hoping you would come by."

"Sure," Sam said, and not wanting to appear afraid he walked by Tidewater, stepping quickly into a square room—Sam could see at once that it was the man's only room—which was very brightly lit. The room measured about ten feet along each edge. The walls, of whitewashed concrete, were bare; the floor, an inch above the level of the cellar floor, was now covered with slats of wood, which were highly waxed.

"Please sit down," Tidewater said, gesturing to an easy chair which was against the left wall. "I'm so glad you came."

"Sure," Sam said, and sat. "Nice layout you got here."

"It's rent-free," Tidewater said.

"It's small, though."

"I'm alone," Tidewater replied, smiling, and Sam remarked to himself that the color of the man's skin matched the color of the walls. At the top, the walls seemed to slope inward, so that the ceiling was smaller than the floor. For the moment, Sam kept his eyes away from the man's face. He concentrated on the room, looking at its furnishings, wall by wall. There was a bookcase next to his easy chair, three shelves high and filled. Then a wooden table, with nothing on it. At right angles to the table, along the wall opposite the door, was a narrow bed, covered with a blue chenille spread. A metal reading lamp was clamped to the bed's headboard, and there was, on the floor next to the bed, a navy blue oval rug; shoes were lined up, evenly, underneath the bed. A table—Sam figured, from the jar of pencils and the bowl of sugar, that it was a combination desk and dining table—filled the remaining space along the wall. Opposite Sam, where Tidewater stood, his hands clasped in front of him like a preacher, the stove, sink, and refrigerator were next to one another—the stove was old and yellow, with sliding trays that could be lifted to cover the gas burners. There was a high slender chest in the far corner—for groceries, Sam imagined—and on either side of the front door, along the wall to Sam's right, was a dresser. The middle of the room was empty.

"I mean," Sam said, nodding to himself, then glancing back at Tidewater, "you have all you need, right?"

"Oh yes," Tidewater said. "As you do."

"Sure," Sam said. "With Ben gone, I don't even use his room, if you know what I mean."

"Of course," Tidewater said. "May I make you some tea? I was about to prepare some for myself."

"Sure," Sam said. "But I can't stay too long—I got something to do—"

Tidewater went to the high closet and took out a tin can, and some cups and saucers. Sam smiled—he'd been right—seeing the dishes and groceries in the closet. Tidewater struck a match and lit one of the burners, then put water on to boil. He sat down in a chair he pulled from under his table and faced Sam. "I'm glad you came," he said.

"I'm a sport," Sam said. He glanced at Tidewater's face, to see if the man would smile. Tidewater seemed slightly puzzled. "Ben must've spent a lot of time here," Sam offered.

Tidewater sighed. "Sometimes I wonder: did I merely use your father during our times together? I loved hearing him tell stories, jokes—" He stopped; his voice became matter-of-fact: "The sound of his voice, in this small room, was so special. You can understand that."

"Oh sure," Sam said. "He had some voice." Sam felt warm. He lifted himself from the chair, sliding his right arm from his mackinaw, and stood to take it off. Tidewater took it from him and laid it across the bed. "I mean, if he wanted, he could have been a pedagogue."

Tidewater stood at the stove, preparing the tea. "I think I understand now why he left."

"Listen," Sam said. "We got on okay, the last five years. We had some good times together. I don't blame the guy. I said that before—with the winters, and his age, and his brother Andy hanging on like—"

"No," Tidewater said. "No. He was worried about you. I told you before. Now that you're here with me, I can see it: he wanted to leave you alone, so that we could, as we have, come to know one another. Don't you see that? He sensed something—he gave you up, you see, despite—"

"Come on," Sam said. "I told you before: I look out for number one. I don't buy that stuff about everybody trying to save everybody else's ass. He did the same thing, finally, looking out for himself. He'll live ten more years, with the air they got out there."

"You are not listening to what I say," Tidewater said angrily. Sam sighed inside himself, and he was ready to leave. Would he tell Stella about coming down to Tidewater's apartment? Tidewater was smiling. "You're like your father in that. I'm not sure how carefully he ever listened to me—but that is no matter. Please, Sam, try to listen to the words I use. He gave you up, his only son—do you understand? He left you to me."

"You're bats," Sam said; then, feeling more confident than he'd imagined he would, he went on. "All that black-white white-black jazz—the way you thought about it all those years—it—" He stopped, not sure of how he had intended to complete his thought.

What he wanted to say, he knew, was that Tidewater should play what was there. He should take things for what they were. But if he said that, he would not, he realized, have been able to explain exactly what he meant. "It turned you bats, that's all. I don't mean completely—but . . ."

"Ben," Tidewater said, with a dreamy look on his face, "might have said that it turned me bats and balls—"

Sam groaned. "I didn't mean anything," he said. "You can believe what you want."

"You were his gift to me," Tidewater said. "He said so."

"I was on special," Sam replied, and laughed to himself. He leaned forward, watching the man's back as he poured tea for them.

"Sugar?"

Sam nodded. "Sugar."

"Lemon or milk?"

"Some lemon, I guess."

Sam took the cup and saucer Tidewater offered him. He sipped his tea and remembered that his grandfather had always put strawberry jam into tea. The liquid entering Sam's chest warmed him pleasantly. The story about his grandfather quitting work one day—maybe Ben had been right about them getting on together, had the old guy lived. Sam's fingertips were cold. "I was looking at your story again—the description of your first game. Your brothers were right, if you ask me—you shouldn't have taken it so hard. From what you say, the runs weren't really earned anyway." Sam paused, shifted his body in the chair. "That's what I think, for what it's worth. You took it too hard."

"Yes."

"I like the way you described things, though." He shrugged. "That's all. I mean, Ben—he could of talked your ear off, I guess."

Sam could see that Tidewater was pleased, and that was all right too, he figured. He'd been nuts before, letting the guy give him the creeps, when all he was, really, was a frightened old man living by himself. There were thousands of them all over the city. Sure. That was something he'd learned from cards but had forgotten to apply to his life: you should never give people any more power than they showed. Most of the time they'd be holding less than you. Things evened out, in the long run.

"But he would not have taken it as seriously as you do. Don't you understand? Bats and balls—of course. He reduced all things to jokes, in his classic Jewish manner. There was nothing—neither God nor the Holocaust—which was immune." Tidewater's eyes found Sam's. "He knew that, like me, you did not find humor in every morsel of life. He knew that you were the one who should have possession of my story. Don't you understand?"

Sam watched the bluish streak on the man's tongue, as the tongue reached out to touch the upper lip. A man—Sam saw his grandfather's face—sits by the railroad station, weeping. Sam listened to his father's voice, acting out the parts. "My God!" the man groans. "My train is gone! What will I do? Everything is lost!" For some reason, Sam now thought that in the joke the word "everything" referred specifically to Ben's two older brothers. "When did it leave, your train?" "Only a minute or two ago," the man replies, his body heaving, tears rolling down his cheeks into his beard. "Is that all?" says the other. "From the way you carry on one would think you'd missed it by an hour!" Sam saw Ben, walking across the green lawns of Pioneer Estates, laughing with his new neighbors, pleased to be able to entertain them, to receive their applause. "I'll tell you the truth," Sam said, aloud. "I'm not sure I got it all. I didn't like Johnson, though, I'll tell you that. I'd cut a wide trail around a guy like him." Sam lifted his cup and drank some more. "I would've steered clear."

"I wondered about his nickname," Tidewater said. "It intrigued me, and when I inquired about it as a boy, my brother Tucker told me the story." Sam settled back. "In Johnson's first game, pitching for the Page Fence Giants against the Cleveland Elites, sometime during the last five years of the nineteenth century, he had hit a man named Dell Corrigan on the side of the head. Corrigan, the story went, had not even tried to duck, and blood had spilled from his ear, wetting the dirt in the batter's box. Corrigan's teammates had, while Corrigan still lay unconscious on the ground, started for Johnson, whereupon Johnson appeared on the mound—nobody had seen him leave it—brandishing a baseball bat in each hand, swinging them around his head and screaming that he would crack six skulls as easily as one. They believed him, and after trading angry words, order was restored, Corrigan removed, and the game continued. Corrigan lay in a coma for twelve days and when he awoke was reported to have asked: "Who hit me with that big brick?" He did not remember Johnson throwing at him, and he did not ever again play baseball or fully regain his senses.

"There were some on the Dodgers who disputed this account—they claimed that Johnson actually had the name before he ever entered baseball, for beating a man senseless with a brick during the robbery of a window-shade factory; this story lost credibility, though, when one tried to fit a jail term into what was known of Johnson's life—of a baseball career that, if his given age were true, had begun at fifteen. No matter which story was told to Johnson, however, he had the same reply: 'That sounds good.' As for myself, I preferred to believe that the name referred to the man's torso, which—a rare thing in a pitcher—was large and square—black, but with a reddish caste to the blackness."

Sam put his cup and saucer down on the table next to him. "I better get going," he said.

"Yes." Tidewater rose, put his own cup and saucer on the table, and handed Sam his coat. They stood in the middle of the room, two feet from one another, and looking into the man's face, being able to reach out and touch the pale skin, Sam thought for an instant that he was in Stella's room, about to touch her. He felt dizzy.

"You work here?" he asked. "Writing, I mean."

"Ah," Tidewater said, and Sam moved away from him. He remembered Flo's smile, when she had approached him upstairs. He felt tired.

"I was just curious," Sam said.

"Your father never asked," Tidewater said, and reached a hand toward Sam. "Come with me. I have something to show you."

"I told you," Sam said. "I got to get going. I got a date."

"Of course," Tidewater whispered. "At your age, you need somebody for that. I understand. But come with me first. I have something to show you. Come with me. It is not an accident that you asked."

"I was just curious," Sam said. "Maybe I was just—no offense—being polite. I mean—"

"Come with me. I promised I would show you, if you recall—the night of Ben's dinner . . ."

Tidewater led the way from his room back into the cellar. "But it can't take too long," Sam said. "I told you—"

"Come with me," Tidewater said, and Sam followed. "I will show you where I work, since you asked."

"Sure," Sam said. "Since I asked."

A few minutes more, he told himself, and he'd be able to get away, out into the streets where he could breathe, even if it was cold. He followed closely behind Tidewater. The man stepped behind the oil burner and motioned to Sam to follow him. Sam was sorry he'd put his coat back on. In the dim light, he could not see Tidewater's eyes. A foot or two behind the furnace, where it would not have been wide enough for the two of them to have stood side by side, the old man was on his knees, brushing the floor with his hands. Sam blinked. He could not decide whether or not to take his coat off again. He remembered how he had felt walking through the snow to the card game Sabatini had set him up for, and he reminded himself to be careful. He heard footsteps on the floor above—Flo, he figured, moving racks of dresses.

Tidewater held an iron ring in his hand, and pulling the ring, Sam saw, lifted up a square section of the floor. "Now you will understand," Tidewater said, "why I said what I said. Are you with me?"

"Sure," Sam said. "What do you want me to do?"

"Come with me." Tidewater reached toward Sam, a hand outstretched. "Don't be afraid."

Sam stepped closer, aware suddenly that the man was already halfway into the hole, his chest only above floor level. Fear was not the right word for what he felt, he knew, and yet he did not want to go below—the thought did cross his mind that, if he did, he might never return. Still, he felt safe somehow, with the cool skin of the man's palm in his hand, with his own sweat dripping along his body, under his clothes. It was all the same to him, even this. "You got a light down there?" he asked.

"Don't be afraid. When they were changing from coal to oil—that would have been just before you and your father moved in—they discovered this door, but thought nothing of it." He paused and Sam, as he let himself down into the hole, finding the iron rung of a ladder with the sole of his right shoe, felt somehow—the association was pleasant—the way he felt when he was in the midst of a good poker game: as if he were both there and not there, as if he were, as he descended below the cellar, watching himself do what he was doing. He smelled chalk. "You are the first to see what I have discovered."

In the blackness, Sam could not tell how big the space around him was. He had let go of Tidewater's hand once he'd started down the ladder and he reached out now with his right hand and touched, not even a foot from the ladder, a dirt wall. He had forgotten to count the number of rungs on the ladder. He reached up, but his hand did not touch the cellar floor. There was light behind him. His foot touched ground, and he realized he had not heard Tidewater's voice or step for a second or two. He turned around, both feet on the ground, his shoulders brushing the dirt wall of the crawlspace, and saw, below him, that another door had been opened and that, in a dirt-walled chamber, perhaps six feet along each edge, the chamber sunk below the level of the earth Sam stood upon, Tidewater waited for him, his head nearly grazing a low ceiling, his hands at his sides. "I work here," he said.

Sam ducked his head, stepped down, and entered the chamber. If he stuck his hands out, he knew, he would touch both walls at the same time. A lightbulb hung from the ceiling, the wire attached by large iron staples. In the corner, behind Tidewater, Sam saw the desk, with a typewriter on it and paper stacked neatly at the side. "How do you get air down here?" Sam asked.

Tidewater motioned behind Sam; Sam looked over his shoulder and saw, in the corner next to the door—to the right—diagonally across from the desk—that there was a round hole in the wall, next to the ceiling. "I wanted you to know," Tidewater said. "This room has been here for over a hundred years."

Sam nodded. He kept himself from saying anything because he did not, where he was, want to anger the man. He wondered if the room had been some kind of storage place for coal, but he didn't ask.

"I buried them there, in that corner," Tidewater said, pointing to Sam's left.

"Sure," Sam said.

"There were only bones, and clothing. The clothing was remarkably well preserved. I buried it with them."

"Sure," Sam said. He looked up, seeing the man's face inches from his own, the bulging eyes looking like hollows in the skull, as if things had been inverted. It was, Sam knew, the light from above which was playing the tricks.

"The rest you can guess," Tidewater said. "There would be no fooling a man of your mind. You are not the kind who listens to the grass grow." Sam saw the man's tongue, inside a smile. His breath, like the room, smelled of chalk dust. "I will, when I have completed my work, join them here."

"Sure," Sam said. "Thanks for showing me. But I got to get going now—I told you."

Tidewater's hands gripped the lapels of Sam's mackinaw. The man hissed into Sam's face, spacing the words, flicking his tongue. "You are supposed to listen to my words, do you understand?" Sam felt himself being lifted slightly from the floor. He touched his right sidepocket, he was ready for anything. But he had to be careful, he knew—when they were bats, people had superhuman strength.

"Who's buried here?" Sam asked, registering Tidewater's sentence for the first time.

He heard Tidewater's breath, felt himself fall; the man's hands came away and Sam stood on the ground again, solidly. He had said the right thing. "Yes," Tidewater said. "You do recall the house I told you about, where Ben and I played—"

"Sure," Sam said, and he heard the pieces fall into place. "I mean, things can happen that way sometimes. My buddy Dutch—he once drew two royal straight flushes, one after the other. Things can happen."

"Ah," Tidewater said. "I knew. I knew you would understand, and yet—" He turned his back to Sam and sat down at the desk, so that Sam found himself looking at the top of the man's head. The hair was straight and sandy-colored. Sam saw no gray. "I have checked, of course, and it is not so unusual—there are many rooms like this in this section of Brooklyn. The church was active in the Abolitionist cause—hypocritical, as most were, but active nonetheless. I have checked old maps. I find no records for this building before 1906, so we are—if you will forgive the phrase—in the dark there, but that is no matter. The wonder of the discovery is grounded in things plausible—"

"Forget it, then," Sam said.

"There were two of them, of undeterminable age, and they sat against the wall, appearing very calm and relaxed." Tidewater stood, pushed his chair under the table. "I feel at home here. You do understand that. And here—there is something I would like you to have—I found it here."

Tidewater bent over, reaching a long arm under the table. His knees remained straight; Sam believed the man had been an athlete. You could see things like that. Tidewater held a bundle made of newspaper in his hands. "They—or one of them—must have worked on it in the time spent here. There was a knife, which I buried also, and this, my gift to you, had already been buried, wrapped in cloth, and so was preserved. I found no wooden chips, though perhaps they had been used to create warmth." Tidewater unwrapped the package. "The work is exquisite. My father—and brothers—would have commended it."

Tidewater held the doll forward. It was, Sam saw at once, beautifully carved: a naked black boy, with a round belly and rounder eyes. The wood was so shiny that, if Sam hadn't been told, he would have thought the doll had been carved and polished only a week or two before. The right hand rested below the belly, covering the boy's nakedness; the face seemed to show nothing in particular: an ordinary, typical Negro boy—full-lipped, broad-nosed, healthy—the kind Sam had seen in illustrated books when he'd been a boy himself. "A pickanniny child," Tidewater said. "From the Spanish *pequeño,* meaning little. We used the term as one of endearment."

"It probably means more to you," Sam said. "Why don't you keep it—?" He stopped, hearing the other thing Tidewater had said. His mind was moving backward, fast, recalling everything it had to. "Christ!" he exclaimed. "Do you mean you're going to come down here in—"

"Here," Tidewater said, smiling at Sam, as if to thank him again for having understood. "I can't be sure whether or not our anonymous craftsman did this for amusement—or for some practical purpose—for carrying a message perhaps. It seems unlikely, in truth. He must have been, for a time at least, visited regularly. Why he was left here in the end, we don't, of course—"

Sam watched the man's long fingers twisting the top of the doll's body. "But here—" Tidewater said. The doll came apart, the boy's torso and head lifted, and inside it Sam saw another doll, identical to the first, only smaller. "The work is exquisite," Tidewater said, pushing his gift forward, in front of Sam's eyes.

"I need air," Sam said, and turned away, toward the entrance. He tripped on the step, forgetting.

"Please," Tidewater said calmly. "Don't be afraid. I'd like you to have it. Please—"

"Some other time, okay?" Sam grabbed the sides of the ladder in his hands. He didn't wait to hear anymore, he didn't bother to think of anything else to say. He climbed, one rung at a time, relieved to find the door at the top still open. He braced his hands against the floor, on either side, and hauled himself up. If Flo stopped him, he decided, he would ignore her. As for Sabatini's buddies—feeling his heart race, and touching his sidepocket—they had better watch out: keyed up the way he was, ready for anything, being scared just enough to give an edge to his reflxes, he'd be more than they bargained for if they approached him now. He stopped at the side of the furnace, before heading upstairs: he did not hear Tidewater coming after him and that was just as well. He dusted his hands, rubbed them against his coat to get the grit off. It was just as well, too, that the doll had stayed down there. Sam took the stairs two at a time and remembered, before he closed the door to the hallway, to turn the cellar light off. Living there for as long as he had, Tidewater would know his way around blindfolded.

Sam did not look up to see if Muriel was still there. He did not glance at the door to the rummage shop. He headed straight outside. He'd let the sweat dry on his body—that was the best way to get cooled off. The light outside, although evening was almost upon him, made Sam raise his right forearm in self-defense—to shield his eyes from the white glare. The streets were clean, free of snow and ice and slush. Mrs. Cameron was not sitting on her stoop. Nate the Numbers Man, when he saw Sam passing, lifted his sunglasses and nodded in greeting. Sam had an idea: he would surprise them—he didn't think they'd really do anything since he was still small-fry—but he wouldn't take any chances. He'd cover all bets this time by taking the offensive. He pulled his mackinaw tight to his body. It was cold out. Steam rose from a manhole cover at the edge of the street, next to the sewer, where, below, the water flowed. Sam saw Tidewater, blindfolded, sticking half out of the hole—and he realized that, in the basement, he had had the sensation that the hole—even though it was a square—had been cut into ice. A blindman's bluff—something to watch out for in poker, if you could get a game.

Sam headed up Martense Street, for Garfield's. He wanted to see Willie the Lump. In front of one of the wood houses, a crowd of men stood around, shooting craps, drinking beer. Something rolled out in front of Sam: a baby carriage. It bumped into a car and Sam heard a mother yelling at her child for having let the carriage go.

"How're you feelin', man?" A black guy, eyes glazed, stuck his hand out for Sam.

"Beat it," Sam said and walked by, not changing his course, bumping the guy with a shoulder. Despite the cold, some black kids were chasing each other in a game, running back and forth across the street in zigzag fashion. He saw one of them jump on the sewer cover. Sam had used it for home plate during most of his childhood. Sure. There was a lot of stuff below the city. He'd read once—in a book he'd given a book report on—that they'd found the ruins of an old circus, when they were building the subway; and old tubes, for trains, which had worked on a vacuum principle. They had known a circus had made its home there because the elephant dung had been preserved. It wasn't so unusual, a room under the floor—you'd see an article in the papers every now and then about workmen finding a place like that. There'd been skeletons in some of them. Tunnels and old pipelines and sewers and wires, abandoned rooms and remnants of old buildings—you could probably find lots of things you wouldn't expect if you started digging under the city. Everybody knew, of course, about the baby alligators that had been flushed into sewers and had supposedly grown up there, living on garbage, but—seeing steam emerge from a grating at the corner of Rogers Avenue, Sam thought of the story Dutch had told him—what people didn't know, since they kept it quiet: that there were mothers, in the ghettos mostly, who'd flushed unwanted kids down, and that sanitation men had actually reported that they'd seen a few of them—like wolves—living below the city and running in packs.

Sam clenched his fists inside his pockets. It burned him to think that anybody could let go of something so small and alive and healthy, when people like Flo—and even Marion—would have given their lives to have had normal kids. Sam didn't like what Tidewater had confided in him: it was the guy's own skin, of course; still, Sam thought, life was precious. There was nothing, he supposed, that he could do with a guy like Tidewater, but if someone like, say Stallworth, who'd almost died and had come back—a black guy who knew what it was all about now that he'd been through his experience—if a guy like that could talk to Tidewater . . . Throwing away life as if it were a gift you didn't want was something no man had a right to do. Tidewater may have had the words, for whatever they were worth, but Sam could feel the anger also.

"I thought I'd stop by and say hello—for old time's sake," Sam said, taking a seat at Willie's table in Garfield's.

"How are you feeling, Mr. Benjamin?" Willie's good eye looked past Sam's right shoulder.

"Now that we don't have business together, I thought we could be—you know—just friends." Sam bit hungrily into the cheese Danish he'd bought.

"Be careful, Mr. Benjamin. Pay up."

"I appreciate your interest, Willie," Sam said. "But you don't have to lose any sleep over me. I look out for number one."

Sam enjoyed the warmth of the cafeteria. He stood and took off his mackinaw, glancing around, then sat again. There were a lot of elderly people sitting at tables and talking, cups of coffee and tea in front of them. Sam wondered what Pioneer Estates had that could match Garfield's. Maybe Tidewater was right, though: at a certain point, memory began to take over—maybe Sam was attached to Garfield's because of all the hours he'd spent there when he'd been in high school, waiting in the back room on Friday nights after basketball games, cheering when the guys from the team would come in carrying their satchels. Nate had always sat down at Sam's table. "You can pay me," Willie was saying. "They told me to tell you, if you came."

"What—?"

"You can pay me. They told me to tell you, if you came. You

have until tomorrow for the first payment. I'll be here from noon until eleven at night."

"You work for them too?"

"You can pay me," Willie repeated. "They told me to tell you, if—"

"Okay, okay," Sam said. "You got a crack in your record." He shook his head, then spoke to Willie in a kindly voice. "They got you from all sides, don't they, Willie? Everybody owns a piece of your body." Sam laughed. "You should hold an auction and get it over with."

Willie gazed into the distance, unmoved by what Sam said. "How are you feeling, Mr. Benjamin?" he asked again in a flat voice.

"Listen, now that I'm off Sabatini's books, you call me Sam. We don't have to—"

"I collect for the others also. You can pay me. They told me—"

"Up yours, Willie," Sam said, matter-of-factly, and drank from his glass of milk. He liked the cold white feeling, as it coated his throat. Sam watched Willie's face, but saw nothing. "But look—I got a friend, an old buddy—if you're looking for some work, for a change, if you know what I mean—I think he'd give you a good deal. He's in real estate, around Brooklyn."

"Be careful, Mr. Benjamin," Willie said, his glass eye focused on Sam's face. "You always treated me good. Pay up."

Sam stood. "This was just for old time's sake—stopping by," he said, pushing his chair back. "You're looking good, Willie. You take care of yourself." Sam slipped into his coat, then laughed and leaned forward, balancing his hands on the back of a chair. "Listen, I got something to ask you—personal: how many kids you got, Willie?"

"You can pay me," Willie said, without showing anything. "They get mean, Mr. Benjamin. Pay me."

Sam hitched his shoulders. "If you change your mind—about seeing my friend—you get in touch, right? Remember—this could be the opportunity you've been waiting for."

At a table by the window, where the man had sat the night of the opening Knick game, scribbling on The New York Times stock page, Sam now saw a young boy, perhaps seventeen years old, trying to raise a cup to his lips. The boy had beautiful straight blond hair to his shoulders. His shirt was open, revealing a smooth hairless chest. His hands trembled uncontrollably. The boy saw that Sam was watching him and Sam averted his eyes quickly; he didn't want the kid coming up to him, trying to make a touch. The boy's eyes, deep blue in color, reminded Sam of Dutch's eyes. If the kid was smart, Sam figured, he could, with his looks, get some older woman to pay his bills.

"How are you f-feeling, Sam?" Milt asked.

"No kicks," Sam said. He took a copy of the *Sporting News.*

"How does your father l-like his new life?"

"Okay, I guess."

"He did the smart thing," Milt said. Milt handed Sam his change and brought his lips to Sam's ear. "Be careful," he whispered. "B-be careful. The word is out."

"I appreciate your interest," Sam said. He thought Milt's eyes, behind the thick glasses, were wet. It might, however, have been the cold. It really got him, though, the way people were watching out for him. But when it came time to put up or shut up, where would they be then? Sam walked away. What mattered was knowing who you could depend on in the clutch, and there—it moved him—Sam knew he could still put Dutch at the top of the list. Even if they didn't see one another for months—for years—Sam knew that Dutch was a friend he could always count on, no matter where, no matter when, and no questions asked.

In the clutch, count on Dutch. Sam walked along Flatbush Avenue. He'd do what he planned to do. It would be nice to sit around Stella's place and have her talk to him, to eat something with her. If she didn't have anything ready, they could send out for pizza. He sighed. In truth, he admitted, if he'd had the money he'd have handed it over to Willie. But he couldn't give what he didn't have. Maybe he'd go see Stallworth and put the touch on him—a guy who'd been given back his life could afford to be generous to others.

The thing was, he told himself, entering Stella's building on Clarkson Avenue, he could understand what Tidewater had felt—he could imagine himself in the man's place, having finished most of his life and missing old friends: guys you'd done things with, guys whom you'd lost, for one reason or another, along the way. Sam could understand the man in that part of him because, like him, he too became angry at the idea that people had, in the course of their lives, to become separated from one another, while at the same time—more like Tidewater than he would ever acknowledge—he wanted most of all to be alone, and to be left alone. That he wanted both things at once had never seemed a contradiction: in his line of work, and living with Ben the way he had, he figured he'd had the best of both. And yet, even while Ben had been there, Sam had known that he'd longed more for each extreme—to be by himself, and to be with someone else—and he'd wondered about himself sometimes.

He pressed the bell to Stella's apartment. The intercom clicked on. "Hello?"

"It's Sam the Gambler," he said.

"Hey, Sam the Gambler—come on up—"

The door buzzed, allowing Sam to enter the lobby. He heard his heart thump, under his mackinaw. His skin was dry. He didn't think about it much—his desire to be with others. Mostly, he took things as they came, as he always had. But with all the stuff they'd been throwing at him lately—Tidewater and Sabatini and Flo and Dutch—it was, he knew, normal to want to get rid of a lot of it, to want some peace. That was why, he told himself as the elevator rose, he'd done the smart thing in coming to Stella's. He felt comfortable when he was there, and that was enough. Let the cards fall . . .

"Come on in—" she called, after he had knocked. "It's open. I was expecting company."

Sam entered, walked down the corridor. "Who?" he asked.

"You, Sam."

"Sure," he said, and took his coat off, hung it in the hallway closet, then walked into the living room.

Stella was out of her wheelchair, sitting in one corner of her couch, her feet tucked under her. "How's tricks, Ace?" she asked, and smiled at him.

His head bobbed up and down. "I can't kick," he said. "It's cold. I've been out walking."

"To get here," Stella said. She swung her neck slightly, so that her hair flipped back, away from her eyes. She was, Sam told himself, as pretty a girl as he had thought on the first night he'd seen her; her smile made him smile. Her hands were in her lap, and he wondered if she'd put them there for his benefit—so that she'd look more . . . normal was the word, he supposed. She wore a soft sweater—a pale violet color—and a black skirt. Sam smelled something sweet. "You can sit next to me," she said. "Take a load off your mind."

"You're sharp," he said. "You must've eaten already." Sam laughed and sat.

"No. I was waiting for you. I told you." She lowered her voice. "You're my company."

"Come on," he said. "Leave off." He let his head fall back against the couch, and closed his eyes. "I've had a rough day—I'm not up to riddles and things."

"I didn't eat yet," she said. "You can eat with me, okay?"

"Sure," he said. "Or we could send out for pizza."

"No," she said. "I've got something in the works."

Sam blinked. "Sure," he said again, then realized that she'd been mimicking him, and he laughed.

"You can sit closer to me," Stella said. "Don't be afraid. I mean, let's face it, with a girl like me a guy is safe, right?" Sam slid closer to her, along the couch. "Put your feet up," she said. "You'll feel better. On the chair."

Sam lifted his feet and rested them on the seat of Stella's wheelchair. He knew the wheels were locked so that it wouldn't roll away. The room was smaller than his own, but slightly larger, he noted, than Tidewater's. Stella worked in the other room, where she slept. "I went to see Tidewater, in his place," Sam stated. He felt Stella's shoulder against his own. Her hands stayed in her lap.

"So?"

"That's all," Sam said. "I was just making conversation."

"Listen," Stella said. "You be careful around him."

"Why?"

"I don't know," she said. "His eyes, I suppose. I don't like the guy's eyes, if you want the truth."

"I'm hungry," Sam said. "I don't want to rush you, I mean—but maybe I could do something, since you're sitting here already—"

"Don't rush me then," Stella said. She moved her head so that it rested on Sam's shoulder. Her voice became soft. "Please?" Sam tensed momentarily, glanced at her, then felt things ease. He nodded, and watched her lips part, as she smiled. "I mean, you'll feel better if you just sit for a while. Take my word for it, okay? You move around too much, if you ask me. You need to take it slow."

"I saw Willie the Lump, on the way here."

"No wonder," Stella said, and closed her eyes. "Didn't I tell you? Didn't I just say it? Tidewater and Willie and me, all in the same day—you move around too much. You want your life to go slower, Sam. Please? I mean, where's it all get you in the end, right? That's what I want to know."

Sam laughed, and—as if it were the most natural thing in the world—he put his right arm around her shoulder and pressed her to himself, affectionately. It was the line she used that always made him laugh—loosen up—and they both knew it. "You left out Flo—I saw her too," he said.

"See what I mean?" she said. "I'll tell you something—you did the right thing, coming here." She blew through her lips, as if exhausted. "Willie the Lump—Christ! Why don't you lay off?"

"I suppose," Sam said. "Where's it get me in the end, right?"

One hand fell from her lap, against his thigh. "I think I need some help," she said, glancing at her hand. Sam took her hand in his, held it briefly, then placed it back in her lap.

"At least my old man lays off—he hasn't called yet. I give him credit there."

"And—?"

"Nothing. He knows there's nothing to say."

"You have nice eyes, did I tell you that?"

"The first time we met," Sam said, and he laughed again. "But Dutch, my buddy, is better-looking. He has those deep eyes— maybe an inch into his face—"

"But he's not here, is he?"

"No."

"So—?"

"You're okay, Stella," Sam said. "I mean—two things you said to me already, in just a few minutes—to be careful, and not to be afraid—the same jazz everybody else is giving me these days, but—" He stopped.

"But what?"

He shrugged. "I don't know," he said. "I'll tell you the truth, I feel better already, just sitting here, away from things, if you know what I mean."

"Sure," Stella said. "You take things too hard, is your trouble. You just close your eyes and relax. Dream about something nice while I fix supper." She sat up, straight. Sam watched her breasts move under her sweater. If you had just come into the room, he realized, and the wheelchair hadn't been there, you never would have thought anything. He liked that: the fact that, in all ways, when she was sitting still, she appeared to be normal, so that he didn't have to think much—when he was with her—about what it would be like to have had her life. "Don't take things so hard, okay, Ace? Listen to yourself—hang loose a little. Let the bastards sweat."

Sam nodded. "You need some help?" he asked.

"I told you before," she said. "Don't be polite around me, okay?" Sam got up, moved the wheelchair to the side, and did as she had taught him to do: he moved her legs so that they hung down, just above the silver footholds at the bottom of the wheelchair; then he squatted and crossed his arms in front of him, his forearms toward her, as if he were going to throw a block in football. She put her hands on his forearms and found her strength there, lifting herself from the couch by pressing down on Sam's arms and, at the same time—she'd done it a thousand and one times before, she'd told him—she stepped onto the metal footholds, shifted, and let her body down into the seat. "See you later," she said, and wheeled away, around the couch to where the kitchenette was. "You take it easy. Put your feet up on the couch, or pull over the hassock. We want you to feel at home here, right?"

"Right," he said, and sat down. He took off his shoes, then put his feet up, over one arm of the couch, his head on two embroidered throw pillows. He didn't have to watch her work around the kitchen—everything was arranged for her. She could, in her own words, really wheel and deal there. Sam closed his eyes, heard Stella humming, and tried to think of nothing. He felt good.

There was no mystery to it really—to why he should feel so good when he was in Stella's place, to why he felt so peaceful when she bantered with him and teased him. It had to do with what he'd been thinking about on the way to her place. There was no point in denying the truth about his feelings: since she was who she was, he supposed that in one part of him he agreed with the rest of the world—he allowed himself to believe that she didn't count somehow as a real person. Sure. That was why he could feel as if he had it both ways when he was with her: he was with somebody, and he wasn't. It clicked into place and his eyes snapped open, seeing what he'd been thinking.

"I think I'm taking you for a ride," he said.

"You don't have a car."

"You know what I mean."

"Forget it," Stella said. "I figure your intentions are as honorable as the next guy's. At least. The odds are pretty good on you, if you want the truth. I've been around."

"Sure," Sam said. "I'm an ace."

"Lie down and rest. I told you—you take things too hard. Don't be so serious your whole life." She appeared in front of him, in her wheelchair. "I mean—come on—look at me—you've got to enjoy yourself, Sam, right? Come on—look at me, damn it."

Sam looked up. "Maybe I should leave you alone," he said.

"You do what you want," Stella said. "But mostly, if you come, don't mope, okay? Enjoy yourself. Christ! Don't they allow us that anymore? If you know what I mean."

"Okay," Sam said.

"Believe me, I don't give away any more than I get." Stella leaned forward in her chair. Her hands were on the armrests. "I've learned that much. You want me to put it in black and white? With me, Sam the Gambler, your account is even up, right? Oh Christ—" She was angry. "If I could, I'd shake your goddamned shoulders—" She breathed out, relaxed. "I would if I could, so consider yourself shaken. You burn me sometimes. It's really crazy, you wanting words all of a sudden." She pushed off, her hands on the chrome rims inside the wheels. "What for, Sam?"

Sam lay back down and closed his eyes. He did not, he knew, feel as if he were both there and not there. He knew where he was—but the other fact remained true. He felt that both extremes met: he had, somehow, as much privacy as he wanted—and he had as much . . . companionship was the word he found. Stella was right, he knew, though he followed her instructions and said nothing. He was pushing too hard, not listening to himself when he should, listening too closely when he had no reason to. If it was true that he did, in one part of him, think of her as being apart from other people—from girls—it was also true that, when he was with her and when he thought about her, she seemed more real than other people. He'd been too quick before, trying to pigeonhole things, trying to find a theory that would tie things together. Since when had Sam Berman ever believed in theories? To want to put an end to it all by saying that he felt as if he were with her and not with her, that she was there and not there, more real and less real . . . Sam shook his head, his eyes closed, seeing nothing: there was, he concluded, more to it than that.

They ate together at the kitchen table—Stella had made steak, french fries, and green beans—and Sam was still as hungry as he had been in Garfield's. Cold weather did that to his appetite. He did his exercises, though, morning and evening: he stayed in shape. Stella didn't press him about any of the things he'd thrown out: not about Tidewater or Willie or Ben or Flo. She talked about her own mother, who'd been trying to visit her more frequently, who'd been after her to get out more. "She wants me to meet other young people," Stella said. "How old are you, Sam?" Sam cleared the table when they'd finished the main dish, and he got dessert for them—ice cream—from the freezer. Stella wheeled away and turned on her hi-fi, then returned. Sam served the ice cream and knew that they were both remembering—listening to the music— what she'd said to him on the first night they'd met, about dancing. He thought of telling her that he didn't like to dance, which was true, but he knew how she would have treated a comment like that, so he said nothing. She said something about the work her mother was doing for the muscular dystrophy organization—and then, getting no response, she apologized for talking so much about her mother. "I think she likes me the way I am," Stella said. "But that's okay. It makes people think she's noble, having a daughter like me. The hours she puts in, carrying around a damned canister—I mean, she doesn't actually carry it all the time, but it's as if she does, as if it's a permanent part of her hand. You want to see a picture I did of her? It's in the other room, on the desk. Forget it." She spoke without pausing.

"You're okay," Sam said.

"Sure. That's what she says. But listen: it's a picture of her, see, holding out a canister, and on the canister is a picture of a girl in a wheelchair—that's guess who—and if you look closely—I'm an ace too, see—you see that the girl in the wheelchair, she's holding her own canister, and on her canister is a picture of my mother in a wheelchair holding a canister. And on the canister—got it?"

"You're an ace," Sam said, taking their ice cream dishes from the table. "I don't know how you get the patience for all the details."

"Help me out," she said, as she wheeled to the couch. Sam let her lean on him. She pushed up, shifted, fell into the corner of the couch, then jerked herself backward. One hand was on the arm of the couch, the other flopped at her side. Sam saw her grit her teeth angrily—strain—and lift the hand to her lap. "That's about two hundred bucks of therapy there, lifting that arm. The guy beats up on me, Sam—he pounds hell out of my muscles."

"He must work for Sabatini."

Stella laughed, but Sam didn't like the hardness in her laugh. He put his arm around her and she let her head drop to his shoulder. "How was supper?"

"Real good," he said. "I like simple meals like that. Ben used to try to make fancy stuff—him and his specials."

"I like that," Stella said. "Too bad he didn't hang around—stealing from the supermarket to keep up with inflation, I liked that." She laughed to herself, more softly. "Listen, Sam the Gambler, how about teaming up with me now that he's gone—I mean, if they wouldn't suspect an old man, think of what we could get away with having me wheeling through the aisles." She paused. "But, since I am who I am, you'd have to do the handy work, right?"

"Forget it," Sam said. "I just wanted to tell you the meal was good, that was all. Lay off on my old man."

Her hand was against his side. Her fingers moved. "Please?" she said. "I'm not so tough, Sam. Please?"

"Sure," he said. He liked the feel of her fingers against him. They were on his rib cage, at the right. He imagined her working at her desk, designing the cards. She'd let him watch her at work one day—he'd been amazed that anyone could draw things so small. "Ben's okay."

"I mean," Stella said. "Can you imagine what she'd feel like—what my life would be like, for that matter—if I wasn't pretty?"

Sam moved away, and Stella's hand fell on the couch, between them. "I don't get you—"

She sighed. "Sorry to lay this stuff on you, but it's okay if I talk some, isn't it?" Her voice was intense. "Christ, Sam, I've got to talk to somebody sometime. Flo's okay—she listens, she loves me, she got me to come that night to meet you, right?—but it's not the same thing. She sees me as one of her kids, one who made it—it's all mixed up with things her life didn't give her. I am, I mean. But I think about it—what I said: I get by, sure—I cope—but if I hadn't been given some talent, and if I was, say, a homely tub of lard, then would you be here? Answer me that—"

"No," Sam said, and repeated himself: "No. I like the way you look. You're a goodlooking girl, Stella."

"Come back," she said. He lifted her hand, moved close to her again. "Sure. You're right. I take what I can get in this life. I'm glad you said the truth, but it's something I think about: it makes things easy that I look the way I do—for my mother too, I suppose. She doesn't want me the way I am—my legs—she'd like me to be like others, and yet she thrives on my sickness, doesn't she? I gave her a purpose for living, didn't I?" Stella waited. Her fingers moved against Sam's side again, nervously. "I'm sorry. You don't have to say anything. I mean, don't think I think this way about myself twenty-four hours a day—I don't know why it came over me." She stopped. "You do like the way I look?"

"I told you. Sure."

"Then look at me."

"I got things on my mind."

"Look at me."

"There," Sam said, leaning back and looking into Stella's face. Her lips were parted and he thought they quivered slightly. Her eyes were a deep brown. He felt, as he often did after a meal, somewhat sleepy. Stella's hand moved upward, pulling on his shirt, drawing him to her. "Sabatini too. He called."

"So what else is new?"

Her sweater seemed to melt under his hand. "His goons are gonna handle me from now on." He felt himself hardening, her leg pressed against his. "They can get mean."

"But you'll handle them, right? You're Sam the Man."

"Sam the Lamb is more like it."

"Don't be afraid," she said, her lips opening, only a few inches away. "I told you, with a girl like me a guy is safe. Even you. You can hide out here, if you want." Her voice seemed to fade away. "My mother would get a big charge out of that."

"You take her too seriously," Sam said.

"You know what? You're right."

Sam relented. "Okay," he said. "Why not?" Then he lowered his face and kissed her on the mouth, moving his left arm around to hold her to him. Her lips gave way and he felt the two of them fall slowly backward, so that her breasts pressed against his chest. She seemed to be humming. Her hand gripped him so hard that he could, lying against her, feel her fingernails through his shirt. Her lips were warm and he could tell that she knew what she was doing. That shouldn't have surprised him, though, since she hadn't, he knew, lost the use of her legs until after she had graduated from high school. He lifted his head and she smiled at him in a way that made him smile too.

"I'll tell you something," she whispered, her head against the corner of the couch, "you did the right thing."

Suddenly, he ached for her—and the ache was so deep that he found himself flinching, tightening his stomach to control the pain. Her fist still held him by the shirt. He stretched out, so that he lay half on top of her; then, as gently as he could, he lifted her legs and raised them so that she lay stretched out also, next to him. He heard his heart thumping and wondered if she heard it also. She said nothing, but while he moved her into position and adjusted himself next to her, she held on, her brown eyes fixed on his face. Sam felt sleepy. He lowered his head and she raised her chin so that he could kiss her on the neck. Her skin was softer than he'd imagined it would be. He pressed his body to hers and her hips moved. He found her lips again and they opened for him this time. He felt fingers against his cheekbone, moving delicately, tracing the shape of his face. His head was spinning and he pressed against her, his right hand moving to the skin under her sweater, at the waist. It had been a long time since a girl had excited him as much as Stella did—and yet, hungry for her as he felt, as furious and passionate as he knew he was, he felt also as if he were tumbling down into something very comfortable, something that would, his eyes closed in the darkness, protect and console him. He reached out with his tongue, tentatively, and licked her teeth. She hummed to him. His tongue moved forward, past her teeth, and when she received him, kissing his tongue with hers, he fell deeper, and then, as if her tongue had been wired with electricity, his head snapped back and his eyes bolted open: she lay beside him, surprised but not scared, and he was certain that he had, a second before, if only for an instant, as her mouth had opened to him, been seeing Mason Tidewater's face, and tasting his sweet tongue.

"I better get going," he said.

She held him by the shirt. "No."

"Listen," he said, sitting up. "You don't know everything."

"Please," she said. "It's all right, Sam."

His thoughts, he felt, were drowning, fighting one another under water. A sitting duck, out of luck. "I got too many things on my mind," he said.

"You'll forget," Stella said, softly. "Turn out the light."

"You don't know everything."

"I'll take care of you," she said. "You'll see."

"Something happened."

"You take things too hard. Relax a little, Sam the Gambler. Christ—what's it all for if . . ."

"Forget it," Sam said, and he saw Ben at the airport, going into the tube. "I better straighten some things out first."

"Take my advice and turn out the light. It'll be worth your while." She turned away then, her face to the back of the couch, and her fist came away from his shirt. "Oh shit, then—move your butt out of here. I don't need anything that bad. Just move it out, right?"

Sam wanted to understand what was happening. "I'm sorry," he said, finding no other words. "I'm Sam the Lamb, I guess."

"I get the picture."

"Can you manage—I mean, get back by yourself?" he asked. Her body was turned from him, her pale skin showing between her sweater and skirt, where he'd touched her. He saw himself covered with fleece, Ben nearby, shears ready. "I can give you a hand. I got a minute, if—"

"Get out!" she cried, spinning toward him. Her eyes shot fire. "And don't lay your hands on me." With an effort that made her face red, and the muscles on her neck vibrate, she pressed her fists against the cushions of the couch and found a sitting position. One foot stayed under her, caught. "For your information, I can even get life insurance—twenty-payment life, but life insurance nonetheless. I checked. Now move it, Sam the Lamb, by your own words—"

"Something happened," he said.

She was breathing heavily from her exertions. Sam thought of Stallworth, lying on his back, his long brown body naked under a sheet in the hospital for twenty-seven days. "I told you. I'll take care of you. I won't say it again. I'm a busy woman, right? There are still a few things I want to see and do in this life."

"You don't know everything," Sam said. His erection, he realized, was gone, but he ached even more than he had before. He wanted to understand—when a thing like that happened, sneaking up on you, you had to figure it out. It made a difference.

"You can't do that, don't you understand?" Stella said. "Get me all—excited, right?—and then just—oh Sam, you're a real prince, did you know that?" She took deep breaths, let her body fall backward, her eyes closed. "You do like it here, don't you?"

"Sure. You know that. It's just—"

"It's just nothing. Oh, one more time, Sam. Don't be a jerk your whole life. Turn out the light and come here. Please." Her eyes opened. "Please."

Sam nodded. "Maybe it was nothing," he said.

"Come here, sweet Sam," she said. Sam nodded again, hoping she would understand. Her voice reassured him. If he told her about it, everything would be ruined—but if he didn't . . . "Come here, sweet Sam."

He turned out the light and sat down, next to her. Her hand touched him, above the knee, and he stiffened at once. He pressed his head to her breasts and cried soundlessly, pulling her so tightly that he feared for her. How could he tell her about what he had seen? And if he started to talk about it, where would it end? It bothered him less, in the dark, that it had happened. He wanted only to press her, to squeeze the life from her. She had, he knew, been good to him. He let the two of them fall again, and lifted her leg, so that they were as before, beside one another. He wanted to be good to her, too. She was right about that. With everything happening the way it was outside, in the streets below, he had more than a right to enjoy some peace. Let the bastards sweat. He tightened slightly, with anger, but when he opened his mouth to speak, he heard the same cry—a helpless cry, he knew.

"Sweet Sam," she said in his ear, and he realized she was crying. He wasn't surprised. He kissed her cheeks, licked her tears, and felt her body heave with relief. He slid his hand under her sweater, and her skin was still cool, firm. "I'm too much, right?" she whispered. "About the insurance—oh Christ, I'm a case sometimes—" Her back arched, her hips moving into him. "Oh Christ, but that feels good, Sam. Oh Christ, you're an ace, sweet Sam. Oh bloody Christ."

Her brassiere unhooked easily and when he took her breast in his mouth, running his tongue around her nipple, she tugged on his hair, and laughed. Her hand gripped him, like iron, between his legs. "Wait a second," he said, and pulled away. "Are you—comfortable here? I mean, I could take you into the other room, if—"

"I can see your eyes," she said.

"Then we'll stay here, right?"

"I have complete confidence in you, Sam the Gambler."

"You're not the first to say that." She kept her hand on his leg as he undressed. He let his clothes drop to the floor, then—with some awkwardness, but without her having to give him instructions—he undressed her, letting her clothes fall to the floor on top of his. She held him in her hands, where he put himself for a few seconds, and then he lay down again, next to her, their chests touching, and he prayed to God that, when they touched tongues again, as he dearly wanted them to, he would be able to do so without tensing, that he would be able to do so as—something he wanted for himself more than for her—what he would have called a free man.

11

Sam saw that Muriel had left the blanket, folded neatly, to one side of his door, and he bent over to pick it up. When he had come in the night before, she had been sleeping on the landing, curled up on her side, blocking her door. Her nose had been red and dripping, but she had seemed to be in such a deep sleep that he hadn't wanted to disturb her. That was why he had taken a blanket from his closet and covered her. Still, he thought, carrying the blanket into his apartment, he would speak to Flo: something had to be done—it wasn't fair for a young kid to be brought up that way, as much as the old woman might have loved the girl.

Sam dropped the blanket on his bed and walked to the window, putting a hand on the radiator. It was barely warm. Damned Tidewater, he thought—so busy with his story he wasn't keeping an eye on the furnace. Flo was right: you hardly saw the man anymore. In the street below, Sam saw some young boys playing— running and then sliding along the sheet of ice that covered the sidewalk, seeing who could slide farthest. Across the street, toward Martense Street, a family—mother, father, four children—were moving, their furniture and cartons on two wooden dollies. The father—a stocky black man in a blue wool hat pulled down over his ears—had the rope to one dolly across his chest, and he leaned forward, straining, steam billowing from his mouth and nose. His wife and one son walked alongside the dolly, making sure the furniture—Sam picked out a wooden table, a green sofa-chair, an unpainted dresser—did not fall. A boy—the man's son, Sam figured—perhaps fifteen years old, but a head taller than any of the others, pulled the other dolly. His sister helped him. Sam saw dishes and pots and clothing. Maybe, with his height, the kid could play ball someday, Sam thought. There was something in the easy way he moved that told Sam he was a good athlete. Sam had told Stella that—how he had, until recently, always regretted not having been a great ballplayer; how he had, as a kid, dreamt of making the pros. But—he didn't want to insist too much, and he wouldn't have said such a thing to anyone else—he was glad now that things had worked out the way they had. He'd been around enough locker rooms to know what the daily grind was like. He pulled for the guys he liked—but he had the feeling that, if they knew him and what his life was like, most of them would have envied him as much as he had envied them. Stallworth was, he'd explained to Stella, the best example, and Sam had told her about him, and about what he had been quoted as saying, about wanting to relax a little in this life.

Sam had the words right—for a change he was glad he could remember things exactly, that way. He banged on the radiator, as he had earlier—then on the steam pipe. He checked the valve, but it was wide open. He unfolded the blanket that he'd loaned to Muriel and put it across his knees. Then he dialed.

"Hello?"

"You up already?"

"Hey, Sam the Gambler," she said. He swallowed, glad he had called. "What's the good word?"

"I was just thinking of you," Sam said. "So I thought I'd call. How do you feel? I mean, after last night."

"Sure," she said.

"Sure," Sam said.

"What's there to say, right?"

Sam shrugged. "You want me to come over later? We could watch the basketball game together. It's like an icebox here. Damned Tidewater—"

"Give me a little time, okay? I got to get things ready."

"Sure."

Sam waited. "You get home okay?" Stella asked.

"Sure. The streets were pretty quiet. People read the papers too much."

Stella laughed. "Last night!" she said, and her laugh was the same as it had been then. "You come over when you want."

"Okay," Sam said. "Take care of yourself."

"Last night," she said again, and laughed. "You're really a prize." Then she hung up.

Sam smiled. He could understand what she meant—he would not, if somebody had told him, have believed that he could have said such a thing at a time like that, but it was what had occurred to him. He was glad now that it had. He liked himself—it was the only way he could think of putting it—for being that way. They had been in bed together, in Stella's room (not in the living room), when she had stopped moving and pushed him off. He had heard the sound then too, at the window, and had pulled the blankets back, to cover them. The guy's nose had been pressed against the glass, his eyes bulging, and Sam had had no idea how long he'd been there, watching them from the fire escape. "Oh shit," he'd heard Stella say. "Shit." He'd reached down quickly to the floor and slipped his knife from his pants, snapping it open, but there had been no need. The guy's face was gone a second later, and Sam hadn't asked why. He'd turned to Stella at once, figuring she would have been scared to death, but he discovered that she was only annoyed. "Just shit," she'd said again, and from the way she said it, he could tell that she had been more annoyed that they'd been interrupted than that somebody had been looking in. "I guess," Sam had found himself saying, as he had put his knife away, "that that's what you got to expect when you live in a neighborhood in transition."

He hadn't intended to be funny—he had wanted, only, to break the ice, to get his own mind away from what might have happened if the guy had wanted to break in—but his remark had cracked Stella up. She had pressed herself against him and roared with laughter. "Oh Christ, I love you, Sam," he remembered her saying, and it was the first and only time that she had let herself say it. "Sure," he'd begun, and she had managed to put her hand over his mouth so that he had not been able to explain himself. He could see her now, her head under him, her hair up—he'd put it there—across the back of the pillow so that it didn't become knotted when she sweated. He had put his head against her chest then, his ear warm against her skin, and had begun laughing with her. "You're my bird, Sam," she'd said, when she'd been able to stop laughing, and though he hadn't said so, he'd agreed with her.

He made his bed, did his exercises, and was eating breakfast when there was a knock at the door. "It's open," he said.

"Still taking chances, right, Ace?" Dutch said, coming into the room. Sam sighed, saw that Dutch had, since the last time he'd seen him, grown a beard; it was trimmed close to his face, and his blue eyes, above the black hair, seemed more deeply set than ever. "I mean, what if I'd been some spook looking to hit you for cash?"

Sam motioned to the sofa. "Take a load off your mind. You want some coffee?"

"Okay." Dutch took his gloves off and blew into his hands. "It's cold as a witch's tit out."

Sam took a cup down from the cabinet above the sink and poured coffee for Dutch. Shimmy had called two days before, to try to arrange a get-together, to offer Sam money—and Sid had left a message with Flo that same day. "What's up?" Sam asked.

"Nothing," Dutch said. "I called a few times, but you never seem to be in so I figured I'd stop by—I thought you might want to come by my place this afternoon, to watch the game. The Lakers go against the Bucks, from Milwaukee."

"No thanks."

Dutch stroked his beard, his chin toward Sam. "Come on—say something at least. What do you think of it?"

"Not bad," Sam said, laughing. "You gonna be a rabbi?"

"Akiba left home at the age of forty, an ignorant man," Dutch said, his eyes looking out over the rim of his cup, scanning the room. "And he returned, the wisest rabbi in—"

"You're not forty yet," Sam said, and sat opposite Dutch.

"I told you before," Dutch said. "You're the one should be a rabbi, the way your mind works."

"Take a walk."

"I mean it, Ace." Dutch leaned forward, on the edge of the sofa. His eyes were beautiful, and as he gazed into them Sam felt the tension leave his body. Poor Dutch, he thought. "The way, when you play cards, nothing interferes—religious men have that kind of concentration. That's why their wives shave their heads and sit on the other side of walls in *shul*—*m'chitzahs*—so that nothing intervenes between them and God." Dutch stood and recited: " 'They tell of the rabbis—Elieser and Joshua and Elazar ben-Azariah, Akiba, and Tarphon—who celebrated the Passover in B'nai Brak and were discussing the story of the going forth from Egypt all night long until their students came and said to them: "Rabbis, it is time for the morning prayers." ' "

Sam could see Dutch, standing in Hebrew School class when the two of them had been eleven or twelve years old, and he knew that Dutch wanted him to be reminded of the past they shared. "Okay," Sam said, looking through the window at the fire escapes on the buildings across the street. "I'll ask again—what's up?"

Dutch seemed puzzled to find that he was standing. He took his coat off. "It's warm here," he said, and sat.

Sam felt far away. "What's on your mind?" he asked. "Come on."

"Nothing—I just wanted to see how you're getting along since Ben left. That's all. Momma asks about him a lot, how he likes it out there."

"He hasn't been in touch," Sam said.

Dutch stood and walked to the window. "Okay. Sure—I'll lay it on the line, Ace—" He turned back. "The word is out that you're in deep, with Sabatini. I wanted you to know that if I could help—in the clutch, count on Dutch, you know what I mean?" Dutch looked at the floor, embarrassed. "I mean, I got a little bread stashed, from before I quit—you can make a touch on Dutch, okay? We don't have to be cagey with each other." Dutch moved away from the window. "You think it over, and—anytime—you let me know." He leaned down and put his hands on Sam's shoulders. "I know what it's like when they get mean, Ace—remember that. I know. If I can help spare you."

"They won't touch me," Sam said, remembering what Tidewater had once said to him. "I got protection." He laughed. "Sure. I'm Sam the Man."

Dutch punched him in the shoulder. "That's my boy," he said. "Enough said, right? If you need me, you know where to come. Since I've been going to *shul* again we got a little extra power on our side, if you know what I mean. In the mornings, when I put on my *tephillin,* I'll think of you, okay?"

Sam waved him off. "You're bats," he said, and smiled. "You don't believe a word of it."

"That's how much you know," Dutch said. "We're in the same boat, you and me—right, Sam?" Sam shrugged. Dutch's voice was intense, passionate. "Those are your own words—they were, that is, when we used to travel together, right? You and me. But listen—we *are* in the same boat, Sam, and that's why I'm here. That's why I'm in *shul* three mornings a week. We can't just be ourselves. Don't you feel that sometimes? We have to be part of something that doesn't die when we die—I know you believe that, Sam, though you've never said it. If everything begins and ends with just our body, then what's the point, right? What's it all for?"

"You can have kids," Sam replied simply.

He looked up and found that Dutch was smiling at him. "That's something—sure," Dutch said, his eyes sparkling. "But not enough. Animals copulate and propagate." Dutch licked his lips. "What makes us different, Sam? 'Be thou righteous,' God said to the first Jew, Abraham, and he said no more. But every Jew bears the weight of that command. 'Who is the righteous man?' the rabbis ask, and they reply: 'He who doeth righteous deeds.' Don't you see, Ace? We Jews believe in this world. None of that adultery-in-the-mind jazz for us—it's your *life* that matters, what you make of it; it's the fact that you're a Jew, whether you like it or not, and—what I was getting at—that does put you in the same boat, even you. We were studying with Rabbi Zanvel last week—on Saturday afternoon—and we read a passage which made me think of you. Listen. In the Talmud they tell the following story: In a boat at sea one of the men begins to bore a hole in the bottom—for what reason, what personal despair, we know not—but his comrades admonish him. 'It's my life,' he replies. 'I am only boring a hole under my own seat.' "

Dutch sat back against the sofa, and Sam wanted to reach out a hand, to help his friend. "Don't you get it?" Dutch said. "We read that portion of the Talmud so that I could come to help you, Sam. It was no accident. I know it. You do understand, don't you?"

Sam shrugged, and crossed one leg over the other. Then something clicked. He smiled: "Sounds boring to me," he said.

Dutch groaned. "Be serious," he said, sitting forward. "Save that stuff for your old man. Listen to me: 'Yes,' his comrades say, 'but

when the sea rushes in we will all be drowned.' Don't you see? 'And
so it is with Israel,' the rabbis comment. 'It's weal or its woe is in
the hands of every individual Jew.' " Dutch paused. "I believe there
was a reason we studied that passage just before I heard about you
and Sabatini. Things like that don't just happen."

"I don't buy it," Sam said, and then, before Dutch could say
anything else, he stood and continued: "Anyway, I don't want to
kick you out but I got something in the works for this afternoon."

"We're in the same boat," Dutch said again, and he stood also,
reciting the line as if he were in a trance. "You and me."

"I look out for number one," Sam said. "If everybody did the
same, we'd all do okay." He stopped, considered what he'd said. "I
mean, those who want to go around helping others—like Flo—
that's okay for them. But there are a lot of birds, if you want the
truth, who, if I found them next to me, I'd heave them right over
the side."

Dutch smiled. "Then think of it another way." He picked up his
coat. "If I was in trouble, wouldn't you be there? Haven't you—you
remember the times—haven't you been there to bail me out of a lot
of tight spots?"

Sam decided. "Christ—you're in trouble now, Dutch," he said.
"But I don't have the time. I'm sorry."

Sam saw Dutch's eyes move swiftly, from side to side. "Me?—I
haven't been near a game or a bookie for months now. You—"

Sam shook his head. "It's all the same. All that stuff you gave me
going out to Herbie's, about why you quit. And this rabbi
jazz—you don't make sense, Dutch, if you want the truth." Sam
sighed. "I mean, some of it makes sense, by itself—but playing all
those games against yourself, and—I *know* you, Dutch, that's all.
With your mother never going out and—" Sam opened the closet
door and took out his mackinaw. "If I had the time, maybe we
could—I don't know. I mean, what good would words do?" Sam
faced his friend, slipped his arms into the sleeves of his coat.
"Anyway, you've been through stuff like this before. You'll—" He
paused, nodded. "You'll probably pull out of it yourself, right?"

"Probably?—what do you mean probably?" Dutch's body
seemed to sag. He put his coat on. "I said it before—you're the one
who should've been the rabbi." They walked onto the landing, and
Sam locked the door. Muriel was sitting in front of her door,

sucking her thumb and holding a blanket across her lap. "It's not like you think, Ace—you should come to *shul* some time on a Saturday afternoon, with the other men. It does me a lot of good—picks me up, if you know what I mean—arguing with these guys about things."

"You were always a good arguer."

Muriel slid backward, closer to her door. Sam waved to her, but Muriel did not respond. Her sandy curls were tangled. "It's not like you think, Ace—" They opened the door to the outside and Dutch shuddered as the cold air hit him. "Sure, I got things on my mind—I couldn't hide that from you—but it's true why I stopped by. About Sabatini, I mean. My own stuff can wait."

Sam stood with Dutch in the doorway. Dutch's eyes were tearing, from the cold. "Sure," Sam said. "I believe you, Dutch."

"What I like about it is the idea of taking a break from life—I mean, the idea that you stop once a week and rest, that you take a break and think a little about what it's all about. That makes sense, doesn't it?"

"It makes sense."

"But it makes more than sense," Dutch went on. "Because we—the Jewish people—we've been doing it, stopping this way to think about life once a week, for over two thousand years. My father and my father's father—"

"Listen," Sam said. "You study for me too, okay? I got to get going now."

"Right, Ace," Dutch said. He took his hand from his pocket, removed his glove, and offered his cold palm to Sam. Sam sighed, and shook Dutch's hand. "It's been real good talking with you again—we don't see enough of each other anymore. I mean—things change, right?—but we should keep in touch."

"In the clutch, count on Dutch," Sam said, and smiled.

"Sure, Ace," Dutch said, and walked off toward Linden Boulevard. "Thanks."

Sam turned to the left. He wondered what Dutch would have thought if he'd known about Stella, and he smiled, for he did know, despite everything, that if he'd wanted to he could have shared what was happening with Dutch. Still, it was better if nobody knew for a while, until things straightened out. Sam glanced over his shoulder and saw that Dutch was waiting at the corner, like a schoolkid, for the light to change. Sam could stop in at Steve's, get another cup of coffee, and then double back and head for Stella's—by then Dutch would have been far enough ahead of him. He didn't like rejecting Dutch because, when he thought about it, he knew that he could never have thought of sharing what was happening with the other guys: Herbie or Sid or Shimmy or Max or Nate. That would really be rich, Sam thought, entering Steve's candy store—Stella sitting around with all the other wives, talking about carpeted wastebaskets.

Sam squinted. The store was very warm inside. He tightened, knowing that his mind could, if he let it, imagine how the guys would treat him if he and Stella stayed together. He could, if he wanted to, hear the words each of them would say, but he didn't want to. He shivered, blinked—as if to clear his head. Why, he wondered, did he feel so angry?

He opened his mackinaw and sat down at the counter. He didn't see Steve. Two black girls were sitting to his left, eating sandwiches, at the far end, a transistor radio on the counter in front of them, blasting rock music. What Sam felt, he realized, was the anger he thought Stella would have felt—the fact that no matter how long they looked at her the others would never stop seeing her wheelchair and her floppy arms and her electric gizmos. She could joke about it until doomsday, but—hadn't Sam felt the same way, and wasn't that why he'd kept going to see her at first?—when you added things up, the fact of who she was, of her condition, would always come out on top. Sure. Stella was right to have set herself up the way she had, so that she needed almost nobody else—and who she needed, she paid. Sam breathed through his nostrils, heavily, feeling what Stella would have felt on a Saturday night at Herbie's house.

A woman—nice-looking, about his own age—looked down at him. "What'll it be?" she asked.

"Just some coffee," Sam said.

The woman nodded. She seemed, somehow, embarrassed to be serving Sam. "You must be Barbara," Sam said. "I'm Sam—Sam Berman. I live up the street."

Her eyes showed pleasure. "Oh," she said. "Oh yes. Steve's mentioned you—you're the one whose father went to live in California."

"Yeah," Sam said. "That's me."

Barbara poured his coffee. "Milk?"

Sam nodded. "Where's Steve—taking a day off?"

Barbara shook her head and glanced toward the two black girls. "No," she said. "I thought you would have heard. He's in the hospital."

"Hey," Sam said, seeing tears in the girl's eyes. "I'm sorry I pried—I was just making conversation, if you know what I mean."

She breathed in deeply. "It's all right. I could have kept the store closed, but it gives me something to do. Steve telephones and gives me directions, and I telephone when I have a question—my father had a luncheonette, in Crown Heights, so I know how to do most things."

"Well, tell him I hope he gets out soon." Sam stirred his coffee. "I mean, I hope it's nothing serious."

"They beat him up," Barbara said, and her head moved up and down, as if to confirm the truth of her statement. "I'm only glad he didn't reach for his gun or they might have done worse. They beat him up terribly, Sam. They beat him up."

"Hey, take it easy now," Sam said, and rose from his chair, his toes pushing off from the silver footholds to reach across the counter. He wanted to console her, to take her head on his shoulder.

"He would have given them the money—they had no reason. He would have given them the money."

"Sure, he's a good guy—Steve's okay," Sam said. "But you calm down."

"I'm all right," she said, wiping her hands on her apron. She looked to her right, but the girls were not paying attention. "Do you want to know what happened?"

"Sure," Sam said. "I mean, if you feel like it—Steve and I knew each other since public school. My father and his father were friends."

"One of them stabbed him in the eye."

Sam's right hand flashed upward. "What—?"

"Yes. There are a lot of bandages now, and Steve is very brave, as always, but I don't know how it will affect him after. His father—"

"You don't got to tell me anymore," Sam said, and he shuddered, imagining the blade of a knife slicing through his own eye.

"Steve won't let me tell his father—I guess because his father warned him to get out before this, with the way the neighborhood's been changing."

"Sure," Sam said. "We talked about it, Steve and me."

"That's why I'm here—to keep myself busy. My mother's watching the children. I close in the afternoons so I can go visit him in the hospital."

Sam thought of telling her to cry if she wanted to. "Listen," he said instead. "You tell Steve I stopped by, and that—which place is he in?—I'll try to go over and visit him, if he likes visitors, I mean. Some guys would rather be left to themselves. I know that."

Barbara nodded. "I'll tell him," she said. "He's at Maimonides. The emergency people took him to Kings County, but my mother knew a specialist and we had him transferred." She looked past Sam. "I'm taking up your time."

"I'm really sorry to hear that it happened," Sam said. "I hope it's not—I mean: do you have hospitalization?"

"Oh yes."

"That's good," Sam said. He could see, from the corner of his eye, that one of the girls was moving her rear end to the music—lifting it from the stool and turning it slowly in circles. "It must have been some guys who were really out of it—nobody from the neighborhood, I mean who knew Steve, would have done it. I'd bet on that."

Barbara moved her shoulders slightly, to indicate her ignorance. "He won't say."

"Is he gonna press charges—if they get the guys?"

"He has to—because of the insurance."

Sam put a quarter down on the counter, and when Barbara had given him his change he stood. "I'll stop by tomorrow—and you let me know what he said. If he wants visitors, I'll go over sometime." Sam moved his shoulders, in the same way, he realized, that Barbara had. "It's no trouble—I mean, I got a lot of free time."

Sam walked along Church Avenue, past the Bel-Air supermarket, the Granada Theater. Shimmy's wife was named Barbara also—it was how he had remembered the name of Steve's wife. He could hear Dutch when they'd been in high school, talking about how much he'd gotten from her, about how he'd dry-humped her on the kitchen floor. There was no point in admitting it to Dutch, but he could, in fact, understand why a guy might want to do what he was doing—start being interested in religion at a certain point in his life. Sam turned the corner at Rogers Avenue and ducked his head down. He should have worn a hat. It was colder than he'd imagined, and if it snowed—which was doubtful—it would become impossible. He had no desire to go to *shul,* or to sit around studying with a bunch of old men, but he did have a desire, he knew, to know about things he could never know about. Most of all, he would have liked to have known what his father's childhood had been like—what it had been like then, growing up with Andy and his grandfather. The story Ben had told at the dinner that last night came into Sam's mind often, especially, he realized, since he'd been seeing Stella, and what he wondered the most about—the things he wished he could have seen—were things physical: the clothes his father had worn, the food he'd eaten, the plates he'd eaten it on, the books he'd carried to school, the hat he'd worn in winter, the stores he'd gone into, what his relatives had looked like, what the apartment they'd lived in had been like, what was where in each room, and when.

It was difficult—he couldn't quite make it, despite the way his mind worked—to imagine his father as a boy playing in the streets. Sam could conjure up the picture of a small boy's body—throwing snowballs, or playing hide-and-seek, or carrying packages home from the store—but what he could not see was the face on that body. He closed his eyes against the cold, and in the blackness he tried to see his father before he had been his father, and though he could visualize a small boy holding onto his grandfather's hand (Sam pictured them at the Battery, near the entrance for the Staten Island ferry), when his eyes got to the boy's face, Sam drew a blank. He could not imagine his father's face as a young face, he could not imagine that it had ever not had things on its mind. Sure. On a day like this, he reasoned, he saw the sense to what Ben had done, leaving.

He looked up, and above the sidewalk he could see Ben under the palm trees, wearing a pink golf cap on his head. *Sunshine and hot competition!* He had an urge to return home, to telephone long distance, to ask him to guess what the temperature was in Brooklyn . . . but if Ben had wanted to be in touch he would have been in touch. *Our greatest asset is our fine year-round weather,* he heard Ben tell him. A week or two before, he would have tightened at the sound of his father's voice, inside his head, but now he didn't mind. Stella made the difference, he supposed. Having her place to go to when he wanted—and feeling comfortable there—made it seem all right that he hadn't made any use of Ben's room, that he'd left it the way it had been. The other room had always been enough for him, anyway.

He spent the afternoon in Stella's living room, watching the game while Stella, in her bedroom, worked on some cards. She would, from time to time, wheel into his room and recite the poems to him, and they would laugh. When the game was over, they ate supper together and talked. Sam told her about Dutch's visit, and about what his own life had been like before he'd moved in with Ben—when he and Dutch had traveled together, playing cards and following the horses. Stella tried to get him to play poker with her, but Sam refused. "I only play for money," he said. "It's best that way."

When the dishes were in the sink, she got out of her chair and they sat together on her couch, watching television and talking about what had happened the night before. Sam stayed to hear the sports on the eleven o'clock news. The Knicks had won again, against the San Francisco Warriors, and while the announcer read off the high scorers (Stallworth was not among them), Sam wondered exactly how far from San Francisco Ben's place was. Stella told him that her physical therapist would be there first thing in the morning, at eight o'clock, and Sam said he would go—did she want him to help her get into bed? She said she would manage. Sam thought, before he left, of telling her about what had happened to Steve, but it was too late. He didn't want to give her bad dreams. It was something that, if he were going to mention it, he should have mentioned when he'd first arrived.

He kissed her goodnight and left, huddled inside his coat, a wool scarf—his mother had sent it to him from the Virgin Islands seven or eight years before—tight around his throat. Stella had been very quiet, he realized as he walked home—and this pleased him. He liked the way she joked with him—the way she had of putting things—but he liked it that she followed her own advice most of the time and wasn't always saying things simply to fill the silence.

Sam enjoyed walking around the old neighborhood at night, when nobody else was out: it was usually like this when he came home from the Garden, or from card games, when there were any. Quieter after midnight, since the buses only ran once an hour then. He walked up Linden Boulevard, smiling. Maybe, shuttling back and forth from his place to Stella's, and being able to choose between them—to stay in whichever one he wanted, when he wanted—maybe that was what they meant by peripheral privacy.

Sam turned the corner at Nostrand, onto his own block, and found that he was thinking of what Tidewater had said Rube Foster had once said to him, about the difference between a player who could stay in for the long pull, and one who was only a flash in the pan. Sam remembered how, as a kid, he had become attached to new guys before the season would start—from what the sportswriters would say about them. He could still remember all the names—guys who were going to be the new Bob Fellers or Joe DiMaggios. Now that Sam had seen the sportswriters sucking around dressing rooms and training camps, he resented what they had once done to him—the way they had preyed upon his willingness to believe. Half of them were rummies, though—and Sam had taken a few of their paychecks the time he and Dutch had stayed at Vero Beach together, for the Dodgers' spring training.

He crossed the street and saw that there were no lights on in the back of the rummage shop. That was fine with him. What he had thought of asking Tidewater, though, was this: what do you see in me? If the guy had known Babe Ruth and all those other guys, and if the rest of his story was the truth . . .

It was all the same to Sam: if what had happened had really happened, or if the old guy had imagined it all. And that included, Sam told himself, the business about the room below the cellar. Sam didn't have to believe that either. He figured Tidewater had found something there, but who knew what it had really been. Sam breathed in. The city air seemed cleaner to him in cold weather. "Hey Sam—!" He stopped, turned, saw nothing. "Over here! Quick!"

When Sam realized that the well-dressed man standing in the darkness of the entrance to the TV repair shop was his Bible Man, he felt himself tense slightly. But Sam walked toward him. "I came to warn you," the Bible Man said. "They got a small contract out for you. They—"

Sam laughed easily. He saw that the man's eyes were bright,

alert, and he studied the guy's clothing. He wore a green felt hat, a rich brown tweed sportscoat, and even in the shadows Sam could see light glisten from the shine on his black shoes. "You're doing okay, I see."

"Sure," the man said. "I'm on easy street now—it's why I'm here. Believe me when I tell you I'm not selling anything this time—I'm giving things away." The man's coat opened, and light flashed in Sam's eyes from a diamond stickpin. "I'm grateful to you, Sam, for helping me out that night, in the snow. I don't know what might have happened if you hadn't come by. That was my low point."

Sam was wary. "You said you were there to warn *me*, that night."

The guy moved forward, eager. "That's just the point—why I'm grateful to you, don't you see? You made me be there, instead of somewhere else. And if I'd been somewhere else—"

"I got to get going," Sam said. "I'm glad you're out from under."

"You can be too, Sam. Just listen to me a minute. It's simple." Sam waited. He thought of how he would tell the story to Stella: that, with the way they were all—Dutch and Shimmy and Sid and Flo and now his Bible Man—ganging up on him, to save him, he might as well have had muscular dystrophy. But he couldn't, in his mind, hear Stella laugh. He remembered hearing Ben tell the Rabbi that Tidewater might as well have been Jewish, but nobody had laughed then either. "You brought me to my senses. Listen. They say the greatest thing in the world is to gamble and win, right?—but we know that the next best thing is to gamble and lose." Sam saw the humor in the saying, and laughed with the man. "So I thought about that. How come, I asked, if I always wanted to win, I always wound up losing? Suppose, I thought—and it seemed crazy and right, there in the snow, after you'd kicked me—I just turned things upside down. Suppose I wanted to *lose*, I asked myself? I must've had some of that bible stuff in my head too, the way I get when I'm out of it—but didn't Christ say that we should not lay up treasures for ourselves on earth?" He held Sam's sleeve. "Just another second, friend—and then you get going, but fast."

"Sabatini?" Sam asked.

"I told you—I'm off his payroll. I gave him my theory and asked for a big stake, and I fooled him—he gave it to me, figuring it would put me that much further into his debt. Where, he must've asked himself, was the gambler ever born who wanted to lose? But I had the answer. Suppose I didn't gamble with the money myself?" Sam stepped into the doorway, to get warm. "I went across the bridge, to Jersey, to a private club where they have a wheel, see, and I took a young guy with me—not a gambler—and gave him a grand, with instructions to lose it as quickly as possible. I stayed at his side. For his work, I told the guy he'd get a hundred a night. The kid was sweet, a college kid, and I let him bring his girl. They had a ball—throwing the money all over the table, and getting cleaned out in thirty-five minutes. The next night I gave him another grand and—he was improving, see?—he lost that in ten minutes." The Bible Man chuckled. "On the third and fourth nights he went under within fifteen minutes, and we sat around drinking the rest of the time. Then, on the fifth night—to tell you the truth, I didn't believe it—he won forty thousand, and when he did, I took the stuff and got out of there, and I'm not going back."

"Sure," Sam said, and thought: tell me another story.

"I paid back Sabatini, told him that this gambler had retired, and I'd like to help you out too—just tell me how much—"

"Forget it," Sam said, and started walking away. "I'll get out my own way."

"But use my theory," the guy said, following him.

"Sure," Sam said. "One of these first days."

"I was serious about the other thing too," the man called. "Be careful. Please—"

Sam looked back and waved. Why shouldn't he use it? What, after all, did he have to lose? He laughed to himself, pleased with his own words, but he tried to keep his mind not on what had or had not happened to the guy, or on what Sabatini might or might not do, but on Stella, on how he'd felt when he was with her, and on what he would do about her when things changed.

He heard the sound of shoes clicking on the sidewalk—metal taps on the heels—and saw a tall man approaching him, from the opposite direction. Under the lamplight Sam could see that the man was dressed in a Chesterfield coat. Sam thought of what it would feel like, were he to run his cold fingers across the velvet collar. He turned to go into his building, one hand on the doorknob.

"Excuse me—"

Sam turned. The man reached him in a few quick steps. His hair was silver at the temples, his mouth thin, his chin almost pointed, and he spoke very clearly—as if, Sam thought, he might have been English.

"I wonder if you could help me—" The man reached into his sidepocket and took out a business card. He looked into Sam's eyes—the two men were exactly the same height—and his tongue flicked his upper lip. "Oh yes," he said. "I see now."

Sam's breath seemed to go even before he heard the sound in his stomach. He saw the man's gray leather gloves, stretched across his fists, and he wanted to reach into his sidepocket, but he couldn't. He gasped for air, doubled over, his hands wrapped around his middle. A gloved hand pressed his jaw, pulled him up straight, and Sam heard the back of his head crack against brick, so that in the darkness, with his eyes closed, points of light sprayed outward. "You'll pay up now, yes?" Sam moved forward, to butt the guy with his head, but he had no chance. The blows pounded against him again, below, where the air was already gone, in sharp, rapid bursts. Sam wanted to cry out but couldn't, and the thought of what he must have looked like—with his mouth open and no sound able to come from it—made him hurt. He spun around, light flying in circles, and knew that he was falling to the sidewalk; he heard the sound of metal clicking down the street, away, and then he felt somebody else touching him. He was on his back, his eyes closed, his knees at his chest. Somebody loosened his belt buckle. "There, there," he heard Tidewater say gently. He'd expected the Bible Man. "You'll be all right. It's just your wind. There, there . . ." Sam could not open his eyes. He wanted to touch the back of his head, where it stung. He felt as if he were sinking beneath water, far below the surface—he saw young boys curling in the water, blood flowing from their ears: South Sea Island pearl divers from movies he'd seen when he had been a boy. He watched a boy's body turn over, in slow motion, long strands of black hair trailing through the water as the boy struggled to get to the surface. The boy had a knife between his teeth, and Sam felt his own teeth biting down on it. The blood, expanding in the water, looked like dust. Sam thought there was somebody with Tidewater, but he didn't know what made him think so—he couldn't tell if he were seeing a shape or hearing a sound. "There, there," Tidewater said, lifting Sam's hips from the sidewalk, the way trainers did to football players on television. Sam heard strange sounds coming from his own throat, and he wanted to curse Tidewater for finding him. "There, there. You'll be all right. You'll come with me now."

12

Flo sat across the table from Sam, in Tidewater's room, explaining her program to him. Sam could tell from the way she spoke that she thought he would be especially interested in the figures. The rummage shop had raised, net, thirty-two thousand dollars during the previous year, and all of this money had gone to support what Flo called the program in independent living. The aim was to get as many of the muscular dystrophy patients as possible out of the hospitals and into apartments. Two of the boys Sam had seen at the Tuesday night parties, for example, were students at NYU, and they were living together in downtown Manhattan. Within the past three years there had been two marriages in which both husband and wife were wheelchair patients. With money that Flo was able to obtain from welfare and medicaid, in addition to the money the shop raised, the program was now able to support seventeen people in independent living. The most interesting statistic, Flo pointed out, was that it cost approximately seventy-five hundred dollars to maintain a couple in an apartment for one year, while, in a hospital, the cost for the same two people would have been over fifteen thousand. Where the patient's family could contribute money, the money was accepted. Stella did not, Flo noted, receive any money from the organization.

Things worked out best, however, Flo explained, when there were two living together. The program provided housekeeping service during the day, usually for five hours, and a person came in the evening—at nine—and stayed through the night. The day person would prepare and serve lunch and supper, clean up, see to the couple's various needs. Transportation to and from work or school was arranged and paid for by the organization. The night person would undress and bathe them, put them to bed, and in the morning would dress them and give them breakfast. The couples were extraordinarily devoted to one another, and it was, Flo claimed, amazing to see what they would learn to do for themselves and for one another.

Most important, though, were the effects on their personal lives—the way in which, in Flo's words, living in the world had lifted their spirits. There was a psychologist working with the program who had known the patients before, and even in those instances in which they had been living at home, and not in hospitals, he had described the change that independent living had wrought as miraculous. Flo asked Sam to imagine the difference it would make in somebody's life, and Sam nodded. It was, he realized, the first time since he had been living there that he had heard Flo talk about why she devoted so much of her life to the store. In a way, Sam was surprised. He would, if he had thought about it, have figured that she would have been more interested in raising money for research—to find a cure for the disease that had killed her husband and two children—but she had, he saw, only a passing interest in research, and hearing her go on about her program, and imagining the difference—between life in a hospital room and life in an apartment—he saw her point. While the doctors worked in their laboratories on cures, and while other women helped raise money to finance the organization's research projects —money which amounted each year to millions of dollars—it was still, as Flo put it, important to pay attention to the living. Otherwise, what was it all for?

"Now," Flo said, putting her coffee cup down on the table. "If I have the strength, my next job is to try to sell the program to other groups—in other cities." She sighed. "But it seems so foolish sometimes—going around and explaining to people, using the psychologist's report, showing them the breakdown financially—it seems so foolish to have to. Shouldn't it be obvious? Shouldn't it, Sam?"

"Sure," Sam said. "It makes sense." Flo looked away, as if daydreaming. "I mean," Sam went on, "if you treat somebody like a human being, then chances are he'll act like a human being." He shrugged, feeling confused somehow, not by what he was saying, but by what he was feeling: he was drawn to Flo, he knew, despite the fact that she was almost twice his age, and despite the fact of what had been happening with Stella. He was aware that he was forcing himself not to look at her chest, at the fullness of her breasts inside her blouse. He remembered what Ben had said, about remarrying. She seemed so wrapped up in her program, and in the store, that he found it difficult to imagine what her life was like—what her face looked like—when she was not doing something that had to do with it. And yet—what made him uncomfortable—he sensed that she did have some other life about which he knew nothing. "Anyway, that's what I think," he added.

"That's lovely, Sam," she said, and put her hand on top of his. "The psychologist says the same thing—only it takes him thirty pages."

"But if you go around to these other cities—" Sam stopped. "I mean, what about the store?"

"Marion," she said. She took her cup to the sink and rinsed it. "And Mason. They'll manage without me." She looked at him from over her shoulder. "And we'll have to think of other things, if the program is to grow. The store has been wonderful, but we can only raise so much."

"I'll make my own move in a day or so," Sam said.

"You're lucky Mason was there. If not, I—"

"No," Sam said, with certainty. "I'll tell you the truth, I'm surprised they even bothered, for what I owe them. There's guys—not big shots either—just ordinary guys with jobs who'll put ten grand on a game, and who get a hundred grand into the hole. I'm just peanuts to them."

"Still," she said. "You're right to get away now."

Sam nodded. "They can get mean," he admitted. "I'm just surprised they bothered with me." He stood, thinking that Flo was leaving. "Anyway, all they did was give me a cut on the back of my head and knock the wind out of me." She moved from the sink to the door, across the small room, and Sam felt that she wanted him to say more. "I don't mind staying here, with him. I'm used to a small place. Is he upstairs now—I mean, while you're visiting with me?"

"No," Flo said. "I thought he'd be here, with you."

"He'll show up," Sam said. "You can count on him."

"Is there anything you need—anything you'd like me to bring down?"

Sam shook his head sideways. "He takes care of everything. We get along okay—but, like I said, I'll make my move in a day or two. Staying in one place—it's leaving yourself wide open, like a sitting duck."

"And Stella?" Flo asked.

"Sure," Sam said, and he was not surprised by the suddenness of her question. "I think about her a lot."

"Yes?"

"That's all," Sam said. "I don't have to say anything else."

"That's right," Flo said. Her voice was cold.

"I mean, you yourself just said she's not part of the program—" Sam laughed.

"You're just like your father," Flo said. She stepped across the room to where he sat, in the corner, and she put a hand on his shoulder, then bent over and kissed him on the forehead. He stared at her blouse, his nose an inch from her left breast. "You take care of yourself."

"Sure," Sam said. "I got brains."

Flo laughed, and opened the door to the cellar. Sam smelled dust. He heard her footsteps on the wooden stairs. In a hole was right, he thought to himself, looking around the room and thinking of the store above. He didn't like the idea of being in a room without windows. He didn't like the idea of others—Flo and Tidewater—keeping a lookout for him. The deck of cards that Tidewater had left for him, unopened, lay on the table where Tidewater had placed it, next to the jar of pencils. That had been a mistake—telling Tidewater that everything would have worked out if only he could have had a game now and then, because the truth, Sam realized, was that he wasn't much interested any more. Instead of cards, he thought of Stella.

He lay down on Tidewater's bed, and slept. He awoke at noon, when Tidewater arrived to make lunch for the two of them. Sam asked him how his work—the story—was coming, and Tidewater said that it would be ready soon. After lunch, Sam started on the dishes, and Tidewater put on his coat. He offered to get a newspaper for Sam. "One thing," Sam said, as he sprinkled soap powder on the dishes. "I was thinking: how come you don't get yourself a piano?" He saw Tidewater smile. "I mean, as long as you're staying. Down here—the noise—it wouldn't bother anybody."

Tidewater's long face, next to his olive green raincoat, seemed ashen. "Ah Sam," he said with affection. "You know—you asked me yesterday why it is that I take such an interest in you. You wondered if it was only because of my feelings toward your father." He moved forward, and Sam kept his eyes on the man's hands, which curled toward him gracefully. "But don't you see? You're rare yourself, Sam. You are—I've thought about it—you are what I would call a man more sinned against than sinning, don't you see? There are not many of your kind left."

"Sure," Sam said. "Whatever you say."

Tidewater left. When Sam had finished the dishes and put them away in the tall closet next to the door, he sat in the easy chair and did nothing. He was surprised at this—that it did not bother him to do nothing. Like his Bible Man, he was ready to retire. He found that it was, below the store, easy for him to sit for an hour or more, not sleeping, not moving, not thinking, not worrying. Letting the others take care of him now—he laughed at the idea—he figured it was his way of keeping up with inflation.

The only thing he regretted, other than not being able to see Stella, was that he couldn't leave to tell Steve's wife about what had happened and why he hadn't shown up to get Steve's message. It angered him to think that Steve might lump him with everybody else—thinking that Sam had not meant what he'd said. He had thought of asking Mason or Flo to leave a message for Steve at the candy store, but the less anybody knew about his life, the better. There was no point in leaving any clues for Sabatini, as long as the guy felt like hunting.

Flo visited him again the following morning. She had spoken with Stella and it was, she said, arranged: Stella would come to the party that evening—Tuesday night—in the rummage shop. Flo and

Mason would, when things were in full swing, bring her downstairs.

"No," Sam said, and he laughed. That, he could have told Flo, if he'd wanted to, would have been carrying things too far.

"But I thought, since they must be watching this building anyway, and it wouldn't seem unusual for Stella to—" Sam watched her trying to read his mind. "I haven't said anything. Just that if she comes, she'll see you. That's all she knows."

"No," Sam repeated. "You tell her I'll be in touch. Tell her—" Sam thought of saying something about the neighborhood, something that would make Stella laugh. "Tell her I'm okay, that's all. I'll be in touch."

"Your friends called again—Shimmy and Sid. I've been doing as you said, telling them you're on vacation." She paused at the door. "It is nice to know people care, though, isn't it?"

"I knew already," Sam said.

"Dutch stops by every morning."

"Dutch is okay."

Flo left. Hearing the names of his old friends, Sam thought of how badly Tidewater had felt about not having known the guys on his team. The last thing he needed, though, was advice from people like Sid. Sid had been the one, he remembered, who, years before, had tried to stop Dutch from running onto the grass at Ebbets Field in order to shake Duke Snider's hand, and if Dutch had listened to Sid . . . Sam could remember cheering as Dutch ran around the outfield with cops chasing him, and—afterward, at school—how good he'd felt, being the best friend of a guy who had done the kind of thing Dutch had done.

When the heat was off, he told himself, he would see to it that he spent more time with Dutch, but for the time being, he had no desire to think about him. If he thought about anything, it was about leaving. Afterward, when things were straightened away, he and Stella could laugh about Flo's scheme. Sure. And maybe, if Tidewater spent all his time below working on his life story—Sam turned the idea over in his head—maybe then the heat would stay off for good.

In the middle of the night, Sam was awakened by the sound of a siren. He sat up in bed, in the darkness. "Mason?" he whispered, but there was no reply. From habit, Sam reached for his pants— held his knife, and waited. He heard the door to the street open, and he listened to footsteps, going up the staircase to his landing. A minute passed, and Sam heard nothing. His eyes were accustomed to the dark, but it made no difference: without windows to let in light, he saw nothing. If Tidewater were upstairs, he would throw them off the trail. Somebody—Sam didn't care who, whether it was Sabatini or Sam's own buddies—was checking on him. But they'd find nothing out of order. Ben's room would be just as it was when Ben had left. The brochure would be there, on the desk, if anybody was interested. Sam laughed to himself, hearing Ben's voice: *People of advancing years gradually—or sometimes suddenly—come to realize that their present home no longer meets their needs in the best way, and that they should think of a change.*

In the morning, when Tidewater did not appear, Sam made breakfast for himself: juice, eggs, bacon, toast, milk. He had offered Tidewater money for food, but the man had refused, and Sam had seen no point in arguing. He'd make it up to him when he got back on top. Although Sam had not seen daylight for six days, he felt good. He did his exercises in the morning and evening, he slept well, he ate well. He felt alert, on edge, ready for anything; the slight dizziness and the pains were gone. There was no point in going above ground and taking chances, but the fact was that they had gone easy with him.

When Flo visited him at eleven, Sam said nothing about what had happened during the night. Flo spoke about her program, and Sam listened. It was something which he was interested in, and it made him feel good to know that the hours he'd put into the store, over the years, though they didn't amount to a lot, had gone for something worthwhile. One of the guys in the program—in graduate school at Teachers College—was going to be the director of a Head Start program for the coming summer, and Sam understood Flo's pride in the fact. He listened to her and remembered one time her voice had not been so sweet. Marion had put up a sign, when Flo had been away, and Flo had been furious when she'd seen it: *I complained because I had no shoes, until I met a man who had no feet.* Flo had been right to take the sign down, Sam thought. Most people would probably have thought that it made sense. Sam smiled, glad to have Flo with him. It took somebody like her to understand why words like that didn't do anybody any good.

"Did Mason tell you about last night?" she asked.

"I didn't see him this morning."

"They took Mrs. Reardon away, you know. I called this morning. They don't think she'll last the day."

It took an instant for the name to register, and then Sam heard his heart thump, off-beat. "What about the kid—Muriel—?"

Flo did not look directly at him. "I put through some calls this morning, to people I know—"

Sam was standing. "What *happened* to her?" He wanted to reach out and grab her, to shake the information from her, but he found that he could only stand stiffly, his hands at his sides. "C'mon. What happened—?" He found the only words which made his point for him: "I got a right to know."

"They took her away this morning. I wanted to keep her—believe me—I tried to—"

"I got a right to know," Sam said again, but weakly. "I mean, I know her since she was a—since she was left here."

Sam allowed Flo to hug him, to press her body to his. His hands remained at his sides. "I know, Sam dear—I know. But it's for the best. She'll be with children her own age, she'll be well fed, she'll have a clean bed." Flo stood back, took Sam's hands in her own. "I had to go inside this morning, with the people from the agency. I'm glad you didn't have to see the filth in their apartment—you wouldn't believe what it was like."

"Why'd you let them? Why didn't you come get me—" Sam turned away from her. He looked around the room, at the ceiling, and imagined Muriel in a room without windows. He did not like the idea of Flo seeing how upset he was. "We could have worked something out to keep them from taking her."

"I'm sorry."

"Sure." Sam's ears were ringing. "I mean, she's just a kid. She's got her whole life ahead of her."

Flo came toward him again, but he swung his hand out. "Lay off me, with your hands. Just leave me alone, okay?" He didn't want to be angry with her, but he could not stop himself from letting the words fall. "You could have stopped them if you'd really wanted to." He nodded. "Sure. You waited till I was down here."

"Oh Sam," she said. Her voice was sad. "Sam," she said again, softly, but he did not make a move toward her.

"Just leave me alone, okay? I got to figure some things out." He blew air into the room, as if he had been holding his breath.

"It's for the best, Sam."

"Sure," he said. "Everything is, if you want to look at it that way." He sat in the chair, spent. "I should've figured something, the way she was sitting out there all last week. I should've figured something myself. I wasn't thinking."

"I'm glad you didn't see the apartment. The odors—"

"Sure," Sam said. "They probably wanted me to be around, to try to stop them—they would have liked that. They could have used that too." Sam shook his head. "You don't have to say anything else. Go upstairs and rummage around, okay?"

Flo did not reply. Alone in the room, after she was back in the store, he couldn't keep the pictures from appearing inside his head: he imagined himself sneaking upstairs, wary of the guys who might be after his skin, and he knew that, if he'd searched for the girl, she would have been gone. He saw himself standing on the staircase, barring the way, and he saw how absurd the scene would have been. Maybe, in a while, he'd come to the same conclusion Flo had come to—that she was better off in a special place, where they were used to taking care of kids like her. Sure. The words were there: she'd be with other kids who were in the same boat she was in.

Except, he knew that he had—even while Flo had confused him—been aware of another solution, though he'd been smart enough not to voice it. Because even if there had been something to it, to taking care of Muriel himself, with Stella, he realized that it was too late. By the time they would have tried to get things worked out, by the time they'd have worked their way through all the forms and, given Stella's condition, the special problems—not to mention the spot he was in with Sabatini—the kid would have been long gone. Sam picked up the coffee cup Flo had been drinking from, and he rinsed it. The truth, he admitted, was that although he may have wished he could have been ready for such a thing, the thought was so new to him, the idea seemed so opposite to the way, if he'd thought about it, he'd foreseen his own life, that he wouldn't have been able to lay odds on its chances of working out. Still, it was what was in his head, and he didn't fight it. He'd see Stella before he left.

He sat down on the bed feeling weak. Later, Flo would forget about the things he'd said to her. Sam pictured her in the hospital, before he'd known her; holding her second baby, he knew she was thinking of the time the first one had had trouble standing up. The kid was smiling, pushing up from the ground with the palms of its hands. Sam was, in truth, glad that he'd been below, where he hadn't been able to see them putting Muriel into a truck. Not that he was afraid—if he'd had to watch, he could have watched. There would have been no great trick to that. But it was better, if you couldn't do anything about something, not to have to be involved in the details.

He was surprised, now that he'd decided about Stella, at how calm he suddenly was; maybe, if he visited Muriel when things got straightened away and he could return—Flo would be sure to know where she was—maybe the kid would remember him. Meanwhile, there was no point in raising the house with the hand he was holding. Sure. But if, he asked himself, he had things figured out so well, and if he seemed to be calm—he could see himself lying there, motionless—why was it that he felt, at the same time, such a shortness of breath, as if somebody were sitting on his chest?

When Tidewater returned and was preparing supper, Sam told him that he had decided—that he was ready to leave. He thanked him for what he had done. "If you could go upstairs and throw some clothes into a suitcase for me—and I'll tell you where I have a few bucks stashed."

"You haven't heard the end of my story," Tidewater stated. He stood at the stove, frying steaks for them.

"You can write to me," Sam said. "I'll leave you an address."

Sam saw the man's eyes bulge. Tidewater raised the frypan in his left hand, to turn the steaks. "Don't be like your father. Everything is not a joke." Sam heard the sizzling, saw Tidewater wince, jerk his head back from hot grease that had splattered him. "You haven't heard the end of my story. You will stay for that. It is the least you can do."

Sam wanted to concentrate on other things. "Whatever you say," he said, and sat down at the table. Tidewater set Sam's plate in front of him—steak, peas, mashed potatoes—and sat across from him.

"Where will you go?" Tidewater asked.

"You know."

"I wish you could have stayed longer." Sam watched the man's fingers as he cut his steak. "It has meant a lot to me, you know, having you here since your father left—having somebody to share this time with."

"Sure," Sam said, hardly paying attention. "Everybody needs somebody, I guess."

"Not at all," Tidewater snapped. "That's your easy way out." He smiled in a way that made Sam shiver. "The Lord chastiseth him whom He loveth."

"Look," Sam said, watching Tidewater's fork pierce a piece of steak, "if you got more for me to read, give it here. I don't have to rush right out. While you're getting my stuff together, I could take a look."

While Sam was eating, Tidewater left for his room below, and a few minutes later he returned and gave Sam the pages. He was, Sam saw, dreaming—a thin smile curved upward in his cracked pale skin. "I remember what Ben said, when I had given him one of my usual speeches—citing those philosophers who have claimed that, given the suffering and injustice of this world, it is better not to have been born. 'Better not to have been born?' he said to me. 'Of course—but how many, after all, are fortunate enough to enjoy such an opportunity? Perhaps one in ten thousand . . .'"

Sam saw tears in the man's eyes. "I don't get it," Sam said. "How can anyone not be born?"

"Ah Sam," Tidewater said. "That's why I chose you to read my story." He started to reach for Sam's hand, but stopped himself. "I was a baseball player," he said. "All of what I have written is true, but that part is also true. I was a baseball player."

"Sure," Sam said. He dipped a piece of steak into gravy. "I never said I didn't believe it."

"Oh I was splendid, Sam," Tidewater went on. "If you could have seen me then, on the mound—oh if you could have seen me!"

"Flo told me about them taking the kid away," Sam said. "It's why I'm not . . ."

"I understand that," Tidewater said. "Things like that have their effect. They do not merely happen when they do." Sam watched Tidewater's gray throat and stopped eating, to listen. " 'There is a certain providence in the fall of a sparrow. If . . .'" His voice trailed off, weak.

"Birds," Sam said. "It's always birds."

Tidewater laughed lightly, and Sam did too, though he was not sure why. "Oh if you could have seen me then, Sam!"

"You can tell me about Babe Ruth too, if you want," Sam offered. "Like I said, I got some time—as long as I get out before the morning comes."

MY LIFE AND DEATH
IN THE NEGRO AMERICAN
BASEBALL LEAGUE

A SLAVE NARRATIVE

CHAPTER THREE

I caress Barton's scarred legs and run my index finger along the inward-folding curves of skin. I ask Jack Henry to tell me about the old-timers, the men who had played before I was born. Jack Johnson, the heavyweight champion, had been a first baseman for the Philadelphia Giants. I give Little Johnny Jones the house he desires; I feed women to Kelly; I make Rose Kinnard's face whole again; I ring the money in for them all and, in my mind, holding them to me with my long arms, reveal to them the man they never knew. ("Nothing shall I, while sane, compare with a dear friend," Horace writes.)

But if he did not show himself, he was not there. My finger glides along skin so thin that I feel I am touching bone directly. It is too late, of course. Even if things could be otherwise than they were—if we could replay those years together—I would never be for them what they have become for me. I reduce their lives to images which please my own mind. In this, I am merely like other men. Why should I perceive the world differently—it is not my eyes or my heart, after all, which are black. Involved in their own lives, and wanting to give me my due as a player, my teammates would doubtless, if asked, remember me fondly. They would (those who are still alive) call me a great pitcher and hitter; they would remark on my quietness, my presumed intellect; they would not allude in public utterance to things private; and they would—clearest of all—not condemn me for my final act. They would have need neither for my gifts, nor for my confession. Why should Barton want me to nurse legs which, deformed though they were, carried him through a career which brought him an income he had never dreamt possible? He would prefer, surely, to be called Little Johnny's sister, and to keep wearing the uniform of the Brooklyn Royal Dodgers.

There remain, then, only facts. I met George Herman "Babe" Ruth some six weeks after the close of the 1924 World Series, and we became lovers. I saw him for the first time on the afternoon of November 26, 1924, when we played his team, the Touring Yankee All-Stars, in Charlotte, North Carolina. When I emerged from the dugout at the city baseball park and glanced, as I always did, toward the outfield to see which way the wind was blowing any flag which might be there, he was at the plate, striding forward with his right foot, his back to me. I tried not to see him. There were no flags, which I must have already known, since the outfield had no fence behind it, but ran to pasture. There were ample stands along the first and third base lines, for whites; ropes had been strung up along the left and right field lines, behind which our own fans stood. Boys—white and colored—had, as always, ducked under the ropes and roamed in the pastures behind the Yankee outfielders, hoping for long drives.

He seemed as real, standing there, as he had been in my mind. I was carrying the photo, now broken along its folds. Bingo called to me, telling me to begin my warm-ups, but I stood and stared, and saw, as Ruth followed through and his profile was, for the first time, revealed to me, just how black his skin was. His turn at bat completed, he picked up his glove and walked in my direction, along the first base line.

"Hiya, kid," he said easily. I looked away. The greeting was, of course, the one he was famous for—the one he gave to the world: to fans, children, friends, teammates, sportswriters. His voice was young and thin—lighter than my own. Though I had known his age (he was ten years older than I was, and had been playing in the major leagues since 1914), it surprised me to see with my eyes that he too was a young man. His skin, though burnt from the sun, seemed especially smooth, and his round features made him appear more boyish than his photographs had indicated. His smile, sincere and vapid, revealed the dumbness my teammates had enjoyed mocking. ("Once," Bingo had told us, "when the fans got on him during an exhibition game—this was in Montreal—they say that they started yelling 'Nigger' at him, and that Ruth, who never did have rabbit ears, only smiled back at them, pleased, remarking to a teammate, 'See—they know me up here too.' ")

I wound up, kicked high, and fired the ball at Bingo; it left my hand too soon, though, from far back of my ear, and I saw at once that it would be wild. I felt faint. Bingo leapt, but the ball sailed above his head and Ruth laughed as his teammates, at the plate, hearing Bingo's cry of "Heads up!" ducked and cowered, covering their ears, unaware of the direction from which danger approached. The ball hit no one, however, but skipped in among the fans. Ruth jogged off in his bandy-legged way, without looking at me again. He tipped his hat to the crowd along the right field line, behind the ropes, and they cheered him.

I saw Johnson then, leaning with one arm on the top of the dugout, some ten steps from me. "Sure now, fair ass," he said, picking at his teeth with a fingernail and smiling in a way which made me burn. "You want to pace yourself."

His voice revived me. I glared at him—at the purple blackness of his skin—and fired the ball at Bingo, stinging him in his glove hand. My weakness was gone as quickly as it had come. I thought of Johnson's age: his perforated face told no lies. In every city in which we played, throughout the southeastern United States, I and not Johnson had been the central attraction. I was the man who, in the Negro press, was already being called "the Black Babe," though my ignorant public could not know that the young man so heralded bore the likeness of one they would refer to, when they had seen him, as "an all gone"—the term deriving from their belief that any Negro of my color would have to have passed through three generations in which white and black had mingled—mulatto, quadroon, octoroon—until, in the fourth, the dark pigment would have been all gone.

I was also, then, a curiosity. After games, young boys would wait outside the ballparks to look closely at me. The brave ones would touch me. I remember none of them—not a single face—though I do recall the voice of one boy who, following me from the park to our hotel, in Savannah, kept begging me to tell him what he had to do to make his skin white. "Oh cap'n," he whined, dancing around me, bowing his head, his hat in hand. "I'd give anything to have skin like yours. What I got to do—tell me please, cap'n. Oh what I got to do to make my skin white."

"For what is this love of friendship?" Cicero asks. "Why does no one love either an ugly youth, or a handsome old man?" I did not, for once, believe that I envied Johnson those things which enabled him to hate me with such an indifferent scorn. I did not listen to Bingo, telling me to take my time. I knew that the Yankee players had stopped around home plate to watch the fast ball they had heard so much about, and I sensed that his eyes were, from behind, even while he joked with his fans, watching my every move, gauging my speed.

I had nothing to hide. I threw with all I had, yet easily. I set down the Yankees—Dugan, Witt, Meusel—in order in the first inning, and my teammates did not need to tell me how good I was. My ears were ringing, yet I heard nothing. Jones's banter was for the pleasure of the white fans, behind our dugout. I burned with pride and did not believe that any man could touch me.

Ruth was the first to face me in the second inning, and as I watched him smile at me from his moon face, I thought that his eyes were playful, that he thought he could toy with me. But it was probably, as always, only his beloved fans he was thinking of; he would have done anything to please a crowd. I reared back and, wasting nothing, fired two strikes across the heart of the plate while he stood, amazed, with bat on shoulder. He hitched his belt then, resolutely—as was always the case in the off-season, and sometimes during the season, he had grown thick around the middle, from too much eating and drinking. As others often remarked, his shape was, incongruously enough for a man of such grace, like that of a pregnant woman. The fans, excited by the confrontation, were silent. I kicked high and threw again, whipping my arm downward and snapping the ball off the tips of my fingers. The ball flew—a brilliant white line, low, toward the knees. He stepped forward and lunged, his bloated torso twisting in vain, for the ball was already cracking the pocket of Bingo's glove even as Ruth was bringing the bat around. I had never thrown faster. The crowd roared; I felt the blood pounding in my ears. Bingo rifled the ball to third base, and my teammates flipped it around the infield. I could not have done other than what I did, but I wondered nonetheless, and it was a moment before I allowed myself to look toward the plate again. He was still there, as if contemplating what had happened to him. His eyes met mine. They showed puzzlement for an instant only, and then he smiled and returned to the bench, clucking to himself: I had pleased him.

In our half of the third inning, I took my first turn at bat and, standing in against Waite Hoyt (himself a native of Brooklyn, as all our fans, receiving reports of the game back north, would have known),

I did not hesitate. The first pitch was letter-high and outside and I moved into it with an ease that belied the energy released: I met the ball solidly and drove it high and far toward right field—Ruth took one step back and then stopped. He turned and watched the ball soar—far beyond him, where the crowd of young boys had also turned and were already giving chase.

I gave all I had. In his second at bat, Ruth set himself for me, and after swinging and missing at the first two pitches, and taking the third pitch for a ball, he timed a low fast ball perfectly and drilled it to right field—straight at Johnson, however, who took it easily. In his third at-bat of the day I took Bingo's instruction and sent the first pitch for his chin, to keep him from crowding the plate the way he loved to. He fell down and sat there laughing, even though the pitch had nearly hit him—a pitch like the one with which, four years earlier, his teammate Carl Mays had killed Ray Chapman. He got up and took his stance, swinging at the air several times, slowly, giving away no ground. I felt nothing and thought of nothing except, as always, of what I was doing. I threw hard, to the inside again. He swung—on time—but the ball, snapped off and breaking, rose in the last twenty feet and passed above the bat. "Oh I feel the breeze," Jones called. I pitched again— a called strike, low on the outside corner—but Ruth continued to regard me with a smile. His shoulders were broad and though one could feel, as he took his practice swings, the power they contained, the great power, as I myself knew, came not from size or strength, but from the energy generated in that moment when bat and ball met and the wrists circled one another, snapping across—breaking was the word the players used—as if straining against an impossibly fierce wind. I felt no fear, though, and with two strikes on him gave him my best—a bullet across the middle, waist-high; he swung, his wrists snapped swiftly, but his bat only grazed the ball—so slightly that the ball did not alter its course. It smacked into Bingo's glove for the third strike. "You own that man!" Jones called. "Oh you own that man now, honey!"

I was thrilled, but not surprised. When the game was over Ruth lingered near his bench and beckoned to me with his hand. I had expected that I would have been able now to stare him down—to disdain, in myself, that very passion which had made me desire, so dearly, to defeat him. In his presence, however, with the game over, I could barely look at him; I was aware of my age, and of how young I must have seemed. "Hey kid," he said. "You really took care of me out there to-

day. How 'bout me standin' ya to a drink?'' I nodded, my eyes fixed
to the ground in front of his feet. ''You come by my hotel later, okay?
Any kid who throws the way you do—I got to stand ya to a drink.''

He punched me playfully on the shoulder of my right arm—the way
he would have done to one of his own teammates. ''See ya later, kid,''
he said, and walked off.

In my hotel room, I took his photo from my wallet and tore it into
little pieces. Yet I could not deceive myself. Although I had proven myself his master as a pitcher and hitter, if only for one day, I grew weak
when I thought of our conversation, when I pictured him at the plate
or in the outfield, when I remembered each detail of our confrontation.

He was, when I arrived, sitting in the lobby of his hotel, sprawled
across an easy chair, entertaining a crowd—a red-headed girl in a low-
cut sequined dress was on one arm of the chair, and Dugan sat on the
other. Ruth was smoking a cigar and laughing boisterously. I recognized
some of his teammates and assumed, correctly, that the other men were
newspaper reporters. I stood in the doorway, watching his large hand
—as he laughed—caress the thigh of the girl. She had a hand on his
neck, her fingers inside the collar of his shirt. ''Oh Babe!'' she
screamed, delighted. I felt an enormous revulsion, but I would not
leave. I waited until, roaring with laughter and looking around the
circle of men who were playing court to him, he spotted me. ''C'mere!''
he yelled, gesturing with the hand that held the cigar. I obeyed and
walked across the lobby. I was wearing a suit and tie, and realized how
out of place I must have appeared.

''This here's the greatest pitcher I ever faced,'' he said at once, as
the crowd parted and I entered the circle of men around his chair. He
pointed his cigar at one of the newspapermen. ''You jackasses can
quote me on that. You tell 'em the Babe says that the greatest pitcher
in baseball is a nigger, and that includes Walter Johnson.'' He sat up
then, as if worried about something. ''Hey listen,'' he said. ''You
drink, don't ya?''

''Yes,'' I said. ''Occasionally.''

He mimicked me. ''Occasionally,'' he repeated, and laughed. ''That's
pretty good. You jackasses hear that? Old stuffed shirt Johnson, he's
so clean—'' He pulled the girl's head down to his mouth and whispered
in her ear so that she howled with laughter. He stroked her thigh. ''He
ain't the Big Train,'' Ruth went on. ''He's the Milk Train!''

When the others had stopped laughing, Ruth shoved the girl off the arm of the sofa. "You get lost now. Me and the boys want to go have ourselves a good time. I'll call ya when I need ya, okay?" He stood up and put his arm around my shoulder. "This here's the greatest pitcher I ever faced. You jackasses can tell 'em that the Babe said so. He hits 'em pretty long too—not as long as me, but he whacked it pretty good today." He put his cheek next to mine then. "But who's blacker, huh? Tell me that. Who's blacker?"

"You got him beat a country mile, Babe," Meusel said.

"You really a colored?" he asked me.

"Yes," I replied, trying to keep myself erect under the force of his arm, which was pushing me downward. "Yes I am."

"Okay," he said to the others. "It's the truth. I seen guys even whiter than him in Baltimore and they were niggers. We had a kid at St. Mary's was a white nigger." He nodded his head up and down, vigorously, as if he were lecturing his friends. His stomach bulged, touching my right side. "Color ain't what counts. It's blood that does it, ain't that so, kid?"

"Yes," I said. "It's blood."

"See?" he said. "Didn't I tell ya?" He laughed again, and the others, for no reason that I could discern, joined him. "I can get even blacker than this, though—ask any guy. You should've seen me in August. Tell 'em, Bob."

"Like the ace of spades," Meusel said.

"Tell 'em, Tony."

"Black as the devil's ass at midnight," Lazzeri said.

"Tony, my baby!" Ruth cried, hugging Lazzeri. I felt myself shudder and could tell, from the way Ruth's other arm lifted slightly from my shoulder, that he had felt it also. "Any guy who strikes out the Babe twice in one day, I got to stand him to a drink, ain't that so?" He paused, then whispered to me in his high boy's voice, "You drink, don't ya?"

"Yes," I said.

He pounded me on the back then, and roared with laughter. "But not like the Babe, I'll bet. C'mon—"

One arm around my shoulder, the other around Lazzeri's, he led us from the hotel—his cigar stuck in the corner of his mouth, pointed upward. The smoke trailed into my face, tickling my throat when I breathed in. Bob Meusel, Herb Pennock, Joe Dugan, Aaron Ward, and George Pipgrass were in the crowd behind us, along with some sportswriters. At the first corner, a group of young colored boys were sitting in front of their shoe shine stands. "I love kids," Ruth said to me, his hand squeezing my shoulder. We waited while he had his shoes shined. He threw a dollar down on the sidewalk. "That's from the Babe," he said, taking me around again as we walked off.

On the next block we entered a small bar. "This here's for whites only," he whispered to me, loud enough for all his friends to hear. "But if you don't say nothing, I won't either, okay, kid?" He laughed out loud and pressed his cheek to mine again. "I mean, how they gonna tell who ya are, unless you tell 'em." He moved away from me and called loudly, "The drinks are on the Babe—and I want everyone to have a good time!"

When his own mug and mine had been filled with beer, he toasted me. "Here's to the greatest pitcher I ever faced," he said. "Even if he is a . . ."

He sputtered, laughing, into his beer, so that the foam rolled over the edge and down across his fist. He drank, then switched hands and sucked on his knuckles. He pulled me to a table at the side. The men who had been in the bar when we arrived would, when he looked their way, all raise their glasses to him. He smiled and raised his mug to them, each time. "Listen," he said in my ear, "anything you want, you come to me. If that jackass bartender says anything—I'll tell him you're a friend of mine. Any friend of the Babe's—" He broke off, turning his eyes to the men around us. "What're you guys all staring at—I ain't gonna give a show." He pounded his fist on the wooden table. "Okay. This is what we're all gonna do. Lazzeri, over here—"

Lazzeri, the Yankees' second baseman, came to him. "Watch this," he said to me. He pulled Lazzeri's head to him and began whispering in his ear. Lazzeri giggled, his eyes wide. "Tony's gonna get a woman tonight," Ruth declared, "so I'm givin' him some pointers—" He pressed Lazzeri's head to him, his hand cupped around the back of Lazzeri's skull.

Pennock spoke: "Lay off, Babe. You know what's gonna happen if—"

Ruth let Lazzeri's head go and he snarled at Pennock. "You gonna do somethin' about it—?"

Lazzeri lay his head on the wooden table. Tears rolled from his eyes, he was laughing so hard. "Sure, Babe," one of the newspapermen said. "Go easy."

"Ain't I doin' just that?" he asked, and I believed him. "I like to see a happy Italian, that's all. It don't do no harm, you guys. It's practice—with us all around anyway to help him out—it's practice so he can learn to—" Ruth leaned over then and said something else into Lazzeri's ear, while Lazzeri's head lay on the table. I tried not to hear the words, which referred to the things Lazzeri was going to do to the whore that Babe would supply him with. "How 'bout you, kid?" he asked, leaning against me. "They got some of the best black cathouses I ever seen right here, just a block away—they got a gal there, she does somethin' called tyin' the knot, you'll think you're goin' through the roof, ain't that so, Tony?" He closed his eyes and drew breath in, through his nostrils. "Mmm—I can smell it from here—"

Lazzeri moaned and then grew limp: his head rolled once, to its other side, and then I heard a gurgling sound. "Do something, you jackasses!" Ruth commanded angrily, but he was already holding Lazzeri's head between his hands. Lazzeri's body twitched and Dugan got him from behind, holding him steady, so he would not fall. Ruth shoved his hand into Lazzeri's mouth and kept it wedged there. Pennock handed him a spoon—light flashed from it as if it were silver—and Ruth inserted it where his hand had been. "C'mon, sweetheart," he whispered to Lazzeri. "It ain't nothing. You'll be all right now. You'll be okay." He shoved me backward, to give himself more room, and then, giving commands to the others to get Lazzeri from the top, he lifted his feet and laid the man out across several chairs. He covered him with his jacket and knelt beside him, caressing the face. There were tears in Ruth's eyes. "It ain't nothing, kid. I didn't mean to excite ya this far. Honest I didn't. We don't have to go to that cathouse if you don't want, okay?" He pressed his cheek to the man's face. "I didn't mean for this to happen, sweetheart, you believe me, don't ya? I just want to see ya get rid of this thing someday. But I didn't mean to excite ya this far." He turned to the rest of us and his eyes were defiant. "Ain't there nobody strong enough to try to stop me? Can't ya see when I let things get carried away?" He spat. "You guys ain't men." He turned his eyes from us. "We don't got to do nothing to no women, my Tony baby, okay? It's whatever you say." Lazzeri's eyes rolled so that, his lids half-open, I saw only the whites. The bartender and the local customers peered over the shoulders of our group. "It's whatever you say, sweetheart." He glanced at us and whispered, "He's comin' around already—I can tell." Looking at the crowd, he began to stand. "Hey, what are you, a regular bunch of goons? C'mon, can't ya see the guy don't feel good—give him air."

"It happens all the time," Ruth said to me some minutes later, when Lazzeri was sitting up, recovered. "It ain't nothin' to get excited about —ya get used to it after a while. What's a guy supposed to do if he's born with a thing like that—stop living?" He raised his beer mug, which was empty. "Hey, kid—you at the bar—let's fill these things up again. We got to drink to our Italian friend's health, don't we?" He smiled lovingly at Lazzeri. "Ain't that right, kid?"

A short while later Pennock, with Ruth's permission, took Lazzeri back to the hotel. The drinking continued. To my surprise, I found that my head remained clear. I did not laugh at Ruth's supposed jokes, and I did not pay any attention to the compliments his friends paid to me, but I was, I knew, despite the man's meanness and vulgarity, happy to be in his presence. "See the way the kid here holds his stuff," he said several times to the others. "You guys take a lesson." He pointed to the newspapermen. "You're a lush, Ziegler. You ain't an athlete. You're just lush. You're a lush, Novak. You're a lush, too, Ellis. You're a lush, Wofford, you asshole." His right arm went around my neck, his beer mug in his right hand, so that he drank while pressing his forehead to me. He put his mug in front of my lips and I drank also.

"I said the truth," he told me, one hand on my leg, above the knee. "I never seen a guy had a fast ball like yours. I was a pitcher too, ya know."

"I know," I said.

"Oh yeah?" His narrow eyes widened. "You knew that?"

"My brothers saw you pitch at Ebbets Field, in the 1916 World Series."

"Oh yeah?" He shook his head, wonderingly. "I couldn't carry your suitcase, though. You got a fast ball like I never seen before."

We left shortly after midnight, his teammates walking behind us along the street, singing raucously. Ruth was very drunk, and in his drunkenness he became affectionate, leaning upon me for support and telling me how sweet I was, what a great pitcher I was, how much he would have liked to have done for a kid like me. "I love kids," he told me. Helping him across the hotel lobby and up the stairs to his room, I felt as if I were, as I had been on the playing field that afternoon, the master of the situation—and yet, as soon as he had unlocked the door to his room and pushed me inside it, in front of him, my confidence vanished.

"Get outa here, you goddamned bitch!" he cursed, seeing that the red-headed girl who had been with him earlier in the evening was lying across his bed, in her underwear. She was barely awake, yet he pulled her by her right leg, jerking her so that she scraped her stomach across the metal railing at the foot of the bed. She screamed. Ruth swung the door open. He ordered me to get her clothes, which were in a pile on a chair, and I did what he said. "Now get your fat ass outa here." He kicked her, his foot thudding solidly against her backside. She tried to get up, but he had grabbed her by one arm and was dragging her into the hallway. "Sure, Babe," she said. "I didn't mean nothing." He took her clothes from me and threw them at her, then tossed some money on the floor. "Here—buy yourself a new ass," he laughed. "Yours is cracked!"

He slammed the door and his anger disappeared at once. He came to me and I found myself backing away, afraid of him. "I ain't so drunk," he said, and smiled at me drowsily. I bumped into a chair and he laughed. "You don't got to be scared of me, any kid got a fast ball like you got." He pressed his body against mine, his arms around my back. "Just tell me if I ain't got power, though?" He held me in a bear hug, his huge stomach pressing into me, his arms locked in the small of my back. "There ain't any guy in baseball got more strength than the Babe, you hear that?" I could not breathe, and there was in me no desire to struggle. I heard him grunting. His head burrowed against my shoulder, he squeezed harder, until I gagged.

He released me then and I fell backward, into the chair, knocking it over. "Hey, I didn't hurt ya, did I?" His arm was around my shoulder. He led me to the bed and sat me down. "I don't know my own strength sometimes, ya know? I didn't mean to go so far." I tried to catch my breath. "You lie down and take it easy for a few minutes." He pushed me and I let my head fall backward so that I was, my stomach and chest heaving for air, staring into his face. He touched my forehead, gently.

"It's all right," I said. "I—I think I'll be all right."

"Sure ya will," he said, and then he roared. "Listen—I ain't so drunk. The Babe can hold it." He pinned my arms to the bed, his hands pressing my wrists down. With a lightness that seemed impossible for a man of his size, he had moved on top of me and was straddling me.

He watched my face for a while, smiling. "Ya like to wrestle?" he asked. I could not reply. "C'mon," he coaxed. "Try to get yourself free. I'll bet you're real strong, a young kid like you." He squeezed against my wrists so that I felt his nails digging into the skin. "C'mon, don't be scared—try to get yourself free. Let's see who's the strongest. Try to get yourself free from me." His thighs pressed inward and the metal of his belt buckle cut against my stomach, above the navel.

He saw then that I was crying. "I didn't mean nothing," he said, lying down beside me. "Honest. I didn't mean to hurt ya so much." I turned my head away from him so that he would not know, from my expression, the real reason for my tears. "I ain't so smart," he said then, very softly, "but I ain't so dumb either." He took my chin in his left hand and turned my head to him. In the dimly lit hotel room I believed that I could see my own reflection in his eyes. I did not resist. His hand went from my chin to the back of my neck; he lifted me slightly from the bed and, my eyes staring into his, and his into mine, he pressed his lips against my own.

He let me go then, but his hand moved across my chest and downward, to my pants. He unbuckled my belt. I did not try to stop myself from crying. He sat up then. "No wonder," he said, as if discovering something important. His smile was one of sheer delight, like the smile I had seen earlier that day, when I had struck him out for the first time. "Sure," he said to himself. "You ain't never done this before, have ya?" He slammed his fist into the palm of his right hand. "No wonder!" he said again. "Now I get the whole thing." He punched me hard, in my right shoulder, and then, for the first time, his voice did not sound boyish. "We're gonna have some fun now, you and me, ya hear that? The Babe is gonna have some fun, and you don't got to be scared." And then, close to me, his lips on my cheek, he was a child again. "My skin's darker than yours," he whispered.

I pitched on the following afternoon, and tired as I was I could summon all my strength when he was at the plate. Although the Yankees beat me, 4 to 2, I struck him out in two of his four at-bats, and got him out easily the other two times, once on a pop-up in foul territory to Dixon, and once on a grounder to Jack Henry. He said nothing to me after the game, but I went to his hotel, when I had finished with my dinner, and he was waiting for me. He had a girl with him, and had selected a girl for me also—a white girl who was younger than I was —and we spent the evening with them, going from bar to bar. We returned to his room afterwards, the four of us, and, listening to him boast and laugh, we did what he asked us to. When we were alone, after he had sent the girls away, he seemed very pleased. "We showed them something, didn't we, kid?" he said. He laughed then, in a way that made me quiver. "Ya see the face on yours when I told her she just done it with a nigger?" He drew me to him. "Ya don't got to worry, though—they'd be scared to say anything 'cause of who I am. It means somethin', being who I am."

Johnson pitched in the third and final game of our series and Ruth had an easy time with him, giving the fans what they wanted: two long home runs, both to deep center field, far beyond Kinnard's reach. I wanted to equal them, but was unable to. Hitting against Bob Shawkey, I found that I could not keep my mind from Ruth, waiting in right field, and that I swung too hard. I connected solidly only once all day, doubling down the left field line.

For the first time, alone after the game, I found that I was angry. Although it was taken for granted by my teammates and by the fans that I would have hitless days, still, I had not wanted to allow him, on the field, even a single victory. I sat on my bed in my hotel room, unable to move. His image was like a fire in my head, and I wished that fire to consume us both. I wanted, already, to be done with him, and yet I sensed that we had only begun, that, no matter how many times I proved myself his master on the playing field, I would, away from the playing field, forever submit myself to him. I wanted to laugh at the sheer clownishness of the situation—the great hero of America lying in bed, locked in that most absurd of positions with a fair-skinned nigger—and yet the humor, ultimately, turned upon me, for I brought him low only by making myself lower. What might have seemed a joke to the world, had it known, held no humor for me, for—I felt this more strongly in the few years of our friendship which were to follow—if anything, his willingness to meet me and to love me, even in his vulgar way, made him seem to me, given who he actually was, brave. And that I felt this way made me realize all the more that I was only another one of that multitude which worshiped him.

Even the thought of simple revenge—of revealing to the world the knowledge that would normally have made it mock him—even this, the instant I had considered it, made me despise myself for having been capable of considering it. The only revenge which could satisfy me had to occur upon the playing field, and yet I had already forsworn the

possibility that that playing field would be one that the large world
could be witness to. Did I, then, in loving him, only desire to do what
I had already learned was impossible—to gain, and sustain, that dream
which I had already surrendered? Or is this merely my way now of
trying to deny what seemed true enough then: that, despite all he was
and no matter my devious reasons, I did love him.

If I despised him for being vulgar, as I did, then I had to despise
myself more for being fascinated by his vulgarity. I must have wanted
the adulation of that world which had made him the most beloved man
of his time, and so I felt sick in my heart to realize not only that I
deserved, by my talents, that adulation, but that I could, had I not
made my initial decision, have had it. And if I had, I wondered, what
then? Would he have loved me more? Was I so vile that I merely
wanted things reversed? Was I so vain and small that I regretted
most that one decision upon which all else in my life had to stand?

I vowed that I would have no more to do with him, and yet, late that
evening, when a messenger came to my room with a note from him, I
could do nothing in my shame but go to him. He was kinder to me than
he had been the night before—he spoke of his home runs, and of what
I had done wrong at the plate. He wished to instruct me. He told me
again that I was the fastest pitcher he had ever faced, and that he
had ordered the New York sportswriters who were traveling with him
to say so in the stories they sent north. And he asked me, for the first
time, what he would ask me almost every time we met. "How come ya
didn't change your name and play with us—nobody ever would've
known, with your color." His question held no malice in it, no sense of
superiority, and I could find in me no words with which to reply or
explain—for even if I could have explained the reasons to myself, I
knew that he would never have understood the workings of my tumbling
brain. "They call me nigger," he said, as we lay in bed together, "and
you ain't half as nigger-looking as me. Nobody ever would've known."
He laughed. "They might've named me after you—that's how come,
when I think about it, I feel for ya, kid."

He sat up, leaning on his elbow, so that the bed creaked under his
weight. "I'll tell ya the truth, I wouldn't've liked it, if you'd been me
and things had got switched. I wouldn't've liked it one bit. I mean—
just look at me: I got everything I want from life—it's just like they
say in the papers—I got everything I want and I started out without
even a real mother and father. They were there—my old lady didn't

kick off till I was seventeen, and my old man got killed just a couple years back, brawlin' like he always did—but I never knew 'em.'' He lay back down. ''I wasn't no orphan like they try to make out sometimes, but I spent a dozen years in goddamned St. Mary's. They called me nigger every day of those twelve years and look at where I got— that's why I'm sayin' all this to ya, kid, so maybe ya can change things if it ain't too late.''

He seemed puzzled suddenly by the line his argument had taken. His dark brow furrowed, and he would not, as his mind tried to figure something out, touch me. ''I'm never in shape after the season ends,'' he explained then. ''We'd be pretty big stuff against one another, if you could play in our league.'' His voice was confident again and he turned to me. ''But I guess, even with the press you get, it's too late, ain't it?'' I felt nothing, and I think he was disappointed; he had, doubtless, expected to see tears in my eyes. ''Like I said, though— they might've named me after you, if ya think about it. That's how come I feel for ya. You could've had it all, just like me.''

We did not see one another again that year. I stayed with my team all winter as we continued to barnstorm, through North and South Carolina, Tennessee, Florida, Alabama, Mississippi, Louisiana, and across the Gulf to Cuba. I thought of him constantly, but did not write to him. I believed, as was probably the case, that as soon as we were apart and he had found somebody new, he had forgotten me. I pitched and hit well, delighting the fans who turned out throughout the South for our games. Even the smallest towns seemed to have their own semi-professional teams, and there was always a holiday atmosphere when we would arrive to play against the town's team, or against another professional team. In some of the smaller towns, the black community would feed us and house us. In the larger cities we might drive down the main street, wearing our uniforms, and honking the horns of our cars. People waved to us, and they stared at me.

I pitched in Birmingham, Memphis, Chattanooga, Columbia, Charleston, Charlotte, Orangeburg, Macon, Brunswick, Bogalusa, Jacksonville, and in lesser known towns whose names I still recall: Jasper, Gastonia, Magnolia, Lydia, Timmsboro, Moultrie, Sylacauga, Andalusia, Milledgeville, Prosperity, Chauvin, Langley, Sherry, Will, Johnston, Grand Coteau, Chataignier, Alexandria, and, unlikely enough, Charenton. I was exposed, for the first time in my life, to the ways in which southern blacks lived, but I remained, for the most part, like

any of my teammates, indifferent to their condition. My head was full
of other things. Jones, when we were going from one game to another,
and would drive past a section of cottages that was particularly poor,
would say as much as anybody ever did: "No more, honey. No more."

My teammates talked a good deal—to the members of the teams we
played against, and among themselves—about how I had, in their
words, handcuffed Ruth. Only Johnson remained, as always, unim-
pressed. The other players teased him about the two home runs he
had given up to Ruth, but he only looked my way and sneered: "Two
niggers in a swamp at night, that's all." My teammates laughed—at
the implied confusions that took place in darkness, and at the joke
this tag line referred to—but Johnson, losing games more frequently
so that Tompkins was pitching as often as he did, found nothing funny.
To the praise my teammates would give me, he would add, "Sure, fair
ass got real brains."

He said nothing else, and yet, when he looked at me I felt that he
knew, and that he said nothing only because he did not believe that
what he knew was worth commenting on. I hated him more than ever,
and not merely because he did not care about what I believed he knew,
but because—my weakness was splendid—I had discovered that I
wanted him to care.

Only once, in the summer of 1925, did he do something which indicated interest, and even then, what he did—what, in actuality, Jones
told me he had planned to do—was no more than he might have done
to any other man. "Don't ask me why," Jones said, when he had come
to my house and awakened me, before the sun had risen. "Old Brick
would as soon cut Little Johnny's throat as not, and he don't need a
reason. So don't ask me why he been bragging on what he goin' to do
to you and the big man, about what he once did before—" He stood
on the porch of my house, refusing to enter, and held his hat in his
hands, as if he were a shy caller. "But I asked myself that even if—
just if is all I'm saying—something might come of it somehow, I
wouldn't be able to sleep nights after, knowing I could've said something before." Even Barton did not know he was there, and he trusted
me never to tell anybody that he had come. He spoke quickly then:
"But old Brick, he been bragging about how he knew a man once used
to—you know—he was a policeman, and he could get you into trouble
if you didn't do it, until Brick," Jones gulped, "he put sand in the
man's jar of vaseline. That's what he did, honey, please don't ask me

why—'' He looked at me very briefly, and then looked down. He was shivering. ''Oh please, you won't ever tell that I come—don't ask me more, I don't know nothing except how you the best pitcher and hitter there is.'' He regarded me then with a look of gratitude that, when I see it now, makes the sweat run cold on my thighs. ''If not for your good arm, honey, I wouldn't never have the money. I say that all the time. I pray for you. You're the man who put the money in Little Johnny Jones's bankbook.'' Jones touched the scar on his forehead. ''I don't got to say no more—maybe you don't got to be the one to be careful of him—I never said so, did I?—but he's goin' to do it to somebody, he been bragging on how he did it, with melting it all together and pouring it back, and with what you done for me, I got to tell you too. But I don't think nothing, honey. You're a good boy. Old Brick, he's a mean man. He *means* to be mean. He's a bad man, honey. . . .''

He talked on and on, and I was not intelligent enough to realize that he would have stood there forever, excusing himself for the thoughts he claimed he did not have, had I not, at last, found my voice and thanked him for coming. He sighed with relief then, and without saying good night, like a boy dismissed from school, he let loose an involuntary cry of happiness and raced off.

I was careful, of course, and Johnson, though he continued to ride me for as long as we were to play together, never did say anything directly to me. He seemed to gather in as much pleasure as he required by asking me why I did not yet have children. ''Foster,'' he would add, ''he got kids.'' I said nothing, and yet—I know it now more than then—his question did matter, for though I may have spent much of my life thinking that I believed in a higher form of love than that which begets children, I would, now, have the children also. I would see something of myself, despite my life and despite the world, remain after me—something which, unlike the memory some may hold of me, could be touched.

I saw Ruth at intervals through the 1925, 1926, and 1927 seasons. Our teams would meet in post-season exhibitions, and during the season, when we were both in New York, he would sometimes send for me. He liked taking me with him to nightclubs, and he could, in the way in which he showed me off—calling me ''the best white-black pitcher I ever faced''—be as cruel as, when we were alone, he could be kind. He was mean and he was dumb, and I must, for him, have been only a diversion—he took from me little more than the physical pleasure he could not do without; still, I did love him—I remained, until the end, in awe of him, and of who, in his world, he was—and, in his way, he returned this love. He derided me for my inability to enjoy myself when, with his teammates, he would go out on the town, eating and drinking and whoring, and yet he never wanted to throw me away. There were things about me—my youth, my abilities as a pitcher and hitter, my fairness—which drew him to me.

My attraction for him came also, I sensed, from things concerning his own origins. He delighted in comparing our skin color, in asking me when I would change my name and play in his league, and yet, even when he would tell me proudly about how they called him Nigger, I remained silent, refusing to question him about those origins which I must have wanted to have remain mysterious. Thus, in the perverse tumblings of my mind, I could consider in infinite ways, and in the language of the game we both played, what, really, was fair, what foul.

Oh but my mind was lovely! If it was not only his glory which drew me, but the possibility that this glory derived from origins which, if verified, would have been the source for his fall—then it was also true that, in loving him, I was only pursuing that same self-love which had always consumed and driven me.

And yet to remember my very capacity for such thoughts is only to realize that I was, despite my fame and abilities, merely another young man whose experience in love followed a familiar and classic pattern. Like many before me, it was the image of my love which I desired—and this image, entering through my eyes, journeyed downward to my heart, where it was ravaged by those very passions which had been created from the darkness of my own origins and the rage which was born of the gifts these origins had brought with them. It is, we know, because she is blind, that love enters through the eyes.

Even now, remembering what I felt when I was with him, his image —the famous smile and dark skin, the graceful stride and powerful swing—makes me grow dizzy. Am I the same man? Was it, in fact, the very mystery of his origins, and not the man himself, which I loved? Did I, in short, remain silent because I wanted to remain in darkness, because I wanted to go on forever being able to ask myself the simple question, did I love a white man or a black man?

"When a man is tempted," we learn in James (1:15), "it is his own passions that carry him away and serve as bait. Then the passion conceives and becomes the parent of sin; and sin, when fully matured, gives birth to death.'' So it was, alas, with me. My life, during the years 1925, 1926, and 1927, was proof of the Bible's claim.

During the 1925 season I won thirty-seven games while losing eight and, playing in the outfield on the days I did not pitch, I hit 54 home runs. In October we won our second World Series in a row, in five games, from the Pittsburgh Crawfords. But I was not satisfied. I felt—and the ache was inexhaustible—as if nothing ever would satisfy me but to return to that time before that first batsman had hit that first ball over the wall in Ebbets Field. I thought less of the dream I had forsworn, and yet I must have felt in some part of me that I could still, if only I were good enough, make the world know. But know what? That I was the best player in black baseball? That our league was superior to theirs? That I was better than the man for whom, in the press, I was being named?

In 1926 I won forty-one games while losing ten, and pitched four no-hitters and thirteen shutouts in the process. I hit 58 home runs. Rube Foster became seriously ill that year, and due to mix-ups—he had refused to let anybody else handle the league's business—there was no World Series. Our team played a longer barnstorming tour—going as far as Santo Domingo, and playing without a break up to the start of the 1927 season. By this time there had been some changes in our lineup. Jack Henry had retired as a player, though he remained our manager. Rap Dixon had left the team, to sign with the Indianapolis Clowns— and he would leave them later in the same year, to play in Japan. Jeannot Massaguen, a strong and beautiful eighteen year old, so striking that I often believed him to be descended from the slaves of Falconhurst, took Jack Henry's place at second, and "Nip" Dell, twenty-six, a first baseman acquired from the New Orleans Pinchbacks—hard-hitting, but not in Dixon's class—now played first.

Jones, Barton, Kinnard, Kelly, and Johnson remained—along with me—the heart of the team, and we were, in a good league, the best. The high point was 1927: our league, with the addition of the Baltimore Black Sox in the Eastern Division, and the St. Louis Giants in the Western Division, was stronger than ever. Our schedule was more regular, attendance was good, and in a one hundred and thirty-two game season, I won forty-five while losing only six. I batted .426 and hit 64 home runs—a figure which was, that year, second to Christobel Torrienti's 67. We won our division title for the fourth consecutive year, and defeated the Indianapolis ABC's in the World Series, four games to one.

Rube Foster, as an indication of his confidence in us, forbade teams while playing to engage in any acts which, in his words, "would demean us as players or men, especially those forms of clowning which the public has long associated with our race." This meant that the standard jokes—presenting bouquets of weeds to the umpire, running around the bases backward, and—the favorite trick of all outfielders—lying down in the outfield and reading a newspaper (the paper would have a hole in it, so that the outfielder would, when he saw the ball coming his way, drop the paper and give chase)—disappeared from our play, to the disappointment of most players and fans.

1927 was also the year in which, from mid-season on, every sportswriter and sportsfan in America—other than our own most loyal followers—believed that the New York Yankee team was the greatest group of baseball players ever assembled, and that he, in the finest form of his thirteen-season career, was proving himself the greatest player of all time. The middle of their lineup—Meusel, Ruth, Gehrig, Combs, and Lazzeri—was called Murderer's Row, and the world could not stop marveling at their power; it could not, then or after, stop recounting the fact known to even that fan who had the mildest interest in the game—that, in his league that year, while his team set a record of one hundred and ten victories, he hit a total of 60 home runs.

What, even when the history of our league will be made known, could ever wipe away the glory that came to surround that team and that number? Even when the season had ended—when Ruth and Gehrig and the others had been (after their World Series victory in four games against the Pittsburgh Pirates) bombarded with ticker tape on the streets of New York—I still found that, except when I played against him and dreamt of his dark face, I relished defeating other teams of black men more than I enjoyed defeating teams composed of whites. Against the most amateur of small town colored teams, I gave away nothing. Against the men who played for the teams I had been defeating all season long—against Buck Leonard and Oscar Charleston and Christobel Torrienti and Mule Suttles and Jelly Gardner and Pete Spackman and Fats Jenkins and Turkey Stearns and Chino Smith and Biz Mackey and Bullet Rogan—I threw harder than I had ever thrown, I hit balls farther than I had ever hit them, and I hated with a relentlessness which, as it seeps through me again, fills me now as then with the same sharp passion, a passion which was, at its heart, murderous. I hated the men I had condemned myself to playing against, precisely because I knew they were the better players; I hated them for not being the men who, inferior to them, I thought I wanted to destroy, but against whom victory would, in the actual playing of the game, mean less.

I wanted, then, as I had for the three previous years, to defeat him —and to defeat him so utterly that he would cease to exist; and yet, even as I desired and acknowledged my desire, I knew how foolish and unreal it was. He would survive any single defeat. Other men had struck him out; other men had outhit him on given days; other men had taken headlines away from him from time to time; I had mastered him before, and the more convincing my victories had been on the playing field, the more shameful my submission had been away from it.

I was now twenty-one years old. I had what I thought I had wanted to have from life—I was the best pitcher and hitter in baseball, and yet, as I read and heard about his team and his feats, I could only despise the man I knew I had become. I longed for our next meeting—a meeting which would come, according to the schedule that winter, in Havana, Cuba—and I longed to beat him, to crush him as I never had before, so that, having done so, I might yet be free of him, and of the feelings for myself which my relationship with him had engendered.

I wanted to defeat him for ordinary reasons: because I had loved him and wanted now to destroy that love; because I had loved him and had not had that love returned; because I had been hurt and wanted him to be hurt. I wanted to defeat him because in so doing I must have believed I could thereby put on what I had thought I did not want—his power and his glory. I wanted—oh so dearly—to defeat him, not, that is, because he had what I wanted, but because he had what I hated myself for wanting.

We arrived in Havana in early February, at the end of our winter barnstorming tour, when we were on our way back to the states from Santo Domingo. We played and defeated the Havana Reds in a five-game series (four games to one), and a team called the National All Stars, composed of members of the (white) Brooklyn Dodgers, Philadelphia Phillies, and Boston Braves (three games to none). The New

York Yankees—called the Touring Yankee All Stars—arrived in Havana on February 13, the day of our final game against the National All Stars, and Ruth himself—to the delight of the Cuban and American fans—came to the game, along with Lazzeri, Dugan, Koenig, and Benny Bengough. I was not pitching that day—being held out so I would be fresh on the following afternoon, when we were to meet the Yankees— and the game was, despite a good pitching performance from Johnson and a barrage of home runs from our bats, dull. We were ahead 8 to 1 by the fourth inning, and the fans eased their boredom by chanting, every few innings "Bam-bi-no! Bam-bi-no!" whereupon he would rise from his seat behind third base and, fat and dark-skinned, wave to the crowd. He had only to tip his hat—a straw porkpie with a bright red sash—to have them roar and stamp their feet, and when I, in the fifth inning, hit my second home run, a line drive over the right field wall, he made a special point of standing and swinging his hat above his head, so that, within seconds, the fifteen thousand or so fans were—with hats and scarves and handkerchiefs—twirling their arms furiously above their heads as I, in shame and anger, rounded the bases and made my way to the dugout. Leaning on Lazzeri and Dugan, and laughing wildly, he collapsed in his seat.

I resolved, when I left the ballpark that afternoon, to refuse to see him. I went to my hotel, ate supper, and then I stayed in my room, waiting for the message I expected to receive, so that I could send one back, telling him that I would see him only at the ballpark. I sat in the darkness and fixed my mind on the game that would take place the next day: I was taller than I had ever been, and I made the ball sing as it flew from my hand and stung Bingo's glove hand. The Yankee players stood there, unable to move their bats from their shoulders, and I pleased myself by noting that, had their faces been dark and their lips full, they would have looked like the plaster statues of faithful house niggers one saw on front lawns. I imagined him with an iron ring in his piglike nose. His smile was fixed in enamel, his form cold to the touch. The skin of paint on his cheeks was peeling, and the white plaster underneath, as I threw the ball past him, slipped like sand down his face.

I was already in bed when somebody pounded on the door. I looked at my watch, on the table beside the bed: it was eleven-thirty. The pounding was insistent and I found that I was frightened. I knew that I wanted to see him and touch him. I knew that he would laugh away my efforts to refuse him. I wanted to call out to him to go away, and yet I was afraid to speak, knowing that my voice would surely have given me away. I felt faint. A fist struck the door again, twice, and I prayed for forgiveness. I could not think. I was sitting up and putting on my robe and slippers; then, like an old man who was fatigued by the least effort, I slid my feet across the hotel room floor and, standing at the door, my fingers on the metal key, I prayed for the impossible—that I would find the strength to stand straight and to say no—and yet, I was wondering at the same instant of what use, being so weak and broken, I could be to him.

I pulled the door open and took one step back, and then I felt as if somebody had struck me in the small of the back with an ice-cold sledgehammer. Johnson's black face moved close to mine and he roared with laughter. He held something massive under one arm and I saw, as he came toward me, that that something was Kelly, who hung forward, unconscious. I smelled the foul odor of liquor and vomit. As Johnson's free hand moved toward my face, I stumbled back against the bed. Johnson was, in the frame of the doorway, a silhouette, and the only light came from his gold teeth and his outstretched hand—the hallway light falling softly on the absurd pink color of his palm. He let Kelly fall to the floor and, swaying from side to side, moved toward me so that he blocked more and more of the light. I could see his face, the cracked skin. Kelly groaned and rolled onto his back. "Sure now, fair ass. I just wanted to see your face." I heard Kelly choke, then retch. "You're pretty, all right," Johnson said, his nose almost touching mine. "But I was once faster than you. Nobody'll tell you the truth, being who you are now, but I was faster." He was no longer laughing. "It don't matter, though. I seen your face at the door, looking out for that other nigger."

He staggered backward, grabbing the back of a chair in order to keep from falling. "Me and Gunboat here been having a good time, but he don't pace himself neither." He reached a long arm to the floor and jerked Kelly upward from the waist, dragging him to the door. "It don't matter." He stopped and shifted, letting Kelly's body slide downward so that he was grasping him under the armpits. His exertions made his chest heave. "Sure now. I saw your face all right, fair ass. I saw your face when you opened that door." Then he howled wildly and left, Kelly's feet bumping down the hallway.

Later, after I had fallen asleep, I awoke, the pillow wet against my face. I had been sweating heavily, and—curiously—I can remember how good I felt. I had been so deep in sleep that, waking, it was as if my body were not there. My arms, clutching the pillow under me, were numb, my shoulders seemed disconnected. There was nothing to decide. I let him in and returned to bed, watching him undress. "How come ya didn't come to see me?" he asked, as if he were genuinely hurt. "I was waiting for ya." I said nothing then, and did not, even as we embraced, feel any longer the things I had felt earlier in the evening. When we woke in the morning, I said what I had planned to say: "This was the last time."

He stood at the sink, naked to the waist. He sloshed water on his face and stared at me. "What for?" he asked.

"No more," I said, surprised at my calmness.

He dried himself and seemed to be studying my words. I stood at the window, looking down at the street below, where, as the day's business began, men and women crowded together, among wagons and mules and carts. "Are ya sure?" he asked, and then, as I was about to reply to what I believed was the sincere hurt in his tone, I felt a pain in my thigh which made me cry out. "Got ya!" he yelled, delighted, and he snapped the wet towel at me again. I covered myself with my my hands, and the end of the towel flicked forward and burned me just under the knuckles of my right hand. "Come on," he said, dancing around me, flicking the towel at me. "Ya got to see if you can get me. Come on—"

I backed away, timed things, and then, as he snapped the towel forward I reached out and snatched it, the tip searing my palm. I jerked and the towel came away. He was, I saw, astonished at my quickness—he backed off, somewhat afraid for a second.

"No more," I said.

He moved toward the sink. "Okay, then. It's your turn—see if ya can hit me."

"No more," I said, and I let the towel drop across the foot of the bed.

He spat. "You ain't got enough spirit, you and your fancy words all the time." He slipped into his undershirt. "Playing the piano like a—" He had found the word, but he seemed puzzled by it. "Sure, like a sissy, no matter what."

"I'm sorry," I said. "But this was the last time."

He laughed at me. "That's what you think," he said. He buttoned his shirt and stepped to me, his nose almost touching mine. "You'll come when I tell ya to come. I know what makes you tick. I know why ya didn't change your name and play with us.'' He jabbed me with his forefinger, just below my throat. ''You were scared, that's what.''

''I'll beat you today,'' I said. ''You'll never touch me. I'll beat you today and every day, whenever we play against each other. I'll hit the ball farther than you ever hit it. I'll—''

He was laughing at me. ''Now I heard everything,'' he said. ''You'll come when I tell ya to come. Sure ya will, and you know why?'' He waited for me to answer, then saw that I would not. ''The Babe may be dumb, but he ain't that dumb. You know why? Because ya like the color of my skin, that's why.'' He watched my face for a second, and then waved a hand at me. ''I had that figgered out a long time back. Shit. I ain't so dumb as you think, with all your fancy words.'' He slipped into his jacket, and then, looking at me from the mirror above the sink, he put his straw hat on and cocked it to one side. ''C'mere,'' he said.

I did not move.

''C'mere,'' he said again.

I stayed where I was, at the other end of the room, next to the window. ''Okay then,'' he said, and he came to me. I had never seen him angry in this way. I had, I saw, reached him, though I did not know what it was that I had said, or done, which had allowed me to. He took one of my ears in each hand and he pulled my head to his. I strained, but he was stronger than I was. His lips pressed against my mouth so hard that I felt my teeth cutting into my lips, drawing blood. His eyes were wide open, and his hands dropped to the small of my back, where he locked his right hand on his left wrist and squeezed. I heard myself moan, and then he let go. ''Shit on you,'' he said. ''I know what you want from me.'' He was at the door. ''Can't even look me in the eye now, like a man. You'll come when I call.'' He shook his fist at me. ''I ain't that dumb.''

When, a few hours later, I stepped onto the playing field, I saw that he was leaning against the third base dugout while he ate a hot dog. I heard his high-pitched laugh and saw that the fans, crowding against one another, were holding hot dogs in the air toward him, above one another's heads. His teammates were on the field, warming up—shagging flies and playing pepper. His stomach protruded and he rested his left hand on it, proudly, grinning from ear to ear. He looked to me, more than ever, like a tanned pig.

Bingo tossed the ball to me for our warm-ups, and I wasted no time drilling the first pitch into the pocket of his glove. The fans on our side of the field whistled and shouted to me in Spanish, telling me how fast I was. Ruth looked our way and doffed his cap in my direction. "Hey kid," I heard him call. "Want a hot dog?" He laughed hysterically then, and his fans laughed with him. I kicked and threw again, harder.

"Gonna melt that arm," Johnson said to me. "Gonna burn yourself out, you go that fast. You want to pace yourself, boy."

He jogged past me without waiting for a response. His body moved easily, powerfully. He joined Kelly down the right field line and Jack Henry picked up a fungo bat and hit the ball in their direction. "You see the way that mean eats," Jones exclaimed, looking over my shoulder. "I heard it before but now I believe it. He ate twelve of them hot dogs already—now I believe it!" He watched me throw a ball. "Ooo-eee," he cried. "Ain't that sweet. We in the money today, honey. You own that man, gonna put him in your pocket."

"All of them," I said.

"That's right too, honey. All of them," Jones said. "I like the sound of that—mean, like old Brick. You gettin' that meanness, by and by. You gettin' it."

"All of them," I repeated.

"Easy now," Bingo called. "Just let it loose. Easy now. Bring it home easy."

When I took the mound for the start of the first inning, I was aware of nothing except my desire to strike out every man who would face me. Jones and Barton and Massaguen and Dell were talking to me from behind, Bingo was cooing to me from in back of the plate, the fans were cheering for the first man—Joe Dugan, the Yankee third baseman—but all the sounds seemed very distant. I kicked, reared back, and fired the first ball for a strike. Then the second. Dugan tried to get set to bunt, but the third pitch was already by him and Bingo whipped it to third base. It sped around the infield and came back to me. Koenig was in the box, and Ruth waited in the on-deck circle on one knee, smiling at the ovation the fans were giving him. "Bam-bi-no!" they chanted. "Bam-bi-no!"

I was beginning to sweat, and the dampness on my skin, under my uniform, felt good. Bingo showed me a spot high and inside, and I realized that he had probably picked off a bunt sign. I pitched it where he showed me his glove, Koenig squared around and, his hands a foot or so apart, he pushed the bat at the ball, popping it weakly toward me. I caught it and returned to the mound. "Give it here! Give it here!" Jones yelled, and then I realized that I was in such a hurry that I had forgotten to toss it to him.

Ruth stepped into the batter's box, on the left side of the plate, and stroked the bat through the air. The crowd was standing, loving him. He tipped his cap, then bent over and picked up some dirt. His legs were extraordinarily skinny, and I wondered for an instant at how I could have loved a man who was so physically grotesque. With Gehrig, who had joined the Yankees in 1925, now a regular, and their leading runs-batted-in hitter (having driven in one hundred and seventy-five during the 1927 season), Ruth, who was faster than Gehrig, was batting third in the order instead of fourth. "He's just posin' for his picture," Jones called. "Everybody know how you own that man. Everybody know."

His stomach bulging, Ruth set himself at the plate, the bat cocked behind his left shoulder, the crowd roaring its encouragement. I pumped and reared back, shifted sideways, kicked, and realized suddenly that something was different—he was not smiling. The ball stuck in my hand. I tried to let it go, but I could not lift my fingers; my left foot struck the ground in stride, my arm still suspended stiffly in back of my ear, my body in a hopelessly awkward position—I strained, and felt the ball scrape by my fingers, low and into the dirt, some twenty feet in front of me. It scudded in the grass, and bounced harmlessly past home plate. The Yankee players laughed at me, the crowd hissed, but he merely stood there, unsmiling. "You take your time now," Bingo said, stepping in front of the plate and rubbing dirt into the ball with his bare hands. "Don't be nervous now. You take your time now, pitch it to me."

I turned away and faced the outfield. Johnson stood nonchalantly in right field, hands on hips, and I could see him smiling. Rose Kinnard adjusted the visor of his cap. Kelly pounded the pocket of his glove and shouted something I could not hear. Did I want to have him hit me? Was it possible that I was trying to succumb to his power on the playing field, so that . . .

I toed the mound and looked toward home plate. He was waiting for me, taking practice swings, wanting to hit the ball. He cared. I closed my eyes, to stop the world from moving in circles, and I squeezed the ball as hard as I could. I tried not to look at him. I pumped again, reared back, and I was suddenly home: I felt the dizziness disappear, I saw the black hole in Bingo's glove, I felt my body loosen, and I let the ball go. It flew. He swung late and missed, his body twisting all the way to the left so that he seemed, almost, to be looking backward. I believe that I smiled then, though I cannot be sure. He glowered at me. I took the ball and fired it again, low and away, nicking the outside corner for a called second strike. He stepped out of the batter's box.

Bingo showed me the heart of the plate, waist-high, and I did not aim. My head was clear, his image gone, and only his penguinlike body waited for me at the plate. I heard myself grunt as I released the ball and saw the white line head downward, then crack and rise. I did not have to wait. He started his swing, but the ball was already by him, and I was walking to the dugout. I saw him hurl the bat down, angrily. In the dugout Jack Henry sat next to me, talking about the Yankee weaknesses, about the book he had on them, but I nodded politely and did not let his words come into my head.

"All of them," Jones said to me, laughing. "You said the word, and I believe that too."

Jones stepped out of the dugout, swinging two bats. Wilcey Moore, who'd led their league in earned run average, was the pitcher, and he set our men down one-two-three in our half of the first. This pleased me too. It would be a good game, and I relished what was to come. In their half of the second, I set down Gehrig, Meusel, and Lazzeri, and Moore set us down one-two-three also, striking out Johnson and Kinnard. Ruth's eyes, I knew, were on me, and I gave away nothing. I tried to make each pitch go faster than the one before, and I felt my body warming to the day, feeling as whole and strong as it ever had. In the third inning I struck out the bottom of their order on eleven pitches.

I batted second in our half of the third, and the crowd cheered for me. The outfield played me deep and straightaway. I let the first pitch go by for a strike. Moore was fast, but my eyes were doing their work and I was able to follow the ball all the way, from his hand to the plate. The second pitch was inside and chest-high. I stepped into it, my left foot a few inches toward third base, and it was as if, a few feet in front of the plate, suspended over the grass, the ball had stopped: I whipped my arms around, delivering all the power that was in me, and the instant I connected, I knew, and the crowd knew, that the ball was long gone. I followed through and then stood at home plate, watching the ball rise against the background of white and red and yellow that were the shirts of the fans in the left field grandstands. I watched the ball continue to rise, above the level of the grandstand, and I was aware of heads turning upward to watch the ball soar against the blue sky, and disappear across the top of the ballpark. Then they gasped—the crowd did—as if they were one man. I started toward first base, my head swimming, and I saw him in right field, unnoticed by everybody else, kicking at the grass.

When I rounded third base, my teammates were out of the dugout applauding for me. Barton, coaching at third, shook his head from side to side as I went by. "I never seen one that far," he said. "I never did." I crossed home plate and, beaming with pleasure, walked to the dugout, remembering to tip my cap to the fans. "Hey Gringo!" one of them called, hanging across our dugout, his hands cupped around his mouth. "You better than Bambino." He was a young boy, perhaps fifteen years old. His features were sharp and small, like a Caucasian's, but his skin was the color of Johnson's skin: a deep dusty black. He turned from me, shouted to the crowd, and they took up his chant, clapping their hands, stamping their feet, and sounding my name. "Grin-go! Grin-go!"

"That ball not goin' to come down till tomorrow," Jones said as I ducked into the dugout. "You laid the powder on, honey."

Jack Henry shook my hand and sat down, somewhat stunned. "I saw John Henry—Lloyd—hit one once when we were playing down here in thirteen, and I didn't think I'd ever see one hit so far again, but you did it." He glanced to his right. "Old Brick has been around a long time too—I'll bet—"

He stopped. Johnson spat tobacco juice onto the dirt in front of the dugout. "Sure," Johnson said, looking at the playing field. "He hits good."

I sat still, urging myself to calm down, trying to concentrate on what was going on on the playing field. Massaguen, batting in last position, singled to right. With Jones at the plate, Jack Henry gave the hit-and-run sign for the third pitch, and Jones poked the ball down the right field line. Then, with men on first and third, Kelly lined out to the third baseman.

I waited as my teammates picked up their gloves and trotted onto the field, and then I forced myself to walk very slowly to the mound. The crowd cheered for me. "Grin-go—Grin-go—better than Bambi-no!" I heard them call and the chant gave me immense pleasure. It

was the top of the fourth inning, and no man had reached first base:
I had given up no runs, no hits, no bases on balls, and there had been
no errors. Three men had batted in each of the first three innings, and
I had only to do the same thing—set the same nine men down—two
more times, and I would have pitched, against the supposed best team
in the world, the perfect game.

The numbers spun around in my head, the nine-inning game divided
into thirds, each third containing three innings, each inning containing
three men, each man receiving three strikes—but the instant Dugan
stepped into the box and I started my motion, my head was clear. I
thought of nothing. I was there. I struck Dugan out on three straight
pitches. I got Koenig on a checked-swing grounder to second. Ruth was
at the plate again, and I could not have been happier. I did not bother
teasing him. I did not even think of him as I kicked and threw. He
swung at the first pitch, and missed. The crowd made noises. He stepped
out of the batter's box and rubbed dirt on his hands. The boy who had
first called me Gringo lay across the roof of the dugout, on his stomach,
taunting Ruth. "Grin-go—Grin-go—better than Bam-bi-no!" he cried,
and I could tell that the shrill voice had slipped under Ruth's skin. I
could sense, also, that my own teammates, poised in the field behind me,
were aware of the special quality of the game—they were quieter than
usual, tensed, and it was—I could hardly believe it—Barton who I
heard yell toward the plate, with a confidence I would never have believed he possessed: "You can't see that ball, nigger man—our man
blows it by you. Oh but you just a poor nigger man, standin' there doin'
nothin'."

I saw Ruth's eyes widen. Jones whooped from third base, and realizing that the word had angered Ruth, he used it also. "You own that
nigger, honey," he called to me. "Oh but you own that man."

Ruth crouched slightly, coiled and ready to swing. I pitched and the
ball moved like a rocket. His anger made him chop at the ball and it
cracked into Bingo's mitt for a second strike. "I feel the breeze," Jones
called. "Ain't never felt so good—that nigger sure fans the breeze!" I
had the ball back from Bingo and I did not wait for Ruth to step out
of the box. His right foot moved, however, as if he wanted to, but he
was too late. I had started my motion and he tried to adjust, to set himself for me, but he was as good as dead. I fired the ball with all my
strength, low, and he lunged forward, only to have the ball hop as it
had never hopped before, hitting Bingo in his glove a good foot above

the spot where Ruth's bat had passed. "Ooo-ee," Jones cried, and he ran from the field. On top of our dugout the boy was standing, his arms stetched above his head, as if he were a *banderillero*, and dancing up and down, he drove invisible darts into a nonexistent animal. I saw handkerchiefs and hats swirling in multicolored circles. I sat in the dugout and watched him run, pigeon-toed, to his position in right field.

We did not score any runs in our half of the fourth, and in the top of the fifth I set down their side again, striking out Gehrig and Meusel, to bring my total of strikeouts for five innings to ten. I batted second in our half of the inning, and slashed the ball toward the hole between first and second. It took a wicked bounce at the edge of the infield grass, and just as I thought it would continue through toward him, I saw Lazzeri fly through the air, spear the ball glove-handed; from a sitting position on the outfield grass, he threw to first base. I was out by a step. "Good wood, though," Rose said to me as I returned to the dugout. He smiled at me with a tenderness I had never before seen. "Take a look," he said, and he pointed to second base where Lazzeri, glove off, was blowing on the palm of his hand.

Bingo's hand touched my shoulder. "Gone to have to soak my hand tonight, but that's okay. You keep throwin'. They ain't gone to touch you."

I nodded and, as I sat by myself, leaning forward so that I could feel the warmth of the sun, I realized that my teammates were feeling close to me—closer probably than they had ever felt. As was the custom, they said nothing to me about the fact that I had given up no hits, but by their very silence I knew that they were aware that I had a perfect game going, and I felt that they knew how intensely important it was to me that I pitch that perfect game. "Goin' to get you some insurance," Kelly said, passing me on his way to pick a bat from the bat rack, but we watched Barton fly easily to Meusel in left; the fifth inning was over, with our team still leading 1 to 0.

Ruth was ambling in from his right field position as I walked to the mound. "Tony stole one from ya," he called to me. "He don't have no fits between two and four in the afternoon." He tried to laugh then, but his laugh was forced. "Grin-go! Grin-go!" the boy called, as Ruth continued toward his dugout. "Better than Bam-bi-no! Grin-go! Grin-go! Better than Bam-bi-no!" I warmed up, preparing to face the bottom third of the Yankee order, and though it was the weakest part of their line-up, I warned myself about not letting up. When Combs stepped into the box to begin the inning, I took Bingo's sign for a duster and fired the ball, without second thoughts, for Combs's chin. He hit the dirt, his bat sailing backward in the air. I pitched again, inside, and though the ball was over the plate, I had Combs backing away for a called strike. He was easy after that: another pitch inside, for a ball, and then two quick ones on the outside and one man was down. Benny Bengough, the Yankee catcher, a shrewd hitter, stepped into the box. My first pitch was perfect, low and away, slicing the outside corner, but Bengough—the crafty Jew, as he was called—was moving with the pitch, and he laid a perfect bunt down the third base line.

I stood there transfixed, watching the ball edge along as if it would take forever to move even five feet. From the corner of my left eye I saw Bengough chugging down the first base line and I was aware that I had not started for the ball. I thought I saw Ruth smiling—but it was Johnson's laugh I heard, deep and raspy. I saw the game dissolving, yet I could not move. Bingo had torn his mask off, but Bengough, a right-handed hitter, had blocked his view, and Bingo was only now —as Bengough must have been halfway down the line—seeing where the ball was, trickling slowly along the basepath, some eight or nine feet from the plate. I thought I heard myself scream, and I could feel the scream tearing through my throat and up through my eyes, but my mouth was not open. The ball rolled along, inch by inch, too far away for me to get it in time. I thought I screamed again, but realized—in the din the crowd was making—that it was somebody else's scream I was hearing. The boy was on our dugout, jumping up and down in a tantrum, and the crowd, on its feet, screamed madly. But the scream I heard, I suddenly realized, came from Little Johnny Jones. Like a mad cat he streaked into view to my right, yelling at me, I now understood, to get my fool head down. I ducked and saw Jones flash by, scooping up the ball barehanded and, in the same incredibly swift motion, firing across the infield, directly above my head, to first base. Were I to pitch a thousand games and strike out every man in every game, I do not believe I would ever see a more perfect and beautiful play: to fly at full speed and scoop up a small piece of leather—to let that ball fly in a direction opposite from your body's motion, with that body, all the while, low to the ground, the back curved forward, the body's balance impossibly maintained so that the ball moves like white lightning to its mark—oh but that was the miracle! Bengough was out by a half-step, and as the umpire gestured, the crowd's noise stopped for an instant, and then returned, cresting and crashing upon me. I turned to Jones and his smile went from ear to ear, filling his dark face. He tipped his cap to me. "All of them," he said. "All of them, honey."

"Ooo-eee!" Barton called from behind, as the ball was whipped around the infield. "That's pretty. Oh yes. That's pretty."

Jones tossed the ball to me. "Nothin' to be scared of, honey—Little Johnny gone to get them all. I get them all—you throw the ball."

He lifted his cap and wiped his hand across his forehead, across the scar in whose groove his perspiration was collecting. The play, of course, had been his, since my follow-through was toward first base, and yet, even if I had had no chance for the play—it had never, as I now saw, been mine—I knew that I had frozen, and had been saved. I would not receive another chance. I threw harder than I had to, and struck out the pitcher, Moore, on three straight pitches.

Kelly doubled to lead off the bottom of the sixth inning, but he was left stranded at second base as Kinnard, Johnson, and Dell made out. I walked to the mound, knowing that, in their half of the seventh inning, I would face him for what I hoped would be the last time. I told myself not to think about him, for that was the surest way to have the two men who preceded him make easy prey of me. But with the ball in my hand and the sun on my back, I was in no danger. Dugan swung late and popped the ball, in foul territory, behind the plate, where Bingo gathered it in for the first out. I put two quick strikes on Koenig, the next batter, and then—as Ruth waited calmly in the on-deck circle—I threw again and Koenig, who had not yet struck out that day, drilled the ball to straightaway center field. My heart dropped. I turned and saw Kinnard moving backward so easily that the ball appeared to slow down—as if it were waiting until he could catch up with it. He caught it in full stride, over his left shoulder. With the crowd, I heard myself sigh, relieved.

"Last time, honey," Jones called, as Ruth waved his bat at me. "You just blow the ball by, like always."

I leaned forward, as if to take a sign from Bingo—Ruth stood there, wanting me to pitch so that he could hit. I took my time, picked up the rosin bag, hitched my belt, then turned to face my team, as if to assure myself that they were in position. Ruth did not move. "Don't fool us, poor nigger man," Barton cried. "Don't fool us with nothing."

Ruth dug the heel of his right shoe deeper into the dirt. I wound

up slowly, and I realized that I was smiling and that he was watching
my smile. The ball was letter-high, like a bullet. He stepped and swung
and I closed my eyes. Bingo's arm, when I opened my eyes, was cocked
behind his ear, the ball in his hand. My smile broadened, and I was
pleased to see that it was angering Ruth. His neck was red. As much
as I may have wanted to defeat him—so much did he want to please
his fans. I reared back and fired again, straight for his chin. His body
dipped backward, but he would not fall. The ball passed an inch or two
from his face, cracking savagely into Bingo's mitt. The crowd became
hushed. He spat across the plate, his spit falling a few feet in front of
the on-deck circle where Gehrig—a man he despised, as everybody knew
—was waiting. I gripped the ball and thought of nothing except that
invisible tunnel to Bingo's glove. I wound up and delivered, low and
outside, and he did not swing. Strike two. On top of the dugout the boy
jumped up and down, then twirled around once and squatted, waiting.
Ruth stepped out of the box, let his bat fall so that he was leaning upon
it, holding the handle. He raised his right hand briefly, pointing toward
center field, and the crowd breathed with delight. They had seen him
make such promises before. I glanced behind, but Kinnard did not back
up. The fans behind him were standing, waiting for the ball they now
hoped would be theirs. I might, at such a moment, have had a thousand
thoughts—and yet I recall having none, and can remember only the
heat my body was generating, and the movements it made as I wound
up, twisted sideways, kicked high with my left leg, strode forward,
and pitched. He seemed to start his swing even before the pitch was
released, and I was, momentarily, terrified. His arms and shoulders, despite his protruding stomach, moved gracefully and powerfully in a
clean arc, waist-high. For a split second I thought the ball had stopped
and that he would murder it, but then it sped on its way and I saw that
I had had nothing to be worried about. I was too fast for him. His bat
did not even graze the white pellet. The crowd gasped as he twisted in
agony, almost falling down from his effort. I had struck him out for the
third time. Jones called to him—something about the pointing he had
done—but I did not hear him. I was, as any of my teammates might
have put it, home free.

It did not even bother me that, hitting in our half of the seventh,
and receiving a standing ovation from the crowd, I found that my desire to murder the ball was gone. With Bingo on first base—he had
singled—Jack Henry, now coaching at third, gave me the hit-and-run

sign. The ball was low, but Bingo was moving with the pitch and I protected him, striking at the ball and pushing it behind the runner, toward the hole between first and second. The first baseman got the ball, too late to get Bingo, but in time to toss to the pitcher covering at first base, and I was out. Moore stiffened after that, and we could not move Bingo in from second base. The seventh inning was over, we still led 1 to 0, and I had only to face six more men.

Now, with each pitch I threw, the crowd roared its approval. I had never felt stronger. I struck out Gehrig and got Meusel on an easy pop-up to the shortstop. Lazzeri, next up, the smartest of the Yankee players on the field, choked up on the bat as I went into my motion and tried to punch the ball to right, but he did not gauge my pitch correctly and the ball, snapping upward, hit the handle of his bat and looped harmlessly to Massaguen at second. Massaguen squeezed the ball into the pocket of his glove and ran from the field, shrieking with joy. His face had never been so beautiful, and I thought, but for an instant only, not of the supposed magnificence of his forebears, but of what the auctions for them must have been like.

The bench during our half of the eighth inning was totally silent. Nobody sat next to me, nobody spoke to me, and yet there was in their avoidance of me, I felt, not merely the custom of the game, but what I hoped was a new respect for me, a kind of friendship now, after the few years we had been together, despite the fact that we had shared little in those years other than the games themselves. I wanted them to hurry, and they did. Moore was still pitching strongly—we had a total of only six hits against him, including my home run—and he gave up no more in the bottom of that inning. Kelly, Kinnard, and Johnson went down easily, on a strikeout, a fly to left field, and a grounder to third base.

As the ninth inning began, Johnson lingered for a minute in the dugout, and I wondered if Jack Henry were going to put one of the younger utility players into the outfield for him. But I saw Jack push him gently from the dugout and I was, I found, pleased to know that he would be with me for the last inning of the game. He trotted by, looking into the sun, which was now behind the right field wall, shining into the eyes of the batters—something a pitcher could not be unhappy about. He stopped at the mound, as if he were going to say something to me, and I smiled at him, hoping he would. But he seemed to change his mind, and it was only when he had continued on that I heard him laughing, and the laugh made me uneasy. I shrugged and tried to pay it no mind. I was, I told myself, beyond that—free of it, also.

I felt loose. I listened to Jones and Barton and Massaguen and Dell and Bingo talking to me. I enjoyed the feel of fresh perspiration sliding down my back, under my uniform. Combs was first up and I had no trouble with him. He went down swinging on four pitches, and I was two outs away from a perfect game. Ruth slumped in the corner of his dugout, thinking, I imagined, of what he would do after the game— of drinking and whoring and eating. Gehrig studied me in his sullen way, and I almost wanted to call to Ruth, to tell him that I understood why he hated a man who was so narrow, who took and gave no pleasure in life. "Cheapest bastard I ever met," had been Ruth's judgment, and it was, as I knew from what other baseball men were saying, an understatement. Bengough was at the plate now, and I recalled what he had done the last time. I glanced briefly at Jones, who played even with the bag at third. The fans were silent. I felt my heart beating and I glanced down, to see if it was making my uniform flutter. I wound up and fired, and the pitch was true. Bengough swung late, however, and the ball cracked weakly against the upper side of his bat—an easy fly to right field. "You take it!" Kinnard yelled toward Johnson, and Johnson stood there, in position, and pounded his glove once as he waited for the ball to come down. I heard the scream—from which of my teammates I cannot say—a long painful "Nooooo," even before the ball had fallen, some five feet in front of Johnson, upon the outfield grass. I could not believe my eyes. The moan from the crowd was genuine, heartsick. Johnson merely shrugged and picked up the ball, tossing it to the infield. Bengough, amazed, stood safely at first base.

My stomach turned over and there must, I know, have been tears in my eyes. Jones was at the mound and I saw that there were in his. "Oh honey, I'm so sorry," he said. "But you still—you still . . ." He knew he was not allowed to finish the sentence. I had not, of course, given up a true hit, but it did not matter. There was nothing to say, or to do. I did not look to the Yankee dugout, for I did not, really, care what he was doing, or whether or not he was happy at my fate. An unknown player—not even a Yankee player—was pinch-hitting for the pitcher Moore, and I worked as swiftly as I knew how. Three pitches to him, and then three more to Dugan and the game was over. We had won, 1 to 0, I had hit the winning home run, I had struck out Babe Ruth three times, I had struck out eighteen men in all, I had proven everything I had ever dreamt of proving, and yet . . .

The players ran by me to the locker room. I stood at the mound. Some boys were on the field, pulling at my glove. One of them leapt up and snatched my hat, running off with it. They asked me questions and spoke to me in Spanish and pigeon-English, but I heard nothing. I stood there, letting them touch me until they had had enough.

It is impossible to say how much time had passed, but when the stands were empty and the field was clear, I saw that Ruth was still sitting in his dugout, watching me. The playing field, without the fans and the players, seemed excessively quiet. I stepped down into the dugout and he stood. I wondered what it was that I had had to say to him. "You pitched good," he said. "I always said you were the fastest pitcher I ever faced." He smiled, and I felt something stir in me; I remembered what he had said to me the night before, about coming when he called, and I tried to wake myself. "But you're a real idiot, playing in your league. I told ya that a long time ago." I was breathing hard. "Ya know how much money I got?" I said nothing. My glove dropped to the ground. "C'mon—take a guess. I mean, a guy's got to have real brains, with an arm and a face like yours, to spend his life with a bunch of niggers." He smiled, to see if he were reaching me, provoking me. He laughed then, in his choir boy's voice, and said what I wish to God he had never said. "You're just a make-believe nigger anyway. Everybody knows that—"

I swung and felt the bone of his chin against my knuckles. My blow had moved so quickly that I had not seen him react. He flopped sideways, his stomach banging into the bench, and his head knocking against it before he fell to the floor.

"Sure now, you got real brains." I turned around and saw that Johnson was standing in the dugout, at the far end. He walked toward me. He was still in his uniform, which meant, I thought, that he had not dared—after his misplay—to go into the locker room. He looked down at Ruth, over my shoulder, and he laughed. "Dumb nigger," he said. His chin almost touched my shoulder. I glared at him, remembering what he'd done. "Sure now," he said, shuffling backward. "Old Brick lost the ball in the sun." Then he howled with laughter, finding his remark so funny that, a second later, he was doubled up, sitting on the Yankee bench, and clutching at his stomach. "Oh, I seen your face, fair ass. I seen it. Old Brick just went and lost the ball in the sun. But I seen your face—" He glanced down at Ruth, lying there like a sleeping child, his head to one side, his right arm caught under it. "Better not get caught here, though—he's still the big boy, no matter what."

He chuckled to himself and started to stand, as if he were finished with
what he had come for. "He told the truth, though. You're a make-
believe nigger all right. I been watching. Only you ain't just a make-
believe nigger—" He was laughing at me. "That's what been shown
to you today." His voice shifted, and he did not smile: "You just plain
make-believe, from start to finish. I seen that."

I saw the ball drop from the sky, and I saw him standing there, hands
on his hips, pounding his glove once, and then letting the white spot
fall in front of him. I had his head pressed against the concrete wall,
and my fingers were locked on his throat. His huge chest swelled and his
hands were on my forearms, but I was, for once, too strong for him. He
gagged, and I thought I heard him apologize to me, but I could not let
go. I heard his voice, telling me what he had waited to tell me. I had
mattered enough to him for that—and for what he had done on the
field. There was no more. I squeezed and would not look at his face,
though I believed, at the time, that I could feel his blackness seeping
into my fingertips. His chest collapsed, and he stopped struggling.

I looked around to see if anybody had seen me. Ruth was still unconscious, snoring now, his body rising and falling in the trench of the
dugout. Johnson did not move. My own body was slack, but I had not
yet released all my hatred. "Oh honey," I heard Jones say, "he was a
bad man, but he wasn't that bad."

I looked at Jones. "I just come out here to see if you was okay," he
said, standing on the grass. "—where you was, that was all." He was
dressed in street clothes, a jacket and a tie. He came forward and bent
over Johnson, listened at the man's chest. "Oh honey, he was a bad
man, but he wasn't that bad. You got to get out of here." He pushed
me, but I could not move. "Everybody's gone, in our place." Ruth
moaned. "Don't just stand there, honey. I'll take care of this." Kneel-
ing, between Ruth and Johnson, he looked up at me. "You got the
money?"

I nodded. "Yes."

"We'll get you out of this place—I mean back to America, or somewhere—you wait for me outside. Ain't nobody gone to come back here
for a while." I stared into Johnson's face, and it seemed wildly absurd
to me suddenly to have dressed this old black man in a boy's costume.
Jones was trying to pull me away. "You got to move, honey. You got
to get out."

I felt tired. I thought that I felt as old as Johnson must have felt,
still running and throwing with boys half his age. But I had no will—

I let Jones tell me what to do. I returned to our locker room and put on my street clothes. I went with Jones, in a taxi, to our hotel, where I picked up my valise and my money. He made sense. He had, he told me, been through similar things before. Nobody was much interested when one nigger killed another.

He found somebody at the waterfront who took me into a boat, below deck. He gave me advice—he told me to change my name, to lay low, not to play baseball again. In a few years, he said, it would—except among players in the Negro American Baseball League—all be forgotten. Thanks to me, he hoped to own his house in Flatbush by the end of the next season. He wished me luck and kissed me good-bye, and I went below deck, not talking to the men who carried me across the water. I slept. When I awoke it was night. I was transferred from the boat I had been in to a rowboat. I gave more money. At the pier—I was told that I was in a town called Naples, Florida, some seventy miles up the western coast—I gave away more money, and was driven to a hotel where all my meals were brought to me; I stayed for three weeks. I did not look in the newspapers to see if there had been any report. I tried, during those weeks, to consider what had happened, but it was difficult to feel anything, either for what I had done to Johnson, or for what I had done to myself.

I never played baseball again. I never saw my brothers or my mother or my sister again. I never saw any of the players from the Brooklyn Royal Dodgers again. I thought, several times, when touring Negro teams would come to the towns I was living in, of going to the ballpark and watching them—but even when I wore a moustache, I had no desire to take the chance of being recognized, even though I believed that my act would probably not, by those who had known me, have been held against me. I lived, in the years after that, in many towns, and held various jobs. For five years during the Depression, I was fortunate enough to find a job as a night watchman at an oil refinery in Livingston, Texas. I lived for thirteen years in the town of Scotlandville, Louisiana, outside of Baton Rouge, where I gave piano lessons and was tutor to the children of wealthy Negro families. I changed my name and was never, so far as I know, hunted by the authorities. During the Second World War, I taught briefly in a boys preparatory school in New England, where I succeeded in passing as a white man. The things that led me to do so need not be mentioned here; I left the school, declaring what I was, after a year and several months.

In 1964 I returned to Brooklyn and secured my present position as janitor. It is a position, I know, which many other stars from my time in the Negro League have also held. My choice, in several ways, has proved to be fortuitous, and I find at the end what I did not expect to find when I started to set these thoughts down: that, except for the fact that I have not been able, over the course of my life, to sustain those friendships which might have been begun in my earliest years, I regret nothing.

IV

Sam the Gambler

"See how different I am from that miserable creature by the river!—all because you found me and brought me to the very best."

"It was my good chance to find you," said Deronda. "Any other man would have been glad to do what I did."

"That is not the right way of thinking about it," said Mirah, shaking her head with decisive gravity. "I think of what really was. It was you, and not another, who found me, and were good to me."

—George Eliot, *Daniel Deronda*

13

Sam believed in Tidewater's story. Nobody, he told himself, could simply have made all those things up. He walked along Bedford Avenue, staying close to the buildings, and he found that he was not trying to forget the things that he'd read. He'd been glad, though, when he'd finished the story, that Tidewater had not been there. This way he'd been able to get out without having to go into any explanations, and without having to have the guy try to protect him in some way.

He turned left on Clarkson Avenue and, a second later, felt the lights of a car, turning the same corner, on his back. He held tightly to his knife and kept walking. The car passed. Sabatini would have somebody keep an eye on the rummage shop, and he'd do what he could to get his money—it was, Sam knew, bad policy to ever let even a single customer get away free—but, with what he owed, Sam was still small fry. There'd be no stakeout, especially at this hour of the morning, when the city was still. Sam saw no lights on in any windows of the apartment houses which lined both sides of the street, no reflections from television sets. Listening to his own footsteps, he remembered Ben's theory on how to deal with muggers, and he smiled, imagining Ben using his voice in front of a class of middle-aged women as he froze a fake assailant in his tracks.

He opened the outside door to Stella's building with the key she'd given him, took the elevator to her floor, and let himself into her apartment. He took off his coat, left it on the couch in the living room, then took off his shoes and tiptoed into the bedroom. He waited, so that his eyes would become accustomed to the darkness, and as he waited he imagined that he could see Tidewater's eyes bulge, when he had opened the door and found Johnson standing there. He'd been right about that too—about what he'd said to Tidewater about steering clear of a guy like Johnson.

He saw the wheelchair next to the bed, and the outline of Stella's body under her covers. She didn't stir. Sam moved forward and knelt next to the bed.

"Hey, Sam—I was just thinking about you."

He leaned forward and pressed his cheek to her forehead. "I wanted to see you before I left."

She turned from her back to her side, facing him, and he could see her eyes. He reached under the cover and took her hand in his. "I'm glad you came," she said.

"I want to be gone before the morning, though," he said.

"Don't take any chances."

"I came to tell you that I'll try to come back."

"Yes?"

"That's all," he said. "I just wanted you to know. I mean, I owe them a bundle and I have to make that up first. But if I do—"

"Why don't you come closer?" she said. "I can't see enough of your face."

"I can't stay long—I told you."

"Come closer and get warm. It must be cold outside."

Her thumb moved gently along the palm of his hand and he laughed. "Hey," he said. "I mean it. Don't start up with me tonight—I got to get going."

"Come on, Sam the Gambler," she said. "Get warm first, next to me."

Sam sat on the edge of the bed and lifted her head to his lap. "I read the rest of his story," he said.

"So?" Her voice was cold.

"So nothing. I read it is all. I mean, I know I read it. I wanted to do it for him before I left, and—"

"You don't have to explain." She snuggled against him. "I'm just jealous, I guess. I want all of you, Sam."

"Sure," he said, and laughed. "You and Sabatini."

"Flo said you weren't hurt too bad."

"That's right."

"I didn't worry about you. I thought you'd appreciate that." She moved backward so that she was leaning against him, her head on his shoulder, her cheek pressing his hand to his chest. "I have great confidence in you."

"Listen," Sam said. "I came here to tell you something, so don't take my mind off—"

"You told me," she said. "You'll come back."

"That's not all," he said. He was, for some reason he couldn't understand, suddenly angry with her—so angry he wanted to hurt her, to crush her, to see her helpless and in pain. And yet, the words which had been in his head, from the time he'd finished reading Tidewater's story, were there, and he let them out: "I love you, Stella. Even if—"

"Shh . . ."

He tried to understand why he had said what he had, and he saw himself on the night things had begun, feeling his heart swell for Stallworth. That, he had thought, had been so easy—feeling for a guy he'd never even have to touch, and yet here, taking a chance at leaving a place he'd been safe in, and touching her, it was easy too, and he wanted her to understand, he wanted to give her words which she could listen to while he was gone. "If I get a stake, and a game," he went on, "—I think I have things figured right—and if I do, I'll—"

"Lie beside me," she said. "Your hands are still cold."

"I'm not promising anything," he said.

"Oh Sam!" she said, and if he hadn't felt her tears running across the back of his hand he would have thought she was laughing at him. "I love you so, Sam. Please. Get warm. Hold me for a while."

"There's no time. I got to be back before—"

Her leg moved against his. "Please—"

"I mean it."

"Please."

"I'll fall asleep."

"I have an alarm clock."

Sam shivered, and remembered how cold he'd been, walking with

Tidewater and Flo and Ben. He imagined that the empty lot, where the Negro men had been huddled around the leftover chimney, was the field where Ben and Tidewater had played when they'd been boys. "Just for a few minutes then."

"You're my bird, Sam," she said.

After a while, when he felt more relaxed than he had before, he spoke to her about the other thing that had been on his mind: about what had happened to him, in his head, the first time his tongue had touched hers, but the story didn't bother her. She held him tightly and whispered: "See—didn't I tell you I knew I shouldn't trust the guy?"

When Sam entered the basement, he saw light coming from under Tidewater's door. He opened the door without knocking and saw Tidewater sitting at the table in a red plaid bathrobe.

"I was worried about you," Tidewater said.

"I had to see somebody," Sam said. "I figured they wouldn't be keeping an eye on me at three in the morning."

"I brought your valise down for you, as you asked me to." Sam took his coat off and sat down. "Would you like some tea, before you leave? It's already made."

"Sure," Sam said, and blew into his cupped hands. "I read the rest of your story," he added.

"Do you know what your father's favorite story was?" Tidewater said. He stood at the stove. "When I was a boy and I heard the less educated colored people singing—for a year or two of my life I believed that the famous spiritual concerned hunters who had gone out in search of game, and had found only birds." Tidewater's eyes flickered with light, and Sam could see his father's eyes, smiling with the man. Tidewater spoke carefully then, in a dialect Sam had never heard him use, humming the tune: "I'm gonna lay down my bird, den . . ."

"Sure," Sam said. "I see what you mean. Ben liked that stuff."

"I wanted to be so different, Sam, do you understand?" The man was pleading with him, bending his narrow body across the table. "It's all over now, but I wanted it to be so different." Tidewater took Sam's hands in his own, and Sam did not try to stop him.

Tidewater's face was old, Sam saw—older than the number of years the man claimed he had. "As different as I was, yet my true vanity lay in this, do you see? That I also wanted to believe that my life—my story—was, with its difference, only the story of my people. Do you understand?" His voice sounded sweeter than ever to Sam. "That must be how I survived all those years—thinking that what I was saving was something precious. Yet now that . . ." He stopped, letting Sam's hands go, and he gave Sam his cup of tea. "Was I not mad?" he asked, "to have wanted to see in the conditions of my own life, marked forever by my face, the conditions of those whose lives were also marked by things outward, by things so opposite that—"

He broke off and began laughing, at himself. "I begin again," he said. "And you've heard my words move along that road, after all." His chin dipped down. Sam waited. If Tidewater had pressed him—had asked—he would have told him that he understood now what he had not understood before—about why, given his birth and the color of his skin, he had chosen the way he had chosen. He knew what Tidewater had meant when he'd written what he had about his head being full. Stella had promised to wait for him. Take care, Sam the Gambler, she'd said to him. "Pushkin was a mulatto, and Dumas an octoroon, most probably." Tidewater laughed bitterly, then bent over and whispered: "Let your father go, Sam—let him go. Let him desert us. You will return, when you can. I know it. The transition doesn't bother you, does it? It is why I have given my story to you. Without offense, you are the city, Sam, don't you see? Despite your leave-taking—"

Sam sipped his tea and shrugged. "I'll take care of myself," he said. "And I'll be back, if I can. You're right about that." He thought of Ben, if he'd had possession of the story, making a joke about the fact that the ball which had fallen in front of Johnson had been hit by a Jew. "What I mean is, I'm glad I read the story now, and I appreciate being able to stay down here while—"

"I wanted to be so different," Tidewater was saying. "And yet I have been useful. You are not the first to stay here. In recent years I have done what I could to help young black men who are now the age that I once was—boys who, like myself, are angry and in flight, and do you know what? If I could control their lives, my instinct would be—am I mad, or merely foolish?—to have them, here, study things which are useless."

"I better get going," Sam said.

"Latin, for example," Tidewater said, holding Sam by the wrist. "It is not difficult to figure out why, after all, I would not have them, proud as they claim they are of the color of their skin, spend their lives learning only of things which pertain to that color. But I say nothing to them, Sam. I shelter them and feed them until it is time for them to move on. At the least, though, I find myself explaining to myself, one would never confuse one's knowledge of Latin with those things, armed with which my young men believe they can change the world. Do you see?"

Sam shrugged, slipped his wrist from Tidewater's grasp. "Ben's the expert when it comes to theories," he said.

"I wanted to be so different," Tidewater said again, standing, getting Sam's coat for him, "when the truth was, all the while, that—excelling as I did in music and sport—I merely possessed those characteristics, in high degree, that my race possesses." He laughed wildly, but spoke very softly. He held Sam's coat for him and Sam slipped his arms into the sleeves. "I had natural rhythm, Sam. I had grace. I was a childlike creature. I was, until the end, inwardly enraged and outwardly docile. I knew, in the end, what my place was, didn't I?" Tidewater sighed. "But you know all this. What I thought I was saving—what I coveted—was not nearly so special. You know me—who I am—after all."

He looked away, as if trying to remember something. "I wanted to be so different, and yet, though without my youth, of course, I'm still—keeping you here—the same man I was, as it were." He looked at Sam. "Sometimes I think, in my fancy, that if I could, I would give one long cry, and ride that cry to the other side. If I could."

Sam said nothing. Tidewater went upstairs and checked the street for him. It was just past five. Tidewater returned to tell him that there was no danger. Sam picked up his valise and then, at the door to the cellar, leaned forward and offered the man his cheek. Tidewater kissed him. They did not speak. Sam could have given himself reasons—what, when he thought about it, did it cost him, after all—but he did not want to. The air outside was ice-cold, so that his skin felt as if somebody were sticking needles into it. He walked for several blocks. In front of Garfield's he managed to get a taxi. He sat in the back seat, hugging himself for warmth. The sliding glass partition that separated him from the driver was locked with a key. The glass was bullet-proof. The cashbox, next to the meter, was bolted to the dashboard.

14

Sam knew that the tiny rectangle of bluish-green directly below his window was a swimming pool; he knew that the small objects farther away, which looked like houses, were houses; he knew that he was seeing lawns and streets, churches and community buildings, palm trees and parks; he knew that the small figures he could see far to his left, on the golf course, were the figures of men; and he knew that the brightly colored buildings, grouped together beyond the private homes and churches and community buildings and lawns and streets and parks, made up the shopping center— and yet, whenever he looked at the place from his window on the seventeenth floor, and even when he had, on his first day there, walked around at ground level, it all somehow seemed less real to him than it had in the brochure. That was why, he would have explained if Ben had asked him, he had stayed inside since his arrival.

Sam turned away from his bedroom window, expecting to find Ben there—but Ben, he knew, had gone in order to leave Sam alone for the evening. Sam walked across the plush green carpeting; when Ben paced back and forth there each morning, reciting his prayers, Sam did not hear steps—and it did not, in truth, bother him that Ben put on his *tephillin* there, with the curtains drawn, while Sam lay in bed. It had, of course, been a mistake—coming here; still, if he made a killing tonight, it all would have turned out for the best.

If not, since he had let Ben put up the stake for him—two thousand dollars—he himself would have lost nothing. Although he had, in the three weeks since he'd arrived, done nothing except eat, rest, and listen to Ben and Andy, he felt tired. Tidewater's story was on his mind. He wondered: would Ben have been happier if Sam were to lose Ben's two thousand dollars? Would he have then felt that their accounts were, finally, even?

The doorbell rang. Sam looked at his watch—it was exactly eight-thirty. He wiped his right hand along his pants to make sure his palm was dry. He felt something heavy on his chest, but knew that the feeling would pass. Stella had given him luck, and he believed that he was all right. He'd kept up with his exercises, every morning after Ben had put away his *tephillin* and left the room. Sam walked from their bedroom, through the living room, then along the corridor. From his second day there, having heard the story from Ben, Andy had been pushing him, had been saying that he could set up a game, whenever Sam gave the word. Flo had written to Ben before Sam's arrival, about what had happened. "A woman who loses her husband is called a widow," Andy had said at breakfast on Sam's second day there. "And a man who loses his wife is called a widower. A child who loses his parents is an orphan, but—our father told us this—there is no word for a parent who loses his child. Do you see?"

"Sam Berman?"

"That's right."

The man looked into Sam's eyes, and Sam stared back. Here we go round the mulberry bush, he thought. The man's hand was in his, the palm dry. "Sol Pinkus is the same, Sam. Pinkus with a 'k' in it. So, let me ask you something—how are you feeling, son?"

"Fine. Come on in and I'll take your coat."

The man was almost as tall as Sam, but much heavier. Sam estimated his weight at two seventy or two seventy-five. He was older than Sam had expected him to be: in his early sixties, possibly more. His upper lip was tucked inside his lower one, so that the inside flesh of the lower lip showed. His nose was large, red, bulbous. Flaps of skin hung down around his chin; his eyes were wide-set, brown, his eyebrows straight. Sam let him go ahead, and he noticed that the man leaned backward slightly as he walked, his shoes pointed outward. He heard him breathing heavily, through his nose. The man struggled out of his coat—a heavy wool overcoat, despite the warm weather outside—and gave it to Sam. Underneath he wore a brown herringbone sport jacket—the cut was old-fashioned, with thick shoulder pads that made him seem even wider than he was.

"In here," Sam said, and led the man through the corridor, into the living room, and then into the dining room.

"Nice place you have here," Sol said. "How much you pay for it, if you don't mind my asking—?"

"It's not mine," Sam said.

"Sure," Sol said, sitting down at the dining room table. He leaned back, so that the chair squeaked. "Sure. I forgot." Sam sat down opposite him. "Just the two of us?" Sol asked.

"There's supposed to be a third—maybe a fourth."

"Sure. I heard four—but if it's just us two, why not? You have any objections?"

"No," Sam said.

Sol looked around the dining room, then for the first time let his gaze fall on the decks of cards, the chips, Sam's envelope. He sniffed in through one nostril and smiled. "So, let me ask you something—how are you feeling, son?"

"Fine," Sam said, and sighed inwardly. He'd met guys like this before, when he and Dutch had traveled together. He'd been right about that, too, he told himself, picturing Sol outside, by the swimming pool in a cabana outfit: California and Florida, if you switched them around one night when nobody was looking . . .

"Maybe the others got held up—on the other side of the highway, going north—I come from up there—there was a big accident. Maybe they got stuck. You don't mind waiting?"

"No."

"You been out here long?"

"No."

Sol's head rocked forward a few times, his mouth turned downward. "What do they call you, you don't mind my asking—Silent Sam?" He laughed.

The problem was—Sam thought of what Tidewater had written—that the better you became, the more you limited your competition. Sam stared at Sol, then let himself smile slowly. "Sam Junior," he said.

"Well, Sam Junior, you don't got to play it cool around old Sol
Pinkus. I been around, you know what I mean? All this business
before—sparring, feeling each other out, jabbing—Oh, I been
through it all, son. Believe me, I was cutting decks of cards before
you were born. I seen things and been places you ain't dreamt of."
He slapped his fat hand on the table and laughed at Sam;
something caught in his throat, however, and he coughed. Sam
watched his face redden, but waited. The man gagged, tried to
smile, gagged again. Sure, he thought. When he was the perfect
poker player—which he might as well have been, with all the games
he'd been getting—he'd wind up playing solitaire.

Sam got up then, walked into the kitchen, directly behind the
dining room, and brought back a glass of water. Sol nodded, took
the glass, dropped his huge head backwards and drank. "Thank
you, son. Ah—that's better. Thank you. You're a good boy, I can
see that." Sam said nothing, and sat down again. "I got children,"
Sol said. "I got grandchildren almost your age. What are you—
thirty-one? thirty-two?"

"About that," Sam said.

Sol pursed his lips, considered. His head rocked forward again
and Sam could see freckles under the few remaining hairs, in the
middle, where the man was bald. "But it's okay—everybody has his
own style, right? And two thousand dollars—that's right, isn't
it?—that's not nickel-dime."

"You do this for a living?" Sam asked.

"Do I do this for a living." Sol sniffed in again. He reached over
to his right, took a deck of cards, and tapped the box on the table a
few times. "That's a good question, Sam Junior, do you know
that?" He laughed. "I'll tell you what—maybe we play a few quick
hands, you and me—to warm up—and if you win, I'll answer you.
A bonus I'll throw in tonight."

"I can wait," Sam said. He saw Ben handing him the envelope,
and heard himself saying that he hoped he could repay it. Ben had
said the usual, about what Sam had once done for him. It had been
a short-term low-interest loan, on Ben's passbook. The interest, if
Ben paid the loan back within thirty days, would amount to
nothing. If not, he explained, he could sell his stock, or take a loan
out against his life insurance policy, though this would mean
cheating Sam of his rightful inheritance. Ben had explained all the

options available to him: social security, medicare, medicaid, a loan against the apartment, the stocks, the life insurance.

"Then we'll wait," Sol said. "We can continue our stimulating conversation." He paused briefly, eyeing Sam. "Or I can keep talking, you can listen. I don't mind. I been around, like I said. I don't got to psyche anybody out—I left that behind years ago. When I play cards, I play cards. When I'm with somebody, I'm with somebody, you know what I mean?" He wiped his mouth with the back of his hand. There was a gold ring with a large blue stone on his left ring finger. "I saw the name on the door—your father?"

"My uncle," Sam said.

"He live alone?"

"My father lives with him."

"They been here long—I mean, I'm only asking, if you want the truth, because my wife—Myra—she wants to get out of the city, and she has some friends here. Your old man, how does he like it here?"

"Fine," Sam said.

"But you don't know what he pays—"

"It's his brother's place."

"Well, it's not cheap, I can tell you that much," Sol said. He stopped, sniffed in. "Look, I'll tell you the truth—it's not the first time I been here, so I shouldn't let on like I know nothing at all. I played here before—not since last summer, but I played here, believe me." He sneered. "Big shots!" He made a bubbling sound with his lips. "What do you think, son, could I earn my keep here—stealing pensions from—" He broke off, laughing to himself, wheezing. "Do a little *shtupping* on the side, why not?"

He looked to Sam for a reaction, but Sam showed nothing. He heard Andy asking him, as he did each morning, what Sam had against older women. He heard, to his surprise, his father giggling at Andy's remarks, and he tried to recall what Andy had looked like when he had been younger—Sam's age—and a lady's man. "It's a thought, though," Sol said, leaning back so that his belly rose almost to table-level. "You got everything you need right here at your fingertips—when you get to my age, I'll tell you the truth, you want things convenient. You want services. You don't want to be running all the time." He closed his eyes, breathed heavily through his nose. "I ran enough for one lifetime, believe me."

The doorbell rang. "You heard of Mickey Cohen?" Sol asked. "This—" he pointed to the cards. "This is bingo after what I seen, believe me, son." He leaned back. "You heard of Mickey Cohen?" he asked again.

Sam left the room without answering. He remembered Ben's story, of course, about the time Ben and Andy had gone to see Lipsky; still, something about Pinkus didn't smell right to him. He wondered if Ben would return before the game was over.

The new player was younger, shorter, very thin. "Sam Berman, right?"

"That's right," Sam said.

The guy blinked nervously with his left eye, looked to both sides down the hall corridor before stepping inside. Sam found that he wanted to laugh. He put his hand out. "Oh yeah," the guy said, and shook Sam's hand, quickly. His palm was very dry. "Yeah, sure. Is the game on?—I don't want to come in if it ain't—"

"It's on," Sam said. The guy reminded him, not of the jockeys Sam had met, but of their stable boys—the white ones—guys who'd save up six or seven months' salary and then blow it all on one race, when they knew something. The guy wore a blue nylon jacket, zipped close, the collar turned up around the neck. Everything in his face seemed to be pointed downward—the tips of his ears, his widow's peak, his thin nose, the cleft above his lip, his chin. "Looks like only three players, though."

"Yeah, I know that," the guy said, and walked in. "I come down anyway."

Sam saw no reason to play it cool with a guy like this. "You from Brooklyn?" he asked.

"That's my business, yeah? Where we playing—?"

"In the dining room. I can hang your jacket up here."

"I'll keep it. What time you got?"

"Ten to nine."

"You start yet?"

"We waited for you."

"Yeah. Well, I ain't got all night, you know what I mean?"

Sam walked into the living room. The guy looked around, as if he were casing the place. "Man, this is some creepy place," he said in a whisper. "I mean, it gives me the willies, all these—I mean, it spooks you, walking around here, you don't see nobody but old stiffs. Let's deal and play so I can get my butt out of here quick, yeah?" He looked into the dining room, saw Sol, and grabbed Sam's sleeve. His breath smelled like wet leather. "He live here?"

"No."

"This is some creepy place," the guy said again. "Wouldn't want to get stuck here—you and me, we'd turn into dead men we stayed here too long." He tried to catch Sam's eye. "I mean—yeah, you guessed it, I'm from Brooklyn too, so we got something in common, we stick together a little, you know what I mean?" Sam said nothing. The guy's left eye twitched.

Sam walked into the dining room and started to introduce the guy to Sol. "I didn't get your name," he said.

"That's right."

The guy took a seat at the end of the table and leaned over, blowing into his hands, as if to warm them. It amused Sam, seeing a bird like this all the way out in California. But he wasn't, he told himself, fooled. Even though Tidewater's story was filling his head, he found himself, to his surprise, able to concentrate. Sol smiled at Sam and winked knowingly. "You young people are always so anxious. What's the rush? Me, I been around, I got time. Where's the hurry?"

"The hurry is I come here to play, and I got things to do."

"Well then, Mr. Noname," Sol laughed, "we shouldn't keep you waiting, although you're the one who kept us waiting—"

"Don't be a wise-ass," the guy said. "And don't call me noname. I got a name as good as yours."

"Ah," Sol said, sighing. "What do you wish us to call you?"

"Call me nothing. Just let's play, yeah?"

"I'll call you Norman, all right? For my eldest son," Sol said, and he looked toward Sam.

"C'mon, c'mon," Norman said. "Cut the gab, and let's move it."

"Five-card draw, you can draw four, nothing wild," Sam said. They nodded their agreement. "Ten and twenty, ten for ante, three raises, you call chip to raise again." He looked at Norman, whose tongue moved out, pointed, and licked his upper lip.

"Yeah, yeah," he said. "You don't scare me. I played Brooklyn-style before. Let's see the deck."

Sol passed an unopened deck to him. He looked at the seal. "Okay?" he asked. Sam and Sol nodded; Norman split the seal with

his fingernail, took the deck out, removed the jokers, fanned the
deck in front of him, closed it, inspected the sides, then passed it to
Sol. "Okay," he said again, and unzipped his jacket. "Here's my
two. Put it in the bank."

"White is ten, blue is twenty, red is a hundred," Sam said.

Sol leaned to one side, pulled a wallet from his left sidepocket.
Sam set the deck down to his right and distributed the chips—ten
reds, twenty-five blues, fifty whites, then took his own two thousand
from the envelope and showed it to them. He stacked his chips to
the left, put the six thousand in the envelope, and laid the envelope
at the far left of the oval table, where the extra chips were. Andy
had supplied the chips. Remember, he'd told Sam before he and
Ben had left for the evening, what's difficult for man is easy for
God.

"I'll deal," Sam said.

Sol looked worried. "That's a big bank," he said. "Six shiny
dimes."

Sam tossed a white chip into the middle, and the others followed,
their chips clicking on the table's wood surface. Sam knew that Sol
had wanted him to say something, but he knew how much good
words were. Sure, Sam thought. His account could be transferred
also. Sam split the deck, shuffled, aware of their eyes on him, of the
cards whirring downward, cascading. His fingertips tingled. Norman zipped his jacket closed, leaned forward, watching Sam. Sam
passed the deck to him, and Norman cut. Sam took the deck; the
cards felt good to him: cold, smooth, firm. He flicked them out, left
to right, five times to each man, and heard his heart pounding
under his shirt. He heard Stella telling him, the first night they'd
met, that if he pulled three ladies, he should think of her. He put the
deck down, reached for his cards, and held the thin stack in his
palm, the edges cutting into his fingers.

He fanned the cards out, and found nothing: no pair, no possible
straight, no possible flush. "Ten more to buy," Sol said, moving a
chip forward. Norman stayed in. Sam set his hand down on the
table, put his ten dollars in also. Sol took three, Norman took two.
"Dealer takes four," Sam said, and dealt three to himself, turned
one card down, then took his fourth.

"I'll chip another penny to the big man," Sol said, talking to
Norman.

"Twenty more to see me," Norman said, and pushed three white chips forward.

Sam looked at his hand—there was nothing there—and turned it face down. "I work hard for my money," Sol said. He turned his cards over and Norman took in the pot. Sam collected the cards, passed to Sol, who moved a chip to the middle, shuffled, dealt. Sam drew a pair of sevens, stayed in. Sol kept three cards, Norman took two again, but dropped out when Sol raised ten, no chip. Sam saw Sol and lost, jacks to sevens, and knew something. He watched Norman shuffle—the guy's fingers were long, and he shuffled beautifully: straight on, not corner to corner. He gave Sam a pair of sixes. Sol drew three cards; Norman took two again and raised twenty plus chip. Sam folded.

"We'll see you this time," Sol said, pushing a blue chip forward.

Norman did not hesitate. "Cost you plate, fat man." Too soon, too soon, Sam thought. Norman slid a red chip into the middle. Sol smiled, moved a red chip forward. Norman turned two cards over—a pair of fives—his eyes on Sol. The guy would be tapped out in less than an hour, Sam told himself, playing like that. It didn't figure.

Sol showed three eights, and pulled the chips in with both hands. He looked at Sam, raised his eyebrows. "No funny looks there, fat man," Norman said, shoving the deck at Sam.

In the next deal, Sam drew nothing again, Norman took two cards to Sol's three, but this time Sol smiled and let Norman take in the forty dollars. "You shouldn't have called me fat man," Sol said, slicing the deck.

"Keep the bottom card toward you—down."

Sam was tired—the excitement he had felt when he'd held the deck for the first time had already vanished. It was a question now of staying in, of waiting. The cards moved around, left to right, left to right, Norman taking two each time, winning a few hands when both Sam and Sol would fold, but not chipping again. On the tenth deal, Sam took his first hand, holding a pair of kings, but the others did not see him. "I'll trust you, Silent Sam," Sol said. "You're a good boy." The pots remained small, Sam drew poorly. In a while he was down two sixty, about even with Norman—Sol had their money—but he wasn't worried. He was playing the cards, as always. If they didn't come now, they'd come later. He thought of his Bible Man, trying to lose, and remembered that there was nothing new there, either: he'd read an article once about a guy who had won at Monte Carlo with the same system.

Sol dealt, Norman passed, Sam passed, and Sol turned his cards down. He passed the deck to Norman—the first time, Sam realized, that that had happened. They raised the house, anted up again, and Sam drew a pair of fours. Norman made it thirty to draw, and Sam put his thirty in, but he drew nothing to the fours and had to let Norman take the pot.

Sam lost a few more, then drew his first good hand. He kept a six, seven, eight, and nine, and pulled the five, raised twenty and chip, then forty more. Sol stayed in, Norman folded. Sam turned the straight over, and as he waited for Sol to show his hand, he tried to show nothing. He knew that Sol was waiting, to see what he would do—if he would make a move for the chips. "Good enough," Sol said, aware of the silence, and Sam took in the chips, stacked them, his fingers steady. He did not smile.

Would he have taken Ben's offer—and let Andy set the game up—if Flo's letter had not arrived? He watched the cards in front of him: two tens. He drew two queens, stayed in when Norman raised twenty and chip. He raised him ten more and Norman saw the ten, raised twenty. Norman blinked. Sam put his money in and Norman turned over three fives. Sam showed nothing, nodded. Watch your ass, Sam Junior, he heard himself saying. Forget Ben, forget Andy, forget Flo's letter, forget Tidewater.

The cards moved around again, and everybody passed. Another hand—nothing again. There were nine chips in the middle, and when Sam reached across for his cards he let his eyes fall on his watch: ten after ten. He was down five hundred—one good hand, though, a few small ones, and he'd be back even. Remember the rules: play it small and play it smart. He drew nothing. Sol bet twenty and chip, and Sam and Norman went out. The cards went around, Sol continued to win, to draw good cards. Sam knew that he was doing what he had to do, playing what was there. Still . . .

He heard a siren. He had, from his window, watched the tiny figures below freeze whenever that sound wailed through the village. About you and your father, Andy had said to him, when Ben was gone one morning, shopping. Remember this, what your grandfather always taught us: one mother can take care of ten children, but ten children sometimes, they can't take care of one mother. Sam saw two queens in his hand, then drew the third. Sol took three cards also. Sam raised twenty and chip, Sol saw him, but Norman went out. Sam didn't hesitate. "Plate," he said. Sol looked at him, put a finger on a red chip and Sam did not move. Then: "Be my guest," Sol said, and tossed his cards into the center of the table.

Sam dealt: another good hand—two tens, and his heart thumped when he picked up his three cards and saw that he'd drawn a third one. He had no choice: he bet as before. Norman stayed with him, but, like Sol, Norman folded when Sam bet plate. Two hands, two hundred—but he should, he knew, have had at least five with cards like that. Something was up. "We'll take a break at midnight," Sol said. "Five minutes."

"I ain't got five minutes," Norman said.

Sol reared back, laughing, then dealt. When he tossed Sam his fifth card, he winked. Sam had four hearts—seven, nine, ten, jack. The others took two cards each. Sam picked up his new card, didn't look at it. "I pass to the power," Sol said. Norman did the same. Sam looked at his card—seven of spades. He didn't fight it: he turned his cards face down, pushed another white chip into the middle and passed the deck. He drew nothing on the next deal, not even a pair, and nothing again on the hand after that, and he felt reassured. Nothing was nothing. You couldn't bet what you didn't have.

Norman, he saw, was trying to prove otherwise. And Sol could, by now, if he'd wanted, have driven out a strong pair by betting heavily. It didn't matter, though. He'd wait for the cards to come. With a pair of aces in his hand, Sam let Norman send the pot to a hundred and twenty. Sol watched them, expressionless. Norman saw Sam, Sam showed his aces. "Yeah," was all Norman said, and he turned his cards down. Sam now had about thirteen hundred left, Norman had fifteen, and Sol had the rest. But a pro, Sam thought, could never play the way Norman was playing and be back a second and third time. Making sure the pot never built, protecting his game—he was up to something else. Sam heard noise in the corridor and Norman's neck snapped to the left. Sam saw that, briefly, Sol had tensed. Sam spun the cards around the circle. "My father," he said.

"I hear women," Norman said. "No women in this room, you hear? They spook me."

Sol laughed. "I like women," he said.

Ben passed the open doorway, and Sam turned, looked at him. It was, he realized, the first time Ben had ever seen him—Sam liked the phrase, and smiled—at work. He looked at the cards: two tens. He glanced up, but Ben was already gone. Sol put a chip in the middle, and Norman did the same. "Make it two," Sam said, still smiling. Sol shrugged, threw a second chip in the middle. "No funny business," Norman said. "They gotta stay far away, you hear?"

"How many?" Sam asked.

Sol asked for three, and Norman took three also. "Dealer takes two," Sam said, and kept a jack with his two tens, picked up his two cards, one at a time: a six, then a king. He closed his hand, waited a split-second. "One and chip," he said, pushing a blue chip into the middle, taking a white one back. He heard a woman's voice—then another. They were laughing. The widows—that, Ben had explained to him was another option: if only the thoughtful senior citizen will take a full and frank inventory of his assets and possibilities . . .

Sol laughed, turned his cards over. Norman touched a chip, looked at Sam. "You don't sucker me," he said, and turned his cards over also. Sam took the stack in, passed the deck to Sol. He went out on the next hand, and the next, then stayed in when he pulled two pairs, nines and jacks. He bet twenty before the draw and Sol and Norman saw him. They each took two cards. "Last card," Sol said, dealing. "Down and dirty." Sam picked up the card, a third jack, and felt his stomach tighten, bounce. Outwardly he showed nothing. "Oh Ben—!" he heard. The woman's voice squeaked. Sam realized that his father's small eyes had been glazed. "We'll pass to the power," Sol said, and Sam bet one and chip. Sol saw his bet; Norman looked at Sol. "Thanks, sport," he said, "for saving me nothing." He went out.

Sam hesitated, but only for an instant; he pushed three chips forward, one for each jack. "Good," Sol said. "I see your three and we'll make it three more."

Sam put three chips forward. "Plate," he said.

Sol's mouth moved downward. "There's twenty chips in there, right?"

"Right," Sam said, and slid two red chips forward.

"I believe you," Sol said. "But I have no choice." He put two red

chips in the middle, tucked his upper lip into his lower one. "So?"
he asked. "I paid to see."

Sam showed the full house. "Good enough," Sol said, and turned
to Norman. "Some young men are polite, you see. It pays."

Sam heard glasses tinkling in the other room. He took his chips
in. Small and smart, and he was almost back even—instead of
being under a thousand, he was over fifteen hundred. He held a
pair of eights, they drew, he bet one and chip, the others folded. He
knew he was all right now: with or without a pair, he could take a
hand.

Sam heard Andy, talking about Ben—something to do with the
taxi, but Sam could not make out the words. It occurred to him that
the two men, more than fifty years before, had been boys, and that
when they had been boys they had slept in the same bed. Andy had
known Rabbi Katimsky.

"Close the fucking door," Norman said. "They bug me."

"There is no door," Sam said.

Norman looked, saw that Sam was right. "Relax, son," Sol said.
"I don't hear a word they're saying."

"Let's pick up the pace, yeah?" Norman said, and he put twenty
in the middle for ante.

"Loser's choice," Sol said, and added a blue chip to Norman's.
Norman dealt, bet twenty again, and then, for the first time all
night, took four cards. Sam had a pair of sevens, drew a third one.

"Plate," Norman said.

"I see your plate, and raise you plate," Sam said.

"Let youth fight its own battles," Sol said, and he went out. Sam
looked at him, and Sol smiled, in a way that made Sam tense.

"I'll see that, smart boy," Norman said, and put in his two red
chips, then two blue ones. He smiled. "And it'll cost you plate again
to see me."

Sam forced himself to pay attention. Norman's left eye was
steady. Sam tried to close off his father's voice in the other room,
but only heard, in his head, Ben talking about what he had willed
his son: about fading in and fading out. He put down five hundred,
took twenty in change, and said nothing. One at a time, Norman
turned over his tens: one, two, three. "It's yours,' Sam said.

His stake was cut almost in half now. The hands moved around:
he paid attention, he ignored the sounds from the living room, he

won his share of hands, but he wasn't fooled. The pots were for forty or fifty dollars, Sam drew well, and his stack went from twelve hundred, to twelve fifty, to thirteen hundred. He drew a flush, against Sol, and reached fourteen hundred, but understood now, with certainty, where things were wrong. With a streak like the one he'd just had, he should have doubled his wins, and been ahead, but he wasn't. Sol played steadily, and though he had not won a big pot for almost an hour, he was still ahead of both Sam and Norman. Neither Sol nor Norman would let the pot build, and Sam couldn't tell when Norman was bluffing and when he wasn't. He didn't like it.

In her letter, Flo had said that she was worried about Tidewater. She had been with him in the basement, in the morning, and then had gone upstairs to the store. He had not, as far as she knew—and she had asked the neighbors—left the building, and yet, when she returned later that day, after locking the store, and had knocked on his door, he had not answered. The following morning, he did not appear. Worried that he might be ill, she had telephoned the landlord, who had come and opened the door to his room. The room had been as it had always been, but Tidewater had not been there. She had inquired in the neighborhood, but nobody had seen him, or heard about him. She had checked all the hospitals, and the police knew of his disappearance. For a day or two after Sam's departure he had seemed unusually depressed, even for him, she said. And then—on the morning she had last seen him—he had looked as good as he had ever looked, and he had been especially helpful and cheerful. She wondered if Sam knew anything—about where he might have gone. There was no point by now, Sam knew, in telling anyone about the other room.

It was past midnight—twelve-twenty—and they had him cornered, Sam saw, pounding into him one at a time, chopping away at him, first one, then the other—testing him, like fullbacks going through the line, first off one tackle, then off the other. When Andy had asked again, the night before, Sam's decision had been there. He wanted to return, even if it was—as it had always been?—too late to do anything for Tidewater. He wanted to win.

He played what he had. Stick to the cards, guard your odds. With two pair, kings over fours, he let Norman raise the pot, then took the chips in. "Norman Noname," Sol said, "you're slipping."

Norman was, Sam saw, under five hundred. His eyes were bloodshot. But it didn't matter. Playing like that, he knew, they could do anything they wanted—anything at all. He had been had: one played steady, one played wild, and if the steady player couldn't win on skill, then the wild player was there, waiting to clean you out when, in the course of the night, he got his two or three lucky hands.

It didn't matter to Sam, though. What they wanted, he supposed, was his swan song, but he didn't figure he was ready for that yet. He had brains. He could, if he had enough time, figure a way out—he believed that. The hands went around, but the pattern remained the same. Every time he raised, one of them would go out—and every time he went out, one of them would stay in. He chipped away at the small pots, and whittled Norman's stack of chips down. When he was under two hundred, though, Norman fooled Sam, and bought into the game for a thousand more, taking the bills from under his nylon jacket. Sam put them in the envelope. He heard somebody approaching, and felt himself tense. He looked at his hand: four cards of an inside straight, jack high. He looked up.

"I was only coming for some water—" Andy said.

Sam realized that he had been glaring at Andy; Sol chipped, asked for one card. Andy slid behind Norman's chair, to Sam's right, and smiled, but his lips trembled. Sol turned his body sideways and Sam saw a ring of sweat under his arm, through the jacket. Norman folded. Sam looked at his card—a queen: he had drawn the straight. "One and chip," he said.

"I'll see your one, and raise you five," Sol said. Andy came back from the kitchen—he was dressed in a flowered silk shirt. Sam felt his anger pass. Let the guy linger if he wanted to. It wasn't costing Sam anything. "I'll see your five," Sam said, and Andy coughed. Sol's eyes fixed Andy momentarily, against the white dining room wall. Andy coughed again, but it didn't matter to Sam. If the guy wanted to use him to transfer some funds, even from his own brother, that was okay with him. Since, thanks to Ben, Sam had never had a brother, he figured there were some things he would never know. "And I raise you plate," he added.

Sol turned his cards over, face down. "But you should relax, son," he said.

Sam took in the pot, and said nothing. Andy had not moved. "I'm sorry," Andy began. "I didn't—"

"That's right," Sol said quickly.

Andy hurried out, carrying a pitcher of water in front of him. All Andy had wanted, Sam realized, was to get some of Ben's money without having to ask for it. Even kicking off, he wanted to stay the big spender in his brother's eyes. Sam wondered if Ben suspected why Andy had set up the game. It didn't matter, though, because Sam would fool him too, as smart as he thought he'd been. "If anything happens to my uncle," Sam found himself saying, "I'll personally take it out of your skin."

"Don't talk big," Norman said. "You could be in the bay like that." He snapped his fingers.

Sam turned the cards over, showing the straight. "That's for free," he said. "Nobody told me anything." It was, he believed, something more than chance which had given him a hand like that at that moment, and he was pleased.

Sol would not return the steady look Sam was giving him. "Of course," he said. "Why should you think—?"

"Let's play," Sam said.

Sol ran through the deck with his thumb. "I don't figure it, though," he said. "A nice young boy like yourself." He set the deck down. "Look. You're almost back even. You play a good game. I respect it, if you know what I mean. Maybe with"—he licked his lips—"maybe we should call it quits for tonight—Norman willing, of course. Then, you think it over, we can play again in a week or so, if you want. You'll call me—"

"Deal," Norman said.

"Well?" Sol asked.

"Deal," Sam said.

Sol shrugged, the cards went around the table, nobody talked. A few minutes later, the voices in the other room became louder, and Sam realized that Andy and Ben and their two women were walking along the hallway corridor. He heard the front door close. Andy was a head taller than Ben—five-eleven, Sam figured—with large brown eyes, a straight nose, a squarish chin; his voice was high-pitched—still, Sam believed that they had come from the same mother. That did not mean, though, that he had to like listening to the guy, to all his sayings, to the stories he told about his women and how they went for him even more when they knew about his illness. Sam saw that Sol and Norman were getting tired. He could wait. Not to win—he would not, he now understood, win with the cards—but to figure the way out.

The pots stayed small: thirty, forty, fifty, sixty—the pattern remained the same, more obviously so. Norman asked for a fresh deck of cards, and Sam passed one to him. Norman checked it, handed it back to Sam, and Sam liked the feel of the new cards, he liked the sound they made whizzing on top of each other, he liked the easy way they fanned apart. And, touching the new deck, he liked it for another reason, which hadn't occurred to him until the deck had been in his hands. Silently, he thanked Norman.

The new cards moved around the table, Sam winning his share of hands. He felt ready for anything. He heard the front door open, the sound of Andy's laughter. The two brothers said good night to each other, and Sam heard the door to a bedroom close. Sam thought of Tidewater again, and heard Ben's voice, in his head, telling him that what mattered in this life wasn't what you knew but who you knew. He had slightly over twelve hundred in his stack, Sol had more than four thousand, Norman had a bit more than Sam had. He sensed that they would make their move soon, and found that he was relaxed. Norman bet three and chip. Sam looked at a pair of kings and saw Norman's bet. Norman bet plate, Sam saw plate, and then saw Norman's pair of queens. He showed his kings.

Norman bet heavily on the next hand, Sam went out, as did Sol. Norman's eye was twitching again. He wondered if Norman would let himself get wiped out a second time, but he did not want to be there if he did. He heard shoes drop to the floor in the living room. Norman anted with a blue chip and Sam saw two lovely ladies in his own hand, robed in tiny segments of yellow and red velvet, a yellow flower in each of their hands. Mirror-images, one in hearts, one in spades, with a pair of sevens guarding them. "Twenty more," Sol said, and smiled. Sam and Norman saw the twenty.

"How many?" Sam asked.

"I'll stick with what I have," Sol said.

"Gimme two," Norman said.

They would, this time, have to go all the way with him. Sam could hear his father, in the other room, wheezing, snoring slightly.

He gave Norman his two cards, dealt one to himself, but did not pick it up.

"Your bet," he said to Sol, and found that he was smiling.

"So it is," Sol said. He did not look at his cards. "Plate again, my friend—and chip."

Sam was almost ready to bet, having assumed that Norman would fold, when Norman surprised him. "Me too, smart boy," Norman said.

Sam tried not to show anything. Sol looked puzzled. Sam picked up his last card, and waited. Again, he told himself to pay attention, to go slow and easy. He knew they were going to make their move but this wasn't the way he had thought it would be. He calculated: he needed at least two grand to do what he planned to do, and he did not want to let them steal it away before he was ready. He relaxed, turned his card over and saw that it was the one he thought it would be: his third lady. "Plate and plate again," he said, and he stopped himself from thinking about what Sol might have been holding. Play what's there, don't bet on air. Norman was in, he knew, to fatten him up—if not for this hand, then for the next—but there wouldn't be a next one if Sam raked this one in, and he figured that Norman didn't know that. "And chip," he added.

"This I must see," Sol said, and put his money in—five red chips—and took twenty in change.

"Yeah," Norman said. "We'll see who—" He stopped, laughed at Sam, and did what Sam wanted him to do. "And I raise plate again to the big shots," he added.

Norman put his chips in the middle, one at a time, but he was shy by more than half the amount, and he stacked the amount of the loan next to his right hand.

"No," Sam said, and Norman went for the chips, thinking that Sam had gone out; Sam put his hand on top of Norman's—it was like ice. "No—I mean, no, I want to see the money. You counted right—nineteen-twenty. You put in eight-ten. I want to see one thousand one hundred and ten dollars, in the envelope."

"What gives—you don't trust me?"

Sam smiled. "That's right."

Norman's chair moved backward. Sam kept his eye on Sol, let go of Norman's hand, and let his own hand drop to his pocket. "If you don't have it," Sam said, "you can borrow it from your partner here—" Norman stood, his eye banging up and down. Sol wheezed. "—who is still in the game, for your information."

"You watch your goddamned mouth," Norman said. "What the fuck do you—"

"Sit down and play, son," Sol said to him quietly. "You were very hasty. He's right: I'm still in. You shouldn't bet what you don't have."

"I got it, I got it," Norman said, sitting. He unzipped his jacket, reached inside. "But I wanna know what he meant—nobody calls me—"

"They've called you worse," Sol said with weariness.

Norman unfolded a pack of bills, bought the exact number of chips he needed. Sam looked at Sol. "I'm out," Sol said. Sam smiled at their system—who could go against such odds, after all: you bet five, you win twenty.

"I see you," he said to Norman, and started, methodically, moving chips forward. Sam was seven hundred shy, and he counted on Norman being too excited to make him do what he had just made Norman do. "Read 'em and weep," Norman said, and before Sam was done counting, and before Sol could stop him, Norman had turned over his cards. One king, one ten, another king, another ten, and then—Sam felt his heart bump—a third ten. He saw Stella smile. She told him that she'd never doubted him.

"Good," Sam said matter-of-factly, and showed his hand. Sol's eyes widened. Sam took in the money: twelve twenty of his own, thirty-eight forty of theirs.

"You play very well, son," Sol said. "You're ahead of me for the first time—we seem to be sharing Norman Noname's bank account."

"Gimme another grand," Norman said. "I ain't dead yet."

"It seems to me," Sol said, leaning forward, "that the game has just begun to be interesting."

"Gimme my grand," Norman said to Sam again.

Sam took the deck in. "That's all," he said. "No more poker."

"What do you mean?" Norman cried. "I'm losing—I got a right—"

"You and me, Sol," Sam said. "We'll see how much of a sport you are, right? You got a little over three grand there. One split of the deck, high card wins."

"I ain't shitting you," Norman said. "You guys don't cut me out. Gimme my grand."

"Quiet," Sol said, turning to him. He looked at Sam, closed his heavy lids, then smiled. "You're a nice young boy," he began. "Why—?"

"One cut, three grand, and we all get to sleep tonight," Sam said.

Norman reached toward Sam, grabbing his shirt sleeve. Sam pulled his hand away. "Stop," Sol said. "I can't think when—stop, stop—" His belly swelled, then collapsed; he ran his finger around the inside of his shirt collar. "All right," he said. "Sure. I can afford it."

"I don't like it," Norman said. "Nobody dickshits me, you hear?"

"You first," Sam said to Sol. Sam shuffled. Norman leaned forward, breathing through his thin nose. Sol wheezed. Sam could not hear Ben. Sol lifted two-thirds of the deck straight up, turned his wrist over: ten of clubs. "Well," he said. "The odds are with me."

"Shuffle," Sam said.

"No," Sol said, as if he had caught him. "As is."

"Sure," Sam said, and without hesitating, he split the deck, knew what he would find, and did: a king of hearts.

"Well," Sol said, and shifted his enormous weight in his chair.

"I don't like it," Norman said, and when he moved his chair backward, Sam was ready, the point of his knife at Norman's chin.

"That makes two of us," Sam said. "Now you'll get up slowly and let everything sit where it is—the cash and the cards—and you'll get out quietly, so you don't wake my old man, who's asleep in the living room."

Sol waved a hand at Sam. "You don't got to do that—you won fair and square. Why—?"

"No words," Sam said. "Just move it. I'll go to the door with you."

"You ain't gonna get away with this," Norman muttered.

"I told you before—around Sol Pinkus you don't got to—"

"Shut up," Sam said. "And move it, quietly." He jabbed the point of his knife into the sleeve of Norman's arm, slicing the nylon.

"What a way to make a living," Sol said to himself, and laughed.

"Keep your hands where I can see them," Sam said, and moved

behind them, through the living room, into the hallway. "Get his
coat," he said to Norman. "The big dark one. Open the closet for
him, Sol."

"I did enough running in my life," Sol said. "I'm entitled also."

"We'll get you, wiseass. Yeah. You ain't gonna—" Norman
began, but Sol grabbed him at the back of the neck, between thumb
and forefinger and squeezed slowly, ferociously.

"Out the door," Sam said. They moved to the door, Sol's hand on
Norman's neck. "Open it."

"You played well," Sol said, letting go of Norman and offering
his hand to Sam. Sam did not move; he kept his eyes on them, the
blade pointed forward, the handle balanced perfectly across his
palm. "I didn't always . . ." Sol began, then shook his head up and
down. "With money so tight—it's hard times, if you know what I
mean. Come. We'll shake and be friends. No hard feelings, all
right?"

"Out the door," Sam said.

"Well. You played well," he said, as they stepped outside.
"You . . ."

Sam closed the door, locked it, and walked back along the
corridor. His knees were, he noticed for the first time, actually
shaking inside his trousers, as if the knobs were disconnected,
swinging from strings like the legs of marionettes. He snapped the
knife closed, and when he did he felt himself shudder, from his toes.

"Did you win?" Ben stood at the end of the hallway, a shadow,
his bathrobe on, his hands in his bathrobe pockets.

"I won," Sam said when he reached his father. "Sure."

Ben looked at his son, the line between his small eyes creasing.
"Enough?"

"Enough," Sam said.

"I'm glad, Sam," Ben said. "I really am." Ben turned and walked
in front of Sam, into the dining room. Sam followed, tried to draw
deep breaths, to stop shivering, but he couldn't. Ben sat down in the
seat Sol had used. "Were they good players?" Ben asked. "What I
mean is—did you enjoy the game?"

Sam shrugged, shoved his hands deeper into his pockets, and
grabbed cloth with his fists. "Look," Ben said, his voice smooth and
deep. "You must be tired—you must want to sleep, working a night
like this. We retired citizens, you see, we have the easy life. Here

in—" He stopped. "Go—go to sleep. I'll put things away." His eye fell on the envelope; some bills were sticking out—the last ones Norman had put in. "My two thousand?" Ben asked.

"I can give it back to you," Sam said, and to himself he thought: let Andy swallow his damned pride and ask for it directly—without having to have them lose any of it to a middleman. Sure. He forgave Andy for having tried, because if he hadn't, he himself would not have been able to get as much as he had, the way he had. Sometimes things worked out—as, he thought, they had with Stella—and you couldn't always figure all the reasons. In the end, he saw, Tidewater had been the one who'd played only what was there.

"Good. It's better that way." Ben picked up the deck of cards. "I didn't say anything before, but I didn't like the looks of them—"

"I'll tell you all about it someday."

"You don't have to."

"You want to play me for the two thousand?" Sam asked.

Ben laughed. "Do I want to play my only son for my retirement money?—of course not. You're too good for me, Sam Junior."

"Not poker," Sam said, and sat down, put his hands on the table, palms down. He felt calmer. "We split the deck, high card wins. Start with any amount you want."

Ben cocked his head to one side. "You don't fool me, sonny boy. With your luck, I—"

"Just for fun then," Sam said. "Go on. Split the deck."

Ben shrugged. "Sure—you're all excited, from the game. Well. I suppose I would be too." He cut the deck: a six of clubs. "See?" he said. "If you had my luck . . ."

Sam cut the deck, his heart pounding, but making him feel warm now: king of hearts.

"See—" Ben said.

"Again," Sam said. "Shuffle first."

Ben shuffled, cut, showed a jack of spades this time. "I'm improving, yes?"

Sam cut the deck: king of hearts, a third time.

Ben looked at Sam, cut quickly, showed him a nine of hearts. Sam shuffled, put the deck down, broke it in half, and again showed Ben the king of hearts. Sure, Sam thought to himself. Christ may have loved losers, as his Bible Man had said, but Dutch and the

Rabbi were right: the Jews—and Sam, unlike Tidewater, was one—believed in this world.

Ben's small eyes, looking at the king, bulged, and then he sat back, sighed, and broke into the most beautiful yellow smile Sam had ever seen. Ben's eyes closed. "My son," he said, his head bobbing up and down. "But—" He looked at Sam, worried, "but why a king—why not—" Then he stopped and nodded to himself again, tried to hold his mouth straight, but could not stop himself from smiling. "Well," he said. "Well—you're a sport, Sam Junior. Nobody could deny it."

He stood, came around the table, let one hand fall on Sam's shoulder. Sam did not look up. "I'll tell you the whole story someday."

"I don't want to hear," Ben said, and his voice shifted. "The important thing, from this man's point of view, is that you're finally starting to listen to your father." He paused—two, perhaps three seconds. "Take, Sam. Take."

Sam wanted to protest: that wasn't all there was to it, he could have said. But if he began to explain . . . He saw the ball drop from the sky, landing a few feet in front of Johnson, and he felt what he thought Tidewater must have felt—not when it had happened, but, looking back, when he'd written about it happening. He ached for the man, but there was nothing he could do or say that would change anything. He had the money for Sabatini, and Stella would be waiting—that was all he knew. "I'm Sam's son," he said to his father's words, wanting to please him, but Ben did not pick up his cue. He left Sam, without saying good night, and Sam listened to his father's bedroom door close.

Sam stayed in the dining room, sitting at the table, trying to think of nothing, but finding that he could imagine more things than he believed possible. Before morning, while it was still black outside, he went into the bedroom and packed his suitcase. Ben was curled up on his side, his mouth open, his arms hugging the pillow. Sam sat down next to him, looking into his face, then shook him.

"I don't want any," Ben mumbled.

"I'm leaving," Sam said.

"What time is it?"

"A few minutes before five. I wanted to get out before breakfast—to get a good start."

"Sure," Ben said. "But why don't you wait, have some breakfast with me. Come—" He started to get out of bed, but Sam put a hand on his shoulder.

"It's okay," Sam said. "We'd only get into a conversation and then Andy would come in, and—"

"Whatever you say," Ben said. "It's all the same to me."

"Here," Sam said, and left the bed. "I'm putting your envelope on the dresser—nineteen hundred. I'm borrowing a hundred, okay? I'll send it back when—"

"Take what you need," Ben said. Sam sat on the bed again, next to his father. "And give me my robe—on the chair. I don't want to catch a chill." Sam handed his father his bathrobe and Ben slid his arms into the sleeves. "You can stay if you want, you know."

"No," Sam said.

"Whatever you want," Ben said. "Last night—it's why I have confidence in you, Sam. I always said that. You're the only one—I'll tell you the truth—you're the only one who hasn't disappointed me, did you know that?" In the darkness he leaned closer, and his eyes seemed to glow. "But do you know what else?" He paused for effect. "I have a feeling that you will." He slid under the covers, onto his back, so that only his head showed. He talked to himself. "Everybody does, don't you know that?"

"They had me down last night," Sam was saying. "They had the noose around my neck, nice and tight."

"Well, you know what I've always said," Ben paused. "No noose is good noose."

"Sure," Sam said. "I set you up."

"Our accounts are even. Go. I want to get back to sleep before I wake up. Say hello to people for me. To Flo, to Mason if . . ."

Ben turned away. Sam reached across the bed, put a hand on his father's shoulder, then stretched his body across, lowered his face, and kissed his father on the cheek. He moved away then, picked up his suitcase, and, since he had nothing to say, left. From the living room he could see the lights on, along the streets of the senior citizen village. Sure. He'd be better off walking through the place when there were no people out. He left the apartment, his coat over one arm, his suitcase in his other hand, and took the elevator to the lobby. He stepped from the lobby into the street, and could see the outline of the row of hedges which surrounded the swimming pool.

He remembered how Flo had scolded him when he had tried to hang up the dresses and blouses which were mixed together on one of the tables. She had explained to him that people preferred it that way: that the same items which had stayed unsold for months on hangers would, when rumpled in a pile on a table, be sold in a day or two. Sure. That told you something.

Sam had never, really, while he was in the bedroom, thought of telling Ben what it was that he had imagined, but he wondered nonetheless what Ben would have thought of it. He had not known that he was capable of having that kind of thing in his head, and it made him feel good to realize that he was. He figured that he wasn't obliged to make too much of it, of course, but once he had imagined it, he had not, in truth, seen any reason why what he had imagined could not happen. When the idea had come to him a few hours before, he had, at first, seen it as part of Flo's letter. One day, he imagined her writing, a week or so after Tidewater had vanished, a group of elderly black men had appeared at the door to the rummage shop; she had invited them in and they had told her that, for some time, they had been looking for a man whom they believed had once been their teammate.

Old Westbury, Spéracèdes, North Hadley: 1969–1973